FROM THIS MOMENT

FROM THIS MOMENT

KIM VOGEL SAWYER

THORNDIKE PRESS
A part of Gale, a Cengage Company

LIBRARY OF CONGRESS CIP DATA ON FILE.
CATALOGUING IN PUBLICATION FOR THIS BOOK
IS AVAILABLE FROM THE LIBRARY OF CONGRESS.

ISBN-13: 978-1-4328-8734-6 (hardcover alk. paper)

Published in 2021 by arrangement with WaterBrook, an imprint of Random House, a division of Penguin Random House LLC.

Printed in Mexico
Print Number: 01   Print Year: 2021

This one is for *the posse,*
with a special nod to *Eileen,*
who planted the first story seed

See, I am doing a new thing!
   Now it springs up; do you not perceive
   it?
I am making a way in the wilderness
   and streams in the wasteland.

                    — Isaiah 43:19, NIV

ONE

Bradleyville, Kansas
Jase Edgar

Jase checked the GPS. Again. The thing showed he'd reached Bradleyville, but it had to be wrong. He scratched his stubbled cheek and frowned out the window. He'd left San Antonio for *this*? He must have lost his ever-lovin' mind.

Thick, hairy grass — wheat, probably — grew on both sides of the road. A little gas station, its wood siding painted bright white with red trim, stood proudly near the two-lane road, but where was the town? There wasn't a single other business in sight. Only a smattering of what appeared to be houses. They formed two uneven north-to-south rows about a quarter mile behind the station. If this was Bradleyville, he'd made a horrible mistake.

Why had he said goodbye to San Antonio, where he'd lived since he was fourteen?

Goodbye to the folks at Grace Chapel, who'd welcomed him into their fold eighteen years ago? And goodbye to Rachel? A lump filled his throat, making it hard to take a breath. Saying goodbye to Rachel . . . that'd been hardest of all. How had he found the strength to turn his back on the love of his life?

He shook his head. He hadn't turned his back on her. What had Brother Tony said? Jase closed his eyes and forced himself to recall every word the wise pastor had said to him during their final counseling session his last evening in San Antonio. *"You'll always carry her with you, Jase, but this fresh start means you're trusting God with the next chapter of your life."*

The problem was, even after twelve months of coming to grips with the fact that she was gone, he didn't want a new chapter. He wanted the one he and Rachel had scripted together. And taking the first step of his so-called new chapter on April first — April Fools' Day — seemed especially inappropriate. He wondered, not for the first time, what God had been thinking to take her and leave him behind.

He scowled at the GPS. According to the lines on the screen, his new boss's address — 207 Bluebell Street — was a bit west and north of where he now sat in the idling U-Haul. Gritting his teeth, he eased his foot off the brake and rolled forward on a pot-holed dirt road. He passed the gas station and came to an intersection marked by a handmade sign indicating Bluebell Street. He could only go right, so he made the turn and drove slowly, scanning both sides of the street while holding the U-Haul to a crawl.

A street called Bush brought an end to the wheat field on the left and led to a block with two small houses separated by empty lots. More wheat on the right. Disbelief weighted his gut. How could they call this place a town? The next intersection was the first four-way intersection he'd encountered so far. A metal building with a cupola filled a good chunk of land on the right. A porta-ble sign sat at the edge of the road. Black block letters spelled out Beech Street Bible Fellowship. So this was where he'd serve as a youth pastor.

He eased to a stop and craned his neck, giving the church a better examination. Now he could see there were actually two long metal buildings standing roughly twenty feet apart. The first one had the cupola, and the second sported a wooden cross nailed to its front. Some sort of enclosed breezeway, the peak of its roof

11

barely reaching the eaves of the other two structures, connected the two halves. Although there wasn't an official steeple or any stained-glass windows, the buildings and the yard all looked clean and well cared for. Not fancy. Not by any stretch of the imagination. Not even churchy. But homey somehow.

Jase's angst eased a bit.

Shifting his focus forward again, he spotted a two-story home with a trio of carriage-type garage doors on its lower level. The front of a ranch-style house stuck out from the far side of the garage. Its paint colors — cream with dark green trim — matched the garage. No other house sat on the right-hand side of Bluebell Street, so it had to be where the pastor lived. Jase pulled in a breath and blew it out, then drove the remaining distance, the growl of the U-Haul's tires loud on the gravel road.

He parked in front of the house and turned off the engine. He hadn't even climbed out of the cab before the front door of the house opened and a smiling couple stepped out onto the porch. The woman stopped at the edge of the concrete slab, but the man — short, heavyset, with gray-streaked hair and a huge grin — ambled down the steps and came toward Jase, his hand extended.

Jase met him in front of the U-Haul. The man's handshake, strong yet not crushing, sent a message of welcome. Jase felt his lips curve into a smile. "Hello. I'm Jase Edgar. You must be Reverend Kraft."

"I am. But call me Brother Kraft. Everyone around here does." The man beamed at Jase, his blue eyes narrowing to merry slits. "I'm sure glad to meet you. And you're right on time for lunch. We were sitting down when Leah heard your truck. She said it had to be our new youth minister." He chuckled and leaned forward slightly, like a child sharing a secret. "She made extra in the hopes you'd be here in time to eat with us."

Jase glanced at the woman. She waited with her hands tucked in the pockets of a yellow-flowered bib apron, her gaze seemingly glued to him. He gave a nod, and she bobbed her head. He turned to Brother Kraft again. "That's awfully nice of her."

"Well, Leah loves to cook. Doesn't need much of an excuse to fix plenty, either. So come in, come in."

Brother Kraft slung his arm up and across Jase's shoulders and herded him along the paved sidewalk to the house. The warmth of the man's arm felt good. Although Jase

13

wouldn't call the temperature in this part of Kansas cold, it was definitely too cool for the T-shirt, cargo shorts, and sandals he'd put on that morning. The weather here was at least ten degrees lower than a typical April day in San Antonio.

Mrs. Kraft, equal in height to her husband but half his girth, pulled her hands out of her pockets and grabbed Jase in a tight hug the moment he stepped up onto the porch. It reminded him of the hugs given by some of the older ladies at the church back home, and he automatically returned it with matching oomph. She patted his back several times, then let go and grinned at him. "Jase Edgar, welcome to Bradleyville. My brother-in-law spoke so highly of you, I know you'll be a blessing in these parts. But instead of standing out here talking, let's get sat down at the table before the meatloaf and mashed potatoes are cold. I hope you're hungry."

Jase's mouth watered. "I am, and that sounds good, ma'am."

"Call me Sister Kraft." The preacher's wife slipped her hand through the bend of Jase's elbow and gave him a little nudge into the house. "We'll get good and acquainted while we're eating, and then we'll help you settle in to your new home."

14

New home. A boulder seemed to drop into Jase's stomach. They were kind words. Welcoming words. Shouldn't they inspire something other than panic?

Merlin Kraft

Merlin forked another slice of meatloaf onto his plate. What had Leah added to the ground beef this time? Yesterday's leftover mixed vegetables? Some of their breakfast oatmeal? Maybe a dab of spaghetti and slices of garlic bread from Monday's supper? All of the above? If it fit through the grinder, it was a potential ingredient. He often teased her that her meatloaf was more loaf than meat, and she never denied the claim. The recipe differed every time, but he could always count on it tasting good. Their guest must've agreed because he also took a second serving. Or was it his third? One thing was certain. There'd be no leftover-meatloaf sandwiches for supper.

Leah picked up the bowl of potatoes and held it to Jase. "More?"

The young man smiled and plopped a spoonful onto his plate. "Thank you, ma'am. Everything's real good."

"Why, thank you. I'm glad you're enjoying it." Leah set the potatoes on the table and offered Jase the green beans. "Help

15

yourself. The youngest of our brood — twins, Stella and Staci — moved out more than fourteen years ago, but I still cook enough to feed the six of us who used to sit around this table."

Jase's eyebrows rose. "Six?"

Pride glowed in Leah's pale blue eyes, which Merlin had come to expect whenever she spoke of their children. She said, "Merlin and me, Stella and Staci, and then our boys, Todd and Matt. They're all on their own now and scattered all over the United States."

Jase jabbed a forkful of green beans and carried it to his mouth. He chewed and swallowed, then grinned at Leah. "They must miss these home-cooked meals."

Leah laughed softly. "Oh, I hope so! My sisters and I were raised by our grandmother. Did my sister Eileen ever tell you that?"

"No, ma'am." Jase cut off a chunk of meatloaf and dipped it in his mashed potatoes.

"Well, Grandma taught us to cook," Leah went on. "She'd lived through near starvation in Russia before coming to America, so she knew to make do with whatever she could scrounge. We didn't eat fancy, but we never went hungry."

Merlin observed Jase out of the corner of his eyes. He listened attentively, respectfully, even while he ate. Tony had been right when he said the young man was personable. Leah was already taken with him. But Leah took to nearly everyone, whether they wanted her to or not.

She sent a sideways glance at Merlin, then settled her gaze on Jase again. "Tony told us you grew up in foster care."

Jase swiped his mouth with his napkin and nodded. "Yes, ma'am. I was lucky, though. I got bounced around a little bit in the beginning, but I landed with a real nice family when I was an eighth grader and stayed with them until I graduated. They took me to Brother Tony's church. That's where I accepted Jesus, got baptized, and met my —" His cheeks streaked pink. He cleared his throat and lowered his head.

Leah touched Jase's wrist. "Tony told us about your fiancée. We're sorry for your loss."

Jase raised his head and looked back and forth from Leah to Merlin. "Thanks. Did Brother Tony also tell you that Rachel and I planned to be church planters after we got married?"

Merlin nodded. "He did. That's why he thought you'd be such a good fit here in

Bradleyville. We're forging new ground by starting a ministry dedicated to high schoolers." He set his fork on his plate and propped his arms on the edge of the table. "You probably noticed there aren't a lot of houses here in Bradleyville."

Jase grinned. "Well . . ."

Merlin chuckled. "We have a population of three hundred and twenty-five."

Leah shook her finger at Merlin. "The count is three hundred and twenty-six, now that Jase is here."

Merlin smiled. "True. Beech Street Bible Fellowship ministers to the people who call Bradleyville home, but we reach out to neighboring areas, too. There's a fairly new housing district a bit north of us, and some of the folks there have started attending services. The students in Bradleyville are in the Goddard school district, so of course we've done some outreach there."

The responsibility of teaching people to move beyond mere religion to truly knowing and serving Jesus created pressure in the center of Merlin's heart, and he inwardly thanked the Lord for sending the help he'd long prayed for. And none too soon. "I'm pleased to say our attendance is increasing, and we have quite a number of people from Wichita who've joined the church in the

18

past four years. I can't see to all of the needs on my own anymore, so you, young man, are an answer to prayer."

An almost-nervous grin appeared on Jase's face. "I hope I won't let you down."

"If half of what Tony told us about you is true, I know we're going to be glad you're here."

Jase ate the last bite of meatloaf on his plate and set his fork on the table. He sighed. "I'm going to need your recipe for meatloaf, ma'am. That was the best I've ever had."

Merlin recognized a conversation change when he heard one.

Leah laughed. "I'll see what I can do."

Merlin winked at her and stood. "Thank you for lunch, dear. If you'll excuse us, I'm going to show Jase to his apartment. Then I'll give him a tour of the church." Leah angled her face and tapped her cheekbone. Merlin gave her a kiss, then turned to Jase. The young man gazed at them with such a forlorn expression that it stung Merlin. He'd talk with Leah later about curbing their easy affection when Jase was with them. No sense in rubbing salt into the new youth minister's still-raw wounds. "Ready?"

Jase nodded and rose. He thanked Leah and followed Merlin out the back door.

19

Merlin led him across the narrow side yard to the outside staircase for the apartment over the garage. He pointed to the garage. "There's a stall available for your car." He frowned at the U-Haul. "I assume you have one."

Jase shook his head. "I left the car behind that I've used for the past year. My car was totaled in an accident." Pain flickered in his blue-green eyes. "Before I got the insurance payout, a church member loaned me a vehicle. Then, after the payout arrived, he told me put my money in the bank and keep using the car for as long as I needed it. I gave the car back the day before I came here. So I've still got that money. I'd like to find a used car as quickly as possible."

"I can help you with that." Merlin started up the creaky stairs, with Jase behind him. "In fact, one of our members owns a family-run dealership in Wichita. You can trust him to sell you something dependable."

"Sounds perfect."

Although the words were positive, the younger man sounded uncertain. Merlin thought he understood. He flicked a glance over his shoulder. "Lots of changes all at once, isn't it?"

Jase released a dry chuckle. "It is. But I'll be okay. I got used to sudden changes when

I was a kid."

Had this staircase gotten longer since the last time he climbed it? Merlin paused with one foot on the square landing and pulled in a big breath. "Jase, I'm sure you already know this, but I'm going to say it anyway. We do not serve a wasteful God. I doubt Tony told me everything you've dealt with in your short life, but he told me enough to know you've had a lot to overcome. Every one of those situations we refer to as trials serves a purpose. Maybe it was to strengthen you. Maybe to give you wisdom. Maybe so you could show someone else how to navigate a tough pathway."

He fixed Jase with a steady gaze, his voice rising in response to his inner conviction. "God tells Moses in Exodus 9, 'I have raised you up for this very purpose, that I might show you my power and that my name might be proclaimed in all the earth.' God raises us up for His purposes so we have the opportunity to experience and share His power in a human life." He placed his hand on Jase's shoulder and gave a gentle squeeze. "Stay open to His leading, Jase. You might feel like your plans have been lost, but His plans are never forsaken. He will use you for His glory, and it'll be for your good, too."

Merlin examined Jase's face for signs of resentment. Had he said too much too soon? After all, he hardly knew the man. Leah sometimes warned him his enthusiasm led him to race ahead of God. Had he raced?

The corner of Jase's lips twitched. Then came a full-blown grin. "Are you this convincing in the pulpit?"

Merlin shrugged, battling a chortle. "You'll have to ask some of the members. It's hard to be objective about yourself."

Jase nodded. "Thanks for the words of wisdom. I'll give them some consideration."

Merlin nearly sagged with relief. He hadn't run Jase off. Yet. He pulled the key for the apartment door from his pocket and held it out to Jase. "I'll let you do the honors since this is your place now. I hope it'll feel like home to you real soon."

Jase took the key and looked at it for several seconds, his eyebrows low. "Me, too, sir. Me, too."

TWO

Kenzie locked her apartment door, jiggled the doorknob, then tucked the key in the zippered pocket of her jacket. Back on the farm in Flourish, Indiana, her family never locked up the house. Or even the barn. But when she left to live in the city, *Daed* had told her to make sure her belongings were secure. So she always locked the door and double-checked the bolt.

Confident her apartment was safe, she made her way down the concrete steps leading to the sidewalk and set off for work at her usual brisk pace. Her coworkers teased her about walking everywhere, but she didn't mind. Didn't mind walking and didn't mind being teased. Growing up with lots of brothers meant getting teased a lot. She'd learned long ago not to let it bother her. As for walking, *Mamm* said if God gave

23

a person good strong legs, then she should use them. Besides, Kenzie didn't have a car. She wouldn't know how to drive even if she did have one. No one in her family's sect operated motorized vehicles. But God had blessed her with strong legs, and she knew how to use them. So she walked.

The clear blue sky promised no rain, and the morning breeze was cool but calm — as close to perfect as a spring day could get. Winter had taken its time departing, with temperatures bouncing up and down like her little brother Caleb on his pogo stick. Kenzie didn't miss trekking to work through patches of slushy snow while a cold wind tried to tear the scarf from around her neck, as she'd done only a few weeks ago. According to the newspaper, by next week the temperature was expected to reach eighty degrees. Summer weather. She wouldn't even need her jacket for her walk to and from work.

An airplane's engine droned overhead, and out of habit she looked skyward. In her two years of living in Wichita, Kenzie had grown accustomed to the sound of aircraft. At first the noise had alarmed her. She'd been certain one of those huge planes would land on her apartment roof, they'd seemed so near. How her naivete must have amused her coworkers, who'd all grown up in this big town. Living in a city certainly differed from being on a farm with nothing but cows and cornfields for as far as she could see. Even though she'd lived in cities — first Indianapolis and now Wichita — for a full decade, the traffic, the close proximity of buildings, and the constant busyness continued to intimidate her. A part of her would probably always miss Indiana's rolling farmland and quiet, but thanks to her connections with her coworkers and the people at church, Wichita was home.

She neared Central Avenue, and her stomach instinctively tightened. She hated crossing the six lanes of traffic. Two lanes flowed east, two flowed west, and two allowed drivers to turn into the businesses on either side. No matter the time of day, all lanes were busy. With no designated crosswalk at Silver Springs Boulevard, she either had to walk another half mile to utilize a crosswalk or make a dash among vehicles. Kenzie glanced at her wristwatch, a gift from her oldest brother and his wife for her twenty-first birthday. Only seven minutes before she needed to clock in at work. She inwardly groaned. No time for the longer walk.

Biting her lower lip, Kenzie zipped her

gaze left and right, searching for a gap in the steady flow of traffic. She sent up a quick prayer for safety and bolted for the median. She paused, her pulse racing, then darted across the second set of lanes. A car honked and whizzed past as she leaped onto the curb, and she blew out the breath she always held while crossing the ridiculously well-traveled street. She offered another prayer — this one of gratitude for having made it without mishap — and trotted through the parking lot where Prairie Meadowlark Fabrics & Quilting was nestled between a beauty supply warehouse and a sporting goods store.

She peeked at her watch and smiled. Three minutes to spare. Lori's car wasn't in the area reserved for employees, so she'd even beaten her coworker. Who said feet weren't dependable for transport? She tapped on the glass door, and moments later the shop's owner, Ruby Key, hurried from behind the displays of cotton fabrics.

Ruby unlocked the door and swung it open, a smile lighting her round face. "Good morning, Kenzie."

Kenzie stepped inside. A nutmeggy aroma filled her nostrils. Thanks to strategically placed bowls of potpourri, the shop always smelled better than her family's barn, where she'd worked for years, helping with the milking. "Good morning, ma'am. How are you?"

"Fine, fine." Ruby put her hands on her hips and tipped her lips into an impish grin. "And you're going to be better than fine when I show you what I have in the storeroom."

Kenzie's heart gave a happy skip. "More clothes?"

Ruby laughed, the sound so merry Kenzie couldn't resist smiling. "My dear, you have yet to see *more*. Come . . ." She headed for the rear of the store, her arms swinging.

Kenzie followed the older woman, excitement stirring.

"The box came all the way from Texas, delivered on a U-Haul." Ruby talked as she walked, her voice carrying over the slap of her sandals' soles against the tiled floor. "I talked about the unique way you support missions last Easter when our family gathered at my sister's place. I've mentioned my Texas sister, Eileen, haven't I? Well, she was so inspired, she wanted to contribute. She's been collecting for almost a year."

Kenzie cringed. "Did you tell her who the clothes were for?" She'd been raised with the instruction to never let her left hand know what her right hand was doing. She

27

wouldn't have told Ruby if the woman hadn't visited her apartment bearing a welcome-to-town casserole shortly after Kenzie's arrival in Wichita. Ruby's fascination with the antique loom taking up half of Kenzie's living room spawned a host of questions, and Kenzie let slip what she did with the projects she created.

Ruby snorted. "No, no. I only said someone from the shop." She shot a soft smile over her shoulder. "You and your humility . . . You are one of a kind, Miss Kenzie Stetler."

Kenzie's face heated, but she wasn't sure if it was embarrassment or pleasure stirring the reaction.

Ruby swung the storeroom door open and gestured to a box sitting in the middle of the room. "Ta-da!"

Kenzie's mouth dropped open. She'd expected a stuffed trash bag, maybe two. But a box that had once held an automatic washing machine? This was beyond imagination. She inched forward and placed her fingertips on the top edge of the box. "Is it . . . full?"

"To the brim." Ruby peeled back a flap and revealed an array of neatly folded trousers.

Kenzie ran her hand over the top layer.

Such quality fabric. It would almost pain her to cut into them, but she'd do it. These would make fine rugs. "I can hardly believe this."

Ruby grinned. "Eileen and her husband had planned to bring the clothes when they visited next Christmas, but then the chance came to send them early, so they seized it."

Kenzie shook her head, her gaze remaining on the clothes. "Please give me her address so I can send her a thank-you card."

Ruby winked. "Will you sign it? It'd give you away."

Even though it seemed Ruby meant to tease, Kenzie took the question seriously. Her grandmother, who'd gifted Kenzie with her beloved loom, was a firm believer in doing good without any expectation of earthly accolades. If Ruby's sister knew Kenzie's name, she might accidentally repeat it, and Kenzie's anonymity could be destroyed. Not even the managers of the shop where Kenzie donated her rugs to support missionary efforts knew her name.

Kenzie sighed. "I'll think about it. But honestly . . . this is such an amazing gift." She shifted her attention to Ruby. "How will I get this box to my apartment? It's too big for me to carry."

Ruby swished her hand, as if shooing away

29

Kenzie's comment. "We'll transfer the clothes to smaller boxes or bags, then load them into the back of my SUV. Where there's a will, there's a way." Someone pounded on the front door, and Ruby rolled her eyes. "Oh, for heaven's sake, I forgot the time. Lori probably needs in." She caught Kenzie by the elbow and steered her out of the storeroom. "Go unlock the door, and I'll get the cash register ready for business."

Kenzie hurried to the glass front door, but her attention stayed behind in the storeroom. Thank goodness this weekend was her Saturday off. Patience might be an admired virtue, but she could hardly wait to sort through the clothes in that big box.

Lori Fowler

"Hey, girl!" Lori stepped into the fabric shop and wrapped her friend Kenzie in a hug. "Thanks for letting me in. I knocked three times. I was starting to worry nobody was here."

Kenzie wriggled free and tugged the waist of her pink T-shirt to her hips. "Sorry about that. Ruby and I were in the storeroom. I guess we didn't hear you the first two times."

Kenzie was a sweetheart — Lori loved her

30

to pieces — but she wasn't much for demonstrative touching. Probably due to her strict upbringing. Somehow Lori always forgot and hugged her anyway. Mostly because Lori needed the hugging. She tucked her purse into her employee cubby under the front counter and grinned over her shoulder. "Did we get in a new shipment?" If so, she knew what she'd be doing today. And she didn't mind. She enjoyed setting up displays, making them eye catching for customers. Ruby always told her she had a knack, and the praise made her heart swell.

Kenzie shook her head, her sleek ponytail swaying. Lori had a hard time not being jealous of Kenzie's hair, yellow as a daffodil and as shiny as silk. If Lori lived to be ninety, she'd never stop ruing the curly rust-colored hair she'd inherited from her mom's side of the family. Kenzie leaned in a bit, her blue eyes sparkling. "Clothes for my project."

True delight exploded in Lori's chest. "Oh, fun! Will you let me help?" She'd assisted Kenzie at least a dozen times in the past year. She wasn't as keen on cutting the clothing items into strips as she was on watching Kenzie turn them into rugs on a loom that had to have come over on the

Mayflower. What was it about the process that fascinated her so? She didn't have a clue, but it was more entertaining than anything on television. Which was good since Kenzie didn't even have a TV in her apartment.

"If you'd like. I'd really appreciate it." Kenzie tugged at her T-shirt hem again. "But you've helped me so much, and I've never really done anything for you. I need to return the favor."

Never done anything for her? Kenzie'd been a faithful friend, one who never betrayed a confidence. But she likely wouldn't see that as a favor. She was just being Kenzie. There was something Lori needed, though. "If you're serious, I could sure use your help with a party."

"What kind of party?"

"Brother and Sister Kraft are hosting a welcome-to-Bradleyville gathering Saturday evening for our new youth minister. An informal time for him to get acquainted with the youth and their parents."

Kenzie's fine brows came together. "I didn't know you worked with the youth."

Lori gave an ominous *ha ha ha.* "I don't. Can you imagine?" She'd had no tolerance for teenage drama even when she was a teenager. Maybe that's why she got along with Kenzie so well. A lot of people considered the former Amish woman standoffish because of her quiet ways, but Lori appreciated her friend's reserved demeanor. Kenzie stabilized her. "But I am part of the kitchen team — helping with fellowship meals and so forth. So Sister Kraft called us to duty for this get-together."

Ruby walked up, arms swinging. "What's my sister put you up to now?"

Lori gave Ruby a hug. "The welcome party for the new youth minister."

"That's planned for Saturday evening, right?"

Lori nodded. Of course Ruby would already know about it. She and Sister Kraft probably talked about everything, the way sisters did. Only having brothers, she had no firsthand experience with such relationships. Something she had in common with Kenzie. "I'm trying to recruit Kenzie to help by making some of her killer brownies."

Ruby laughed. "Baking brownies is one of Kenzie's many talents. Speaking of which . . ." The woman looked at Kenzie. "I laid out a new quilt kit in the sewing corner. It's cuter than cute — three strip-pieced cats, all done in primary colors. I took the liberty of cutting the fabric into strips, but I'd like you to sew it together. And please

33

do it as quickly as possible. It'll be darling hanging in the front window as a sample."

Kenzie bustled off, and Ruby turned to Lori. "As for you, someone made an absolute mess of the embroidery thread display. Would you straighten it out? I'll be in my office, working on the summer order, if you need me."

Lori shot a glance around the neat sales floor. Were she and Kenzie the only two employees on the schedule for today? "Who'll tend to customers?"

"Barbara will be here by nine, and she'll handle customers." The woman's face clouded. "Assuming we have some."

Lori gave a mock salute. "I'll get right to it." She hugged Ruby again, then scampered in the direction of the craft area. Ruby's expression lingered in Lori's memory, and worry attempted to take hold. She pushed it aside. The fabric shop had been a mainstay for three decades. A slow period didn't need to spell gloom. Of course it didn't.

THREE

Bradleyville
Jase

One good thing about not owning lots of stuff was that it didn't take too long to get organized. Shortly before noon on his second day in Bradleyville, Jase flattened the last of the emptied boxes and plopped it on the stack by the door. As soon as he carried the tower of cardboard down the stairs to a recycling dumpster, the open-concept kitchen, dining, and living area of his apartment would be as neat as a pin. The way he liked it.

When Brother Tony told him the church would provide his living quarters, Jase didn't know what to expect. Yesterday after lunch when he'd followed Brother Kraft up the set of outside stairs to the second-floor landing, he'd mentally prepared himself for disappointment. How nice could a place be if it was part of a garage? But the paint,

35

carpet, and tile were so recently updated that the "new" scent still lingered. All in all, it was much brighter and fresher than his old townhome. Despite its size — less than half the space he'd had in San Antonio — he found a place for everything he'd brought with him. If any youth group kids or parents wanted a tour, he wouldn't be embarrassed to let them in.

Jase still had to organize his dresser drawers and closet. A person shouldn't live out of suitcases for more than a day or two. Sure, the rest of the place looked neat, but not until his clothes were put away would it really feel like home. He'd used the same measuring stick when he was a boy, bouncing from foster home to foster home. Except back then he'd carried everything in a black garbage bag. Still, if he got to unpack, he knew he'd stay. At least for a while. His urgency to get fully settled battled against his resistance to adopt Bradleyville as his new home, making his insides twitch.

His stomach rumbled, reminding him he had organized the kitchen cabinets instead of eating breakfast. Bless Leah Kraft's heart, she'd fully stocked his fridge with milk, apples and oranges, assorted lunch meats and cheeses, plus a half dozen whipped topping and butter tubs containing leftovers from her own kitchen. She'd even loaded the door with basic condiments. The Krafts were good people — thoughtful, generous. He already liked them a lot.

He selected a tub and peeled back the lid. A single slice of meatloaf and a lump of mashed potatoes waited inside. Perfect. He bumped the fridge door closed with his hip, took a half step to the mini microwave on the counter, slid the container in, and pushed Start. He wasn't much of a cook, but he knew how to operate such a simple appliance. When the thing gave a tinny *ding!*, he transferred the steaming food to a plate, then sat at the little table tucked against the pony wall separating his kitchen from his living room. He folded his hands and bowed his head.

"Dear Lord . . ." A lump filled his throat. Why was praying so hard these days? He used to talk to God as easily as if they were seated across a table from each other. Now even thanking Him for a meal left him tongue-tied and empty worded. Maybe even empty hearted. And he was going to lead young people?

Suddenly the food didn't hold the same appeal. He scraped it back into its tub and returned it to the refrigerator. As he rinsed his plate, someone knocked on the door. He glanced at the clock hanging on the soffit above the sink. One o'clock already — the time he and Brother Kraft had agreed upon to turn in the U-Haul and then do some car shopping.

Jase put the plate in the sink, grabbed the towel he'd draped over the oven door handle, and hurried to the door. He opened it and gestured the minister inside while drying his hands. "I lost track of time. Let me get my jacket, and —"

Brother Kraft whistled through his teeth, his gaze roaming the room. "Look at this place." He scuffed across the freshly vacuumed carpet and touched the frame of the Spurs poster Jase had hung dead center above his faded brown leather sofa. "Decor items up and everything. It looks like you've been here for weeks already."

Jase folded the towel and lay it over the pony wall. Then he snagged his jacket from a hook behind the door and shrugged it on. "I think better when I'm not in the middle of a mess." He wasn't as obsessive about neatness as he'd once been, but he'd probably never completely recover from the total disarray in his earliest memories. He'd probably never forget the piles of garbage and clutter that accompanied his mother's mental illness and led to his removal by the state. Rachel had understood his need for order and hadn't ever made fun of him the way his college roommates had. He'd found his soul mate. And now she was gone.

He pushed aside thoughts of mess and of Rachel. This was his new chapter, remember? "Besides, I figured some parents might want to come up, see where I live, since their kids will probably hang out here some."

Brother Kraft turned and faced Jase, his expression solemn. "If you did all this work for that reason, I'm sorry. I should've told you . . . all gatherings with the kids will take place at the church. In this day and age, having kids to your apartment?" He brushed his toe against the nap of the carpet, pushing the shaggy strands the wrong way. "It isn't that I don't trust you. You were given a glowing recommendation by someone I hold in respect, so it isn't personal. We just have to take extra precautions."

Jase understood. During his tour of the church building yesterday, he'd determined there was plenty of room in the fellowship hall for activities, and even the smaller room designated for the youth was adequate for Bible study and small-group meetings. In all honesty, he didn't mind keeping his apartment his private domain.

He smiled. "No worries. I wouldn't want to open the door to any kind of scandal or ill conjectures toward Beech Street Bible Fellowship. Or you, by default. I'll plan to hold all our activities at the church."

"Good." A breath of relief eased from the preacher's mouth. He picked up a short stack of flattened boxes and opened the door. "Let's get these things cleared out so you won't have to trip over them, and then we'll head into the city. I told Ronnie to expect us at his dealership around two. He's got a couple of cars picked out for you to give the once-over. I'll take my car, you drive the U-Haul, and I'll lead the way."

Jase scooped up an armful of cardboard. "Sounds good. I'll follow."

I'll follow. Isn't that what he'd said the night at church when he went forward with Rachel and committed himself to becoming a church planter? And look where God had led. He hoped Brother Kraft would prove more trustworthy than God was.

Wichita
Kenzie

Kenzie plopped the last bag of clothes in the middle of her living room floor. Six trash bags meant two trips each for her, Lori, and Ruby. The pile astounded her, and her mind

40

spun, imagining the stack of rugs that would grow from this generous donation. She put her hands on her hips and heaved out a mighty "Wow."

" 'Wow' is right." Lori sagged onto Kenzie's floral love seat, reminding Kenzie of the way Caleb collapsed on the lawn after a long day of playing. "Girl, you really need to live in a first-floor apartment. Or bug the landlord to put in an elevator. Carrying those things up the flight of stairs did me in."

Ruby shook her finger at Lori. "I'm more than double your age, and you don't hear me complaining."

Lori rolled her eyes, snickering. "Yeah, well, you boomers have a stronger constitution than us spoiled millennials."

"You got that right."

Kenzie grinned at her boss and coworker. Although she never participated in the teasing sparring matches that played out between them, she enjoyed spectating. "I appreciate your help bringing it all up. And, Ruby, I've decided to write an anonymous thank-you note to your Texas sister. May I put the store's address on the envelope for the sender instead of mine?"

Ruby shrugged and headed for the door. "That'd be fine. In one of those bags is an envelope with a note from her. If her address isn't written in it somewhere, let me know and I'll get it to you."

"Thanks."

"And for now . . ." Ruby opened the door with a flamboyant gesture. "I'm outta here. Strong constitution or not, I'm pooped."

Lori and Kenzie waved goodbye. Then Lori slid from the couch and sat cross legged on the floor. She began untying a bag's plastic strings. "I'll make a deal with you."

Kenzie reached for the ties on the bag closest to her. "What's that?"

Lori gestured toward the kitchen. "I've helped you often enough to know how to categorize by color and type of fabric. Fix us some sandwiches and then bake a pan of brownies while I organize these clothes into stacks."

Kenzie raised her eyebrows. "You really think a couple of sandwiches and a pan of brownies is a fair exchange for . . ." She flapped her hands at the mountain of bags.

Lori laughed. "You underestimate the scrumptiousness of your brownies. Honestly, Kenz, I've never had richer, fudgier, more chocolatey brownies than yours. You could patent the recipe." She dug into the first bag. "What's your secret?"

Kenzie hunched her shoulders. "If I tell, then it won't be a secret anymore."

Lori gaped at Kenzie for several seconds and then hooted with laughter. "Did you just joke with me?"

Kenzie blinked several times, replaying her last comment. She tapped her chin with her finger, the way Ruby often did when she was thinking. "Um . . . did I?"

Lori laughed harder.

Kenzie couldn't help but smile, even though she hadn't intended to make a joke. She'd learned the brownie recipe from her mother, who learned it from her mother. Kenzie intended to pass it on to her daughter. If she ever had a daughter, which became less likely with each birthday that slipped by. How could she be twenty-eight already and still unmarried? If she'd joined the Amish church instead of moving to Indianapolis after her *rumspringe,* would she have a husband and children by now? Most likely. But would she be any happier than she was now? There was no way to know for sure, but she doubted it anyway.

She loved her family and missed them more than she knew how to express. Yet when she remembered living under the strict rules of their sect — rules that were supposed to give her the assurance of

43

righteousness — her stomach churned. She'd been a good girl. Always a good girl. But not until her rumspringe, when she met a group of college kids doing a mission project in the city, did she learn about grace. Accepting the grace made possible by Jesus's death at Calvary had swallowed the feelings she'd always had about not being good enough for the almighty God. She wasn't good enough. Not nearly good enough. But thanks to grace, her position as God's child was secure. As much as she loved her family, she could never go back to the system of hoping to earn her right to heaven.

Lori flicked her fingers at Kenzie. "Scoot. Go. Sandwiches first. Chicken salad, if you have any left. It was delish yesterday." Still chuckling, she peeled back the black plastic and removed a blue plaid shirt. "Then . . . secret-recipe brownies."

Standing, Kenzie kicked off her tennis shoes and left them beside the front door. Then, stocking footed, she padded to her compact kitchen. In her first apartment in Indianapolis, she'd nearly climbed the walls of her little kitchen, it was so tight compared to Mamm's spacious kitchen in their farm-house. But a decade of functioning in a small space had eliminated the cramped

44

feeling. Now, since she only cooked for herself, she appreciated having what she needed close at hand. If she got married and had a family, though, she'd want a kitchen more like Mamm's.

Funny how her "when" thoughts about marriage had changed to "if" thoughts. And how silly to think about it at all, considering there wasn't a single prospect for matrimony on her horizon. Technically, she was now an *Englischer,* but somehow the men her age still saw her as set apart. Lori often teased that one could take the girl from the Amish but not take the Amish from the girl. Maybe Lori was right. Being alone wasn't so bad, though. If she were married and had children underfoot, she wouldn't be able to weave. Maybe God wanted her to be a weaver instead of a wife and mother. She could be content with His desire for her. He'd done so much for her. Should she complain about serving Him?

She spread the last of the chicken salad on slices of bread, cut the sandwiches in half, and arranged them on plates. The sandwiches looked sad all alone on her secondhand denim-blue stoneware, so she added a handful of chips and a dill pickle spear. Simple fare, especially for an evening meal, but Lori had confided she never

45

cooked — unheard of from Kenzie's point of view — so she cheerfully consumed anything homemade.

Kenzie put the plates on the table and peeked around the corner. The sofa already held several stacks of neatly coordinated items. Lori was definitely earning her sandwich. Even though Kenzie knew Lori wanted the brownies to take to church, Kenzie vowed to bake a batch that was all for Lori tonight. She'd bake another pan for the church get-together on Saturday so they'd be fresh.

"Lori? Supper's ready."

Lori jumped up so fast, her springy curls bounced. She screeched the chair legs on the linoleum floor and sat, then folded her hands. Kenzie sat, too, and imitated Lori's gesture. They both bowed their heads. Kenzie silently recited the Lord's Prayer. When she lifted her head, Lori was looking at her. And frowning.

Kenzie glanced at the food. "Is something wrong? Oh — I forgot drinks." She stood and headed for the refrigerator. "Milk or water?"

"Water, please. Thanks."

Kenzie pulled out two water bottles from the fridge and returned to the table. She set one in front of Lori and slid onto her chair's vinyl seat.

Lori tilted her head, her brow furrowing. "Can I ask you something?"

Kenzie shrugged. "Sure."

"How come you don't pray out loud?"

Kenzie picked up one of the sandwich halves and bit off the corner. "I was taught prayer is private. It's boastful to let others hear what you say to God."

Lori continued to frown across the table. "So . . . you never pray out loud?" She took a big bite of her sandwich and followed it with a chip.

Only one time had Kenzie prayed aloud, when she was seven years old. Mamm was laboring to deliver her seventh child, and Kenzie — or, more accurately, Mackenzie — had climbed into the barn loft, the closest spot to heaven she could reach. She'd opened the vent window and yelled her desire to the blue sky, fully aware that all her brothers from the oldest, Timothy, to the youngest, Caleb, were also in the barn and would hear every word.

Her childish voice rang in her memory. *"Dear God, let my baby sister be born fast and healthy!"*

Mamm's labor continued for another nineteen hours before the newest brother finally arrived. The midwife declared him

47

healthy, but Seth was never as robust as the other Hochstetler boys, and he succumbed to a fever when he was not quite eight years old. After the long, difficult labor and delivery, Mamm never conceived another child. Although Kenzie's minister had assured her God's sovereignty had already determined the course of Seth's life, Kenzie would never stop wondering if his condition was her punishment for making bold demands from the barn loft. She wouldn't risk it again.

Kenzie shook her head.

"Do you think you ever will?" Lori tapped the edge of the plate with her pickle, turning a thoughtful look on Kenzie. "I mean, you've left a lot of your Amish behind — you don't cover your hair, you wear modern clothes and use modern technologies." She grinned impishly. "Well, sort of. Seriously, Kenz, skirts all the time, and no TV?" She pointed at Kenzie with the pickle spear. "It'd be okay to totally unbend, you know."

Kenzie laughed. "I totally unbent during my running-around period, believe me." She hadn't gone as wild as some of her friends, but she'd sampled enough of life's temptations to know what she was missing by living more conservatively. "Wearing skirts and not having a TV have nothing to do with how I was raised. I'm more comfortable in skirts than in blue jeans, and I can't afford cable."

"Makes sense." Lori didn't sound convinced.

Kenzie waved her hand toward the living room. "Stop and think . . . if I had a television in there, would I be lazy and watch it after work instead of using my loom?"

"No." Lori shook her head. "No."

Kenzie gave her friend a rueful smile. "That's kind, but sometimes I think your opinion of me is higher than it should be. I'm not perfect."

Lori rolled her eyes and laughed. "Did I ever say I thought you were perfect? Nuh-uh." She bit into her pickle, still grinning. "But you're dedicated. You're what I'd call an old soul. Earning money to send to missionaries is too important to you to set it aside for a little TV watching, so your loom will always come first. Am I right?"

Kenzie lowered her head, trying to hide the warmth flooding her cheeks. "You're right." If the mission team in Indianapolis hadn't shared the good news of Jesus with her, she'd still be lost in a pit of insecurity and worthlessness. No one should spend her life so entangled. As she wove, she

49

always prayed for the lost — including her daed and mamm, her brothers and their families, and those living in her former community. She'd weave rugs until she was too old to thread the warp, even if she could afford cable.

"Thought so." Lori sounded smug.

Kenzie glanced at her friend. A grin curved Lori's full lips and brought out her dimples. Kenzie shook her head, smiling. "You're a mess, you know that?"

Lori laughed. "I've been told that before." For a moment, her expression clouded, but her grin returned so quickly Kenzie wondered if she'd imagined it. "Let's hurry and eat so I can get back to sorting and you can get the brownies baked, okay?"

Kenzie picked up her sandwich. "Okay."

Lori stayed until past ten and organized all but the last bag of clothes. She squealed in delight when Kenzie presented her with her very own pan of brownies, and she gave Kenzie a hug that stole the breath from her lungs.

After Lori left, Kenzie cleaned up the kitchen while her radio crackled out tunes broadcasted by a contemporary Christian music station. With everything restored to order, she started for her bedroom, intending to put on her pajamas and ready herself

50

for bed. But as she passed the living room, the lone stuffed bag seemed to beg to be emptied. She changed direction and dropped to her knees next to the bag. The ties already dangled, loose, so she tugged the opening wide and emptied the entire contents. All men's trousers and blue jeans. What a wonderful gift.

She used any donated fabric that could hold together, but the heavier fabrics made the sturdiest and, therefore, the most desirable rugs. She sorted the pants into stacks by color, her hands moving so deftly and instinctively she didn't even have to think about where to place them. When she finished, she picked up the crumpled bag, folded it, and put it with the others near her front door. She'd take them to work. They were still usable. Waste not, want not, *Grossmammi* always said.

She returned to the stacks and picked up the pile of gray-toned items. As she laid them on the stack Lori had sorted, she felt something hard. Often she found loose change or other small items, from petrified wads of chewing gum to packages of dental floss, in the pockets of donated pants. Making sure the pockets were empty before she applied her scissors was part of her routine. She pulled the pair of trousers from the pile

51

and let them unfold. Then she reached into the pocket. Her fingers encountered something round, but it didn't feel like a coin.

Frowning, she pulled the item free. She held it to the light and gasped. She dropped the pants, and they puddled on the floor at her feet. She gaped at a single diamond attached by four prongs to a wide band. She pinched it between her fingers and tilted it, watching the light bounce from the stone's facets. Was it real? One of the older women from work, Van, wore a cubic zirconia solitaire necklace to church every Sunday. The man-made stone looked so real that if Van hadn't confessed it was an imitation, Kenzie would never have known.

Maybe this ring also wasn't as valuable as it appeared. She angled the band and looked at its underside. Another gasp left her throat. A tiny stamp reading *14K* indicated this wasn't a cheap gold-plated band. An engraving in a flowing script hinted at a story Kenzie longed to uncover.

She read the words aloud. " 'From this moment into eternity.' " She hadn't intended to whisper, but her voice emerged low and husky, almost with reverence. She stared at the ring until the words wavered. She blinked several times, then stared at it again. She was holding someone's wedding ring. It was too small and delicate to be a man's ring. Yet it had come from the pocket of a man's pair of trousers.

Her pulse pounded so loud in her ears that it muffled the song playing on the radio. If this was a real gold-and-diamond ring — and it certainly seemed to be — she needed to return it to its owner. Ruby had said her sister had been collecting clothing items for months. Would she remember who'd donated this particular pair of pants? She'd talk to Ruby on Sunday after church. In the meantime, she'd better find a safe place to keep the ring.

FOUR

Bradleyville
Jase

Jase checked his reflection in the full-length mirror attached to the bathroom door. He was going to a party, not a church service, so he didn't need to dress up, but he didn't want to look slovenly. After all, first impressions were important. His tan khakis and soft chambray shirt were comfortable but not over-the-top dressy. They'd do. He wasn't sure about his leather flip-flops, though. In San Antonio they'd be fine for this time of year, but in Kansas? His loafers or some sneakers might be better.

He headed for his closet, finger-combing his hair away from his forehead as he went. Despite the application of mousse, the strands wanted to droop. Maybe he should have gotten a haircut in Wichita yesterday. He snagged his tan canvas sneakers, sat on the end of his bed, and swapped the shoes.

54

And what about his beard? Should he go ahead and shave it all the way off? He liked his short whiskers because they hid the acne scars along his jawline. Rachel had approved of what she called his "studly stubble," but what would the mothers of the teenagers in his youth group think?

His hands stilled in the middle of switching shoes. *His* youth group. As of today, he was responsible for a group of teenagers. Of mentoring them, counseling them, helping them grow in faith. Chill bumps broke out over his arms. He returned to the mirror and gave himself a firm look.

"What would Brother Tony tell you right now? He'd say all things work together for good for those who love God and are called to His purpose." Had he been called to this purpose? Well, sort of. He'd definitely been called to church plant. He knew that with every fiber of his being. Both he and Rachel had received the same prompting at the same time, shortly after he'd told her he wanted her in his life forever and she'd declared she wanted that, too. But the door slammed closed with Rachel's death. Then *this* door opened, and Brother Tony was so sure the position at Beech Street Bible Fellowship was God's redirection for Jase's life.

He stared at his uncertain expression and

contemplated the other part of the biblical stipulation concerning for whom all things worked for good. He couldn't say he didn't love God, but he also couldn't say he wasn't plenty angry about how things had turned out. He still wanted the life he and Rachel had scripted together. He probably always would. They should be together. Either here or in heaven. It wasn't fair that he —

A knock on his apartment door brought his ruminating to an end. He hurried through the apartment and swung the door open. Brother Kraft stood on the little landing, his hands in his pockets and his trademark smile in place, but his cheeks were splotchy and perspiration dotted his wide forehead. Jase gestured him in.

Brother Kraft entered the apartment and crossed to Jase's sofa. He sat, his breath wheezing as his body lowered to the seat. "Party'll start soon. Leah's been over at the church for an hour already." The man laughed, winking. "She's the head of the kitchen team, and, let me tell you, every one of our events that includes food is top notch."

Jase didn't doubt it. For lunch, he'd heated the contents from one of the tubs she'd put in his refrigerator. He wasn't completely sure what all had been in it —

tuna, rice, peas, and some kind of cheesy sauce under a crunchy topping — but his taste buds had celebrated every bite.

Brother Kraft placed his palms over his widespread knees. "I thought you might be a little nervous, so I came up to pray with you beforehand. If that's okay with you."

Jase rubbed his knuckles on his prickly jaw, chuckling. "You thought right. That's more than okay with me."

The minister extended one hand to Jase.

Jase had never been one to hold a man's hands, not even in prayer, but he sat on the sofa, took hold, and bowed his head.

"Our dear Father . . ." Brother Kraft addressed God reverently yet with a familiarity that sent a spiral of longing through Jase's middle. Would he ever regain his closeness with God? Or would Rachel's unexpected departure be a permanent wedge between him and God? His chest ached in loneliness for the girl he still loved and the God he'd come to resent.

Brother Kraft asked a blessing over the gathering and specifically for Jase and the young people. He requested that Jase and the teens would be bound together in Christian fellowship and that Jase would follow God's direction in leading the youth. Jase squeezed his eyes closed so tight that pain pricked in his forehead. What would the man say if Jase interrupted and told him he might not be able to encourage the kids to follow a God who'd carved such a painful pathway for him?

"Lord, setting off on a new course is exciting but also scary. Ease Jase's fears. Remind him that he does nothing in his own strength and that Yours is sufficient in all of life's circumstances. We're so thankful to You for bringing him to Bradleyville. You have answered my prayers. I praise You, my Lord and Savior, for Your gift of a partner in ministry."

The sensation of having a bucket of warm, scented liquid poured over his head struck Jase with intensity. He opened his eyes and looked for evidence of moisture. He saw none, yet he couldn't deny feeling as if he were wet. Not wet and cold, the way he'd expect if doused, but wet and . . . what? He couldn't define what he felt, but he knew something unusual had happened during Brother Kraft's prayer.

The minister finished with a husky "Amen," released Jase's hand, and opened his eyes. He met Jase's gaze and smiled, but the smile quickly faded to a confused frown. "Are you all right?"

Jase cleared his throat and shook his head

slightly, trying to clear the odd sensation he'd experienced. While less acute, it lingered. He touched his hair. Dry. He must have imagined it. Whatever it was. "Yeah. I think so."

The jovial man's smile returned. "Still nervous?" He clapped Jase on the shoulder. "I think you'll forget all about it —"

Would he also forget the strange feeling of wetness?

"— once you get to the fellowship hall and start meeting people. We're a pretty friendly bunch here. None of us have ever bitten a newcomer." His blue eyes sparkled with mischief. "Yet."

Jase gave the expected laugh. "Well, let's hope I don't give anyone reason to make me the first." He opened the door for Brother Kraft, then followed him down the wooden stairs to the grassy yard that hadn't yet turned green. The fellowship hall portion of the church was closest to the pastor's house, its door propped open with a rock the size of a loaf of bread. Happy noises met Jase's ears before he and Brother Kraft reached the square concrete stoop. Was everyone here already? Nervousness knotted his belly.

Jase paused and allowed Brother Kraft to enter first, then trailed on his heels, scanning the room as he went. Someone had put up a volleyball net, and four teens, apparently boys against the girls, whacked a ball back and forth while shouting playful insults at one another. In the far corner, four girls sat at a round table, laughing and talking. A pair of older boys slouched against the wall not far from the girls. One wore his ball cap with the bill angled over his right ear. Jase dubbed him Cool Dude — or maybe Cool Dude Wannabe. The kid reminded him of himself at that age. He probably gave bunny ears to the person standing next to him in a group photo, just to be a pill. The other boy, with thick glasses and uncombed hair, didn't fit with the first one, in Jase's opinion, but the two seemed to be joking with each other.

He did a quick tally of teenagers. According to the membership list he'd been given, they were two girls short of the total count. He searched the room for them, but the others present appeared to be parents or maybe adults helping with the gathering. The clock hanging above the kitchen's serving window showed five till seven, so it wasn't quite time to start. The other girls would probably arrive soon. Given how many were already there, though, he should have made an effort to come earlier. He hoped none of the parents would think ill of him for waiting until closer to the start time.

Brother Kraft put his hand on Jase's shoulder and guided him in the direction of the circle of people Jase had presumed were parents. The group ceased talking and turned toward them, their attention shifting to Jase. He pasted on a smile and searched their faces, noting friendliness in all expressions. The tight knot in his gut loosened a smidgen.

"Everyone, meet our new youth minister, Jase Edgar." Brother Kraft beamed at Jase the way he imagined a proud father would look upon his son who'd hit the tie-breaking home run. "Jase, I forgot to ask how you'd like to be addressed. Brother Jase? Pastor Jase? What do you prefer?"

Pastor felt entirely too stuffy and beyond his abilities. "Brother Jase is fine, thanks."

By turn, the gathered adults shook Jase's hand and introduced themselves. Thank goodness they wore stick-on name tags on their shirts. He'd never remember them all, even though it wasn't a huge crowd. He smiled and thanked each for their kind welcome.

Brother Kraft folded his arms over his chest. "We're waiting for the Greens. You met Ronnie on Thursday, remember?"

Jase still couldn't believe the deal he'd gotten on his car. Even though the car was fifteen years old, the former owner had taken good care of it. Ronnie had teasingly claimed it'd only been driven on Sundays, below the speed limit. A standard car salesman joke. But clearly the vehicle had never been left out in the elements. The dove-gray interior complemented the shiny exterior and, given its pristine state, had probably never had greasy fries dumped on its seats or floors. Jase would make sure it never did.

He nodded. "Yes. I'll have to thank him again. I hadn't expected to find something so nice for the cash I had in hand." And he had enough left to pay for tags, taxes, and a full year of insurance, plus a little extra he'd already set aside for an emergency fund.

Brother Kraft clapped Jase on the shoulder. "I'd say the Father blessed you."

Jase gave a little start. He hadn't thought so when he got what he'd deemed a pretty minimal insurance settlement, considering all he'd lost, but now guilt pricked. He'd underestimated God's goodness. Again. How many times had Brother Tony told him he needed to let go of his preconceived notions about earthly fathers and trust God to be the best, most attentive, most compassionate Father he could ask for?

The minister slid his hand into his trouser pocket. "Ronnie's daughter, Sienna, brings her friend Kaia with her. In the past, she invited a young man named Brent, who's become a regular attendee of all of our youth-focused activities. He's the blond-haired boy in the green T-shirt who's playing volleyball."

One of the dads — his name tag read *Rick* — leaned in a bit. "My son, Zackary, is a senior this year, so he'll graduate out of the youth group at the end of the summer. But if you need help corralling Brent, call on Zack. He's helped Brother Kraft, here, with the youth for the past two years, and I think Brother Kraft would agree he's been a good influence."

The teen with the uncombed hair and glasses looked enough like the serious man peering through Coke bottle lenses at Jase that there was no question which boy was Zack.

Brother Kraft nodded. "Absolutely. Zack's a strong Christian and a good example for the other kids." Then he shrugged, a smile creasing his round face. "I think you'll discover, as a whole, we have really good kids in the youth group. And with your leadership and encouragement, the group should grow both in number and commitment to the Lord."

"Amen," Rick said, and several others murmured their agreement.

Jase's stomach panged. He hoped he wouldn't disappoint anybody. All at once, he remembered the feeling of being washed in a warm flow, and he spoke without thinking. "The students and I will teach each other. We'll grow together."

Their approving smiles and nods both bolstered and challenged Jase. He'd need to live up to the statement.

A flurry of activity at the fellowship hall entrance caught Jase's attention. The car salesman, Ronnie Green, with a petite woman and two young teen girls — one short with Ronnie's wavy sandy-brown hair and blue eyes, the other tall and slender with straight dark hair and an olive complexion — rushed to the group.

The woman held her hands out in a defeatist gesture. "Sorry we're late. You know how girls are, can never decide what to wear, and I made the mistake of having them pick up all the discarded items from the bedroom floor before we left. So you can blame it all on me if we've held you up."

The shorter girl groaned and rolled her eyes. "Mom, you didn't have to tell them that!" She adjusted the collar of her pink-and-white-striped top and turned a bright smile on Jase. "Are you the new youth pastor? I'm Sienna, and this is Kaia." She drew her friend forward, and the second girl offered a bashful grin. "Kaia's family moved to Wichita from Arizona last year, but they're originally from Bangladesh." Silver braces flashed as Sienna talked, competing with the sparkle in her eyes. "Kaia's the first generation in her family to be a natural-born American citizen. Isn't that the coolest?"

Jase smiled first at Sienna, then at Kaia. "Absolutely the coolest. It's nice to meet both of you."

Brother Kraft put his arm around Sienna's shoulders. "Brother Jase, now that you've met the shyest member" — he coughed a laugh, and Sienna groaned — "of the youth group, how about we round up the whole gang and have her make the introductions?"

As if fired from a cannon, Sienna shot off across the tiled floor, and after a moment's pause, Kaia trotted after her. The parents separated, forming a makeshift half circle, while Sienna darted from group to group, pointing in Jase's direction and jabbering. The kids made their way over, some sauntering, some nearly trotting, and one — a Hispanic boy — dragging his heels. He reached the group last and went to Brother Kraft's side.

Brother Kraft slung his arm around the boy's shoulders and aimed a smile at Sienna. "All right, social director, do your thing."

Sienna pranced to Jase and lifted both of her hands toward him, like she was making a presentation. "Everyone, this is Brother Jase, our new youth minister." She began to clap, and the others all joined with applause, some more enthusiastically than others. Sienna made a slow sashay around the circle, pausing at each young person and announcing his or her name as she went. She reached the Hispanic boy and said, "Last but not least, this is Raul." She folded her arms over her chest, blinking up at Jase. "Do you wanna know what grades they're all in?"

One of the older girls — Leesa, if Jase remembered correctly — poked Sienna in the ribs with her finger. "He'll figure it out as we go along. Let him learn our names first."

Sienna grinned and shrugged.

Jase sent a smile to each student by turn. "It's nice to meet all of you. Thanks for the welcome."

"Yeah." Cool Dude, whose real name was Cullen, shifted the bill of his cap back and forth. "Sister Kraft said we couldn't have any snacks until everybody showed up. Now that we're all here, can we eat?"

The woman standing near Cullen gasped and nudged him with her elbow. "Be polite."

Cullen made a "What did I do?" face and slunk away from her.

Brother Kraft laughed. "Now, Starla, he wouldn't be a typical teenager if he wasn't hungry all the time. Cullen, how about you let Sister Kraft know we're ready for the snacks?"

"Sure thing!" Cullen took off, and the woman named Starla covered her face with her hand, shaking her head.

There wasn't a man with Starla, which left Jase wondering if she was a single parent or if her spouse was somewhere else. And why had Raul gone to Brother Kraft? Seeing Brent standing with the Greens let him know the boy had a connection to them. Did Raul not have a connection with anyone other than the minister? He had so much to learn about the kids. Brother Tony had told him that before he could teach them, he'd have to reach them, which meant becoming acquainted.

The parents and youth ambled in the direction of the kitchen's serving window, and Jase caught snippets of talk as they passed him.

From a teenage girl, "He's really hot, isn't he?"

From a dad, "Seems like a nice enough young man."

From a mom, "I predict half the girls will have crushes on him."

From Brent to Zack, "Figure he'll do more activities an' fun stuff than Brother Kraft did with us? That'd be cool."

And Zack's response, "We can't ignore the Bible study, though, bud. That's the most important."

Jase didn't hear Brent's reply, but he didn't need to. When he and Rachel had attended a workshop about church planting, they'd been told activities and music and food were great tools for drawing people in, but teaching the true gospel of Jesus Christ should be their greatest focus. Gaining and growing hearts for the kingdom — that was the goal.

Maybe this youth pastor gig wouldn't be as different as he'd initially feared. Even so, the weight of responsibility bore down on him. In his earlier prayer, Brother Kraft had called Jase a partner in ministry. But with these kids, he'd be on his own.

"Yo, Brother Jase."

Jase turned in the direction of the call.

Cullen gestured him over. "Gonna miss out on the good stuff if you don't hurry. Come on, bro."

Pasting on a smile, Jase headed over.

FIVE

Lori

Lori had peeked out the serving window at the new youth pastor already. Twice. And she'd determined he was good looking. But up close and personal? Yikes trikes, as ruggedly handsome as Prince Harry. She gawked at him across the short stretch of countertop while he made his selections from the variety of snacks. The platters and bowls were considerably picked over since the teens had already loaded their plates.

His hand hovered near the serving spatula for the brownies. The kids had dug in the pan and left the few remaining brownies looking more like lumps than cut squares. Not appetizing in appearance, but in this case, looks were deceiving. She should know. Half the pan Kenzie had baked just for her was gone already, and she hadn't shared a single piece with anyone.

She braced her hands on the edge of the

counter and leaned in. "Go for it. You won't regret it."

His gaze — were his eyes green or blue? — met hers. A slight grin lifted the corners of his mouth. "Oh, yeah? Did you bring them?"

Lori chewed the inside of her lip. She'd brought them, but her yes would make it sound as if she'd baked them. "No, but I know who did, and believe me, they're incredible."

His grin grew, revealing a pair of dimples behind his smattering of neatly trimmed copper-colored whiskers. "Then I'll take two." He slid two lumps onto his plate, put down the server, and stuck his hand across the divide. "Hi. I'm Jase Edgar."

Lori stifled a giggle and swiped her hand the length of her apron before taking his. "Lori Fowler. It's nice to meet you."

"Nice to meet you, too." His palm was wide and warm, and he let go before she wanted him to. He moved to the platter with chicken-salad-and-sweet-pickle sandwiches on cocktail buns. "What about these? Worth the risk?"

She laughed. "Sister Kraft made those, and the cherry cobbler."

"Then I know not to leave either behind." He took a sandwich and scanned the containers on the counter. "Which is the cobbler?"

Lori wrinkled her nose. "You're too late. The kids . . ." She waved her hand in the general direction of the teens, who sat on the floor under the volleyball net. "They emptied the whole thing."

"Well, I guess it's true what they say." He shrugged. "You snooze, you lose."

She drew back. Her dad used that phrase. Usually to be derogative. How strange to hear it spoken so nonchalantly from someone else. She managed a jerky nod. "I guess so. Next time, try to be first in line."

"Ah, but what does the Good Book tell us? 'The last will be first.' " His eyes — they were definitely green *and* blue, the most incredible combination against his red-gold hair — twinkled with mischief. "I'm sure everything else is good, too." He took a second sandwich, then spooned a blob of pistachio-pudding salad onto his plate.

Lori inched along the kitchen side of the counter, staying in step with him. "I realize tonight is all about the youth, and it should be, but in case nobody's mentioned it, we have a pretty active young-adult group here, too. A mix of married couples and singles. Just 'cause you're with the youth during Sunday school and on Wednesday evenings doesn't mean you won't be welcome at our social gatherings."

He sent her an interested look from across a pan of coconut cake. "Oh, yeah? When do y'all get together?"

The *y'all* sounded so quaint and friendly, she couldn't hold back a little giggle. "The third Thursday of every month. Sometimes we meet at a member's house, sometimes at a restaurant or coffee shop. The location's always on the church calendar, though, so look for it there, and I'll try to remind you, too."

"I'd appreciate that."

In tandem, they reached the end of the counter. He piled carrot sticks and cucumber slices on his plate, topped them with a huge dollop of chive dip, then aimed a dimpled smile at her. "Well, Lori, I look forward to getting to know you and the other church members, but right now I better go join the youth."

She leaned against the counter and watched him cross to the circle of teenagers and sink down on the floor, his plate balanced on his palm the way waiters carried trays. He picked up a carrot stick and used it to gesture as he said something, and all the kids laughed. Even bashful Raul.

She sighed. He was perfect.

An arm curled around her waist, and she tipped her face slightly, meeting Sister Kraft's knowing grin. Heat filled Lori's cheeks. She used the skirt of her apron and wiped at a few crumbs on the counter.

"Dreamy, isn't he?" Sister Kraft's eyes twinkled with humor.

"Yeah." Continuing to scrub at non-existent messes, Lori raised her head and peeked at Jase through her fringe of bangs. "Oh, yeah." And he'd been so nice to her. He hadn't acted put off by her pudginess or her wild hair. Not to mention he had dimples, like she did. Only his were cuter with those whiskers shading them. Not that she'd want whiskers to shade hers. Yikes trikes, that would be awful.

"And still in mourning."

Lori jerked her focus to Sister Kraft. "What do you mean?"

Sympathy pursed the older woman's face. "His former church family ministered to him for the first year after a devastating loss."

Lori sucked in a sharp breath.

"His fiancée was killed in a car accident."

Lori's heart constricted, and her breath wheezed out on a sorrowful sigh. She zipped her attention to Jase, who sat munching and chatting and behaving as if he didn't have a care in the world. Was he pretending, or had time erased the greater burden of grief? She knew from experience how losing someone special carved a hole in a heart that never seemed to close up. Not that she'd lost a fiancé, but she'd never stop missing her mother. Tears stung, and she blinked hard and fast. "Oh."

Sister Kraft gave Lori a little squeeze. "Now it's up to all of us to help his heart continue to mend."

Lori nodded slowly.

The minister's wife stepped away a few inches and put her hand on her hip in a saucy pose Lori'd seen countless times before. "For now, though, Ruby asked if you'd wash up the pans used for the barbecued beef and baked beans."

Lori stifled a groan. Those pans would have caked on tomatoey sauces, which were so hard to get off and made the dishwater absolutely gross. But she wouldn't say no and risk Sister Kraft's disapproval. "All right."

Sister Kraft flicked her fingers, giving Lori a mock scowl. "Go on, then. Shake a leg."

Lori grinned, bounced her foot a few times in Sister Kraft's direction, then headed for the sink. As she went, she sent a look over her shoulder at Jase. After Mom died, so many things changed, and it seemed like nobody really loved her. Did Jase at least have someone besides his fiancée who loved him? Or was that something else, besides dimples and red hair, they had in common?

Kenzie

Kenzie kept her purse strap looped across her body all through the Sunday service. She probably looked ridiculous. Every other woman in the sanctuary put her purse under the pew in front of her or on the bench beside her. But was any other woman toting a valuable ring that really didn't belong to her? Doubtful. Her stomach whirled, imagining the panic of the person who'd lost it. She had to get it back to its rightful owner as quickly as possible.

After Brother Kraft's closing prayer, she gripped her purse, ready to rise and locate Ruby. But Brother Kraft asked everyone to stay put, and he invited the new youth minister, Brother Jase, onto the platform. He made a formal introduction to the church members. Lori had called Kenzie last night, gushing about the new minister's red-gold hair, unusual green-blue — green-blue, *not* blue-green, she'd emphasized — eyes, and masculine stubbly beard. Kenzie would have recognized him even without the introduction. She had to agree with Lori concerning the man's appealing exterior. But what mattered to her was his heart. She settled into the pew and watched Brother Jase move behind the podium.

"Good morning, Beech Street Bible Fellowship." His voice was warm, low in timbre with a slight twang, the kind of voice that blended well with a guitar's strum. "It's great to be here. All y'all have made me feel very welcome."

Lori, seated a few pews in front of Kenzie, turned around and mouthed, "Y'all," then rolled her eyes and grinned. Kenzie waggled her brows at her friend, smiling to herself, and Lori faced forward again.

"I'm available twenty-four seven, especially if you're baking brownies."

Light laughter rolled through the congregation, and Lori whirled around and met Kenzie's gaze, with her mouth forming an O. Kenzie's face went hot, although she wasn't sure why she should be embarrassed.

"You think I'm kidding," Brother Jase was saying, a teasing smile turning up the corners of his lips, "but I need the baker of last night's brownies to share the recipe with me." More laughter rolled, and several people looked at Kenzie. Her face was probably glowing like a stoplight. She wanted to crawl under the pew. Then he held up his hands and shook his head. "In all seriousness, I want the youth to feel free to be in touch with me if they need a listening ear, a word of support or advice, or someone to p-pray with them."

Kenzie frowned. Did he stumble over the word *pray,* or did she only imagine it?

"The same applies to parents of the youth. If you have concerns or suggestions, give me a call, text or email me, or catch me here. The deacons have graciously set up an office for me in the church, and I plan to keep regular hours, so don't hesitate to stop in. Y'all are my family now, and I always have time for family. Thank you."

He stepped back to the floor. Applause broke out, and Kenzie joined in, her trembling hands clumsy. For reasons she couldn't understand, his comment about always having time for family stabbed through her with a physical pang.

Brother Kraft's booming voice carried over the applause. "You'll want to be here this evening. Brother Jase will share his testimony. For now, come give him a holy handshake before you leave today."

People milled toward the front of the sanctuary, but Kenzie eased in the opposite

78

direction. She had no connection with the youth department, and with so many other people greeting the new minister, she wouldn't be missed. She needed to find Ruby. Not surprisingly, her amiable boss was one of the first in line to shake Brother Jase's hand. Kenzie waited at the rear of the sanctuary, keeping her gaze locked on Ruby. When she bustled up the side aisle in her familiar determined gait, Kenzie waved her over.

Ruby gave Kenzie a quick embrace, then straightened, her smile wide. "Did you meet Brother Jase? Oh, he's a nice young man. I doubt Tony and Eileen could have sent a better leader for our youth." A worried frown erased her smile. "Is something wrong?"

Kenzie nodded and led Ruby around the corner to an empty Sunday school classroom. "When I went through the bags of clothes your sister sent from Texas, I found something. But I'm not sure what to do with it." She slipped her hand into her purse and pulled out the ring. She held it up, and Ruby's eyes widened. "I'm pretty sure it's real. What do you think?"

Ruby took it and turned it this way and that, her forehead puckering. "Oh, my, I think it is, too. How on earth did I not see it in the box when I took the clothes out of there?"

"It was in the pocket of a pair of pants."

"Ah. That makes sense." Ruby closed her fist around the ring, frowning. "Well, that explains why I missed it, but it doesn't explain what it was doing there. It was loose in the pocket? Not inside a jeweler's box?"

Kenzie shook her head. "Just by itself. I'm sure whoever left it in there is frantic, wondering where it went. I need to return it, but I don't know exactly how to go about it. Should I ship it to your sister?"

"Gracious, Kenzie, how will she know whose it is? She took clothes from people all over San Antonio and neighboring communities. Plus, she shopped at garage sales for bargains all summer long. It could've come from anywhere."

Dismay filled Kenzie's chest. "But maybe someone contacted her. If I'd lost a ring like that, I'd sure try to figure out where it went."

Ruby nodded. "You're right. I should at least ask Eileen. I'll give her a call this afternoon." She pressed the ring back into Kenzie's hand. "In the meantime, put that in a safe place and don't say anything to anyone about it. As much as I hate to admit it, there are unscrupulous people who

80

would try to cheat you out of it if they thought they could get by with it."

Kenzie gaped at Ruby. "You think someone from here would —"

Ruby waved her hand. "No, not necessarily someone from the church, but people talk, and with social media, information can spread like wildfire. Especially when there's a mystery surrounding something. Anyone could contact you and say it's theirs, and we wouldn't have a way to prove otherwise. It's best to keep this to ourselves."

"All right." Kenzie put the ring in the little zippered pocket inside her purse, then held the bag snug against her ribs. "Would you please call me after you talk to your sister? I don't like hanging on to something that doesn't belong to me. It feels . . . dishonest."

Ruby gave Kenzie another hug, this one longer and tighter. "And that, my dear, is why I love you. Moral to the core." She pulled back and smiled. "And apparently already popular with our new youth minister. Are you going to give him your brownie recipe?"

The thought of sharing a recipe with a man she didn't know made Kenzie's pulse pound. She shook her head.

Ruby laughed. "I wouldn't have expected

otherwise." She looped arms with Kenzie and escorted her to the foyer. "That big-hearted sister of mine always invites someone over for lunch on Sunday, so I need to give her time to serve and clean up. But I'll call her midafternoon. Eileen and I will put our heads together and figure out what to do with your unexpected find."

SIX

Wichita
Kenzie

When she lived at home, Kenzie never took the cover off Grossmammi's loom on a Sunday. Daed wasn't a harsh disciplinarian, not like some of the fathers in their strict community, but he would have punished her severely for dishonoring the Sabbath. Even now, hundreds of miles and several years distant from her family's home, she cringed as she slid the protective layer of muslin free from the 1930s loom on a Sunday afternoon.

Daed might not understand or accept her reasoning, but Kenzie didn't view using the loom as work. She found joy in turning strips of cloth into something beautiful and useful. Lori had once suggested Kenzie quit her job and weave full time. She'd said, "Specialty shops'll snatch these rugs up. Or you could open an online store and sell them yourself. I bet you'd make a fortune!" Kenzie appreciated Lori's enthusiasm, but she didn't want weaving to become her job. Grossmammi had told Kenzie the Lord had gifted her with a special ability and she should use her gift for Him. Besides, she crafted her rugs from donated materials. Would it be honest to make a profit from someone else's generosity?

Kenzie folded the muslin into a neat square and draped it over the armrest of her sofa. There was already too much dishonesty in the world. Back home, sometimes people from nearby cities tried to cheat the Amish. Many traded fairly, but others thought people who lived a simplistic lifestyle were simpleminded, and they employed tricks to get the better end of a deal. How often had Daed come home from the market seething because someone had attempted to pay him less than his asking price? Mamm always listened to Daed's rant. Then she would remind him they needed to repay evil with good, saying "Instead of getting angry, Alan, you must should pray for those who try to cheat you. They need a heart change."

Gentle Mamm . . . As kindhearted as Grossmammi. Kenzie ran her finger along the woven rows stretched tight across the beam, seeing in her mind's eye Grossmammi's wrinkled, bent fingers making the same trek. Neither Grossmammi nor Mamm would approve of using this old loom for personal gain. Nor would they approve of keeping a ring that didn't belong to her. She closed her eyes and sent up a silent prayer that the owner would be found. Then, with peace wrapping around her heart, she settled on the stool and picked up the shuttle, with its thick wrap of sewn-together strips of denim, twill, and flannel.

As she added rows to the rug in progress, her mind wandered backward in time. Grossmammi had let Kenzie feed the shuttle through the shed when she was very small. How she'd giggled as she'd pattered on bare feet back and forth behind Grossmammi's stool. Her cheeks tickled in memory of her *kapp*'s ribbons bouncing as she darted to and fro. She'd made it a game to reach the opposite side before Grossmammi pulled the beater bar the third time. Even now, her favorite part of the process was sending the shuttle through, pulling the bar snug, one, two, three, then sending the shuttle through again.

Cutting the strips, stitching the ends together, winding the shuttle, stringing the weft and warp, even cutting the rug free and tying it off . . . those tasks were *work*. Kenzie never did the work part of weaving on Sunday. But flipping the shuttle, pulling the bar and hearing the musical thud-thud-thud, then watching the pattern emerge on the weft . . . those actions were pure joy. Humming to herself, she developed a rhythm, her bare feet pushing the pedals and her hands tossing and catching the shuttle without conscious thought. Caught up in the wonderful creative process, she almost missed her cell phone's ring.

She gave the beater a quick pull, leaped off the stool, and snatched the phone from her purse. Ruby's number showed on the screen. Her pulse quickened, and she slid her finger across the glass to connect the call. As breathless as if she'd been racing back and forth behind her grandmother's stool, she gasped, "Hello? What did she say?"

Ruby's husky laughter sounded. "You are eager to unload that ring, aren't you?"

Kenzie hunched her shoulders, embarrassment striking. She crossed to the sofa and sat, pulling her feet to the side and hugging a throw pillow to her chest with her free hand. "I guess I am."

"Well, I hate to disappoint you, but no

one has contacted Eileen about a missing ring."

Kenzie's spirits fell. "She didn't have any idea where it might have come from?"

"She didn't know how to pin it down, considering how many individuals and groups contributed to your cause."

Kenzie rested her chin on the pillow and sighed. "So now what do I do?"

"Eileen and I discussed some possible ways of reuniting the owner with the ring. You have a social media account, don't you?"

"I have one on Facebook." Kenzie grimaced. "But I'm hardly ever on it. I basically opened it so I'd know what was going on at Beech Street."

"Eileen suggested making a post about finding a ring. She said not to mention how you found it, but only that you found it. It's all right to say it's white gold with a gemstone, but beyond that, keep the description vague. The real owner will know that it has a wide band, that the stone is a round diamond, and that it bears an inscription inside the band. If someone can give you all those details, you'll know you've found the rightful owner."

Kenzie considered everything Ruby had said. "I think I only have about thirty friends. Will posting to them do any good?"

Ruby's laughter came again. "Oh, honey, I'm sorry. Eileen will actually post it, so her name will be attached to it, not yours. Then she'll encourage others to share it. Hopefully the post will get spread around — what they call going viral. And if we're lucky, eventually the right person will see it and contact you."

Kenzie sighed. "Do you really think it'll work?"

"It's worked for other things." Confidence tinged Ruby's tone. "People have been reunited with lost relatives or purple hearts or even teddy bears through social media sharing. So it's worth a try, don't you think?"

"I suppose, but . . ." Daed's stern voice blasted in Kenzie's mind — *"Don't be foolish, Mackenzie, and open yourself up to mistreatment. Protect yourself. The world is full of thieves and evildoers."* She hugged the pillow tighter. "You said unscrupulous people would try to claim it if they knew about it. I'm kind of uneasy about making my contact information available to people I don't know."

"Oh, trust me, Kenzie, you won't be in any danger. You won't put any of your personal information on the internet. We'll word the post very carefully and set up a secondary email account where people can reach you."

"Um . . ." Kenzie released an embarrassed laugh. "I don't really know how to do that."

"I can help you. We'll do it after work tomorrow. All right?"

Eagerness to return the ring to whoever lost it propelled Kenzie to her feet. She set the pillow aside and nodded. "All right. Thanks so much for your help, Ruby. I appreciate it."

"You're very welcome, and both Eileen and I are proud of you for wanting to give it back. You're a good person, Kenzie. Goodbye now."

The connection went silent, but Grossmammi's voice filled the void. *"You're a good, good girl, my Mackenzie Faith. I know God loves you very much."* The memory should have brought a smile to Kenzie's face, but pain stabbed her heart. When she was a child, it was always so important to be *good* and thereby be found favorable by the almighty God.

She didn't want to return the ring to its owner in order to win favor from God. No deed, no matter how big or important, could ever be enough. She'd been given undeserved grace, and she wanted to do right to please the One who'd saved her soul from sin's damnation. She believed that Ruby understood Kenzie's motivation. But would Grossmammi, Mamm, and Daed understand?

Bradleyville
Merlin

Merlin awakened with a start. He sat up in his recliner and blinked across the dusky room to Leah. She smiled at him from her chair next to the unlit floor lamp. An open book rested in her lap. She clicked on the switch, and light flooded the area.

He pointed to the book. "Have you been reading in the dark?"

She chuckled. "No. I was napping, too, until you started to snore. I had my book ready for when you woke yourself. I knew you would. Not only were you snoring, you were kicking at something." She tilted her head, her brows rising. "Bad dream?"

He couldn't recall what he'd been dreaming, but he'd probably kicked because his foot was tingling. An annoying sensation that had become far too common. The doctor told him it was a side effect of high blood pressure. Wasn't his new medicine supposed to help bring it down? As was hiring someone to relieve some of his responsibilities.

Merlin snapped the recliner's footrest into its frame and sat up. "I'm sorry I disturbed you. I can't believe I fell asleep like that. How long has it been since I took a Sunday afternoon nap?"

"June 16, 2013."

He burst out laughing.

Leah shook her finger at him. "You think I threw out a random date. But check it. You'll discover it's correct."

"I'll save time by acknowledging you're always right." He chuckled at her smug grin. "But how do you know?"

"That was the last time you didn't have to deliver the evening sermon. We had a missionary couple here, visiting from Ghana. They did a presentation of their work at the hospital in Tamale, remember?"

Merlin gawked at his wife, his jaw hanging slack. How had she remembered so many details about something that had happened almost seven years ago? And had he really delivered every morning and evening sermon since then? As well as counseled, wrangled the youth, guided the deacons, visited the sick, comforted the weary and mourning . . . All God's work, all things he'd been called to do and, truthfully,

91

delighted in doing. But no wonder he was tired.

"Whew." He shook his head. "If that's true, then I guess I deserve tonight's break."

"I won't argue with you." Leah set her book aside and leaned forward slightly, linking her hands over her knee. "Merlin, now that Jase is here, maybe you could schedule specific Sundays for him to preach. Morning or evening — whichever you prefer. You'd have a chance to be fed instead of always being the one pouring out."

He rubbed his chin with his thumb. "You don't think the congregation would think I was being lazy?"

Her eyebrows came together. "If anyone calls you lazy, they better not do it where I can hear."

He swallowed a grin.

She sat back, and a thoughtful expression replaced her frown. "What if you handed off the responsibility on months that have a fifth Sunday? Not only would you get a little bit of a break, but more people than just the teens in the church would really get to know our new youth pastor." She gave him a pensive look. "Unless you've already outlined some other responsibilities for him to assume and don't want to overburden him."

Merlin sighed. "Of course I don't want to overburden him. Even considering he's been given a rent-free place to live, his salary package isn't what we'd call extravagant. Not a full-time salary, for sure."

"It's the most our congregation could offer."

"I know. I'm not criticizing our financial team for the amount they budgeted. But he might end up having to take on a part-time job somewhere else to make ends meet, depending on his other responsibilities — school loans, personal loans, whatever. I don't want to put full-time responsibilities on someone who's receiving a part-time salary."

She folded her arms and scowled at him over the top of her reading glasses. "You've been handling what equates to two full-time positions for decades. I think even the Lord would agree you have the right to delegate some of what you carry."

Her tart tone made Merlin fight another smile. "I'll pray about it." He stood and stretched, bouncing his heel against the floor to chase away the persistent tingle. He crossed to her chair, leaned down, and placed a kiss on her forehead. Remaining nearly nose to nose with her, he winked. "Thanks for worrying about me."

"I'm not worrying. I'm being realistic. You aren't exactly young anymore —"

He barked out a short laugh.

"— and you've been burning the candle at both ends for too long. Keep it up, let your health fall apart —"

His pulse skipped a beat. Did she know? Or only suspect?

"— and you won't be able to do anything."

His back was starting to hurt. He braced his palms on her chair's armrests and nodded. "Advice taken. As I said, I'll pray about it, then have a discussion with Jase in a couple of weeks, after he's settled in some."

She nodded. "Fair enough. But May has a fifth Sunday, so don't put it off too long." She cupped his cheeks and delivered a gentle smack on his lips. "Now, let me out of this chair so I can put some supper on the table. We need to be at the church in less than an hour."

He pushed himself upright and glanced at the clock. Past five already? He'd slept longer than he realized. "Okay. But something light, huh?" He rubbed his fist on his breastbone, where a touch of indigestion burned.

She stood, her frown fixed on him. "Are you all right?"

"Oh, sure." He leaned in for another kiss,

one that lingered for several seconds, then gave her a wink. "Heavy food makes me sleepy. I wanna stay awake during Jase's sermon tonight."

Uncertainty flickered in her blue eyes, but she nodded and headed for the kitchen.

Merlin sank into her chair and put his head in his hand. Leah was astute. Even at sixty-six, she was as sharp minded as she'd been at thirty. He wouldn't be able to keep her in the dark for long. Those pills the doctor had given him better kick in fast.

SEVEN

Wichita
Kenzie

Kenzie gnawed on a hangnail on her left thumb and watched as the words Ruby was typing with her two-finger peck method appeared in the blue box she'd created using a computer program. Ruby finished, then leaned back in her chair and held her hand toward the screen. "There. What do you think?"

The announcement looked so important in white letters on the bold background. Kenzie pressed her linked hands to her rib cage and read the post aloud. " 'Found: Ladies' white-gold, gemstone ring. Respond with description to claim.' " She shrugged. "Is there enough information to clue in the owner?" Maybe they should change *gemstone* to *wedding.*

Ruby rocked in her desk chair, her forehead furrowing. "We don't want to feed too

96

much to the public. If we come right out and say that the gem is a one-carat round diamond or the band is inscribed, it doesn't leave much else to define. I realize you'll likely have to wade through quite a few responses that aren't connected to the ring you found, but I think it's best to be ambiguous."

Kenzie frowned. "What's 'ambiguous'?" She might have hesitated asking someone else the question, but Ruby never treated Kenzie as if she were unintelligent, even though she hadn't been allowed to go to school past the eighth grade. Most people wouldn't hire her because she didn't have a high school diploma. Ruby hadn't even batted an eye after contacting the owner of the shop in Indianapolis and receiving her recommendation. Kenzie appreciated the way her boss listened to questions, answered patiently, and never made fun if Kenzie didn't grasp something unfamiliar the first time.

Ruby patted Kenzie's clenched fist. " 'Ambiguous' . . . vague or undefined in nature." She smiled. "Honey, it'll let you know without doubt you've found the rightful owner if they can give you all of the details, plus the inscription."

Kenzie nodded. "Okay."

Ruby turned back to the computer. "Now, we need to set up an email account for you to use. Let's go with one of the free ones. What name do you want to use? Your real one or a fake one?"

"Not my real one." She never went by her birth name, Mackenzie Hochstetler, anymore. And she didn't want her new legal name floating around the internet, either. "My email name is Loves2weave, but for this one maybe just Weaver. Or WeaverGirl."

"Hmm . . ." Ruby pecked Weaver and then variations of WeaverGirl into a box, muttering under her breath. "It looks like those are taken." She tapped her chin with her finger, glowering at the screen. Suddenly she brightened. She leaned over the keyboard. "What about . . ." She tapped on a few keys and then crowed, "Aha!" She beamed at Kenzie. "FinderznotKeeperz is available."

Kenzie leaned close and frowned at the name. "Shouldn't there be *s*'s instead?"

Ruby's eyes twinkled. "For the *z* in Kenzie. Okay?"

Kenzie couldn't help but laugh. Ruby seemed so pleased with herself. "Sounds fine."

Ruby smiled, wagging her finger at Kenzie. "It's better than fine. And a lot better than some variation of *weaver.* Because there's no way anyone could trace this to you. Your identity will remain completely private."

Kenzie grabbed the end of her ponytail and twisted it over her shoulder. "I like that idea."

"All right. FinderznotKeeperz it is." Ruby filled boxes on the screen. Then she used the mouse and directed the little arrow to a rectangle marked Submit and clicked it. "An email box is reserved for you, but we'll still need to connect it to your cell phone so you can receive the messages. If you don't mind, I'll come by after work and help you set it up."

Kenzie wouldn't know how to do it. "I'd really appreciate that."

"You got it. For now, though, let's get this show on the road." Ruby opened Facebook on her computer. "Eileen gave me her log-in information so we can post as if we're her."

Kenzie felt a little sneaky, pretending to be someone else, but if Eileen knew about it, then it would be all right.

Ruby brought up her sister's Facebook page on the computer screen. Using the mouse, she placed the blue box on the page and clicked a button on the mouse. Then she sat back, a smile breaking, and clapped.

"Done!"

Kenzie's tummy did a funny flip. "You mean the post is up?"

Lori entered the office, a bounce in her step and a big smile on her face. She'd been smiling since she arrived that morning, still glowing about the new youth minister's talk at church last night. "What post? What're you two doing?"

Kenzie hadn't gone to last night's service — she'd forgotten to arrange a ride — but the way Lori had raved about the new youth minister's testimony and short sermon made her wish she had. She also wished she'd checked to make sure she and Ruby were completely alone before she asked about the post. Ruby had told her not to say anything to anyone. She didn't know how to answer Lori.

Ruby spun around in her chair. "I'm helping my Texas sister with a project, and Kenzie was kind enough to give me a hand on her break." She closed the screen and rose. "Did you need something, Lori?"

"Yes." Lori's gaze zipped from the computer screen to Ruby's unsmiling face. "There's a customer who wants to order some fabric, but it's out of stock, and she's kind of upset about it. I'm not sure what else to tell her, so . . ." She hunched her

100

shoulders, her full lips forming a pout.

Ruby moved toward the door. "I'll take care of it." She paused and turned to Kenzie. "In answer to your question, yes."

Kenzie released a breath of both relief and apprehension. "Okay. Thanks."

Ruby patted Kenzie's arm and strode out the door.

Lori gazed after Ruby for a moment and then gave Kenzie a puzzled look. "Since when do you help Ruby's Texas sister with stuff?" Understanding dawned. "Oh, I bet it has to do with the clothing she collected, doesn't it? Is she getting you more?"

Lori was half-right, but the half-wrong part left Kenzie floundering. "I guess I'll find out. If you're on break, I better go to the floor." She headed for the door, but Lori put out her hand and stopped her.

"I have a favor to ask." Lori bit her lower lip and gazed intently into Kenzie's eyes. Whatever the favor was, it would be a big one.

A memory verse from Matthew 5 trickled through Kenzie's mind — "But let your communication be, Yea, yea; Nay, nay: for whatsoever is more than these cometh of evil." Strange how even more than a decade after she'd left behind the strict sect of her childhood, rules taken from God's Holy

Word still hounded her. She couldn't commit to or refrain from anything unless she knew what it was. "What is it?"

Lori clasped her hands beneath her chin and pleaded with her eyes. "If I come to your place tonight and I promise to pay you for the ingredients, would you teach me how to make your brownies?"

Suspicion bloomed in the back of Kenzie's mind. "You want to bake some for Brother Jase, don't you?"

Lori giggled. "I really do. He liked them so much he even ate the crumbs from the pan before he handed it over for washing Saturday night. They say the way to a man's heart is with food, so . . ." She tipped her head and smiled sweetly. "Please?"

Kenzie couldn't hold back a chortle. "I'd be happy to bake another batch for Brother Jase, but I can't do it tonight. Ruby's coming over, and . . . um . . ."

"Oh."

Lori's crestfallen expression pierced Kenzie. She hated keeping a secret from Lori, her best friend in Kansas. Maybe even the best friend she'd ever had. Kenzie had laughed more with her than with any other person she'd known, including Grossmammi or her brother Caleb, whom she'd teasingly declared was part monkey.

Kenzie cupped Lori's elbow. "I can't tonight, but what about tomorrow? Then you can take the brownies to Brother Jase on Wednesday evening when they're still fairly fresh. Okay?"

Lori's bright smile returned. "Oh, that's an even better idea. Thanks, Kenz." She grabbed Kenzie in a hug. "Okay, tomorrow. And I promise to help cut up some clothes while I'm there to repay you."

Kenzie stepped free and moved backward toward the door. "Not this time. We'll bake and have fun."

Lori waved, beaming. "Perfect."

Bradleyville
Jase

Jase spent a fair portion of Monday, his scheduled day off, learning his way around the area of Wichita closest to Bradleyville. The busyness of Wichita didn't feel much different than San Antonio. Today's weather pretty much matched up, too. He wore his favorite cargo shorts and flip-flops, adding to the feeling of familiarity. Since he didn't know where to find groceries or gasoline or everyday stuff like toothpaste and toilet paper, he went out in search of convenient shopping options.

To his relief, he located a supercenter

where he could buy everything from car tires to canned soup. And only ten miles from his apartment — a reasonable distance. He browsed the aisles for over an hour, filling his shopping cart with what he considered necessary.

Now back in his apartment, he put everything away. The little freezer section of his refrigerator was stuffed full of microwaveable dinners and cartons of off-brand butter brickle ice cream, his favorite flavor. And his cupboards held boxes of cereal, snack cakes, cans of ravioli and macaroni in meat sauce, and little plastic cups of pudding. He'd need to buy things like bread, milk, and lunch meats more frequently, but he had staples to last for at least a month.

As he closed the cabinet door, he remembered Rachel telling him he really needed to learn how to cook. But why bother? Ready-made meals were so convenient. Besides, if he learned to cook, he'd need more pots and pans and fancy things like spatulas and mixers. He shuddered. Not today. Not even this summer. Maybe next winter, when he'd be cooped up more. Or maybe not. Canned pasta wasn't that bad. A whole lot better than some of the stuff he ate before the state took him away from his mom. The one sandwich he'd never eat

104

again, no matter how hungry he got, was oily canned tuna on stale white bread.

He left the kitchen area and scuffed barefoot across the carpet to his sofa. He settled at the end closest to the lamp table, where he'd stacked his Bible and several study books Brother Kraft had given him for perusal. Most recently, Brother Kraft had been teaching the youth from the book of Proverbs — sound material, for sure. Jase had contemplated continuing where the man left off, but Brother Kraft had made up his own curriculum. Jase didn't have the seasoned minister's ability, so he'd borrowed some books from the preacher's shelves. He liked the one focused on John's gospel the best. Lots of meat, lots of solid doctrine, lots of looks at Jesus. Didn't they all need that?

He flopped the book open across his lap and began reading. Studying. Looking for nuggets that spoke to him because if they spoke to him, he'd be passionate about sharing them with the kids. But he couldn't seem to focus. His mind wandered backward to his college years. Sometimes being poor had its benefits. And, as Brother Tony had pointed out way back then, maintaining a good high school GPA paid off, too. Trinity College had offered him enough in scholarships and grants to cover all but a small balance, which he'd been able to pay, thanks to his part-time job at the town's bowling alley.

He'd chosen a major in communication management and a minor in religious studies, coursework Brother Tony had recommended because Jase had expressed the desire to know God at a deeper level and to share His love with others in a meaningful way. He'd done well in college — even graduated summa cum laude. Not bad for a foster-system kid. He stared across the room, his focus inward. Back then, he'd been so single minded in purpose, so determined to do well. To succeed. To prove to his foster parents and his church family and even his social worker that the time and effort they'd poured into him hadn't been in vain.

So had he done it for God, for them, or for himself?

The question jolted him, and the book slipped to the floor. Grunting in aggravation, he leaned forward and snatched it up. It had landed facedown, crimping several pages. He tried to smooth them flat with the heel of his hand, but the creases remained. He scowled so hard his forehead hurt. Partly because he'd damaged Brother

Kraft's book, partly because he didn't like the uneasy feeling his internal query had raised.

When he and Rachel had committed themselves to ministry, he'd been so certain his chosen degrees had been God's means of preparing him. Why couldn't he recapture that certainty now? Did he really even belong in this town, bearing the title Brother Jase and being a spiritual leader? Brother Tony thought he did. Brother Kraft and his wife seemed to think so.

He pushed himself upright, as slow as an arthritic ninety-year-old might move, and trudged to his bedroom. He opened the top drawer of his bureau, reached beneath a stack of T-shirts, and pulled out the framed photograph of him and Rachel. Just a candid shot taken at a church picnic. Nothing formal. Their chance for formal engagement or wedding pictures had been stolen from them. But he liked this image, her looking up at him, the two of them laughing at something. He couldn't recall what they'd been laughing about, but he remembered her laughter. She'd used her laugh freely, and he could never resist joining her, because it was always such a joyful sound.

He sighed, his warm breath briefly fogging the glass covering the image of her precious face. "I know where you are, Rachel, and even if I could bring you back, I don't think I'd be selfish enough to do it. But I sure miss you. I wish you were here. It wouldn't matter to me if your body was permanently broken or your mind forever changed." The doctor's solemn words, meant to indicate the blessing death provided for her, hadn't assured him then, and they didn't assure him now. "At least we'd be together. I just don't think I can do this alone."

"Surely I am with you always, to the very end of the age." Jesus's promise from the book of Matthew roared through Jase's mind. Brother Tony had used the passage to comfort him during the first weeks after Rachel's death, reminding him that even though she was gone, he wasn't alone. Jesus was there and would always be there for him.

Jase pressed Rachel's photo to his chest and looked up at the ceiling. "You say You're with me always, but right now . . . I'm not feelin' it. So You might wanna step up Your game." He cringed. Had he really challenged the Son of God? Surely God would smite him for it. But his feelings were honest, and God knew them even if Jase never said them out loud, so he might as well lay it all out. "If You're here, show up. Show up where I can see You and feel You and trust You again."

His throat went tight, and he forced his last words out. "Jesus, who's with me to the end of the age, prove Yourself to me. Because" — he gulped and hung his head — "I need You."

EIGHT

Jase

Jase glanced at the round plastic clock loudly tick-ticking from its spot on his office wall and gave a little jolt. Five o'clock already? His first official day as youth minister for Beech Street Bible Fellowship was all but gone. At least he was fully prepared for his first real youth gathering tomorrow evening. Remembering what Brother Tony'd said about reaching them before teaching them, he'd chosen an activity called "Introductions." Pairs of kids would interview each other and then share what they learned with the group, revealing a bit about themselves in a fun way. At least, he hoped they'd think it was fun. He was sure Sienna would approve. The shyer ones? Might be a little harder for them, but he'd always found talking about someone else easier than talking about himself. Surely he wasn't the only one who felt that way.

He examined the schedule, which he'd typed into an organizational program on his laptop. When Brother Kraft told him he'd get two hours with the kids every Wednesday evening, he'd been a little concerned. How would he fill the entire time? But looking at it written out gave him more confidence. After all, the first thirty minutes were for eating and chatting. Sister Kraft and a few volunteers took care of the meal, and there'd be no formal structure needed during supper. He'd allotted forty-five minutes for the lead-in activity, which left another forty-five minutes for Bible study, maybe some singing — according to Zack's dad, the teen was willing to accompany them on his guitar — and, for sure, prayer.

Eventually he'd trim back the lead-in activity to a half hour so he'd have more time committed to the meatier side of things, but for now he was satisfied with the schedule. He hoped Brother Kraft would be okay with it, too. His boss said he'd come by the apartment around seven thirty to talk through Jase's plan and answer any questions. The minister was nothing if not supportive and helpful. A lot like Brother Tony. The brothers-in-law could be real brothers based on their personalities. But not on looks.

Jase chuckled, comparing Brother Tony's lean frame and dark hair and eyes indicative of his Hispanic heritage to Brother Kraft's obvious German coloring and rather paunchy shape — no doubt the result of eating Sister Kraft's good cooking for so many years. But where it mattered, in heart and dedication, the two men were nearly identical. Already Jase felt drawn to the pastor of Beech Street Bible Fellowship and believed he'd learn as much from him as he'd learned from Brother Tony during his years at the San Antonio church.

Longing to see and talk to the people from his former congregation struck hard, and Jase turned on his web browser, then logged into his social media profile. He didn't have a lot of friends on his account, but the ones who were there mattered to him. He clicked to his news feed and scanned the entries, smiling at memes and jotting down the prayer requests he encountered. His scrolling uncovered some sort of notification. The white block letters set against a blue rectangle stood out like a billboard.

FOUND:
LADIES' WHITE-GOLD GEMSTONE
RING.
RESPOND WITH DESCRIPTION TO

Brother Tony's wife had posted it. In the comment area, she encouraged others to spread the word. Warmth filled his chest. Whoever'd lost the ring was lucky someone with honesty had found it. He clicked Share. For the most part his friends were all in Sister Eileen's circle of acquaintanceship, but he knew enough about algorithms to know that the more shares, the better coverage it would get. He'd do his part.

Someone tapped on his door, and he closed his laptop and called, "C'mon in."

The door creaked open, and Brother Kraft peeked around its edge. His usual grin lit his round face. "Leah just called, said for me to bring you home for supper if you don't have plans."

Jase rose, unplugging his laptop's power cord at the same time. "My only plan is to chat with you this evening, so I won't turn down her invite."

Brother Kraft pushed the door all the way open and stepped inside. He sent a slow look around the small room. "Hmm . . . Bringing in a desk and a couple of shelves doesn't do much to mask the truth that this was a storage closet. What else can we do to make this feel more like a place where you want to hang out?"

Jase rounded his metal desk, his laptop tucked under his arm. He gave a glance, too. Small, sure. And plain, considering its bald fluorescent fixture, tan walls, and scuffed tile floor. But it had a desk, Wi-Fi, and a pair of dented metal shelves. The shelves had probably held cleaning supplies in the past, but they adequately housed his books and a few personal effects — his framed college diploma, a posed photo of him in his high school basketball uniform, and the trophy he'd won for pitching a winning game in Little League. The office met his needs. "I don't think it's that bad."

Brother Kraft raised one eyebrow and tsk-tsked. "Believe me, Jase, it's pretty bad."

Jase snorted under his breath. If the man had spent nights in a homeless shelter, he might have a different opinion about the room.

"If you're going to do counseling sessions and other kinds of meetings in here, we need to make it, well, *more inviting* is what Leah would say." He slid his hands into his pockets and tapped his right heel against the floor. "We spent so much time readying your apartment, we kind of forgot about your office, where you'll spend almost as much time. After supper tonight, let's pick Leah's brain on how we can spruce up this room for you. She's always got good ideas."

Jase believed Sister Kraft would have ideas. But he wasn't convinced it was necessary. "If that's what you want to do, I won't argue."

"Good." The man gave Jase a light smack on the shoulder, then gestured to the hallway. "Let's get going. I have it on good authority Leah made spaghetti and meatballs for supper."

Sister Kraft's meatballs were as flavorful as anything Jase had tasted. Between the spaghetti, garlic bread, and salad made of so many raw veggies Jase couldn't even recognize all of them, his stomach was achingly full. He used his last chunk of meatball to swipe up the remaining sauce from his plate and shot her a grin. "Ma'am, if there was a cooking prize, it'd go to you hands down." He popped the bite into his mouth and made a show of enjoying it, the way he'd seen Opie on *The Andy Griffith Show* do over Aunt Bee's cooking.

She laughed. "I'm glad you enjoyed the meatballs, because you'll be eating them again tomorrow."

Jase wiped his mouth with his napkin,

115

then wadded it and tossed it onto his empty plate. "Oh? Why's that?"

"It's what we're serving for the youth supper." She rose and stacked their plates. "Spaghetti is an easy way to feed a crowd, and when that gang of teenagers swoops in at six for supper, it feels like a crowd." She turned in the direction of the kitchen doorway.

Brother Kraft held his hand toward her. "Leah, can you hold off washing those dishes? We need your thinker for a problem Jase has."

She returned to the table, set the plates in front of an empty chair, and sat. She fixed her gaze on Jase. "What's wrong?"

Jase scratched his jaw, holding back a laugh. "Nothing. I mean, Brother Kraft thinks there's a problem, but I'm really okay."

Her attention shifted to her husband. "Well?"

Brother Kraft patted her wrist. "I'm sorry I made it sound more troubling than it is." He explained the starkness of Jase's office. "Can you come up with ways to spruce the place up? Make it feel less like a closet?"

Sister Kraft's white brows pulled down. "I've forgotten. Why did the deacons set him up in the storage room?"

116

"Because it was the closest room to my office."

"Isn't there a Sunday school room we could use as Jase's office?"

"Now, Leah, you know those rooms are all in use."

"Of course they are, but could a couple of classes be combined to free up a room for Jase?"

Jase sat quiet and still, shifting his eyes from speaker to speaker. The pair seemed to have forgotten he was with them. Their easy way of tossing comments back and forth with hardly a pause for breath reminded him of how he and Rachel used to talk. As if they didn't even really need to think so much as respond instinctively. He'd thought they were unique in the ability, but maybe all couples possessed this ease. He wasn't sure if he appreciated or resented the realization.

"No, I don't think so." Brother Kraft puffed his cheeks and blew out a breath. "There really isn't anyplace else to put him. So we'll have to make the storage room work. Somehow." The minister's final word was tinged with gloom and doom.

"Pffft . . ." Sister Kraft waved her hand and pursed her lips. "Where there's a will, there's a way." She turned to Jase. "Do you

117

need to use your office tomorrow night when you're teaching the youth?"

Jase shook his head.

"Well, then, after we get the supper mess cleaned up, I'll take a couple of the kitchen team members to your office and we'll do some brainstorming." She grinned. "If we get all our heads together, we'll come up with something. But, Jase . . ." Her expression turned serious. "There's not a window in that room, so the door is the only way to see in or out. When you've got someone in there with you, you need to leave the door open."

He frowned. If he was counseling someone, they'd want privacy.

"Now, don't get me wrong. I'm a good judge of character, and I don't see you as the kind of young man who would take advantage of anyone."

Heat blazed in Jase's face. He understood her concern, and guilt smacked him, even though he hadn't done anything wrong.

"I also don't think any of our youth are the kind who would make a false accusation, but to protect yourself as well as any of the young people who might come to your office, leave the door open when you have someone in there with you."

Brother Kraft cleared his throat. "And it's

probably best to schedule any one-on-one sessions when either Leah or I are also in the building."

Sister Kraft nodded hard. "Yes. Merlin doesn't even meet alone at the church with someone. I make sure I'm at my church-secretary desk the whole time." She reached across the table and put her hand over Jase's. "In this day and age, it behooves one to exercise caution. Remember what Jesus told His disciples — we're to be as wise as serpents but as innocent as doves. This especially applies to young, single, attractive youth ministers. There's no sense in giving cause for speculation, right?"

Jase gave a stiff nod. "Absolutely. Right."

"Good." Brother Kraft stood. "Let's go the living room and you can tell me what you have planned for tomorrow night." He gave his wife's shoulder as a squeeze as he passed behind her chair. "Thank you for the good dinner, for your willingness to make Jase's office a more pleasant place for him to work, and for your wise counsel. When God designed you, He must've been showing off."

She laughed and shooed him away, but the sparkle in her eyes let Jase know she appreciated her husband's compliments. Jase cringed. He should've said things like that to Rachel. During his early years, shuffling around to wherever someone would put him and Mom up for the night and then being passed from foster home to foster home, he'd experienced more rejection than affection. Even as an adult, he struggled with expressing his deepest feelings. But maybe it didn't matter anymore. Rachel was gone, and he wasn't looking for another woman to share his life.

He trailed Brother Kraft to the cozy living area of the parsonage. Brother Kraft sank into the scoop-shaped cushion of one of the two matching recliners. Sister Kraft usually took the other one, and she might join them when she was finished in the kitchen, so Jase sat on the sofa. He crossed his leg, curling his toes to keep his flip-flop on.

Brother Kraft shifted a bit in his chair, linked his hands over his belly, and gave Jase a bright smile. "Well, what did you decide for a course of study?"

Jase told him the title of the book he'd selected and outlined the lesson, taken from the first chapter of John. Brother Kraft listened intently, his hands occasionally rising and pressing against his chest, then returning to his stomach. Jase suspected the man was experiencing heartburn and considered asking him if he'd like to take an antacid. Would the question be too personal? After all, he'd only known Brother Kraft for a few days. Maybe it was an unconscious gesture and he'd embarrass the minister by pointing it out. In the end, he chose to ignore it.

When Jase finished sharing his intentions, Brother Kraft nodded and smiled. "Sounds like you're on a good track. Keep in mind, some of these kids didn't have the privilege of going to Sunday school when they were small, so they won't necessarily be up on what we consider common terminology. They might be hearing some of the stories from John for the very first time. Don't be afraid to slow it down, to take time for definitions or further explanation if needed. Teens aren't always the best at asking for clarification, especially when most of the others seem to get it. They don't want to look dumb. But you'll learn to recognize by their expressions or their lack of participation whether or not they're with you."

Unease created an uncomfortable ache in Jase's stomach. Would he recognize their needs? Did he have what it took to meet those needs?

"It might take a bit to settle in, but I'll be in the sanctuary, leading the adult Bible study, while you're leading the youth. If questions come up, poke your head in and ask. Wednesday evenings aren't so formal that they can't be interrupted if need be."

Jase hoped he'd never have to interrupt. He'd look like an inept dolt if he did.

Brother Kraft sat forward and put his elbows on his knees, hands still linked. "Let's pray, okay?"

Jase nodded and started to bow his head.

Sister Kraft hurried into the room. "Merlin, I —" She came to a halt, her gaze jerking from her husband to Jase and back. Her face flooded with pink. "Oh, I'm so sorry."

Brother Kraft chuckled and reached for her hand. "We hadn't started yet. Now you can join us." He gave a little tug, and she crossed in front of him to the second recliner and sat. "What were you going to say?"

The color in her face faded. "I went ahead and called a couple of the ladies who help in the kitchen on Wednesday night, and Lori — Jase, you might remember her from your welcome party. Lori Fowler . . . red headed? Gregarious?"

An image of a dimple-faced young woman with thick, curly hair, a round smiling face, and a bubbly demeanor flashed in Jase's memory. He nodded.

"Well, she promised to take a look at the

122

office and make a list of ideas for fixing it up." An unreadable expression flitted across the woman's face. "Lori seemed particularly eager to be helpful. I suspect she might, well . . ." She sent a glance at Brother Kraft, then faced Jase again. "I think she has a little crush. If you think it's better for her not to be involved, I'll find a kind way to tell her, and I'll ask someone else to help."

Jase rubbed his knuckles against his jaw. "I'd hate to turn away an eager helper, and I sure don't want her feelings to be hurt. It'll be okay."

Sister Kraft sighed. "All right. I've already let her know you aren't in the market —"

She'd done what? Heat filled Jase's face. He didn't much like having his personal life discussed behind his back.

"— and I hope she'll take the hint. I don't want you to be uncomfortable around her."

Well, being uncomfortable was a certainty now.

Brother Kraft cleared his throat. "Let's go ahead and pray."

That suited Jase fine.

NINE

Lori fingered her cell phone in her pocket and stared at the partially completed rug in Kenzie's loom. Greens, blues, and yellows played against one another, with a random strand of red giving a splash of unexpected color. Kenzie sure knew her craft. This rug would brighten any room. A sly smile quivered on the corners of her lips. What if . . .

She bounded around the corner to Kenzie's little kitchen, a question ready, but the oven timer interrupted. Kenzie pulled the pan from the oven and set it on a stack of hot pads. The rich scent of chocolate rising from the brownies drew Lori like a magnet. She leaned over the pan and admired the crackled top while inhaling the aroma. Her mouth watered, and temptation to cut a piece for herself tugged hard. But these

124

weren't for her — these were for Brother Jase. As much as she loved food, giving up the whole batch would be a sacrifice, but she'd make it. Would Kenzie be willing to sacrifice for Brother Jase, too?

"Mmm, those smell so good. And look so pretty with the crackly top." Lori shot Kenzie a mock frown. "When are you going to give me your recipe so I can make these myself and not have to bother you?"

Kenzie dropped the oven mitts in a drawer. "A place for everything, and everything in its place" seemed to be her motto. Lori admired it but also found it annoying. Yikes trikes, she loved Kenzie, but did she have to be so perfect?

Kenzie closed the door with her hip and gave a one-shoulder shrug. "I don't know. It's a family recipe, so I guess I feel a little . . . territorial."

Lori burst out laughing.

Kenzie's face pinched into a frown. "What's so funny?"

Lori stifled her amusement. She touched her friend's arm. "I'm sorry, but you've given up almost everything else from your family. You don't follow their religion anymore. You wear skirts, sure, but they're nothing like the solid-color homemade dresses you had to wear when you were a

125

kid. And you haven't visited them in how many years? So does the recipe really matter that much?"

Kenzie lowered her head and fiddled with the hem of her T-shirt. "Maybe it sounds a little dumb, but I . . . I want to keep it." She lifted her face. "I'm willing to bake them whenever you want some."

Lori grabbed Kenzie in a hug. "Okay, I'll quit bugging you about the recipe." She let loose and stepped back, glancing at the brownie pan. They smelled so good the temptation was almost overwhelming. "Can we go sit in the other room? I wanna talk to you about something else."

"Sure."

One thing about Kenzie — she was always quick to forgive. And forget, it seemed. Something Lori maybe needed to learn to do. She might actually be able to get along with her dad if she could forgive and forget. Lori caught hold of Kenzie's hand and drew her to the sofa. She plopped down, and Kenzie sat at the opposite end.

"Sister Kraft called a little bit ago. She asked for my help with a project." Well, she hadn't specifically asked for Lori's help. She mentioned she'd be recruiting help to decorate Brother Jase's office, and Lori volunteered. But that detail wasn't very im-

126

portant.

"What kind of project?"

Lori wriggled on the cushion. "Fixing up Brother Jase's office so it feels more welcoming. Can you believe they stuck him in an old storage closet?" She waved one hand, wishing she could erase the question. It didn't sound very kind. "It really isn't anybody's fault. There's only the one pastor's office in the church, and Brother Kraft has it for his study, as well he should. But now Brother Jase is here, too, and they couldn't stick him in with Brother Kraft, or even in the secretary's office Sister Kraft uses, so they took the only room available for his office. The problem is it's not very office-y, and it needs to be."

Kenzie picked up a throw pillow and hugged it, settling more fully into the corner. "So how're you going to fix it up?"

"Well, for starters, a better paint color than institutional tan. Sister Kraft said we could ask people to buy or donate some nicer shelves, a couple of chairs where visitors can sit, maybe some framed Scripture prints for the walls. And . . ." Lori bit her lower lip and aimed her gaze at the loom. "I wondered if you'd maybe donate the rug you're making. It's pretty without being girlie, and it looks like it's gonna be kind of

127

long, so we could lay it out in front of his desk. You know, to break up the monotony of that awful gray-speckled white tile, which Sister Kraft said has to stay."

Kenzie didn't say anything.

Lori looked at her and caught her examining the rug. She waited a few more seconds, but when Kenzie still didn't speak, Lori couldn't stay quiet. "Kenz? What do you think?"

Kenzie pulled her ponytail over her shoulder and twisted the strands. "Since I always donate my rugs anyway, I guess it would be all right. I'll just make a monetary donation to the mission fund in its place."

Lori slid forward several inches and grabbed Kenzie's hands. "No! You're already giving up the rug. You shouldn't pay money, too." Lori wanted that rug for Brother Jase's office. It would add color and warmth and personality to a dull space. She blurted the only compromise she could think of with short notice. "How much would the shop get if they sold the rug? Maybe I can buy it from you." Then she could gift Brother Jase with it. A hopeful shiver rattled her frame.

Kenzie's face turned bright pink. "I can't sell it to you. You're my friend. That would feel —"

"Dishonest." Lori rolled her eyes. Then

she grinned. "You already bake brownies for me without asking to be reimbursed for the ingredients. I don't want to take advantage of you. So . . ." She yanked on Kenzie's hands. "How much would they get?"

Kenzie pulled in a breath and let it out through puckered lips. "A rug of that size? They'll probably ask between a hundred and fifty and two hundred dollars."

Lori gasped, let go of Kenzie's hands, and collapsed against the backrest. "Wow . . ."

"Yeah." Kenzie's expression turned apologetic. "Listen, I know what a big expense that would be to me. I can't ask it of you."

Lori huffed, plopping one hand on top of her head. "I couldn't give it." Not all at once. But maybe she could pay it out a different way. She sat up again. "About how much fabric is wrapped up in that rug?"

Kenzie grimaced. "It's hard to say, really, since I don't use actual lengths of cloth but clothing items cut into strips. That one has several pairs of jeans and khaki pants, maybe a dozen flannel shirts, some long johns —"

Lori's mouth fell open. She spluttered, "Did you say . . . long johns? Aren't those underwear?"

Kenzie folded her arms. "Listen, a lot of long johns are mostly wool, which is great

129

fabric for rugs."

Lori laughed at Kenzie's defensive pose. She gestured to the rug. "So the red in there . . . that's from long johns?"

Kenzie nodded.

Knowing she'd need to locate at least one pair of men's long underwear complicated Lori's plan, but she could scour secondhand stores and garage sales for most of the clothes. "Okay, so what if I agreed to find enough jeans and shirts and" — she snickered — "long johns to make another rug the same size as that one? I realize having the fabric is a small part of the whole rug-making process. The weaving part takes a lot of time. But if I bought the clothes and cut them all into strips and stitched the strips together for you, would that be a fair exchange?" She held her breath and stared into Kenzie's face.

Kenzie looked toward the ceiling, like she was seeking guidance, then gave a quick nod. "Okay. That sounds fair."

Lori squealed and lunged for a hug.

Kenzie squirmed. "But the rug isn't finished yet. You can't have it right away."

Lori straightened. "How long?"

"A few more days, if I can get three or four hours a day at the loom."

Lori bounced up and pulled Kenzie from

the sofa. "Well, what're you waiting for? There's still a couple hours until bedtime. Go. Weave." She teasingly pushed Kenzie to the loom.

Kenzie laughed and sank onto the old-fashioned piano stool. "What is your deal? I mean, you get excited about random stuff all the time. It's one of your charms."

Lori gave a little jolt. It was? Dad said her excited outbursts were annoying.

"But over a rug for —" Her blue eyes widened. She swiveled the stool until she faced Lori. "I thought you were impressed with him as a minister, but you're impressed with him as a . . . a man."

Hearing it stated so plainly made Lori's knees go weak. She perched on the edge of the little table beside the sofa and folded her arms over her chest. "And that's dumb." Not a question. A proclamation.

Kenzie tilted her head, her ponytail swinging across her shoulder. "Why is it dumb?"

Lori flung her arms wide. "Kenzie! You have eyes. Look at me."

Confusion clouded Kenzie's expression. "Look at what?"

Lori hugged herself, battling tears. "At dumpy, goofy, ugly me."

Kenzie stood so quickly the round seat on the stool spun. "Lori, you aren't any of

131

those things."

Lori launched from the table and stomped to the opposite side of the room, then whirled and faced Kenzie. "I admit it, I think Brother Jase is very attractive. And he's so nice. The way he talked to me the night of his welcome-to-Bradleyville gathering . . . he made me feel so normal. Like I was real."

Kenzie's forehead crinkled. "Why wouldn't he? You are real."

Lori snorted. "I mean a real woman, with feelings that matter."

Kenzie slowly sat again, her gaze locked on Lori's.

Lori swallowed hard. "Yikes trikes, Kenzie, my own father doesn't think I matter. He acts like he's embarrassed to even claim me. I know I'm nothing to look at." Not like slim and pretty Kenzie. She hung her head, battling a wave of jealousy, followed by a wash of guilt for being jealous of someone so kind and unassuming.

" 'Favour is deceitful, and beauty is vain: but a woman that feareth the LORD, she shall be praised.' "

Lori blinked, baffled. Then she realized Kenzie'd shared a verse from Proverbs.

"You deserve the praise, Lori, because you try to honor the Lord with your life. You're always doing nice things for people, like helping with the dinners at church, giving me rides wherever I need to go, and even fixing up Brother Jase's office." Kenzie's blue eyes flashed. "You're a good person. I know God the Father is pleased with you."

Kenzie's sincerity pierced Lori. "That's really nice of you to say, but let's be honest. How many men look at a woman and think, 'Oh, wow, doesn't she revere the Lord? That's the girl for me.' No, men want a pretty girlfriend or wife. I bet that was true even in your Amish community. Didn't the pretty girls get courted first?"

Kenzie turned her gaze aside. Even though she didn't say a word, the action let Lori know who'd won the bet.

Lori sighed. "And I bet Brother Jase's fiancée was drop-dead gorgeous. She'd have to be to match him."

Kenzie shot Lori a startled look. "He's engaged?"

"I said *was.*" Lori returned to the sofa and sat on the edge of the cushion, her shoulders slumping. "The night he shared his testimony, he told everybody about her dying in a car accident. Sister Kraft had already told me. I think she was trying to warn me off, like it's too soon for him to think about dating someone else, but she warned me too late. I'm . . . smitten." Her chin wobbled and tears made her vision go wonky. "And it's so dumb because he's too good looking for me."

Kenzie jammed her hands on her hips. "If he thinks that, he's not worth crying over."

Lori released a chortle. She sniffled and rubbed the tears away with her fists. "Aw, thanks, Kenz. I don't think I was crying over him as much as crying over . . . me." Why couldn't she have been born blond haired and blue eyed? For Jase, but mostly for her father. Would he love her then?

Kenzie stood and took hold of Lori's elbow, pulled her from the sofa, and led her to the piano stool. "Well, stop crying now and have a seat here."

Lori dropped onto the stool and gave Kenzie an apprehensive look. "Why?"

"Because if you're going to gift Brother Jase with this rug, you need to at least have a hand in crafting it."

Lori raised her hands like she was under arrest. "I'm too clumsy. I'll probably mess it up or break something."

Kenzie grabbed Lori's hands and guided them to the loom. "You won't break it. Trust me."

Lori blew out a breath. "Better stay close."

Kenzie patted her shoulder. "Don't worry.

I'll stay for as long as you need me. I think you'll discover the rhythm of weaving is very soothing. Let me show you what to do, and once you get the hang of it, I'll check and see if the brownies have cooled enough to be cut. We can sample them."

"But they're for Brother Jase."

Kenzie winked. "If we arrange them on a plate, Brother Jase will never know he didn't get the full pan. Sound good?"

Food was Lori's favorite go-to when she was blue, and Kenzie's brownies were her favorite food. She nodded. "Sounds great."

Kenzie nodded and leaned close. "Okay, then, this is how you work the loom."

TEN

Kenzie

Lori, under Kenzie's supervision, worked until well after eleven o'clock. Her rows weren't as even on the ends as the ones Kenzie had done, and Lori bemoaned the imperfections with every fling of the shuttle through the shed. Kenzie repeatedly reminded her she was a newbie and shouldn't expect to be perfect on her first attempt at weaving.

Two brownies with a glass of milk seemed to erase Lori's deepest angst, and Kenzie wrapped one more brownie in a paper napkin for Lori to take home with her. Lori accepted the package with eager hands, but when Kenzie tried to give her the pan of remaining brownies, she refused. "If I take those home, I'll eat all of them and Ja— I mean, Brother Jase won't get any. So you better keep them here."

"All right, if they'll tempt you that much,

they can stay here." Kenzie placed the pan on the counter. "I'll put the last dozen on a pretty plate and have it ready when you pick me up for church tomorrow, okay?"

"Perfect." Lori pointed at Kenzie. "Sister Kraft is always in the kitchen by five thirty, so let's try to get there then, too. She'll have a key and will be able to sneak the brownies into Brother Jase's office before everybody shows up. If the kids see them, they'll eat them before he gets any. And it'll be a nice surprise for him."

Kenzie tilted her head. "Surprise? Aren't you going to tell him where they came from?"

"No." Lori's dimpled cheeks turned apple red. "Yes." She hunched her shoulders. "I don't know. What do you think?"

Kenzie laughed. "I think you should tell him they're from you."

Lori pulled in a big breath, then let it out. "Okay. I'll make a little note to put with 'em."

The girls hugged at the door, Lori uttering repeated thank-yous in Kenzie's ear for the rug, and Kenzie assuring her friend she was very welcome. After Lori left, Kenzie changed into her nightclothes and readied herself for bed, yawning as she went through her usual nighttime routine. She rarely stayed up past ten thirty because she was such an early riser, and tiredness tugged at her. But even after she'd said her prayers, read her evening portion of Scripture, and crawled under the covers, her body refused to relax. Or maybe her mind refused to shut down.

Lori's comments about her father's rejection troubled Kenzie. Lori'd mentioned growing up in a male-dominated household after her mom died, but Kenzie hadn't realized her seemingly confident, happy-go-lucky friend harbored such insecurities. Kenzie's strict upbringing, so different from what the majority of the people she encountered on a daily basis had experienced, left her feeling out of place in most social situations. But when she lived on the farm in Indiana, she'd never questioned whether her parents loved her. She'd honestly say her childhood had been secure, even if outsiders saw it as rigid.

More than Lori's insecurities, though, a simple question about the brownie recipe taunted Kenzie. Why wouldn't she give Lori the recipe? She hadn't joined the Amish church. She no longer practiced many of the rules she'd followed so stringently when she was growing up. As Lori had pointed out, she'd cast aside nearly every bit of her former life. So why hold so tight to the recipe passed down from mother to daughter? She ruminated well past midnight and finally fell asleep without coming to a conclusion.

Her alarm clock blared at six Wednesday morning — her usual wake-up time even on her unscheduled days, which included today. She slapped it silent, then flopped against her pillows. After her restless night, she had no desire to rise and shine, as Mamm used to encourage, but her longtime habit brought her out of bed anyway.

A long hot shower revived her, and she felt fully alert for her morning Bible reading and prayer time. She chose a simple breakfast of cold cereal and orange juice, and while she ate, she checked her email.

Three junk messages and one note from Beech Street Bible Fellowship waited in her regular inbox. She deleted the junk ones. What did she need with car insurance, discount airfare, or crypto-currencies, whatever they were? She opened and read the email from church, a reminder about the youth supper that evening and an encouragement to invite any young people who weren't regular attendees to come. Kenzie didn't know any youth apart from the ones at church, and she didn't know those teens well, so she deleted that message, too. Then, out of curiosity, she opened the second email inbox Ruby had set up for her to receive messages about the ring.

When the screen loaded, she drew back so sharply that milk sloshed from her spoon down the front of her T-shirt. She grabbed her napkin and dabbed at the splatters while counting the responses. Seventeen. And the post had only been put up on Monday afternoon. How could so many people know about it already? Her pulse galloped in a rush of panic she didn't understand. Would the ring's owner be somewhere in this list?

She set the napkin and her bowl aside and read each email. Slowly. Carefully. Seeking any hint that the real owner had sent the message. But not one description mentioned an inscription. So none of these had come from the owner. She sent a pat "this ring isn't yours" reply to each, deleted the messages, then sat back and frowned at the empty inbox. Had all of those people really lost a ring, or had some of them sent her a query hoping they might get close enough to fool her? She hated the cynical thought. It reminded her too much of Daed's angry grumbles about being cheated. Yet the pondering was understandable. Some people tried to swindle other people. Sad, but true.

What if the rightful owner never came forward? What would she do with the ring then? She pushed the idle thoughts aside and carried her bowl, spoon, and cup to the sink. Hadn't Ruby prayed for the owner to be found? And wasn't Kenzie praying the same thing? They'd find the person eventually, but she needed to exercise patience. In the meantime, she might as well put her hands to the loom. If she worked hard, she might be able to finish weaving the rug for Brother Jase's office. She doubted she could get it freed from the loom and tied off before Lori arrived to drive her to church, but she'd accomplish as much as possible until then.

Her gaze drifted over the rows caught in the weft as she settled on her stool. What had Grossmammi said about weaving? Seeing the colors come together was like seeing a person's life emerge — dark colors for hard times, light colors for joyful times, each color a gift from God because it represented a day to serve Him. Kenzie smiled at the memory. But as her hands set to work, her smile faded. She missed Grossmammi. And Mamm and Daed and her brothers. Would today bring each of them a dark or a light color for their life's weaving? For the first time in a long time, she wished she could see for herself.

Bradleyville
Jase

Jase escorted the youth group members up the hallway to the front double doors. Despite ending their time together on a serious note — prayer time that lasted past their planned cutoff time of eight — the majority joked and laughed, and the boys playfully socked one another's shoulders on the way. They reached the doors, and Jase held one open with his hip. Several of the kids raised their hands for high fives as they filed out, and the others gave him shy or not-so-shy smiles. Only Charmaine scuttled out without acknowledging him. But he wasn't offended.

He'd learned during the introduction activity that Charmaine, although only a sophomore, spent most evenings and all night with her dad's elderly grandmother. She probably needed to get to her great-grandmother's place and relieve the daytime caretaker. He made a mental note to tell her if things went late again, she should go ahead and leave whenever she needed to. He waved goodbye to the last two, Sienna and Kaia, whom he'd inwardly dubbed Lucy and Ethel for the television best friends. If he ever said the nicknames out loud, he had no doubt everyone would guess who was Lucy and who was Ethel. As he watched them head for the parking lot, Sienna tripped over her own shoelaces. Kaia prevented her from falling, and then they threw their arms around each other's waists and moved on, both laughing.

Chuckling, he turned in the direction of his office and discovered Brother Kraft standing only a few feet behind him. He glanced at his wristwatch, grimaced, and sauntered over to his boss. "I'm sorry if I held you up."

The man smiled, but it lacked its usual sparkle. He looked tired. "No problem. The kids all seemed happy. Things go okay tonight?"

Jase didn't want to toot his own horn, but he thought the evening had gone better than okay. "Yes, sir, I'd say so. The kids were pretty open during our share times, listened during our study, and some even volunteered to pray during our prayer time." He'd been relieved to see that many felt comfortable praying out loud. He wouldn't have to be the one to always lead prayer.

"Glad to hear it. So . . . Cullen cooperated

with you?"

The seemingly nonchalant question set Jase's senses on alert. "Yeah. Shouldn't he?"

Brother Kraft chuckled. "Well, let's just say Cullen can be unpredictable."

A senior girl, Leesa, had introduced Cullen to the group. Jase tried to remember what she'd said that would explain unpredictable behavior. Cullen liked baseball, didn't have a dad . . . and was he the one who hated hot dogs? Jase inwardly groaned. Why hadn't he recorded the intros somehow? He should go to his office and write down everything he could recall before he forgot all of it.

"A lot of his acting out is a bid for attention." Brother Kraft was talking, and Jase forced himself to listen. "He's better than he was a few years ago, but he's not fond of change. Several of us were worried he'd give you some trouble, so I'm glad to hear he did all right."

"He did." Jase inched in the direction of his office. "The whole evening actually went real good. Real smooth. I think the kids and I are going to get along fine." Thank goodness.

Brother Kraft moved alongside Jase. "Just so you know, the adults in Bible study this evening prayed you'd have a good first night, and we prayed for each of the kids individually. At the end of prayer time, people took names and committed to praying through the summer for their teens."

Jase should appreciate the concern and support, but a snide question flitted through his mind. Were they worried he wouldn't be able to handle things without extra prayers? He cleared his throat, an attempt to eliminate the unkind idea. Hadn't he given up looking for the worst in people to instead look for the positive? Brother Tony would be disappointed with the direction his thoughts had gone.

He paused and gave Brother Kraft an honest smile. "That's real nice of y'all. The prayers of the faithful . . . they avail much."

An odd expression creased the older man's face. "Yes. Yes, they do." Then a smile broke. "Well, everyone else is gone, so we can head home."

Jase cringed. "Actually, I'd like to do a little work in my office, if that's all right with you. I'll lock the door when I leave." The church didn't even have a security system, so locking up only meant turning a key in a dead bolt.

"How 'bout I take care of the front doors, then you let yourself out the west door and lock it behind you when you go?"

"Works for me." Jase lifted his hand in a wave and set off for his little office in the northeast corner of the church. As he turned at the end of the hallway, the sweet scent of chocolate teased his nostrils. Odd. They hadn't had anything chocolatey for their youth supper. He opened his door and flipped the toggle light switch up. The overhead fluorescent tubes flickered, then steadied, and he spotted a foil-wrapped plate in the middle of his desk. Was the chocolate smell coming from whatever was under the foil?

He hurried to the desk and lifted the crinkly cover. Brownies. His mouth watered, and he pinched up one of the rich-looking squares and took a bite. At once he remembered tasting these before — the night of his welcome-to-Bradleyville party. Rounding his desk, he took another bite and settled into his chair. The corner of a piece of paper stuck out from under the plate. He popped the last of the brownie in his mouth, swiped his hand down his pant leg, then slipped the paper free and unfolded it.

Brother Jase,
  I hope you'll enjoy this treat. They can either be celebration brownies (Woohoo! The night went great! Eat chocolate!) or

commiseration brownies (So things didn't go great. Eat chocolate; it helps). I hope, for your sake, they're the former instead of the latter.

God bless your ministry with our youth.

— Lori Fowler

Funny how her perky personality came through in the note. It was nice of her to think of him. He should write her a thank-you note or, at the very least, tell her thanks when he saw her on Sunday. And — he chuckled — make sure she knew they were celebration brownies. But for now, he had other work to do. He plucked another brownie from the plate, stuck it between his teeth, and sealed the rest under the foil. Then he set the plate on the shelf behind him. These things were addictive, and he'd empty the plate if they stayed close. He ate the brownie while gently rocking in his chair and recalling details from the kids' introductions.

The brownie gone, he rummaged in his drawer for a pad of paper and pen, laid the paper out in front of him, and bent over the page. "Cullen," he muttered as he wrote, "doesn't like hot dogs . . ."

ELEVEN

Merlin

Leah had already gone to bed, most likely reading while she waited for him, and Merlin should go, too. Wednesdays were long days. Counseling sessions in the morning, preparation for Bible study in the afternoon, then leading prayer and intense study in the evening. Yes, bed sounded good. But he stayed in his recliner, a watchful eye aimed out the window for Jase's return from the church.

In his younger years, Wednesdays energized him. The way Jase had seemed tonight, all twitchy and eager to get to his office and work some more. Lately, though, the busyness depleted Merlin. Were years of pastoring catching up with him? He was close to retirement age. But lots of preachers stayed in pulpits well into their seventies. Or even eighties. Why, his old mentor, Estel Hines, who was now enjoying his reward in heaven, had led weekly Bible studies when he was in his midnineties.

No, preachers just didn't seem to retire. Unless they had to. Merlin idly rubbed his chest. Would he have to?

Jase's comment about the prayers of the faithful availing much rolled in the back of Merlin's mind, stinging him. He'd decided to keep this health issue to himself. Why worry Leah until he knew for sure what was going on inside his chest? Why concern the congregation? He was their leader, the shepherd of the flock. *He* should bolster *them,* not the other way around. But was he doing them a disservice by not opening up and allowing them to pray for him?

A thought crept through his mind. *If God already has life pathways mapped, does prayer change the circumstance?* He'd pondered it time and again, knew all the book answers, but in his heart, he hadn't really settled it completely for himself. Some of his congregants would probably be shocked to know that even ministers didn't know it all. And that was part of what kept him quiet about this potentially life-impacting situation. The other part was that if he talked about this health challenge, it would be more real. He wasn't ready for it to be real.

A shadowy figure crossed the grassy expanse between his house and the church. Merlin leaned forward for a better look. The garage's motion-detecting light came on, illuminating Jase heading for the staircase to his apartment. Merlin sighed out a breath and pushed the footrest down. Jase was home, safe and sound. All was well. With Jase, at least. Time for bed.

Wichita
Kenzie

Ruby opened the door for Kenzie at the fabric shop on Thursday morning, then put her hands on her hips. "Well? Any responses?"

Kenzie nodded. She slipped off her light jacket and wrapped it around her everyday fanny pack. "Quite a few. More than I expected so soon."

"Any likely prospects?"

"I'm afraid not." Kenzie crossed to the counter and put her pack and jacket bundle in her cubby. Only three days and already the new email address was starting to get junk mail, which meant more to sort through. But she wouldn't complain if the post actually connected her with the ring's owner.

Ruby followed her, tapping her chin with

150

her finger. "Well, if you're getting responses, there's no sense in boosting the post. Eileen was willing to pay a fee to help it get to more people, if necessary."

Kenzie straightened, smoothing her skirt as she rose. "I don't want her to do that. If you think it'll help, I'll pay for" — what had she called it? — "boosting. But it isn't her responsibility."

Ruby grinned. "I figured you'd say that, and I already told Eileen you would refuse, but she said to offer anyway."

"That's really nice. Please thank her for me." Kenzie had never met Eileen, but she already liked her. She must be as kind and helpful as her sisters, Leah and Ruby. And maybe as spunky, too. They were lucky to have one another. Kenzie would never stop wishing for a sister, but at least she had Lori and several women from church she could count on the way Ruby seemed to count on Leah and Eileen. Would she be close to her sisters-in-law if she had the time to get to know them? She didn't need to let her thoughts go there. Not now.

She checked the duty roster laid out on the edge of the counter for her assignment. To her surprise, all of the shop's employees were listed for today. They hadn't all come in on the same day since the weeks between

Thanksgiving and Christmas. She sent Ruby a puzzled frown. "Is there something special happening today?"

Ruby reaffixed the corner of a poster in the plate-glass window closest to the front door. The wind currents always seemed to tug at the one hung there. "No. Why?"

Kenzie pointed to the roster. "Everyone's on duty. I wondered if you were having some sort of flash sale. Or an event." She'd be mortified if she had forgotten something so important. She needed to get her mind off the ring and her family and pay better attention.

"Check the hours. You and Lori are on the schedule for the full day, but Van and Barbara will only be here a few hours this afternoon." Ruby spoke with a casual tone, but Kenzie sensed tension in the way she pressed the tape to the glass with the heel of her hand.

"Oh." According to the schedule, Kenzie was supposed to cut pieces for quilt kits. She turned in the direction of the worktable, watching Ruby over her shoulder. "Then everything's okay?"

Ruby sent a tight smile in Kenzie's direction. "There's something I'd like to discuss, but I plan on asking everyone to stay over a few minutes after closing for a quick person-

152

nel meeting. Will that work for you?"

Worry attacked, but Kenzie nodded. "Sure, that should be fine."

"Good. We'll chat then." She shifted her attention to one of the sample quilts hanging in the window.

Kenzie took the hint. She hurried to the workstation, the rubber soles of her sneakers squeaking on the tile floor as she went. As she pulled bolts of floral and solid fabric from the shelves for crib-sized quilts, the bell signaled the door opening. Moments later, Lori's laughter carried from the front of the store. A mutter of voices let Kenzie know Lori and Ruby were discussing something. Then the patter of footsteps approached.

Lori breezed around the shelves and went straight to the cutting table. She pressed her palms on the table's edge and gave Kenzie a worried look. "Ruby's calling a staff meeting," she whispered, her green eyes wide.

Kenzie smoothed a length of calico cotton. "I know. She told me." She didn't bother to whisper. "What's the big secret?"

Lori shot a glance over her shoulder, then scuttled close to Kenzie. "I think she's gonna fire one of us."

Kenzie's hand froze midway to the scissor

holder. "What? Why?"

" 'Cause business has been slowing down and slowing down. She probably can't afford to keep all of us anymore."

Kenzie chose a pair of scissors and toyed with the handle. She couldn't argue with Lori's statement. This shop didn't get near the business as the one where she'd worked in Indianapolis. And the building that housed the shop wasn't exactly new anymore. Its shabby appearance didn't invite new people to visit, so Ruby was dependent on the faithful customers she'd developed a relationship with over the decades. Could they keep the shop open?

Kenzie sighed. "Don't let your imagination run away with you. She could want to talk to us about all kinds of things."

"Like what?"

Kenzie thought about some of the ploys her previous employee had used to draw people in. "Like doing workshops, or putting in a quilting machine for customers to use, or —" Another thought struck. "Or maybe she's retiring and selling the shop." Kenzie'd lost her previous job due to an ownership change. The change propelled her to Kansas. If Ruby sold the shop, would Kenzie have to move again?

"Oh, Kenz . . ." Lori nibbled on her lower lip.

Kenzie patted Lori's hand. "But we don't know. That's all speculation. And there's no sense in borrowing worry. Nothing's gonna happen that God doesn't already know about." How many times had Grossmammi or Mamm told Kenzie the same thing? Funny how many of their words of advice found their way from Kenzie's mouth. "So get to work, keep yourself occupied, and we'll know what's up at the end of the day."

Lori's worried expression didn't fade, but she ambled off.

While Kenzie cut strips of fabric for the quilt kits, she listened for the musical *ding-dong-ding-dong* that played each time the door opened. With every four-note melody, she smiled and sent up a prayer that Ruby's cash register drawer was filling every time someone came in. She spent the entire day laying out fabric, using a rotary cutter to separate three-and-a-half-inch strips from the bolts of fabric, then making stacks of coordinating fabrics.

The cutting table was nearly covered with strips by the time Barbara and Van arrived around three o'clock. They helped Kenzie sort the strips of fabric into groupings and arrange them for packaging. Kenzie had learned a layer-and-fold technique in Indiana, and she'd shown it to Ruby, who immediately adopted it. Exposing at least a full inch of each fabric discouraged customers from opening the packages to get a better look at what was included. A neatly arranged grouping sold better than a willy-nilly jumble.

Kenzie enjoyed putting the fabrics together into appealing bundles, and most of the time she preferred to work alone. Today, with the uncertainty of what they might hear at closing time, she appreciated the older women's help sorting, layering, and folding. She had their company, but their usual chatter and banter was achingly absent, evidence that they, too, weren't sure what Ruby might tell them. But at least the task went smoothly, and by closing time, they'd cleared the table of fabric strips and had an entire stack of quilt kits ready to sell in the store or online.

Two shoppers came in a few minutes before closing. Ruby told Lori, Barbara, Van, and Kenzie to go to the break room and wait for her — she'd see to the customers. Barbara and Van sat on the squeaky vinyl sofa, and Lori joined Kenzie at the round table. The two older women visited quietly, heads close together, and Lori drummed her fingers on the table while staring at the door and chewing her lip. Kenzie was reminded of a line from a book she'd read, something like the tension being so thick it could be cut with a knife. At the time, she hadn't understood the phrase. Unfortunately, on this early spring afternoon, it made too much sense.

When Ruby finally came in, Kenzie emptied her lungs with a relieved sigh, and all three of the other waiting women did the same.

Barbara folded her arms. "All right, Ruby, skip the fabled line 'I suppose you're wondering why I gathered you here' and get to it before we all explode from curiosity."

Ruby pulled the third plastic chair from the table and sat. "I'm sorry if I've caused any angst. That wasn't my intention. I've actually needed to have this meeting for several weeks, and I kept putting it off, hoping . . . well, hoping for a miracle, I guess."

Lori fidgeted, and her chair squeaked — an obnoxious intrusion. "One of us is getting fired, aren't we? Is it gonna be me?"

Ruby aimed a mild frown at Lori. "Let's not be melodramatic, please."

Lori slunk lower in her seat, this time making the chair squawk. "Sorry."

Ruby reached over and squeezed Lori's

wrist. "I don't intend to fire anyone."

Another round of sighs followed Ruby's firm statement, and Kenzie's taut muscles unknotted. With the threat of losing her job gone, much of her anxiety released.

Ruby crossed her leg and linked her hands in her lap, a relaxed pose that further eased Kenzie's concern. "It's true that I'm bringing in less revenue every month here in the shop. I'm sure all of you have noticed the decrease in traffic. I blame some of it on our location. This isn't exactly a prime area of town, not like it was when I opened in 1990. The culture has changed, too. People buy instead of make their own clothes, and they don't tend to engage in the craftsy projects of previous decades. The younger generation doesn't seem all that interested in quilting or embroidery or knitting or even sewing their own curtains."

Van sat forward, her wavy blond-dyed bangs flopping forward and partially shielding her blue eyes. "I'm confused. If you're losing revenue, then you need to reduce expenses. Are you sure one of us isn't getting the boot? I'll volunteer to go if you need to cut a position."

Ruby held up both hands like a crossing guard. "Give me a minute, okay? When I'm done telling you everything, we'll discuss options."

Van flicked her bangs to the side and flopped against the sofa's backrest.

"Today's shoppers do more online than in person." Ruby went on as if no one had interrupted, leaving Kenzie wondering if she'd practiced her speech. "As you know, I've had an Etsy shop for a couple years already, and the majority of the ready-made quilted wall hangings and quilt kits sell there. It makes sense to increase my online presence and boost those revenues. Of course, that means giving the online shop more attention. Consequently, someone's position here will need to shift from floor work to online work." She raised one dark eyebrow. "Any takers on that?"

Kenzie inwardly shrank back. She didn't know enough about computers to do an adequate job. She glanced at the other employees. Lori was examining her fingernails, Van seemed interested in the ceiling tiles, and Barbara was squinting in Ruby's direction.

Suddenly Barbara humphed. "Well, if no one else is gonna speak up, my college-age grandkids have been pestering me to get more proficient on the computer so they can connect with me on Instant-book or Face-gram, or whatever those crazy things are. If learning to manage the online store will help me get better, I'm game. But you'll have to train me. I'm an old dog, and new tricks don't come easy."

Ruby laughed. "It isn't rocket science. I'm sure you can learn it. Thank you."

Barbara sighed. "Whatever I can do to help. I love this store. I'd hate to see it close after all these years."

"I don't want to close, either." Ruby lowered her head slightly. "I really think upping the online sales will help a lot, but there is another change I need to make. As Van said, I need to reduce expenses. Obviously rent, utilities, and keeping the shelves stocked are requirements. So the reduction will have to come through paid positions."

Lori flung her hands outward. "I knew it! I just knew it. Someone *is* getting fired."

Ruby's chin rose sharply, and she scowled at Lori. "I told you I'm not firing anyone, and I meant it." She grimaced. "But I do need to cut back employees' hours. Either take a few hours a week from each of you or cut someone to pretty much part time."

Lori's frantic expression didn't clear. "But which one of us can survive on a part-time salary? I know I can't. I'm barely making my rent and car payment now. If my hours get cut even a little, I'll have to look for another job to make up the difference. Do you know how hard it is to find a job with flexible hours? If I can't find one, I might have to move in with my dad." Tears swam in her eyes. "If he'd even let me."

Ruby patted Lori's hand. "That's a lot of *ifs,* Lori. Let's talk things all the way through before panicking, hmm?"

Van crinkled her face. "I'll be honest, Ruby. I'm the one who does the books, and if you take hours away from each of us, all of your employees will drop below thirty hours a week, which the government defines as part-time status. You could be charged with trying to avoid paying benefits, even though we know that's not the case. I think the wiser thing is for one of us to drop to part time and leave the other employees' hours as is."

Barbara nodded. "I have to agree. The last thing you want is to open yourself up to litigation from the IRS."

"Well . . ." Ruby angled a slow gaze across each attentive face. "If we go the route of one person cutting hours here, there is a flexible part-time job opportunity I know about. I happen to be on a first-name basis with the people in charge, and they've promised to give one of my employees first dibs at it, if any of you are interested."

Kenzie was the newest hire. If anyone was going to make a sacrifice, it should be her. She gathered her courage and asked the question she was sure the others wanted answered. "What's the position?"

A smile quivered on the corners of Ruby's lips. "You all know Jim from church. He's been the custodian since he retired from teaching, about seven years ago I believe. He's done a great job, but his wife wants him to quit. Kathy told me they'd like to do some traveling before they get too old to enjoy it. Yesterday he turned in his resignation with a promise to continue serving until someone is found to replace him."

Lori gasped, then sucked in her lips. Kenzie looked at her friend, puzzled by the reaction.

"It's a part-time position," Ruby went on, "but it does come with health-care benefits through a private Christian medical-share program the church participates in. Leah and Merlin won't advertise for a new custodian until they know whether or not any of you are interested. So . . . anybody?"

Kenzie was the last hired. She should volunteer to go part time. She pulled in a breath, wriggled her fingers, and —

Lori thrust her hand into the air. "Me!"

TWELVE

Lori

Lori had raised her hand so fast her shoulder popped. Everyone in the room jolted and then stared at her, but she didn't care. As her father always said, "You snooze, you lose." She wouldn't lose out on this chance.

Ruby angled her head and raised her eyebrows. "Did you want to ask a question?"

Barbara and Van chuckled, and even Kenzie grinned.

Lori lowered her hand to her lap. "Do you think I could do it? The custodial position, I mean. I know how to vacuum, mop, and scrub bathrooms. I do it here all the time. I don't turn up my nose at dirty jobs." She'd learned to deal with gross messes after years of taking care of Dad. When he got drunk, he got messy in lots of ways. "But are there other duties I wouldn't be able to do?"

Ruby turned away from Lori. "Van, Barbara, Kenzie . . . why don't you think about what I suggested as far as cutting hours? If you want to jot down some ideas for bringing in customers, I'd be interested in hearing them, but not tonight. I've kept you long enough. Let's come together again next Monday for another meeting, all right?"

Lori blinked rapidly. Her nose stung and her eyes teared up. Was Ruby dismissing her as a potential custodian for the church? Maybe Ruby didn't think she had the smarts, as Dad would put it, to handle such an important position. Everyone appreciated Jim, even looked up to him because he took such good care of what Brother Kraft called God's house. If she was the custodian, then the members of Beech Street Bible Fellowship would hold her in esteem. Which is why she'd leaped at the chance. Their trust in her might show Dad she was worthy of admiration.

The other three left the break room, and Ruby sat quietly until the front doorbell chimed, signaling the women had gone home for the night. Then she shifted sideways in her chair and smiled at Lori. "All right, let's talk about the custodial job."

The smile erased Lori's momentary worry. Ruby handed her a list of duties someone — probably Jim, or maybe Brother Kraft —

had written on a piece of paper.

Keep the entire church from floor to ceiling and everything in between clean on a weekly basis.

Be available to set up for weddings, funerals, and other church functions.

Do the cleanup after all of those events.

Lori chewed her lip, considering each task. Nothing sounded too tough. She slid the paper across the table to Ruby. "Do you think I could do it?" She searched Ruby's face for signs of skepticism.

Ruby shrugged. "I doubt the duties at church would be more than you could conceivably do. As you already pointed out, you and Kenzie have covered custodial duties here and you've always done well."

Lori puffed up at the compliment. Praise felt so good.

"The question is whether you're willing to make yourself available for an unpredictable schedule that will probably affect your schedule here. It's a salaried position, so if there's a month where there's more going on and you spend extra hours, you won't receive extra money for the extra time. It could mean some late nights or early mornings. It would require some juggling and . . .

well . . ." She offered a sympathetic grimace. "A lot of organizing."

Lori cringed. "I hear ya. I know I'm a flibbertigibbet." When she was really young, Dad laughingly called her the funny word, turning it into an affectionate nickname. During her teen years, his biting tone let her know it wasn't for fun anymore. "But when I have to focus and get things done, I can." She leaned forward slightly and gave Ruby her best pleading look. "Will you ask Brother and Sister Kraft to give me a chance? I'd like to do it. I really would."

Ruby pinned a thoughtful gaze on Lori. "I've never heard you express any interest in working at the church. I'm curious about your reasoning now. Is it because it would let you spend time each day with the new youth minister? Leah said you two were making some pretty good sheep's eyes at each other across the serving counter."

Lori jolted. Sister Kraft thought Jase had made sheep's eyes at her? "I . . . He . . ." She gulped, then shook her head hard. She pushed her hair behind her ears. "I wasn't even thinking about Brother Jase when I volunteered." She held up her palm, courtroom style. "Honest." She was thinking about him now, though.

Ruby's expression relaxed. "I'll let Leah

know you're interested. She'll probably call you and arrange a time for you to chat with her and Merlin. Does that sound okay?"

Lori smiled so big her cheeks hurt. "It sounds more than okay." Then she sobered. "I hope you don't think I'm interested in the other job because I want to get away from here." She'd started at the fabric shop after she graduated from high school and never worked anywhere else. A lump filled her throat, and she swallowed hard. "I love working with you and Barbara and Van. You've all been so nice to me. I really love you. All of you. And when Kenzie came, it was like we added a sister to the family." Yes, family. More of a family than she'd known since her mother died.

For a moment, her resolve to be the church custodian wavered. Could she make such a drastic change to her schedule? Would the friendships she'd made with the women at Prairie Meadowlark Fabrics & Quilting dissolve if she wasn't here as much? What was better — being part of the Prairie Meadowlark family or taking a position of importance at the church and maybe scoring more time with Brother Jase?

Ruby tapped Lori's knee with her finger. "Hey, where'd you go?"

Lori blinked several times. "What?"

Ruby grinned. "You drifted off some-where, Miss Flibbertigibbet." Warmth and affection came through in her voice. "Are you having second thoughts?"

"No, not second thoughts. Just . . . thoughts." Lori pulled in a breath and blew it toward the ceiling. She shoved an errant strand of hair behind her ear and shrugged. "I'll talk to Brother and Sister Kraft. I'm sure they'll help me make the right decision."

Ruby stood. "Good. And as for decisions, I'm going to make an executive one for you right now. Go home. It's past your suppertime, and you're on the morning schedule tomorrow."

Lori laughed at her boss's mock scowl, stood, and saluted. "Yes, ma'am. I'll see you in the morning." She gathered her purse and jacket, then headed to the parking lot and her waiting car. But when she slid in behind the wheel, she decided to go to Kenzie's. She wanted to see how Brother Jase's rug was coming along.

A delightful shiver rattled her frame. If she got the custodian job, she'd get to clean Brother Jase's office. Somehow she'd talk Kenzie into sharing her brownie recipe, and she'd leave brownies on his desk every week.

Kenzie

When the knock on the door came, Kenzie knew without peeking out the little peephole that her visitor was Lori. She opened the door and welcomed her friend in.

Lori shot straight past her and went to the loom. She froze for a moment, then spun and gawked at Kenzie. She waved one hand at the loom. "What happened to it?" Her shoulders slumped. "Oh. I bet I know. I messed it up, and you had to throw it out."

Kenzie frowned, trying to make sense of Lori's comments, and understanding dawned. She hurried across the floor and touched Lori's arm. "Stay here." She darted into her bedroom and got the rolled rug she'd tucked behind the door. With the bulky tube under her arm, she returned to the sitting room and grinned at Lori. "Look." She grabbed the end and let the rug unroll, then held it high enough that the fringe barely dusted the carpet.

She couldn't see Lori, but she heard her squeal. Moments later the rug was snatched from her hands and laid aside, and Lori grabbed her in a stranglehold of a hug. "Thank you! Thank you! Thank you!"

Kenzie laughed, wriggling. "You're welcome, you're welcome, you're welcome, but let go so I can breathe."

Lori giggled and stepped back. She bent down and spread the woven rug flat across the floor. "Oh, Kenzie, it's wonderful." She walked around it, as if participating in a cakewalk, seeming to examine every square inch. Then she shot Kenzie a shocked look. "I can't even tell which rows I did. They're all so . . . perfect. Are you sure this is the same rug?"

Kenzie pointed. "See the strips from the long johns? It's the same one."

"But how can it be so perfect? I know my rows weren't quite right."

Lori's astonishment tickled Kenzie but also concerned her. "I stretched them a little bit so they'd be more aligned." She moved to her friend's side and laid her hand on Lori's arm. "But even if they weren't all perfectly straight, the rug would still be beautiful. You don't have to be perfect to be beautiful. Not in God's eyes, for sure, and not in mine."

Lori's eyes flooded, and her smile quavered. "Aw, thanks, Kenz. I love you, too." She hugged Kenzie again, then fixed her gaze on the rug. "It's gonna look so good in Jase's office. Can I take it now?"

Kenzie rolled it back into a tube and handed it to Lori. "Of course." She gestured to the sofa. "Are you really gonna be the

170

church's janitor?"

Lori sat and placed the rug across her lap. She finger-combed the fringe, making the strings lay like bangs. "I'm going to tell them I'm interested. They might not hire me, but if they do, it'll mean the rest of you won't have to give up hours at the fabric shop." She flicked a grin at Kenzie. "And if they do hire me, I'm gonna start bugging you again for your brownie recipe."

Kenzie's chest constricted, but she couldn't hold back a soft laugh. "You think you'll need them for energy, or what?"

Lori shook her head, a sly smile dimpling her cheeks. "No. I'll bake them for . . . for the church staff every week." Wistfulness flitted through her eyes. "That'll make me popular, don't you think?"

Kenzie surmised Lori was more interested in being popular with Brother Jase than with Brother and Sister Kraft, but she wouldn't say it. Lori needed to be bolstered more than she needed to be teased. "I don't think you need to bake brownies to win friends." Kenzie accompanied her words with a smile. "Your kind heart, bouncy personality, and sense of humor endear you to people. All of those things are appealing. And they're calorie free."

Lori burst out laughing. "That's really

171

nice, but I think it's your roundabout way of telling me you won't give me the recipe."

Kenzie shrugged, still grinning. Lori was right. She didn't want to share the recipe, and she had to be honest even if it meant disappointing Lori.

Lori stood and tucked the rolled rug under her arm. "It's okay. I've got the rug, and that's good enough." She winked. "For now."

Kenzie trailed Lori to the door. "I'll see you tomorrow?"

"Yep. We're both on the schedule for all day." Lori seemed to freeze for a moment. Then she slowly turned and faced Kenzie. "If I do get the job at church, I won't see you as much at the shop. We'll still get together, won't we? I'd really miss you if we didn't have our gab sessions."

"Of course we'll still get together. Nothing's gonna change between us just because you're not at the shop as much." Kenzie spoke with conviction, but an unnamed worry gnawed at the back of her brain. She pushed it aside and patted Lori's shoulder. "No worries. You're stuck with me, pal."

Lori smiled big. "Thanks, Kenz." She left whistling and with a bounce in her step.

Kenzie stayed on her little landing and watched until Lori got to her vehicle. Lori put the rug in the back seat, placing it as carefully as Kenzie used to lay her sleeping little brother on his bed. When Lori moved to the driver's seat, she glanced up and caught Kenzie watching. Lori's smile broke across her face again, and she waved. Kenzie returned the wave, but with less enthusiasm than Lori exhibited.

Lori drove away, and Kenzie stepped inside and closed the door. She turned the lock out of habit, then ambled to the loom. She needed to restring it and start a new project. The basket under the loom overflowed with strips of denim, which she planned to weave into a set of place mats. They'd been very popular at the mission store. But she didn't reach for the strings. She had no desire to work the loom. A different longing tugged at her, one that had plagued her days.

She entered the kitchenette and pulled her cell phone from the little pocket inside her purse. What would happen if she called her parents? They didn't have a telephone in the house, but Daed had one in the milking barn. At this hour of the evening, if he followed the same schedule as during her growing-up years, he would be washing down the milking room walls. He'd never hear the telephone over the noise of the powerful spray hose. But if one of her brothers was still there, puttering around in the barn, he'd hear it. Answer it. And she'd be able to talk to someone from her family.

Gripping the cell phone in her hand, she contemplated the wisdom of making a call. She called twice a year — on Mother's Day and at Christmas. Her family expected the calls then. She might frighten them if she called on an odd April day. But Easter was this coming Sunday. Traditionally, her family would spend the weekend socializing with friends and breaking tomorrow's Good Friday fast. So maybe a phone call wouldn't seem out of place.

She pulled up her list of contacts, located the one marked *Daed & Mamm,* and pushed the number. A ringing met her ear. There was no answering machine in the barn, so she could let the phone ring until someone answered. But if it went beyond ten rings, she'd hang up. By the tenth ring, if no one answered, they weren't close enough or interested enough to pick it up.

She counted. Seven, eight, nine . . . With a sigh, she lowered the phone and started to punch the disconnect button.

"*Guder daag.* Hochstetler Dairy. Can I help you?"

Kenzie yanked the phone back up, her

pulse pounding in rapid beats. "Yes. Hello — er, guder daag. This is Ken— Mackenzie. Is this Daed?"

Laughter rolled. "Do I sound as old as Daed? It's Caleb, Mackenzie."

Kenzie's mouth fell open. Caleb? The little brother who teased her by jumping on her bed to wake her up and tormented her by chasing her around the yard with a dead garter snake dangling from his fist? He sounded like a man. How could he sound like a man? But then, he was twenty-two years old already.

"Caleb . . ." His name emerged on a note of regret and wonder. "How are you?"

"*Gud.* How are you?"

"I'm good, too." She swallowed. She was fine, wasn't she? "How are Daed and Mamm? Grossmammi? The boys?" Not that any of her brothers were boys anymore, but calling them anything else seemed unnatural.

"All gud. Grossmammi is a little slower. She'll be eighty in June, and it shows."

Kenzie closed her eyes, envisioning her beloved, gentle grossmammi.

"Jayden and Sharlene just announced a new baby coming. In September, I think, the same month their oldest will turn six."

Kenzie searched her memory. "Is that

three for them?"

Caleb's laughter rang. "Four. As many as Job and Deedee have, but still not as many as Trenton and Patty or Tim and Stephanie."

"What about you?"

"Me?" He laughed again. "I'm not married yet. Why should I be? I have a good thing, living with Daed and Mamm, helping in the dairy. What for do I want a wife and a bunch of kids to take care of?"

Did she hear a hint of bitterness in his tone? Caleb had joined the church after his rumspringe. He knew the expectation was to marry a girl approved of by Daed and Mamm and raise a God-honoring family. So why was he still living at home? She didn't know what to say, and it bothered her. Shouldn't a sister know how to comfort or advise her younger brother?

"What for did you call?" Caleb's puzzled query intruded on her thoughts.

"Oh, I was just thinking about all of you and decided to . . . check in." Tears distorted her vision. "I was missing everyone."

"We miss you, too, Kenz." The old nickname, identical to the way Lori shortened her name, made Kenzie's chest ache. "You ever gonna come see us? Mamm keeps your room ready, just in case."

176

She did? Why hadn't someone told her? But would it have made any difference? She'd checked on bus routes from Kansas to Indiana. A bus could carry her to Indianapolis, but it was expensive and took more than a day to get there. Then she'd have to find a way to reach Flourish, a full hour-and-a-half drive northeast of Indianapolis. Another expense. She couldn't do it. "I wish I could, Caleb. I really do. I can't afford it, though."

"*Ja,* I understand. Why don't you get your own car now that you're an Englischer?"

She was sure he meant to tease, but a hard note underscored his light words. "Cars cost a lot of money, Caleb."

"So do our buggies."

Kenzie gave a slow nod. Caleb was right. Horses and buggies cost dearly.

"But with a car, you can go to far places. Farther than in a buggy, for sure. Englischers with their cars have freedom."

Kenzie's freedom didn't come from being an Englischer, and it wouldn't come from owning a car. "Caleb, freedom, real freedom, is found when —"

"Daed is waving at me through the milking room window. I better go see what he needs."

Disappointment struck hard, but Kenzie

knew better than to argue. If Daed needed Caleb, he had to go. "All right. It was good to talk to you. Please give everyone my love. I'll try to call again soon."

"All right. *Mach's gut.*"

Kenzie repeated the common farewell, then carried the phone to the charger and plugged it in. She stood staring at the little piece of technology she'd never dreamed of owning when she was growing up. Caleb seemed to believe having worldly things would make him happier. They'd definitely made her life easier, but her joy was found in something much more important and permanent than a cell phone or an automobile.

Caleb had been a little boy of twelve when she'd left home. The two oldest Hochstetler boys, Trenton and Tim, were already married by then, and Tim and Stephanie were the parents of two little boys. Over the years she'd been away, the family had grown, adding sisters-in-law and nieces and nephews. And she didn't know any of them. She really didn't even know her brothers that well anymore.

"Mamm keeps your room ready, just in case." Caleb's words played over in her mind. Kenzie sank down at the table and

put her head in her hands. *Dear God, I think I want to go home.*

THIRTEEN

Bradleyville
Jase

Jase adjusted the knot of his tie. He always dressed neatly for Sunday morning service — trousers or a pressed pair of khakis and a nice polo or Hawaiian-inspired button-down shirt — but he rarely wore a dress shirt. But today was Easter, and the day's meaning inspired a greater reverence and formality than a typical Sunday. So white button-down shirt, black trousers, and his one and only tie.

He leaned close to the bathroom mirror and inspected his cheeks. His skin still looked blotchy from the razor marks defining his short beard, but the ruddiness would probably be gone by the time Sunday school began at nine thirty. He hoped so. With his reddish hair and red stripes on his tie, he had enough of the color on display. He ran his hand down the length of the smooth fabric. The red and black stripes made him think of sin and the blood Jesus shed to cover it.

A lump filled his throat. Sinless Jesus had shed His blood for him, a cast-aside urchin whose own parents hadn't thought enough of him to feed and dress him appropriately. He hung his head and closed his eyes, offering a silent prayer of gratitude. There were a lot of things he still questioned about God and His ways, but his confusion and, yes, his bitterness toward the Father couldn't erase his appreciation for the sacrifice the Son had made for him.

He whispered "Amen" and glanced at the clock. A quarter till nine. Early, but not too early. He was teaching the youth Sunday school class for the first time, and he wanted plenty of time to get comfortable in the room before the kids arrived.

As he walked the short distance from his apartment to the church building, he went over in his head the instructions he intended to give at the close of their lesson. Last Sunday morning, he'd noticed the high school kids sat in a group on the west side of the sanctuary in the front pews near the hallway door. The bathrooms were across the hall on the other side of the door, and there'd been a steady flow of traffic back and forth throughout the service. If it had distracted him, it likely distracted others. So today he'd lay down the law and put a stop to the practice. They were all plenty old enough to sit through an hour-long church service.

He used his key and let himself in through the back door, then traveled the narrow hallway leading to the fellowship hall and church kitchen. He rounded the corner from the hall and nearly collided with Lori Fowler. His feet slid to a halt, as did hers, and all of a sudden he remembered he hadn't sent her a thank-you for the brownies he'd found in his office last Wednesday. He choked out an embarrassed laugh. In his usual style, his intentions had been grander than his follow-through. Mostly because he really didn't like writing anything personal. But here they were, face to face, so he could remedy the situation now.

"Lori. Hi."

Her cheeks glowed as red as the stripes on his tie. "Yikes trikes, Brother Jase, you startled me."

What a unique exclamation. And she'd startled him, too. Why was she here so early? The kitchen team weren't preparing for a dinner after service, were they? He crunched his lips into an apologetic grimace. "Sorry about that, but actually I'm glad I ran into you. I wanted to say thanks for the brownies. I ate the last of them this morning for breakfast."

The red in her cheeks faded to pink, and she grinned. Her dimples really showed when she smiled. "You've got great self-control if they lasted a whole four days. I'm glad you liked them. Did you use them to celebrate or to comfort yourself?"

He laughed, this time heartier. "They were definitely celebration brownies."

"Oh, I'm so glad."

She meant it. He could tell by the sincerity in her tone and expression. Beech Street sure had a lot of nice people. "Me, too. It was a great way to top off the night, so thanks again for thinking of me." He peeked into the kitchen. The light was on, but no one was inside. "Is there some kind of get-together here after church today?" Whatever it was, Sister Kraft wasn't involved, because she'd invited Jase to join their family for Easter dinner. All four of their kids and their families were in town, so he'd given a polite "No thanks." He'd feel like a fifth wheel intruding on their big family gathering.

Lori shook her head. "Not that I'm aware of. And if there was something, I'd know because . . ." Pride glowed in her eyes. She stuck out her hand. "I'm Lori, the new custodian here at Beech Street Bible Fellowship."

Stifling a chuckle, Jase shook her hand. "Nice to meet you." He gave her outfit a glance. She wore an ankle-length skirt covered in flowers the size of dessert plates, a loose yellow sweater-type top, and white sandals — different from anything he'd ever seen a janitor wear. "You don't look much like the previous custodian. Or any custodian, for that matter."

She linked her hands behind her back. "It's my first day, and my only responsibility today has to do with opening and closing up the building. I was actually going to unlock the back door when you came in, so you helped me out. Tomorrow when I come in to clean, I'll be dressed in something more custodial." She wrinkled her nose. "Custodianish? Oh, well, you know what I mean."

Jase grinned. "Sounds like a plan. And speaking of plans, I've got some work to do before the kids get here." He eased around her, aiming his feet for the row of Sunday school classrooms. "So if you'll excuse me . . ."

She waved at him, and keys jangled from a pink plastic spring around her wrist. "If you need something, like extra chairs or whiteboard markers or . . . or . . ." She laughed. "Well, anything. Just gimme a holler."

"Thanks, I will." He turned and hustled up the hallway to the youth room. He dug a marker from the top drawer of the bedroom dresser that served as a storage unit and began writing a list of Scripture references on the dented whiteboard attached to the wall. A sound at the door stole his focus, and he peeked over his shoulder. Lori again. Automatically, a grin tugged at the corners of his mouth. What was it about her that made a person want to smile?

"Brother Jase, pardon me for intruding."

He turned fully and faced her. "You're not an intrusion. Whatcha need?"

"Well . . ." She crossed the threshold and sent a slow look around the room while she talked. "I wondered if you had plans for . . . lunch."

She stood with her face angled to the side, and her thick, curly hair completely hid her profile from him. But he suspected she was blushing to beat the band. He cleared his throat to remove any humor from his tone. "Not really."

"Kenzie and me . . . Kenzie's my best friend, the one who bakes the brownies . . .

185

we always go to lunch together on Sunday." She fiddled with the corner of one of the posters on the wall. "I wondered if you'd like to join us."

Jase wished they could have this conversation facing each other. He crossed to her and waited until she turned her head. Sure enough. Blazing red cheeks. Sister Kraft had speculated Lori had developed a crush on him, and her behavior seemed to validate it. He shouldn't encourage her. He wasn't in the market for a new girlfriend. But neither did he want to hurt her feelings by turning her down. Rejection always stung.

He sought a friendly but not overly friendly reply. "If you and Kenzie usually go by yourselves, are you sure I won't be an intrusion on your time together?"

Lori shook her head. "Kenzie and I always go, but sometimes others from the young adult Sunday school class go, too. With today being Easter, people who have families in town will probably be with them. But neither of us have family to be with —"

They didn't? Why?

"— and since you don't, either, I thought . . ." She waved her hands and turned toward the door. "Never mind, it's last minute and you probably have plans."

He hurried after her. "Lori, wait." She

186

turned, and the hopefulness mingling with doubt in her green eyes stung. He knew the feeling. He'd experienced it a lot as a kid, wanting so much to be accepted but fearing it would never happen. "If you're sure I wouldn't be intruding on your time with your friend, I'd like to go, to get to know y'all better."

Joy exploded in her expression. "That's great! I'm gonna make an open invitation in Sunday school in case there are others who don't have lunch plans."

If others came, too, it would make the whole potential crush situation easier to handle.

"And if for some reason something changes between now and lunchtime and you need to do something else, no hard feelings, okay? The invitation's open, but you aren't obligated."

"Sounds great." He really needed to finish getting ready for class. He touched her arm, hoping she'd interpret the gesture as a gentle nudge. "I'll meet up with you and" — what was the friend's name? — "Kenzie and whoever else decides to go in the main foyer after church."

She went to the door, her steps bouncy. "Remember, I have to lock everything up, so I can't leave right away, but yes, I'll be in the main foyer when I'm able to go. See you later. If you don't end up with other plans. Have a good class time, Brother Jase." She fluttered her fingers in a little wave, then exited the room.

He peeked out to make sure she'd moved on, then closed the door. She was a nice girl, very bubbly and friendly, and cute with her wild hair and dimples. But she'd sure derailed his train of thought. He returned to the whiteboard, smiling as he went. One thing he could count on, lunch wouldn't be boring if Lori Fowler was along.

How long did it take to use the bathroom? Jase sent another scowl toward the side door. Some of the high schoolers had rolled their eyes when he told them to make use of the restrooms after Sunday school and stay put during the entire service, but none had openly complained. However, midway through the sermon, Cullen had tapped Jase on the shoulder and whispered his need to go. Jase had reminded him of their agreement, and the boy had wriggled. "I got a medical condition, bro. I can't wait." Jase didn't know if it was true, but if it was, he couldn't make the boy suffer. So he'd whispered back, "Then go. But hurry."

Fifteen minutes had passed, and still no

sign of Cullen. Was he sick in the bathroom? Was he really in the bathroom? Jase still didn't know these kids well enough to know what to expect from them. Brother Kraft's comments about Cullen's unpredictability coupled with the length of time he'd been missing convinced Jase to check on him.

He'd put himself in the middle of the group of kids, and it took some doing to work his way out of the pew. He exited the sanctuary and hurried to the door of the men's room. The men's restroom was small, with only a single toilet and a wall-mounted sink, so if Cullen was in there, the door would be locked. Jase gripped the doorknob and twisted. It opened.

Swallowing a groan, he peeked inside. Sure enough. No Cullen. He paused for a moment, listening to Brother Kraft's warm yet authoritative voice carry from the other side of the wall. Then he heard laughter, not from the sanctuary but from the foyer. He hurried around the corner and down the short hallway toward the sound. Aggravation immediately rose when he spotted Cullen with the usher who'd been assigned hall duty for the morning.

He marched directly to Cullen, who leaned against the welcome center counter with his back to Jase. He put his hand on the boy's shoulder and turned him around. "What are you doing?"

Surprise widened Cullen's eyes. He jammed his thumb in the deacon's direction. "Talking with Brother Phil. What're you doing out here? Is the sermon over?"

"No, the sermon isn't over, and I'm out here because you didn't come back. I was afraid you might be sick in the bathroom, given your *medical condition*." Jase tempered his tone, hiding his annoyance with the kid. "Why didn't you come back in?"

Cullen shrugged, innocence blooming on his pimpled face. "You told us in Sunday school how it's disruptive for us to leave and come back. I'd already disrupted by leaving. I didn't want to disrupt again. So I stayed out here with Brother Phil." A smirk twitched on his lips. "I guess we could go back in, but it'd probably cause another disruption since two make a bigger noise than one."

Jase looked at Brother Phil, who was watching Jase as if measuring his reaction. He took a deep breath and gave Cullen a firm look. "Disruptive or not, we're going back in. And we are going to honor the no-leaving-the-sanctuary-during-service rule from now on."

"But my condition," Cullen whispered,

panic rasping his voice. "What if I can't hold it? You want me to have an accident right there in the pew?"

"I'll talk to your mom about how best to deal with your *condition,* but —"

Cullen shot for the hallway. "Never mind, bro. Let's go."

Jase caught up and put his arm across the boy's shoulders. Cullen shrugged loose and stepped out of Jase's reach. His stomach in knots, Jase reached the door first. Singing carried from inside — a hymn, "Christ the Lord Is Risen Today." The congregation always stood to sing, so his and Cullen's entrance wouldn't be as noticeable during the hymn. He opened the door and waved Cullen through, then followed.

Back in their pews, he sensed Cullen's glare on the back of his head as he raised his voice in song, but he refused to let it cow him from joining his new fellowship of believers in singing his joy that Jesus overcame the grave.

Brother Kraft closed the service with prayer, and the pianist played the hymn again while the congregation filed out. Jase scanned the room for Cullen's mother. He doubted the boy had a medical issue preventing him from sitting for an hour. After all, he'd gone the whole hour and a half during youth group on Wednesday without needing a bathroom break. But he'd get confirmation rather than operate on assumptions. He spotted her near the main doors, Cullen fidgeting beside her, and headed in their direction. But by the time he worked his way to the opposite end of the sanctuary, she and Cullen were gone.

Brother Kraft caught his eye and motioned for Jase to join him, so he crossed to the minister. He shook hands with people who filed out, returning their "Christ is risen" with "He is risen indeed," just as he'd done at the church in San Antonio. The traditional Easter greeting brought back pleasant memories of his years at Grace Chapel. Without warning, a wave of loneliness washed over him. He missed Brother Tony and Sister Eileen, his foster parents, and many others from the church who'd made him feel welcome and loved. Maybe he'd give Brother Tony a call in the morning. He didn't want to bother his old mentor on Easter Sunday, but tomorrow would work. It'd be good to hear his voice.

He'd make another call tomorrow, too. To Cullen's mother. He wanted to set up a private meeting with her and Cullen. He'd get to the bottom of this medical condition claim, and while he was at it, he'd address

Cullen's practice of calling him "bro." At first it had seemed like an affectionate nickname, but already it rankled, feeling more disrespectful than friendly.

The line of departing congregants reached its end, and Sister Kraft escorted Brother Kraft out the door, teasingly scolding him for letting their lunch get cold. That left Jase and a blond-haired young woman, who stood beside the welcome center, alone in the foyer. Was she Lori's friend Kenzie? If so, he'd wait with her. He ambled to the opposite side of the high counter.

"Hi. Are you waiting for Lori?"

She turned to face him. A nervous smile quivered on her lips. "I am. She's got to lock up the building before we can go to lunch."

"Yes, she told me. She also invited me to join y'all." He glanced around, frowning. "Will it be just the three of us? She said she was going to ask everyone in the class to go."

The woman shrugged. "She asked, but everybody else had plans."

"Ah." Jase wondered if he should bow out, too, but the idea of a frozen dinner or canned spaghetti for Easter lunch didn't appeal to him. "I hope you don't mind me going along."

"No. No, not at all." Her tone wasn't as certain as her words. She extended her hand. "I don't think we've officially met. I'm Kenzie Stetler."

He gave her hand a quick shake. "Jase Edgar. It's nice to meet you."

"Yes. Thank you. You, too."

Compared to Lori's vivaciousness, this woman acted like a scared rabbit. She was pretty. In fact, with her shining blond hair, bright blue eyes, and petite frame, she resembled Rachel. But he would never have used *timid* to define his outgoing fiancée. He wanted to put Kenzie at ease, but he wasn't sure how. She wouldn't even look him in the eyes. Maybe he should go to his apartment instead. He took one step toward the doors, forming an apology.

Lori came around the corner. Her beaming smile landed on Jase. "Oh, good, you're both ready. Let's go."

FOURTEEN

Wichita
Kenzie

Lori and Brother Jase chatted across the table. Kenzie tried to pay attention and contribute, but her mind refused to remain in the booth. It traveled over the miles to Indiana, to a trestle dining room table with benches on both sides and sturdy chairs at either end. A table around which Daed, Mamm, Grossmammi, her brothers, and her brothers' families were now gathered, eating a good dinner and probably especially enjoying it after Good Friday's time of fasting.

Had her nieces and nephews colored eggs, the way she and her brothers did when they were little? Mamm always made egg salad sandwiches for Easter Monday lunch. Her mouth watered as she thought about the chunks of hard-boiled eggs, green onions, and sour pickles mixed in Mamm's home-

195

made mayonnaise and served on hearty wheat bread. They were the best sandwiches in the world. When she called home next time, she would ask for Mamm's mayonnaise recipe. Then maybe she could make her own egg salad.

Lori nudged Kenzie with her elbow. "Earth to Kenzie."

Kenzie shifted her attention to her smiling friend. "What?"

Lori laughed. "I asked you a question and you acted like you didn't hear me. Are you napping?"

Kenzie shook her head, heat flooding her face. "I'm sorry. I was thinking about . . . something. What did you ask?"

"If you wanted some dessert."

"Oh." Kenzie shook her head. "No, I've had enough to eat."

Lori shifted her grin from Kenzie to Brother Jase. "Kenzie's always thinking, and she has one of the most creative minds I've ever met. She's a real artist."

Brother Jase sent her an interested look. "Oh? Are you a painter, Kenzie?"

"No. I —"

"Kenzie's a weaver." Lori beamed at Kenzie. "She makes beautiful rugs on an old loom. It belonged to her grandmother, right, Kenz?"

Kenzie nodded.

Lori aimed her gaze in Brother Jase's direction again. "Kenzie grew up in Indiana, on a farm. And she's Amish. Sort of."

Brother Jase's eyebrows rose. "How can you be sort of Amish?"

"Because —"

Kenzie put her hand on Lori's arm. "My family is Amish. But I didn't join the church. So I'm not Amish, or even sort of Amish. I'm just . . . a Christian."

Brother Jase nodded slowly, a smile curving his lips. "How interesting. I've never met anybody who grew up in the Amish church. I'd like to hear about your upbringing sometime." He wiped his mouth with his napkin and dropped it onto his plate. "One of the things I want to do with the youth is have people come and share their testimonies. You'd probably be a good one since your background is very different from the way the kids are being raised."

Kenzie drew back, her stomach fluttering. "I'm not a speaker."

Lori squealed and clapped her hands. "Oh, Kenz, you'd be great. Some of the things you've told me, about living on the farm and doing everything by hand, would fascinate the kids, I bet."

Kenzie gave Lori a frown she hoped would

silence her outspoken friend. "Kids who have cell phones and computer games and cars won't find churning butter or riding in a buggy or sewing your own clothes fascinating." She offered Brother Jase an apologetic grimace. "I'm sorry. I don't think I'd have anything of value to tell the kids."

His forehead pinched into furrows, his green-blue eyes narrowing beneath his thick red-brown eyebrows. "Every person's journey to faith in Jesus holds value. I agree with Lori that the kids would find the contrast between your upbringing and theirs interesting. Would you at least consider sharing your testimony? I'll give you plenty of time to think about it — no pressure — but please don't say no right away. All right?"

When he looked at her that way, as if she held the key to something precious and vital, she understood Lori's attraction to the man. But his intensity also made her uncomfortable. She lowered her gaze to her napkin. "I'll think about it."

"And pray about it," he said.

She jerked her head up and met his gaze again. His smile invited her to smile back. She nodded. "Yes. Of course."

"Good." He angled himself onto one hip and reached into his back pocket. "Since y'all wouldn't let me pay for your lunch, at least let me leave the tip for the server. Then I should let you two go. I can't believe we've sat here and talked for almost two hours."

"What's your rush?" Lori sat forward, lacing her fingers together. "There's no service at church tonight, so we don't have to hurry off."

Kenzie pointed to the group of people milling near the checkout counter. "I think we need to leave. We're done eating, and there's a lot of people waiting for a table."

Lori glanced over and made a face. "Oh. Well, all right." Then she brightened. "But maybe we could go someplace else and talk. You said you wanted to know more about Kenzie's background. Could we go to your apartment, Kenz, and hang out for a while? You could show Jase your loom."

Kenzie forced a laugh. "I doubt Brother Jase is interested in my loom."

Brother Jase chuckled, too. "I wouldn't mind seeing it someday, but for now, I think I should head on home." He stood and dropped a five-dollar bill on the table.

Lori sat gazing up at Brother Jase. Kenzie gave her a little bump with her elbow, and with a sigh, Lori got out of the booth. Kenzie climbed out after her. The three of them walked out together, and Brother Jase escorted them to Lori's little green Chevy.

He stopped next to the car's hood and bounced a smile from Kenzie to Lori. "Thanks again for including me today, ladies. I enjoyed the company."

Lori giggled. "I did, too." She hit the unlock button on her key fob, and Brother Jase reached forward and opened the door. She giggled again and slid behind the wheel. "Such a gentleman. Thank you."

Brother Jase looked at Kenzie across the top of the vehicle. She quickly opened the passenger door and got in. He leaned down and peered past Lori at her. "Be sure and give some thought and prayer to sharing your testimony with the youth, Kenzie. Bye now. It was very nice meeting you."

Kenzie snapped her seat belt in place. "You, too. Happy Easter."

He closed Lori's door, waved, and trotted off.

Lori started her car's engine, but she sat staring out her window in the direction Brother Jase had gone. Kenzie waited several seconds, then tapped her friend on the arm. Lori gave a start and looked at her.

"Ready to go?"

Lori's gaze didn't shift. "Kenzie, do you believe in love at first sight?"

Some people might laugh at a question like that, but Kenzie took it seriously. Grossmammi had told her she'd known from the moment her daed introduced her to Grossdaadi that she wanted to be his wife. Storybooks often had heroes and heroines falling in love right away. Although Kenzie had never experienced an immediate attraction to anyone, she couldn't deny its reality. "Yes, I think it's possible."

Lori zipped a hopeful look in Kenzie's direction. "Really? You do?"

"Sure. Why not?"

A huge smile dimpled Lori's cheeks. "Right. Why not? It can happen. And I think it has happened. To me, I mean. I think it's happened to me."

Kenzie squeezed Lori's arm. "I know. And I'm happy for you. Now that you'll be at the church every day, maybe he'll get the chance to know you better and he'll grow fond of you, too."

" 'Grow fond.' " Lori sighed. "Yes, that has a sweet, old-fashioned ring to it. I'd like that." She turned sideways in the seat and fixed Kenzie with a pleading look. "Are you on the schedule at the fabric shop tomorrow?"

"In the afternoon. So are you. And we have the staff meeting at closing, remember?"

Lori groaned. "Oh, I'd forgotten about

the meeting. Thanks for reminding me. But since you'll have tomorrow morning free to do what you want, would you be willing to bake another batch of brownies today? Brother Jase and Brother Kraft take Monday off, but I'm going to the church tomorrow to clean. I'll put the rug you made in Brother Jase's office while I'm there, but I'd like to leave some more brownies, too. He said he ate the last ones this morning for his breakfast."

Brownies for breakfast? Kenzie cringed. The sweetness would give her a stomachache. "I don't mind baking some, but I used up my Dutch cocoa on the last batch, and I think I need more butter, too."

Lori's eyes glittered. "Hmm, real butter? And Dutch cocoa? Are you divulging secrets?"

Kenzie pretended to zip her lips, and Lori burst out laughing.

"Okay, how about we go to the grocery store before I take you to your apartment? I'll buy the ingredients since I'm the one always begging for these things."

"Will something be open? It is Easter Sunday."

Lori rolled her eyes. "Business is business, Kenz. Just like restaurants are open, the supermarkets will be open."

"Okay." Kenzie frowned, worry striking. "Lori, instead of going to the store, wouldn't you like to go see your dad? It is Easter, and families get together at Easter. Won't he look for you to come?"

Lori groaned. "Aw, do you have to ruin my day by talking about family? I know it's hard for you to understand, but my dad doesn't like me." Sadness sagged Lori's face. "He won't miss me."

"Are you sure? Not even on a holiday?" Kenzie tipped her head. "At least think about it, okay? If there's a chance of building a relationship with your father, wouldn't you like to take it? Maybe he just needs you to make the first move." If her parents were in the same town, even if they were Amish and she wasn't, she'd try to spend as much time with them as possible.

Lori stared at Kenzie for several seconds, her expression unreadable. Then she gave a quick nod. "I'll think about it. No promises, but I'll think, okay? Now, can we go get the stuff for brownies?"

Kenzie stifled a chuckle. "Okay. If you're sure a store will be open."

"I'm sure. Wait and see."

As Lori drove, Kenzie gazed out the window at the traffic. The streets were as busy as always, store parking lots crowded with cars. How convenient to have whatever she wanted available any day of the week. So why did being able to buy Dutch cocoa and butter on Easter Sunday make her feel sad?

Bradleyville
Merlin

After lunch and much conversation around the table, Leah invited the girls to the kitchen for cleanup and girl talk, the grandkids clattered down to the basement to horse around, and Merlin led his sons and sons-in-law to the living room. He settled into his recliner, and Todd flopped into Leah's. Merlin's sons-in-law, Raymond and Michael, slumped at opposite ends of the sofa, but Matt stretched out on the love seat with his feet hanging over the armrest. They all rubbed their bellies, and Merlin couldn't hold back a little groan. He'd overeaten. The way he always did on holidays. The way he did too often on regular days. A habit he needed to break. For lots of reasons.

Matt adjusted one of the throw pillows under his head and sighed. "Mom outdid herself. If that's even possible. I won't need to eat for a week."

Todd smirked at his brother. "Betcha ten bucks you'll be digging in the leftovers

Mom sends with you before you get home."

Matt snorted. "No bet. I'd lose for sure. Especially if she sends dinner rolls. Why are hers always so much fluffier and . . . what's the word I want? . . . creamier than anybody else's?" He flipped his hand in the air as he spoke. "Seriously, Dad, Mom missed her calling. She needs to run a restaurant somewhere. Why should we be the only people to get fat from her cooking?"

Merlin forced a laugh. "Your mother wouldn't be happy cooking in a restaurant. She enjoys cooking for people she loves, like family and friends." Which is why he couldn't tell her what the doctor had told him about changing his diet. At least the pills were easing the tightness in his chest. He wasn't struggling to draw a breath anymore — a huge improvement. If he started eating less, it should eventually help with his weight. Shouldn't it? "Cooking in huge batches and then charging strangers to eat it would ruin the fun for her."

"You're probably right." Matt linked his hands behind his head and closed his eyes. "So, Dad, how's the new youth pastor working out? Cassidy said he did a good job in Sunday school and" — he tilted his head and peered at Merlin through squinted eyes — "was easy to pay attention to because he's, as she put it, 'a full meal deal.' " He sat up and swung his feet to the floor. "And to be honest, I'm not sure how I feel about my fourteen-year-old daughter using that kind of term when speaking of a minister."

Merlin chuckled. "We didn't include 'full meal deal' in the list of qualifications for a youth minister, but sometimes you get a bonus. Sure, he's a good-looking young man, and he probably knows it, but he isn't conceited about it. Someone who grew up like he did, without a real home or family, could capitalize on his looks and use it to his advantage, but he doesn't."

Acid burned in Merlin's throat. He adjusted the angle on his recliner. It helped. Helped so much he might sleep out here tonight. Nah. Leah would never put up with that. "I think as the kids get to know him, they'll focus less on his exterior and appreciate his knowledge of the Scriptures, his goal of growing their faith, and his heart for furthering the gospel message. Those were the things that solidified my belief he'd be a good fit here."

"From what I could see," Michael said, "the teens were a lot better behaved this morning than the last time Staci and I attended. Only one kid got up and left, and there wasn't any whispering or note passing. They seemed to pay attention to the sermon."

Raymond nodded. "I noticed the same thing. I guess having an adult sit right in the middle of them makes a difference."

Three years ago, Merlin had instructed the youth to sit together in front to his right so he could keep an eye on them while he preached, but when he got wound up, he focused on his message instead of the ones who were supposed to receive it. "Yes, Jase asked approval for a no-bathroom-breaks-during-service rule. I wholeheartedly endorsed it."

Michael applauded. "Great idea. It's gotta be distracting watching people come and go during the sermon."

Merlin raised one eyebrow. "The biggest distraction is watching people's heads turn and follow the person out, then follow them back in." He held up both hands and slowly swept them first left and then right, tracing the movement with his gaze. "Like choreography."

The younger men all laughed. Matt aimed a warm smile at Merlin. "I'm glad you've hired another pastor, Dad. We've been worried about you carrying so much responsibility on your own for so many years. You aren't" — he fake-coughed into his hand —

"as young as you used to be. You deserve to slow down some."

Merlin swallowed against the sting of acid. "Deserved or not, it was time." The cardiologist had been emphatic about it. "Your mother's pleased about having someone else pick up some of the slack, too. We've talked about it and prayed about it for years. Getting the church council's approval and the congregation's commitment to financially support a second minister took a little longer than she wanted, but I think in the grand scheme of things, the timing is perfect."

He rotated his fist against his breastbone. Yes. God's timing was just right.

FIFTEEN

Lori

Lori shivered as she wriggled the key into the lock for the church's front door. From low eighties at the end of last week to mid-fifties at the beginning of this one — Kansas weather couldn't make up its mind. Kind of like Dad when it came to moods. Another shiver shook her, this one unrelated to the cool, damp wind pressing at her back. Most parents would want to see their kids on a holiday, but Dad wasn't like most parents. Not anymore. Not since Mom died.

His so-called greeting rang in her memory. *"Well, look what the cat dragged in. I guess you do know where your old man lives."* No teasing smile, no warmth in his tone, only sarcasm. She'd stayed all of half an hour before escaping. She'd hoped, given the fact that yesterday was Easter and it'd been weeks since they'd seen each other, he'd be happy to find her on his doorstep. She

209

should've known better. All the wishing in the world would never change him because it couldn't bring Mom back. At least Kenzie had been available to console her after her dismal encounter with Dad. Who needed family when she had great friends?

The lock finally clicked, and she blew out a relieved breath. She grabbed the rolled rug and pan of Kenzie-baked brownies she'd set aside and then bustled into the foyer. She bumped the door closed with her hip and sighed again, grateful for the building's warmth. Then she gave an internal start. Should it be this warm at seven o'clock on Monday morning? Jim had told her all the thermostats were preset for best energy efficiency, which meant when no one was on duty, the temperature would be cooler on cold days and warmer on hot days. As cold as it was outside, shouldn't it be cold in here?

She hurried up the hallway to the closet Jim jokingly called the operations room and checked the thermostats. She let out a huff. Someone had overridden the control for the hallway, the row of Sunday school classrooms, and the pastor's office. Jim's lecture about keeping the electricity bill manageable echoed in her ears. She hadn't adjusted the system, so who had?

"Lori?"

Lori squealed and nearly threw the pan of brownies over her head. She spun toward the sound.

Sister Kraft stood in the doorway, her brow pinched in puzzlement. "What are you doing here so early?"

Lori stumbled from the closet. "I'm supposed to be here. Cleaning. Remember?"

Sister Kraft released a little laugh. "Of course I remember. But Jim never came in before nine. I expected to be by myself for another hour at least. I probably would've finished by then."

Lori's pulse was returning to normal. "I'm on duty at the fabric shop at one. I wouldn't be able to get everything done here if I waited until nine to start." She finally noticed Sister Kraft's clothes. Baggy sweatpants, a stretched-out T-shirt, and — were those slipper socks on her feet? Lori'd never seen the minister's wife in such sloppy clothes. Was this her usual Monday attire? She zipped her gaze to the woman's face. "What're you doing here?"

"Painting." She turned and padded up the hall in the direction of the offices.

Understanding clicked in Lori's brain. She hurried after Sister Kraft. "Why didn't you tell me you wanted to paint today? I could've helped." She turned sideways and edged past the shelves, desk, and other items that had been in Brother Jase's office.

Sister Kraft paused at the room's threshold. "It's a small space, Lori. When I use the roller on its longest handle, I have to be careful not to bump another wall. There's not enough moving-around room for more than one painter. I'd hoped to be done before you got here."

"But I really wanted to have a hand in it." Lori hadn't intended to sound so woebegone, and she cringed at her own tone.

"You will." Sister Kraft spoke crisply, almost impatiently. "When this paint is dry to the touch, which — according to the information on the can — will be early afternoon, you'll help carry in the furniture, hang pictures, and otherwise get the room in order so it'll be ready for Jase's use tomorrow morning."

"I won't be able to this afternoon." The rug started to slide from her grasp, and Lori tightened her grip. "I'll be at the fabric shop."

"Well, then, I'll get Merlin or Jase himself to help me."

Lori glanced at the metal desk and shelves. "Isn't he getting new furniture?"

"Eventually, yes. People are gathering

items. But for now, these things will have to go back in or he won't have any furnishings at all." Sister Kraft wrinkled her nose. "I wish there was a window in here to let the fumes out. Could you find a fan? It'll at least blow the smell into the hallway."

"Where I get to enjoy it."

"You did say you wanted to have a hand in it."

"A hand. Not my nose."

Sister Kraft laughed.

Lori put the brownies on the corner of the desk and leaned the rug against the wall. "I saw a tower fan in one of the adults' Sunday school classrooms. I'll get it and be right back."

She lugged the fan — it was heavier than it looked! — to Jase's office and peeked inside. Three of the four walls were now a greenish-blue hue that closely matched his irises. She smiled. "I like the color."

Sister Kraft glanced over her shoulder. "It's called Restful. I thought it was masculine without being cold."

"I agree. And, ohhhh . . ." Lori set the fan on the floor and hurried to the rug Kenzie had woven. She brought it to the doorway and let it unroll across the threshold. "Sister Kraft, look! The color you picked goes really good with the yellows, greens, reds, and

213

plaids in the rug."

"Well, look at that." Sister Kraft's wide-eyed astonishment made Lori smile. "Did Kenzie make this?"

"Yes, ma'am. Won't it be perfect in front of Brother Jase's desk?"

"I think it will. She did a great job with it."

"I helped." Lori couldn't resist bragging a bit. "She showed me how, and I did about a half-foot-long section." A half foot sounded so much more impressive than six inches.

"This will definitely warm up the room and add some color and texture. Good choice." Sister Kraft bent over and lifted the rug. She handed it to Lori. "But it's too soon to bring it in. I might drip paint on it. So bring the fan instead, please."

Lori rolled the rug and set it aside. Then she carried the fan to the far corner, careful to avoid the handle of Sister Kraft's roller, and set it a couple of feet from the wall. She plugged it in and hit the On button. The motor whirred to life, stirring the wet-paint aroma. She scurried to the doorway. "I'll get out of your way. I'm going to clean the bathrooms. Feel free to come get me if you need help."

"I'm fine for now." Sister Kraft dipped the roller and aimed it at the wall. "Thank you for the fan. Now scoot and let me work."

Lori began easing past the furniture in the hallway.

"Oh, Lori?"

Lori leaned back and peeked around the doorjamb. "Yes?"

"That pan out there . . . Is it full of brownies?"

"Yes."

"Kenzie's brownies?"

"She made them for Brother Jase." And this time, even though Kenzie had sent the pan with her yesterday evening when they were still warm and aromatic, Lori hadn't eaten any. All sixteen were in the pan. She was so proud of herself for staying out of them, even after her disappointing encounter with Dad. She'd consoled herself with a bag of potato chips instead.

"Take them to the kitchen, please. I haven't had my breakfast yet, and if you leave them within reach, they might not be here when you come back."

Laughing, Lori did as Sister Kraft requested. As she placed the foil-covered pan on the counter, her stomach growled. She hadn't had any breakfast, either. Temptation tugged hard. The brownies were so good. And those salty chips hadn't erased the memory of Dad's scorn for her showing up late in the day. He'd said, "Look at the time. Past seven. You waited the whole day before coming over? I guess that tells me how much your brothers and me really mean to you." She'd cringed, shame flooding her, but what about him coming to her? Did he ever think about taking the first step toward reconciliation? The sadness that always hit when she thought about the chasm between her and her father created an aching emptiness she couldn't ignore.

She peeled back the foil from the pan and dug out a middle brownie with her finger. She ate it in two bites, almost swallowing the chunks whole, her ears tuned for Sister Kraft's approach. The first brownie went down so fast she hardly tasted it. So she ate a second, and it was so good she compulsively gobbled a third and then a fourth. She licked gooey chocolate from her finger, then reached for another one.

Her hand froze midway between her mouth and the pan. She gasped. What had she done? These were supposed to be for Jase. Groaning, she buried her face in her hands. Oh, she loathed herself when she gave in to these feeding frenzies. But in the lonely, empty moments, she only thought of one thing. Filling herself.

Well, she was full now. Her stomach hurt

from overfullness. And her chest ached from guilt. She slammed her fist on the counter. No more! She would never do this again. She aimed her gaze at the ceiling. "I promise, God. I'm done with it." How many times had she already made that promise? God was probably weary of hearing it. Weary of seeing her gorge herself like a pig at a trough. Weary of her. Like Dad.

Pursing her lips, she blinked against tears and grabbed the rumpled foil. She folded it over the mess of remaining brownies, then slid the pan on top of the refrigerator. Out of sight, out of mind. Later she'd transfer the nicest ones to a plate for Jase. She didn't dare remove them now or, the way she was feeling, she'd eat the whole pan even if it made her sick as a dog.

Inwardly berating herself with every motion, she gathered the basket of cleaning supplies Jim had shown her and headed for the bathrooms.

Jase

Jase carried his basket of clean clothes up the staircase. The folded stacks stood at least six inches above the rim of the plastic container and teetered with every upward step, but he balanced the piles against his middle and prevented them from going over

217

the edge. The next time he went shopping, he'd buy a second basket. Pretty stupid to pay to wash and dry everything and then send half the clothes tumbling down the staircase.

He set the clothes on the landing and dug in his pocket for his key. Sister Kraft had told him he could use her washer and dryer. She'd even given him his own key to get in the back porch, where the appliances were hooked up. But he didn't feel right about intruding into what was really part of their house. Besides, he could wash several loads at one time at a laundromat and not tie up a whole morning, which appealed to him. Laundry wasn't his favorite chore.

He put his clothes in drawers, tucked the empty container in his closet, then headed to the kitchen table, where he'd left his laptop. Before leaving for the laundromat, he'd sent out several emails, including one to Cullen's mother, asking for a conference. He wanted that over with as quickly as possible, so he hoped she'd responded already. He tapped the mouse, and the screen lit. A little number two was next to his email icon. He clicked on it, and the messages came into view. Sure enough, one was from Starla Wade.

Sliding into the kitchen chair, he opened

the email and read silently.

Mr. Edgar, I'm a single mom who works two jobs. I send Cullen to church so he isn't home alone so much. I don't have time to go to church most Sundays and I don't have time to come to a meeting. If you have a problem, talk to Brother Kraft or Zack's dad. They know Cullen as good as I do and he'd prolly listen better to them then he would to me. Sorry I can't help. Starla Wade

Jase sat up, frowning. Brother Kraft had said a lot of Cullen's issues were cries for attention. Based on this email, Jase was inclined to agree. Would Brother Kraft or Rick have Cullen's medical information? Somehow he doubted it. He bent over the keyboard and tapped a second message.

Ms. Wade, I'm sorry your schedule is so hectic. I'm sure that's a hardship for you and for Cullen. I wanted to ask you about Cullen's health. He told me he has a condition that requires frequent bathroom visits.

He grunted. The email read like a preteen kid tattling on a classmate. There had to be a better way of asking. He sat and thought

219

for several minutes, but nothing came to mind. With a sigh, he saved the email as a draft and clicked out of the program. He'd contact her later. No sense in interrupting her day again. He wouldn't see Cullen until Wednesday evening anyway.

He got a bottle of water from his refrigerator and returned to the computer, then opened his social media account. The last post on his profile was the one he'd shared from Sister Eileen about the missing ring. According to the statistics under the picture, it'd been shared 141 times and viewed more than 15,000 times. With numbers like that, it could very well go viral. Wouldn't that be something?

He added a comment to the post —

Way to go on spreading the word!
Wouldn't it be great if the gospel got
around so fast?

— then looked again at the contact email. How many emails had FinderznotKeeperz received? Reading about someone else's lost ring reminded him of a special one he'd purchased — Rachel's engagement ring.

He hadn't had the heart to take it back to the jewelry store right after she'd died, and there was probably some kind of limit on returns, so it was too late for that now. It wouldn't matter anyway. He couldn't bring himself to take it back or sell it. It was Rachel's ring, one he specially chose for her. It didn't belong on someone else's finger. He had no idea what he should do with it now, but he didn't have to do anything with it. It was safe in its little velvet box in the cedar whatnot box he'd made in woodworking class in high school. And that's where it would stay.

SIXTEEN

Jase

Jase fixed a slivered ham sandwich for lunch, ate it while watching a television game show, then dusted his furniture, cleaned his bathroom, and ran the vacuum cleaner. By half past one, he was out of things to do and was bemoaning his day off. What would he be doing if he was still in San Antonio? The answer to his inner reflection tripped through his brain, and he released a little snort.

Before he met Rachel, he hung out with a group of single guys from church. After he met Rachel, she consumed every minute of his free time. And after she died, he was mostly alone. Like here and now. So why did the aloneness make him feel more restless here? He needed to get to know the folks close to his age at Beech Street. Lori'd said activities were listed on the church's monthly calendar. What was going on this month?

He dug the bulletin and its inserts from the inside flap of his Bible, flopped onto the sofa, and looked for activities involving the young adult class. On the sixteenth — the third Thursday, just as Lori'd said — the group planned to meet at a bowling alley for pizza and bowling. He nodded, smiling. Yeah, he liked pizza, and he liked to bowl. Perfect. He'd attend the gathering and get acquainted with the Sunday school class members. But the gathering was still three days away, and he had the rest of this day to fill. So what now?

His cell phone buzzed in his pocket. He pulled it out and blinked in confusion. Why was the church calling him? There shouldn't be anyone over there today. He accepted the call and pressed the phone to his ear. "Hello?"

"Brother Jase, it's Sister Kraft. What are you doing?"

For reasons he didn't understand, he quickly stood and squared his shoulders. "Nothing important."

"Good. I could use your help. I finished painting your office, and even though it isn't cured yet, it's dry enough for us to bring in your new furniture."

Jase gave a start. "New furniture? Already?"

A sly chuckle rumbled. "When I want things done, things get done."

He believed it.

Now laughter spilled. "The truth is, one of our members had offered Merlin a set of used office furniture several weeks ago, but Merlin didn't want to swap out what he has. You know how we get comfortable with things, yes? He remembered the offer, though, and called Brother Don this morning. Brother Don, bless his heart, still had it and was more than happy to give it to you."

Jase scratched his jaw. These people were nothing if not generous. "That's really nice of him."

"He and his wife, Ann, are both very nice people. He's here now with the furniture in the back of his pickup truck. We already put your old furniture in the youth Sunday school room to get it out of our way. If you don't want it in there, we'll haul it off later this week. Everything that had been in the desk or on the shelves is in boxes on top of the desk, waiting for you." A sigh came through the connection, and he envisioned her swiping her forehead with the back of her hand. "So now it's a matter of bringing the new stuff in, but I'm not strong enough to lift these pieces out. Merlin had an appointment in Wichita at one, so he isn't here to help. Are you able to come?"

"Of course I'll come."

"Good. The back door's propped open." The connection went dead.

Jase dropped his phone into his pocket and trotted down the stairs. What perfect timing. Reorganizing his office would fill an hour. Maybe more. He crossed the grassy expanse, utilizing his longest stride. When he was halfway to the church, Sister Kraft peeked out the doorway.

She beckoned with an insistent wave of her arm. "Hurry now, Brother Jase. Shake a leg!"

"Yes, ma'am!" He broke into a jog, closed the distance quickly, and entered the fellowship hall.

She took off like a shot, yakking as she went. "Now, about this furniture, it isn't new, but it's still very serviceable and much nicer than the old metal stuff you had in there before."

"I'm sure it'll be fine." Jase double-stepped to keep up with her. For someone whose age qualified her as a senior citizen, she had a lot of energy. "I really appreciate the trouble all y'all have gone to for me."

She huffed. "We don't consider it trouble, so put that thought out of your head."

He choked back a laugh. "Yes, ma'am."

They reached the hallway that split, leading to the offices or the foyer. The smell of paint hung heavy. Sister Kraft turned toward the foyer, and Jase followed, waving his hand in front of his nose. She led him out the front doors to the concrete slab that served as a kind of patio between the two buildings. A pickup truck, its tailgate open, was parked as close to the slab as it could get without being on it. A tall bald-headed man with an easy smile waited beside the truck. A wood desk, a matching low shelf, and a pair of small side chairs covered in a yellowish fabric sat in the bed of the truck.

The man took a step in Jase's direction. "Hey there, Brother Jase. Sorry to pester you on your day off."

"It's no problem at all." Sunshine glinted on the wood surface of the desk. Brother Don must have given it a good polishing before loading it. Up close, the furniture was even nicer than Jase had first presumed. The desk and shelf were stained solid wood, maybe maple, definitely not veneer-covered particle board. Not quite old enough to be antique, but vintage, built during a time when quality meant something.

Jase whistled. "Wow, this is really nice. Are you sure you want to give it away?"

Brother Don rubbed his hand across the

edge of the desk's top, his smile warm. "I bought it when I opened my accounting office in 1972 and used it right up until my retirement last year, so it's been well used. But there's still lots of years left in it, and I don't need it anymore. To be honest, I was pretty disappointed when Brother Kraft decided not to take it. Seemed so perfect to me, with the extra deep desktop and inset for visitors to pull up close on the opposite side. You know, half desk, half conference table. But now I'm thinking it was God's way of saving it for someone who needs it more."

The feeling of warm liquid flowing over his head and down his frame touched Jase. He ran his hand through his hair and then touched his short beard, surprised to find it all dry. What was that sensation, and why was he experiencing it? He forced himself to ignore the warmth and extended his hand to Brother Don. "I sure appreciate the gift, sir. I'll take good care of it."

"Oh, I know you will, son." Brother Don squeezed Jase's hand and let go. His grin lifted higher on the left side, giving him an impish look. "And let me tell you, you're going to earn your keep helping me carry this in. Even with the drawers empty, it weighs half a ton."

Brother Don might have exaggerated the desk's weight, but not by much. Jase made use of every arm, leg, and back muscle wrestling it out of the pickup and then carrying his end all the way through the church to the back corner, where his newly-painted empty office begged for furnishings. They set the desk to the side, rested for a few minutes while panting like a pair of dogs who'd been on a hunt, then went after the shelf. Sister Kraft brought the chairs, and she directed the men where to put everything.

Jase swallowed a chortle. Was this her office or his? But when they were done, he couldn't fault her reasoning. Her arrangement left the greatest amount of floor space open and gave him a view into the hallway. The only outlet in the room was conveniently located on the wall between the desk and shelf — perfect for plugging in his laptop.

Brother Don settled the chairs side by side under the wide knee hole at the front of the desk, but Sister Kraft shook her head.

"Not yet. There's something that needs to go in front of the desk first." She bustled out and returned a few moments later carrying a thick colorful tube. She unrolled it across the tile in front of the desk. Jase looked from the rug to Sister Kraft, who stood smiling at it with her hands on her hips. She gave a satisfied nod. "Yes, that's exactly where it should go, just as Lori planned."

Jase examined the rug. He didn't know a lot about rugs, but this one didn't look factory made. He scratched his jaw. "Did Lori's friend Kenzie make this?"

Sister Kraft smiled. "Yes, she did. On an antique floor loom, by hand. You won't find another one like it anywhere, and it's exactly what this space needed to make it not feel like a closet."

Brother Don chuckled. "Well, now, I think the furniture helps with that, too. But you're right. It's a very nice rug." He nudged Jase with his elbow, winking. "A pretty snazzy gift, I'd say."

Jase would say so, too. Should he accept something that must have taken several weeks to complete? But it was perfect with the stained desk, and even he could see how it made the yellow-toned chairs look right with the color on the walls. He couldn't define the wall color, but he liked it. It was . . .

"I hope you like the color of the paint." Sister Kraft touched her fingertip to the matte surface. "It's called Restful."

Restful. Jase couldn't have chosen better himself. "I like it very much. Thank you." A lump filled his throat. He was so unworthy of everything these people had done for him. If they knew his inner struggles to truly trust God, would they still have done all this? Maybe the fact that they had was God's way of letting him know he was loved.

He cleared his throat. "I guess I should get my stuff and bring it back in, get things put away and organized."

Brother Don grinned at Sister Kraft. "That's our cue to go, I think."

Sister Kraft laughed. "You might be right." She exited the room but stopped outside the door, seeming to examine the hallway floor. "Oh, goodness, Lori's going to need to come back and vacuum again before Wednesday night. We tracked in dried grass."

Jase stepped out behind the others. "I can run the vacuum when I'm done organizing. I'll probably bring more in when I fetch my laptop and a few more books from the apartment and bring them over here."

Sister Kraft set off up the hallway. "If you want to do that, I'm sure she'd appreciate it. She was here several hours this morning and is working at the fabric shop this afternoon. I don't know what tomorrow's schedule looks like for her." She paused beside a door and patted it. "The vacuum cleaner is in here, so help yourself. And now . . ." She waved and walked backward toward the fellowship hall. "I want to see if Merlin's home."

Jase remembered she'd said he was at an appointment. "Is everything okay with him?"

She flicked her fingers. "Routine checkup. He needs them from time to time for our insurance. No worries. Thank you again, Brother Don. Brother Jase, have fun settling in." She turned and hurried off.

Jase walked Brother Don to the front doors, thanked him, and then locked the doors behind him. Alone in the quiet church, he brought the boxes of his personal items into his office and placed them carefully on top of the desk. He didn't want to scratch the freshly polished surface. He opened a drawer, intending to transfer items from the box, but the quiet was too . . . intense. He needed some company.

His portable CD player was in one of the boxes, but he hadn't brought over any CDs. No problem, though. He'd use the FM radio option. He plugged in the player, set the dial to a contemporary Christian radio station, then sang along to the staticky songs while he worked. The sectioned drawer organized his standard office supplies, and the deep file drawer was perfect for housing his CDs and player when they weren't in use. He'd never liked the way the black plastic box looked on display.

He emptied all three boxes, carried them to the hall, then stood in the doorway and admired his office. *His* office. He never would have imagined having such a nice space to call his own. The open corner needed something. A standing lamp? No, he'd have to run an extension cord along the wall, which would look messy. Maybe a potted artificial ficus tree. With no window bringing in natural light, a real one wouldn't survive, but they made some nice fake ones these days. Then some pictures up on the walls — should he hang his Spurs poster in here? — and people wouldn't even remember the room had once been used as a storage closet.

An odd idea struck. What if he put his photo with Rachel on the shelf? They were supposed to serve together. Maybe having her picture in his office would be encouraging. Comforting. Like she was still with him, at least in thought. His heart twisted into a knot. Yes, he wanted her picture in here.

He went to the hallway and stomped the

boxes flat, then tucked them under his arm and strode up the long dark hallway in the direction of the fellowship hall. He dropped the flattened boxes next to the big trash canister just inside the doors, then headed for the rear exit.

As he passed the kitchen serving window, a scent caught his attention. Chocolate. But not chocolate bars or even chocolate cake. He smelled the rich dark chocolate aroma of Kenzie's brownies. Funny how he recognized it after eating them only a couple of times, but they were distinct. Like her rug.

He made a sharp turn and entered the kitchen, flipping on the lights as he crossed the threshold. No pan or plate sat anywhere on the counters, but he smelled brownies. They were here somewhere. He checked behind the door marked Pantry. No brownies there. Disappointed, he closed the door. He turned a slow circle, searching every surface, and spotted a foil-covered pan stuck above the refrigerator.

With a little half skip, he hurried to the fridge and lifted down the pan. Even before he peeked under the foil, the smell gave the contents away. He pulled in a deep breath, savoring the aroma, then lifted the foil aside. He jolted. What a mess. Whoever got into the pan hadn't used a spatula. Or even a fork. Had an animal dug through the pan? Maybe that's why it'd been put up high — to protect it from another invasion. But then why hadn't the brownies been thrown away? Who would want them after a dog or some other pest got into them? He for sure wasn't that desperate.

He covered the pan and put it back where he'd found it, then headed for his apartment.

SEVENTEEN

Jase

Jase pushed his key into the lock, twisted the knob, and stepped inside his apartment. Then he stopped, his heart firing into his throat.

Cullen Wade slouched in the middle of Jase's sofa, knees widespread and arms stretched along the sofa's back. He didn't even move when Jase entered, only offered a lopsided smirk and said, "Hi."

Jase looked at the keys in his hand, then at Cullen. "How'd you get in here?"

Cullen shrugged. "Pretty easy if you've got a nice stiff library card. Which I do."

His next expenditure would be a dead bolt. Jase dropped his keys into his pocket. Remembering what Sister Kraft had said about having kids up here, he left his door open even though it let in the cold air. He folded his arms and aimed a stern frown at Cullen. "It isn't cool to let yourself in at somebody's place when they aren't there. It's a good way to get yourself accused of breaking and entering."

Cullen swung his arms down and sat up, clamping his hands over the knees of his torn jeans and glaring at Jase from beneath thick brown bangs. "Does it look like I broke my way in? Besides, you told everybody at church that you were always available, twenty-four seven. But maybe you didn't mean it."

The challenge in the boy's tone set Jase's teeth on edge. Did he have to test Jase at every turn? But he realized the real reason Cullen bugged him. Cullen reminded Jase too much of his teenage self, using cockiness to hide unworthiness, rejecting others before they had the chance to reject him. If Jase's foster parents and Brother Tony and Sister Eileen and so many others at Grace Chapel in San Antonio hadn't loved on him in spite of his unlovable ways, how might he have turned out? Cullen didn't need Jase's anger. He needed Jase's love. Maybe his tough love.

Jase took two steps and perched on the arm of his sofa. He gave a nod. "I did mean it. I'll be there for you when you need to talk, but from now on, you gotta call first. Set up a time. And we need to meet in my office, not here" — he sent a quick glance around the living room — "in my home."

Cullen rolled his eyes. "Sheesh, didn't know there was a bunch of rules to follow. All I wanted to do was tell you I kinda fibbed to you yesterday."

"Oh, yeah?" Jase eased onto the sofa.

Cullen slid to the opposite end. He angled himself on the seat and aimed his pimply face in Jase's direction. "Yeah. About my medical condition." He fiddled with the ragged cuff on his hoodie sleeve. "See, I don't exactly have a problem with my bladder. What I have is a problem with sitting so cramped together. I get . . . sort of twitchy. You know, like there's bugs or something crawling under my skin. And I gotta go to where there's more space. You know what I mean?"

"You mean you get claustrophobic."

Cullen nodded. "Yeah. That's the word. After a little while of being all" — he bounced his bent arms like he was doing the chicken dance — "close, I need to be far. That's why I get up and leave during church. Everybody's too cramped together."

Jase gazed at Cullen for several seconds, and Cullen stared back, unblinking, as if measuring him. Jase leaned forward, resting his elbows on his knees. "You know, Cullen, there's an easy solution to your problem."

"Yeah?"

"Yeah. Don't sit in the middle of the pew." Jase used a conversational tone, the way Brother Tony had addressed Jase during his rebellious moments. A gentle answer turns away wrath, the proverb advised, and it'd worked for Jase more than a dozen years ago. "From now on, we'll put you at the end. And to make sure nobody gets too close, I'll sit by you and give you plenty of space. Will that help?"

Cullen pinched the bill of his cap and shifted it back and forth, his blue eyes never leaving Jase's face. "I generally sit by Zack. Him an' me, we're tight."

Jase fought a grin. "But I didn't think you wanted to be tight."

Cullen ducked his head, but not before a glimmer of humor sparked in his eyes. "You know what I mean."

Jase laughed. "Yes, I do know what you mean. I was giving you a hard time."

Cullen played with his cuff again.

"Cullen?" He waited until the boy looked up. "I'll talk to Zack, and we'll work it out so you don't feel hemmed in. Fair enough?"

Cullen scrunched his lips to the side, but he nodded. "Okay." He started to stand.

Jase put out his hand. "Wait a minute.

While we're talking, I'd like to ask you a favor."

Suspicion glinted in the boy's eyes.

"You're a junior, right?"

Cullen nodded.

"Which means you're one of the older members of the youth group. That kind of puts you in a leadership position."

Cullen snickered.

Jase decided to ignore the response. "The younger kids watch you. They watch your example, and they'll follow it. So don't you think it'd be best to set a good example?"

Cullen scowled. "What do you want from me?"

Jase smiled. "Nothing more than you're able to give, I promise. I'd like you to call me Brother Jase instead of bro."

Cullen rolled his eyes again and stood. "Is that all? Yeah, sure, I was just trying to be friendly."

Jase knew what Cullen had been doing, and friendliness wasn't the motivation. Arguing, though, wouldn't help. He stood and met Cullen's arrogant gaze. "Brother Jase is friendly enough." He stuck out his hand. "Deal?"

Cullen jammed his hands into the pocket of his hoodie and sauntered to the doorway, sidestepping around Jase. "All right, Brother

Jase, I gotta vamoose. See ya Wednesday." He paused and sent a lip-curled glance around the room. "Nice place. Glad I got to see it." He scuffed out.

Jase went to the landing and watched Cullen clump down the stairs and disappear around the corner. He let out a big breath and stepped inside, shutting the door behind him. He turned and stood for a few moments. Shame struck. He should've prayed with Cullen before letting him go. Clearly the boy was searching for guidance, for somebody to care. He'd blown it.

Jase stomped to his bedroom and to the drawer where he'd tucked away the photograph of Rachel and him. He pulled it out, stared into her upturned smiling face, and sighed. "I'm out of my league, Rachel. Working with these kids should be easier than planting a church. Maybe God took you home because He knew I wasn't cut out for service."

The strange sensation of something warm being poured over him returned, and his hands trembled. He put the photograph on the dresser and rubbed his hands as if applying lotion. The tremble stopped, and a chill shuddered through him. With his gaze locked on Rachel's sweet image, he forced words past his gritted teeth. "I need you,

Rachel. I need you with me. I don't want to do this life alone."

His whatnot box from high school rested in his peripheral vision. Still looking at Rachel's image, he stretched his hand toward the box and lifted the lid. He pawed inside and located the square velvet box from the jewelry store. He gripped it in his fist and settled it directly in his line of vision. It'd been a year since he'd looked at the ring, but an image of it was burned into his memory. A wide band and a single diamond. A round full-karat stone. He'd bought the biggest diamond he could afford, and it'd been so pretty against the gleaming white-gold band.

He tried to smile at her photo, but his lips quivered too much to cooperate. "Rachel, you loved the ring so much when I proposed. And you would've loved what I had engraved inside the band when I had it sized for you. You'd have seen those words as my commitment to you, and you would have accepted the ring as your commitment to me." How unfair that she hadn't gotten to read the inscription. The chance to even wear the ring had been stolen from her by a driver who'd had too much to drink and couldn't recognize that a red light meant stop.

His heart pounding, he angled his head. "Would . . . would you like to read it, Rachel?"

Underneath, he knew it was a ridiculous thing to do. Really? Show a ring to the image of a person? But for reasons he couldn't explain, in that moment, he needed to show her the engraved promise. And there was no other way to do it. Trembling from head to toe, Jase positioned his thumb against the box and pushed. The lid popped open. The box was empty.

His fingers lost their grip. The box hit the floor, bounced, and landed on its hinged side, wide open, resembling the munching figure from the old video game *Pac-Man*. Jase jerked around and gaped toward the living room. One name roared through his mind.

Cullen . . .

Merlin

Merlin accepted the glass of tea Leah offered, then took a sip as she settled into the chair across the table. She was silent, but worry lines creased her brow. She'd be even more worried, maybe even mad, and certainly not silent when he told her what the doctor had said. But he didn't have a choice anymore. The jig was up. Did people even say that anymore? Not that it mattered. His thoughts were procrastination, pure and simple, and he shouldn't — well, he couldn't — keep the truth from his wife anymore.

"I'm waiting." Leah's voice cut into his thoughts. "What did the doctor say?"

Merlin set down his glass and reached for her hand.

She drew it back. "Is this going to be bad news?"

He shook his head. "Not entirely." He turned his palm up and waited. After a moment, she placed her hand in his, and he curled his fingers around it. The doctor's declaration, although grim from one side of the coin, offered assurance on the flip side. He prayed Leah would focus on the positive. "After the first of the year, you suggested I go to the doctor because I was having so much acid reflux, remember?"

She gave a little huff. "Suggested? I insisted. You wouldn't have gone otherwise."

He chuckled and squeezed her hand. "You're right. You insisted, I went, and after I told him what I was experiencing, he did a complete physical. When he listened to my heart and lungs, he got a little concerned. He said it didn't sound right."

Her fingers went stiff in his grip, and her blue eyes widened. "What do you mean, didn't sound right?"

"Well . . ." He lowered his gaze to their joined hands. He'd held this woman's hand for more than forty years, and he wasn't anywhere close to being ready to let go. "He said there was fluid in my chest, constricting my lungs and putting pressure on my heart."

Leah jolted from the chair and jammed her fists on her hips. "Merlin! Congestive heart failure?"

Of course she'd guess. What a wise woman he'd married. He rose and rounded the table. "Now, honey, don't get yourself all worked up."

"Don't get myself —" She glowered at him. "You knew this three months ago and didn't tell me?"

"There wasn't any reason to worry you. The doctor said I wasn't in imminent danger, that he'd put me on medication to reduce the fluid and things would improve."

Her breath whooshed out and she seemed to wilt. But the angry glint in her eyes didn't fade. "You should've told me."

"I'm telling you now."

"You should've told me then."

Maybe he should have. But it was too late now. He gently massaged her shoulders, and although she stood rigid beneath his touch,

244

she didn't pull away. "I didn't want to say anything until I knew for sure what was going on with my heart. Why have two of us stressed and worrying?"

Tears swam in her eyes. "What does Galatians 6:2 say? 'Carry each other's burdens, and in this way you will fulfill the law of Christ.'"

Ouch. The scripture stuck with so much force she might have stomped on his toes.

"You denied me the chance to carry your burden. We're supposed to be a team, Merlin. I'm very upset with you."

He nodded. "I know. You have every right to be upset, and I'm sorry I didn't say anything before. At the time, I thought it was better to wait."

"Well, it wasn't."

"You're right. I'm sorry."

She glared at him for several silent seconds. Then she lunged and flung her arms around his middle. Given his girth, her arms couldn't quite reach all the way around, and her fingers dug into his back. She burrowed her face into the curve of his neck. "What did the doctor say this morning?"

He doubled his arms around her shoulder blades and rested his cheek against her warm hair. He loved holding her this way. Like being home. "He said the diuretic is helping some, but I need to do more. He's starting me on medication to lower my blood pressure, and he wants me to make some changes in my diet."

She lifted her head and gave him a squinty-eyed look. "What kind of changes?"

Oh, how this woman loved to cook. She loved on people with food. This would be more painful for her than it would be for him. "Things like cutting way back on sodium, no more fried foods, less red meat and more chicken." He grimaced. Not even Leah would be able to make chicken taste like meatloaf. He'd sure miss her meatloaf. "He sent me home with a packet of information. There's more details in there."

"Then I guess I better look at it." But she didn't move. Kept her hands on his waist and gazed into his face as if she were memorizing him.

He cupped her jaw with his palms and smiled. "Honey, I'll be all right."

"You better be."

Her tart tone made him chuckle. He leaned forward, intending to give her a peck on the forehead, but she grabbed him around the neck and pulled him into a kiss that spoke of both intense love and intense worry. He rubbed his hands up and down her spine and tilted his head, deepening their contact. He wouldn't have minded this kiss lasting forever, but a knock on the back door interrupted.

She pulled free and turned her back, running her hands through her snow-white bob. "Would you get that, please? I need to check my lipstick."

Lipstick. He grabbed a napkin from the holder in the middle of the table and cleaned his mouth as he crossed to the door. Through the uncovered window he spotted Jase waiting on the porch. Merlin opened the door.

Jase had his hands in his pockets and a sheepish look on his face. "I'm sorry. I knocked before I realized — Before I saw what —" He angled his gaze to the side. "I didn't want to just disappear after knocking, but I'm sorry I interrupted. Especially on your off day."

"Even on my off day, I'm available for emergencies." Merlin tried not to sound impatient. But the day's stress colored his tone anyway. "What's up?"

The younger man hung his head. "I think I have a problem. And his name is Cullen."

EIGHTEEN

Lori

Lori unlocked the front door and held it open, then gestured Kenzie into the dark foyer.

Kenzie stepped inside. "Are you sure it's okay for me to be with you? I don't want to get you in trouble."

Lori locked the door behind them. "Will you stop worrying? I'm the custodian. I can be here whenever I need to." What a heady feeling, having a key for the church and being able to come and go at will. Brother and Sister Kraft and all the deacons trusted her. She loved having their trust, and she wouldn't do anything to betray it. "I had to leave before Sister Kraft was finished in Brother Jase's office, so I didn't get to see what the rug looked like in there. You should get to see, too, since you made it. Aren't you curious?"

Kenzie hugged herself, glancing around

248

the shadowy space. "Sure I am. But I could've peeked in on Wednesday, when the lights are on. It's kind of creepy in here at night."

Lori laughed. "Creepy in a church?" She glanced toward the black hallway. Maybe it was creepy. A little. "Lemme get the lights. That'll eliminate the creep factor." She hurried to the switch plate and flicked up all four toggles. Light flooded the foyer and illuminated the hallways. "There. Better?"

Kenzie nodded.

"Then follow me." She set off for Jase's office, eagerness putting a bounce in her step. After she'd shown Kenzie the rug, she'd go to the kitchen and do something with the brownies she'd left hidden above the refrigerator. She got so focused on cleaning earlier that she forgot about them, but she could ready a plate and have them waiting for Brother Jase tomorrow morning.

The door to Sister Kraft's secretary office and Brother Kraft's study was closed, but Brother Jase's was ajar. Sister Kraft probably left it open to let the paint smell escape. But the light on inside the room gave her pause. As did the mumble of voices coming from the other side of the open doorway. She stopped, and Kenzie stopped, too.

"What's the matter?" Kenzie whispered.

Lori pointed ahead. "Brother Jase's office light is on. And I think I hear somebody in there."

Kenzie shrugged. "Maybe he's working in there."

They continued to whisper, adding an element of suspense to the moment. Lori shivered. "With all the other lights in the church out? And it's his day off. He shouldn't be —"

"Lori? Kenzie? What're you two doing here?"

Lori spun around at the sound of Jase's voice. He stood half-in and half-out of his office, furrows of curiosity lining his brow. She released a shrill giggle. "We, uh, I mean, *I* was here this morning. Cleaning. And I noticed Sister Kraft was getting your office in order, but she wasn't done when I left, so I didn't get to see if it needed dusting. Or sweeping. Or anything."

Yikes trikes, she was babbling like an idiot. And acting guilty. She had no reason to be guilty. She was a paid employee who had permission to be here, the same as him. She gave her hair a cavalier flip. "I came back to . . . see." The mumble of voices continued from the office. She angled her head slightly, trying to peek inside. "Is there someone with you?"

"Nope. Just the radio."

Thank goodness they hadn't interrupted a counseling session or something. Lori looped her arm through Kenzie's. "Well, do you mind if Kenzie and me come in for a minute? We'd like to see if Kenzie's rug fits the room okay, and I'll make sure nothing needs cleaning."

He stepped aside, gesturing with his hand. "C'mon in."

Lori guided Kenzie to the office and gave her a little nudge over the threshold. She paused in the doorway and smiled up at Jase. "I didn't expect anyone else to be here. You're awfully dedicated, working on your day off."

He shrugged, a grin lifting the corners of his lips beneath his neatly trimmed mustache. "I didn't have anything else to do. Besides, it's easy to focus when no one's around and it's quiet."

"But the radio is making noise."

"White noise. Hardly notice it."

He probably wouldn't classify her and Kenzie as white noise. They should get out of his way. "Well, we won't bother you for —" She took a step into the office, and her mouth fell open. What a transformation in such a short period of time. "Yikes trikes . . ."

Jase burst out laughing. "I take it you approve?"

Lori nodded, twisting her head back and forth and taking in every detail. "It looks great in here. Sister Kraft and I were going to try to find some framed prints, like maybe Bible verses or something, to hang up, but you've already got that covered." She crossed to a huge poster with *San Antonio Spurs* printed in bright white on a sheeny black background. The words repeated in an upside-down slant in pale gray at the bottom half of the poster, reminding her of a pond's reflection. She touched the black plastic frame. "You must miss your hometown." She shifted to look at him, and she caught sight of another framed picture, this one on the middle shelf behind the desk. She swallowed. His hometown wasn't the only thing he missed.

She couldn't tear her attention away from the image. Jase and a woman, captured in a moment of joy, their smiles as bright as the sun must have been, given the glow on their faces and hair. And in their eyes, locked on each other with such affection and admiration.

Would a man ever look at Lori that way?

She aimed a shaky finger at the photograph. "Is that . . . your fiancée?" Kenzie had been examining the rug, but at the question, she jerked her focus to the image, too. She sucked in a little gasp, which Lori completely understood. The woman in the photo looked enough like Kenzie to be her sister.

Jase leaned against the doorjamb, sliding his hands into his pockets. "Yes. That's me and Rachel. The picture was taken at a church picnic." His tone and expression didn't resonate with deep emotion, but somehow Lori knew he was hiding his feelings. He was too casual. Too composed. Underneath, he was aching. She just knew it.

"She's . . ." Lori swallowed again. She wished she could get rid of the lump in her throat. "Lovely."

Jase nodded. "I always thought so." He pushed off from the jamb and took one step into the room. "Kenzie, what do you think? Does the room do your rug justice?"

Kenzie scuffed her sneaker-covered toes against the slightly curled edge. "It looks good in here."

"It has long johns in it." Lori blurted the comment.

Both Kenzie and Jase gawked at her.

She wanted to slap herself silly. What a

dumb thing to say. Couldn't she ever think before opening her mouth? Dad was right. She didn't have any more brains than the Scarecrow from *The Wizard of Oz.* She flapped her hand at the rug. "The red parts. That's from long johns. They're wool, so they make good rug material. That's what Kenzie told me."

Kenzie ducked her head, and her shoulders shook slightly.

Jase's lips twitched like a rabbit's nose. "Well, I suppose she knows what she's talking about."

Kenzie sent a grin in Jase's direction, then moved to Lori's side. "Maybe we should let Brother Jase get back to work."

Lori nodded. "Yeah. Yeah, it looks good in here. No cleaning necessary." Except cleaning her brain of ugly self-recrimination. "Let's go."

She steered Kenzie out of the room and up the hallway, moving as quickly as if they were escaping a fire. She'd intended to plate the remaining brownies for Jase, but she changed her mind. She drew Kenzie to a halt at the foyer. "Kenz, would you wait here for a second? I need to get . . . something . . . from the kitchen. Then we can go."

"Sure."

Kenzie moved toward the front doors, and

Lori took off for the kitchen. The soles of her sandals clapped like applause against the fellowship hall's tile as she rounded the corner into the kitchen. The pan was right where she'd left it. She grabbed it, located a black plastic trash sack from under the sink, and slid the pan into it. She twisted the open end into a knot and tossed the bag over her shoulder like Santa's pack. Then she set off for the foyer, smacking off lights as she went.

She hurried to Kenzie's side, groping in her pocket for her key. "Okay, I'm ready. Let's go."

Kenzie turned an interested look on the bag. "You're carrying home garbage?"

Lori opened the door. "Not garbage. Something that needs washed." Guilt pricked, but she hadn't really lied. The pan would need washing once she'd emptied it.

"Can't you wash it here?"

"I could, I guess." Lori urged Kenzie out the door and locked it. "But why hang around here and do it when I have other dishes to wash at home? Let's go."

To her great relief, Kenzie didn't question her further. Desire to numb her emotions nearly overwhelmed her. She couldn't wait to get home and drown her sorrows in the pan of brownies.

She dropped Kenzie off near the staircase to her apartment. Ordinarily she waited and made sure her friend got into her apartment before leaving, but not this time. So many thoughts cluttered her mind. Jase was still hung up on Rachel. *Rachel.* Such a pretty name for a pretty girl. Slender. Blond haired, blue eyed. As unlike Lori as a girl could be. She bet nobody ever tormented Rachel with nicknames like Roly-Poly or Homely or Lowlife. Even though none of the nicknames rhymed with her given name, kids still made it work. And why not? The names fit.

She turned into the parking lot of the rows of former motel rooms converted into efficiency apartments. Run down and dismal, but still more peaceful than living under her dad's roof. She parked the car near her door and got out.

With the bag gripped in her hand, she clomped up the cracked sidewalk and let herself in. Music with a strong beat vibrated the wall separating her apartment from the girl's next door. She'd banged on the wall a few times in the past, but it never helped, so why bother? Instead, she turned her attention to the bag. The brownies would help her forget the brain-jarring music, her loneliness, her unworthiness . . . her wishful thoughts.

She set the bag on her eating bar, clawed a hole in the plastic, and pulled the brownie pan free. The aluminum foil had come loose and the brownies were all scattered inside the trash bag. No matter. As she'd told Jase the night of his welcome-to-Bradleyville party, they tasted as good in chunks as in cut squares. She grabbed a sizable piece and lifted it toward her mouth. Slowly. Salivating. Anticipating.

Her cell phone rang.

She froze with her mouth open and the brownie in front of her face. It rang again. Should she ignore the call? Might be a junk call. But it might be Ruby or Kenzie or even Sister Kraft. Ring number three. The aroma rising from the brownies tormented her, but she could eat after she took the call. She dropped the moist chunk and snatched up her phone as it rang for the fourth time. Her heart jolted at the name displayed on her screen. She jammed her finger against the accept icon and shoved the phone up to her ear.

"J-Jase. Hello."

"Hi, Lori. Am I bothering you?"

Her knees went weak. She staggered to her sofa and sank down, holding the phone with both hands. "No. Not at all." Thank goodness she hadn't shoved that brownie in her mouth so she could speak clearly. Well, sort of clearly. Her voice was shaking, the same way her whole body was shaking. "What can I do for you?"

"I wish I'd thought of this when you and Kenzie were here. The young adult class has a get-together this Thursday, right?"

She closed her eyes, envisioning the church calendar. Then she nodded. "Yes. This one's a bowling and pizza party."

"Are you planning to go?"

Turn down pizza? Not this gal. "Uh-huh."

"What about Kenzie?"

Lori licked her dry lips. "We usually go together to the parties."

"That's what I kind of figured." If Dad had made the comment, it would've been snide, like Lori couldn't handle doing anything on her own. But Jase didn't sound unkind. Not at all. "Would you two mind if I tagged along? I feel kind of funny showing up alone since I haven't really gotten acquainted with any of the others in the group. But I know you two. After our lunch together and all."

Lori's pulse thundered so hard she wondered if he could hear it. "Sure, you can go with us. I always drive because Kenzie doesn't have a car. She walks everywhere, but the class is meeting at the bowling alley on North Rock, and it's too far for her to walk. So I'll pick her up." She clamped her mouth closed. Did she always have to prattle?

Jase's chuckle came through the connection. "That's nice of you. So . . . how should we meet up?"

Lori forced her rattled mind to think. "I was going to clean at the church Thursday afternoon. Maybe you could come with me afterward. We'll get Kenzie and go." Too late she realized she'd want to run home and shower before the get-together. "Or —"

"That sounds like a good plan. I'll stick around Thursday until you're ready to go, then leave with you."

She swallowed a moan. Could she manage a wash in the church bathroom?

"Lori? You there?"

No way would she tell Brother Jase she'd need a shower before she put him in the car with her. "Yeah, I'm here. Sorry about that. Just thinking. I'll come by your office Thursday when I'm done, and . . . maybe you can follow me to Kenzie's. Since you live in Bradleyville and I live in Wichita, and . . ."

Another chuckle, warm and a little embarrassed. "I should've thought about the inconvenience of you bringing me back to Bradleyville afterward. Good idea for me to follow you."

She cringed. "It wouldn't be an inconvenience. Really. How about you leave your car at Kenzie's apartment and we all ride together to the bowling alley? Okay?"

"Sounds good. I appreciate it, Lori. Thanks a lot."

"No problem at all." What a fib. Not being able to clean up, refresh her makeup, and change into decent clothes before the group's get-together was a problem she needed to solve. But what a gift she'd been offered. Time with Jase. "See you Thursday. And probably Wednesday. I'll be there for Bible study, and of course you'll be there with the youth." She was prattling again. She started to say goodbye.

"Hey, Lori, about the youth . . ."

She held her breath.

"The group's got a lot more girls than boys in it, and I feel a little out of my league. When I envisioned serving, I never thought I'd be alone."

The picture of Rachel — of beautiful sunshine-haired Rachel — flooded Lori's mind.

"The girls will probably get tired of the activities I plan. I tend to, you know, think like a guy." The chuckle again, the one with a self-deprecating undertone, rumbled in her ear. "It probably wasn't that long ago when you were in the youth group. Could you maybe write down some things I could do with the kids that would appeal to both boys and girls?"

Yikes trikes, was he asking for her help? Lori swallowed. "Yeah. I'll do some thinking. And if you ever wanna split them — you know, boys do this thing and girls the other — I'd be happy to lend a hand." What was she saying now?

"Oh, that'd be great. Thanks. You're a good friend, Lori."

Warmth flooded her. She closed her eyes and savored his comment.

"I should let you go. I'll talk to you later, okay?"

"Okay. Bye for now, Brother Jase."

She disconnected the call, then slumped against the sofa back. The beat of the neighbor's music matched the pound of her pulse and seemed to announce a repetitive message.

Time with Jase. Time with Jase. Time with Jase.

"Yikes trikes . . ." She needed to celebrate. And she knew how. She bounded off the sofa and reached for the trash bag.

NINETEEN

Bradleyville
Jase

Jase dropped his cell phone into his pocket and let out the breath he'd been holding. That hadn't been so hard after all. Maybe he should have clarified that he wasn't asking Lori on a date, but surely she was smart enough to figure out he wasn't. After all, Kenzie was going, too.

He swiveled in the squeaky old desk chair, the only piece of furniture that hadn't been replaced, and turned off the radio. Silence fell like a wool blanket. Or maybe like a pair of wool long johns. Despite his worries about Cullen and angst over Rachel's missing ring, he chuckled. Kenzie's face when Lori mentioned long johns . . . It'd been all he could do to hold back his laughter. When Lori was around, it was never boring. The way it'd been with Rachel, who was so spontaneous, so joyous, so overflowing with life that she touched everyone around her. For those few minutes Lori was in the room, he hadn't missed Rachel with such intensity. But he couldn't expect Lori to replace Rachel. Unfair to Lori, and unfair to Rachel.

With a push of his hands against the sturdy desktop, he raised himself from the chair and scuffed to the door. He turned off the light but left the door open. It still stunk in there. By tomorrow morning the paint smell should be pretty much gone. But it'd be a lot longer before the ache in his heart died away.

He walked up the hallway, his steps slow, his mind on Rachel. Seeing that empty ring box had been like losing her all over again. Brother Kraft had cautioned him not to make accusations against Cullen. After all, there was no real proof the boy had taken the ring. He'd been in Jase's apartment, sure, but Jase couldn't prove he'd gone anywhere but the living room. Nothing had seemed out of place on his dresser or in any of his drawers or cabinets. If Cullen did rustle through things until he found something valuable, he was wily enough not to leave a trail of any kind.

On top of that, when Brother Kraft asked, Jase couldn't honestly say the ring hadn't gone missing in San Antonio. How many people had been in and out of his town-house before he moved? The landlord showed the place to several potential rent-ers. He'd packed the whatnot box without looking inside. The ring might've never made it to Kansas.

Consequently, Jase had agreed to keep the incident between them and pray for discern-ment. Well, Brother Kraft was welcome to pray. Jase would be quiet and keep an eye on Cullen for signs of guilt. He'd do a couple of other things, too. He might as well send a query to FinderznotKeeperz. Since the post originated with Sister Eileen, it stood to reason the ring had been found in San Antonio. A long shot? Sure. But it wouldn't hurt to ask. And he'd file a report with the police. They would notify pawn shop owners and other channels, so if the ring turned up somewhere, Jase would find out about it.

In the meantime, Brother Kraft had sug-gested searching through the whatnot box, his dresser drawers, anyplace else the velvet case might have been where it could've been bumped open and spilled the ring. But if that was true, the actual ring box would still be open. It wouldn't shut itself, would it? Then again, maybe it could. The spring was pretty strong. Too strong to be bumped open?

He shut down his inner voice. It was talking him in circles.

He flipped the hallway light off, plunging the church into darkness. He stood in the deep shadows, staring into nothing. The initial shock of realizing the ring was gone had faded, and fury crept in. Wasn't it enough that he lost the woman he loved? Did he now have to lose his last link to her? He'd begged God to prove His presence to Jase, and instead of showing up and giving peace, He'd taken something else away.

A growl found its way past his clenched teeth. The next lesson for the youth was from the latter verses of John's first chapter. Specifically, the part where Jesus's disciples invited those who doubted that anything good could arise from Nazareth to come meet Jesus and see for themselves. *"Come and see . . ."* Could he really invite the kids to come and see Someone from whom Jase was feeling increasingly distant? How could he convince them that Jesus would always be there for them when he wasn't completely sure about it himself?

"It's not fair, God. It's not fair that I lost Rachel and now I've lost her ring. *Her* ring!" His words echoed against the walls, stinging him with the reality. "It's . . . not . . . fair."

He'd said the same thing after Rachel died. He still didn't understand. They were in the car together. He'd suffered bruises, a broken arm, and a concussion. No life-altering injuries. She'd died. Side by side yet miles apart in the damage done. Again and again he'd questioned it, railing against the unfairness of it, and finally Brother Tony, his wonderful minister and mentor, had grabbed him in a vice-grip hug and declared in his ear, "Life isn't always fair, Jase, but let me tell you something — God is always faithful."

Brother Tony's voice returned again, just as forceful, just as confident, just as tough loving. Jase hadn't believed it then. Oh, he believed the unfairness part. If life was fair, he wouldn't have been born to an unmarried, mentally ill woman who'd neglected him. If life was fair, he would've had a stable home and a family to call his own. He knew without a doubt life wasn't fair. But God *always* faithful? No. In his deep sorrow, he hadn't believed it then. And he didn't believe it now. Maybe he never would.

Wichita
Lori

Lori stared at the few remaining moist

266

crumbs stuck to the sides of the pan. Had she really eaten every remaining brownie? The equivalent of a dozen in all. And out of a trash bag, at that. Her stomach hurt. But more than that, her soul hurt.

Why did she do this to herself? Time and again she reached for food. She ate when she was happy. She ate when she was sad. She ate when she was confused or angry. Time and again she was left with guilt and more pounds and self-loathing. Time and again she promised God she was done. When she said it, she meant it — she was really done with gorging herself. But over and over she failed Him. She failed herself.

She'd told herself she was celebrating Jase asking to go to the get-together with her. But underneath, she knew the motivation for chowing down on those broken chunks of brownies. She'd seen the one Jase loved. The girl with shiny, straight blond hair instead of unruly red curls, with a trim figure instead of a pudgy one, with sky-blue eyes instead of pond-water-green ones. How could she possibly compare with someone who looked so perfect?

The emptiness brought on by inadequacy gnawed at her, and she couldn't rest until she'd somehow filled that gigantic hole. Her stomach was full now. Achingly full. Sickeningly full. But the emptiness was still in place.

She was a special kind of fool to fall for a minister, a man who had it all together. She'd be an emotional drain on him, the way she was to her dad during her teenage years. Dad had told her too many times to count that if she couldn't get her act together, there wasn't a man in the world who'd take her on. And he was right. Especially when it came to Jase. Jase was too good for her, and that was a fact.

She pressed her finger to a crumb, turned her finger upside down, and carried the bit to her mouth. She put the crumb in her mouth. Let it sit on her tongue for a few seconds. Swallowed. Then she turned off all the lights, curled up into a ball on the corner of her sofa, and stared into black nothingness.

Kenzie

Kenzie spread Lori's outfit across the end of her bed. The women had arranged for Lori to take a quick shower and change into fresh clothes at Kenzie's before going to the bowling party. Kenzie smoothed wrinkles with her palms. The tunic and leggings had been rolled up in a sack with a makeup pouch all day, and it showed. But even wrinkled, the pieces were cute — floral leggings and a kelly-green tunic with ruffled bell sleeves. Kenzie could never wear something so flashy, but it was perfect for her perky friend.

She put Lori's makeup pouch on the bathroom vanity, then went to the living room. She'd already washed up and changed for the get-together. A customary T-shirt, this one baby blue, over a midcalf-length broomstick skirt and her tennis shoes. Compared to the ankle-length plain-colored dresses she'd worn throughout her childhood and teen years, even this outfit was flashy. But compared to the clothes worn by the women her age at church, even though they dressed modestly, she usually looked plain.

She didn't belong in her Amish community anymore. But did she really belong here? Why was she questioning it so much these days?

Voices on the stairs alerted her to Lori and Brother Jase's arrival. She opened the door as they stepped up on her small landing, and she welcomed them in. Lori gave Kenzie a quick hug, then darted for the bedroom and closed the door. That left Kenzie with Brother Jase, who remained just inside the door with his hands in the pockets of his tan cargo shorts. Lori had told her she'd need to entertain him, but until that moment she hadn't quite realized it meant they'd be alone.

She stared at him, uncertain. When she'd checked her email after work, she'd been surprised to find one from him, sent to her FinderznotKeeperz account. She wished she could have told him she had his ring, but his description, although close, hadn't included an inscription. Ruby said the real owner would know about the words etched inside the band. Even though she'd already sent her standard "Sorry, not your ring" message to him, she was tempted to ask him about the ring he'd lost. But then he'd know she was FinderznotKeeperz, and he'd surely ask where she had found the ring. If she told him the ring was in the pocket of some donated clothes she used for her rugs, she might let slip what she did with her projects. *"But when thou doest alms, let not thy left hand know what thy right hand doeth."* The biblical instruction of Matthew 6:3 was as woven into her being as the strips were onto the loom's strings. Worried that it might sound like she was bragging about her mission work, she held her tongue.

He grinned and bobbed his head in the direction of the sofa. "Do you mind if I sit?"

Some hostess she was, staying as silent as a statue instead of talking to her guest. A nervous giggle escaped. "No. No, please, make yourself comfortable." She moved out of the way, and he ambled to the center of the living room. She started to close the door, then instead pushed it flat against the wall. The mild day should be enjoyed. And she wouldn't feel so hemmed in with the breeze flowing through the room.

She turned around and found him examining her loom, hands still in his pockets. She crossed to the half wall and leaned against it.

He bobbed his chin at the rows of denim strips. "Are you making another rug?"

"Place mats. They don't take nearly as much time, and they're really popular because they're so sturdy." What could she talk about besides her projects? "Would you like something to drink? I have milk, cherry Kool-Aid, or water."

"Thanks, but I'm good." He removed his hands from his pockets and headed for the sofa, glancing around as he went. "This is a nice little apartment. Reminds me some of the one the Krafts have above their garage."

Relieved he'd left the loom, she followed and perched at the far end of her sofa. "Oh?"

"Mm-hmm." He sat the way men did, with his knees spread and his arm stretched across the sofa's back. He angled his head toward her, an easy smile on his whiskered face. "How long have you lived here?"

"Since I moved to Wichita a little over two years ago."

"And you grew up in Indiana? Is that right?"

She nodded. "A little town called Flourish."

"Never heard of it."

She lifted one shoulder in a sheepish half shrug. "Most people haven't."

He smiled at her. "You're a long way from home. What brought you here?"

"God, I guess."

His eyebrows rose.

His reaction seemed a silent invitation to explain. "After my rumspringe — you know, my running-around period — I decided not to join the Amish church. I moved to Indianapolis and worked at a fabric-and-quilt shop there. An Amish woman owned it, so it didn't bother her that I didn't have a high school diploma."

"You didn't?" He sounded surprised.

Kenzie shook her head. "I still don't."

"Not even a GED?" Now he sounded

shocked. "How did you get a job without it?"

She smiled. "Well, as I said, it wasn't a problem with the original owner. She didn't have one, either. But when she sold the store to an Englischer, the new owner insisted on all employees having at least a high school diploma. So I got let go."

"Well, that stinks."

At the time, Kenzie had thought so, too. "It's okay, though. I saw an ad for a shop here in Wichita. My former boss gave me a good recommendation, and Ruby — she's Sister Kraft's sister who owns Prairie Meadowlark Fabrics & Quilting — hired me, sight unseen. I've been here ever since."

He gazed at her intently, slowly nodding. "Pretty brave of you to move across states to a place where you didn't know anyone."

She held out her hands. "Isn't that what you did, too?"

Surprise registered in his eyes, but he didn't say anything.

She shrugged, offering a shy smile. "I'd never imagined myself in Kansas, but I'm really glad God opened the door for me to come. Ruby, Barbara, and Van are like aunts to me. Lori's become the sister I never had. Brother and Sister Kraft and the people at Beech Street welcomed me in and made me feel at home. I'm h-happy here." Why had she stuttered?

His gaze narrowed. "Are you sure?"

She looked aside. "Sure I'm sure." She bit her lip. "I mean, I've always been sure, until . . ." He was a minister. He'd told the congregation they could come to him. Did he mean even people who weren't part of the youth ministry? She jerked her attention back to him. "Can I ask you a question?"

He rubbed his jaw with his knuckles. "Sure."

"How do you know when God is stirring you to do something?"

His eyebrows pinched together. "Can you be more specific?"

"Well, when I moved to Kansas, I thought it was circumstances. You know, a job opportunity, somebody who'd take me even with my limited schooling." She toyed with the hem of her T-shirt, seeking the right words. "But then I settled in, and I could see His hand in it. Like, just this past Monday, Ruby asked us to brainstorm ways to help boost traffic at the shop, and I told her some of the things we did at the store in Indiana. She loved the ideas, and she told me I was a godsend." Warmth flooded her in remembrance. "So I can see how God used me to be of service here."

He lowered his arm from the sofa back and loosely linked his hands in his lap. "It seems to me you already know the answer to your question, if you see how God is utilizing you in Wichita."

She shook her head. "That's the thing. I can see *now* how God is using me here. But I didn't know it was God's doing before I actually came and got involved here. And now I keep getting this weird feeling . . ." How could she explain something she didn't understand herself? Maybe if she had more education, she'd be better at expressing herself. She sighed and hung her head. "Never mind. It's too hard to put into words."

"Try."

One little word but uttered with such kindness it invited Kenzie to raise her head and look at him.

"What are you feeling?"

"Like I'm being pulled." Yes, that was it. She released a huff of amazement and nodded. "Like something, or maybe Someone, is tugging my heart. Tugging me back to Indiana."

He rubbed his jaw again, his expression thoughtful. "Do you know why?"

A chill wiggled its way from Kenzie's scalp down her spine. "Maybe. I think God wants me to tell my family about grace." She threw her hands wide. "But I'm not a missionary. Not like the people who told me about salvation. I don't exactly know what God would expect me to do once I got there. And I don't have money to get myself there, either. Right now it's just this uncomfortable tug with no real guidance. So . . . is it really God pulling at me, or is it me worrying over or missing my family?"

Brother Jase sat gazing at Kenzie, not frowning but not smiling, either. Almost as if he'd slipped away somewhere and wasn't listening at all. She waited for him to say something, but when he didn't, embarrassment hit. She started to stand, intending to go to the kitchen and pour herself a drink. Something to break the uncomfortable silence.

"Abraham."

Kenzie eased back onto the sofa and sent him a puzzled scowl. "What?"

"Abraham. From the Old Testament." Brother Jase's reddish brows tipped together, as if he had a headache. "Listen, Kenzie, I'm going to be honest with you. I don't have all the answers. I probably have more questions about God's leading than you do. But God does speak to His people. He told Abraham to go. He didn't tell Him where or how. Just to go. Abraham knew he was being sent, so he obeyed. If you know you're being sent, you have to obey."

Kenzie's mouth went dry. "But . . . but how? I don't have the money to get myself to Indiana."

"Do you have anything you could sell?"

Nothing except a ring that didn't even belong to her, and she wouldn't sell that. "No, not really." She puffed her cheeks and then blew out a noisy breath of frustration. "Why would God ask me to do something I can't physically do?"

Brother Jase shrugged and slumped in his seat. "I don't know. But if He's doing the calling, I reckon He'll provide the means. You just have to wait. And trust."

TWENTY

Jase

He must be the biggest hypocrite in the world, advising Kenzie about the call of God on a person's life. At least his brain had regurgitated a biblical answer. He'd learned a little something from his years of study. Now she sat there biting her lip and looking scared and forlorn, so even if he'd given the biblical answer, he hadn't provided much comfort. Proof of his inability to shepherd. What was she going to do? And what was he going to do?

"I'll think about what you said." Kenzie spoke slowly, her voice barely above a whisper. Jase had to lean a little closer to hear her. "And I'll pray about it, too. I probably should ask Ruby and my Sunday school leader, and maybe Lori, to pray with me. Right?"

He inwardly cringed. A minister would offer to pray with her. He'd failed with Cullen.

He shouldn't add to his list of failures by not offering to pray with Kenzie. He gathered his courage and offered his hand. "How about we pray now?"

She hesitated only a moment, then placed her hand in his. Her fingers were trembling, which was good because it'd mask the quiver in his own hand.

He cleared his throat. "God, You spoke to people in the past. You speak to people today." *Why can't You talk to me? I kinda need You, too.* "Kenzie believes You're speaking to her and asking her to return to Indiana, but she has a lot of questions. She doesn't know how to get there. She doesn't know what to say once she arrives. You tell us in Your Word that You give wisdom to those who seek it and power to the weak." *Yeah, I know the verses. Now prove 'em to me, God.* "If You're calling her to go home, then give her the answers she needs. Provide the means for her to get there. Assure her that You're the one prompting her so she has no doubts she's following Your will." *Doubt is awful, God. Rid her of it. And rid me of it, too. Please.*

A knot formed in his throat, almost strangling him. He gruffly cleared his throat and finished with a ragged "Amen."

He looked up and found Kenzie gazing at

him, her eyes bright with unshed tears. A smile quavered on her lips, and she squeezed his hand hard.

"Thank you, Brother Jase."

He forced a nod. "You're welcome." He placed his free hand over hers and battled the urge to thank her. He'd needed to say that prayer. And not only for her.

The bedroom door flew open, and Lori breezed into the room. "Ta-da! I'm ready!" Her gaze fell to their joined hands, and her bright expression changed to confusion. "Is everything okay?"

Kenzie slid her hand free of his and stood. "Everything's fine. You look cute. And smell good, too."

Jase rose and forced a laugh. "I agree with Kenzie. What is that scent — apples?"

Lori didn't smile. "It's called Pearberry."

"It's nice. Very nice." Jase searched for a safe topic. "Almost as nice as the aroma of Kenzie's brownies." He angled a teasing grin at her. "When're you gonna bake some more of those?"

Kenzie's eyebrows shot up. "You're done with that batch already? I only gave it to Lori on —"

Lori bounded forward and caught hold of Kenzie's elbow. "Let's not waste time talking about brownies. We're going to have pizza, remember?" She laughed, but it sounded a little shrill and almost desperate. The wide-eyed glance she sent Jase furthered his feeling she was trying to hide something. "Everybody ready?"

"I am." Kenzie looked at Jase. "Are you?"

He nodded.

Lori pulled Kenzie toward the door. "Then let's go."

Lori

Lori managed to keep Kenzie and Jase distracted during the drive by sharing the names of all the members from the young adult Sunday school class and telling a little something about each of them — "So you won't feel out of the loop when you meet everyone." When they reached the bowling alley, most members of the class were already there, gathered in a chatty, laughing group near the front doors. Lori dove into introductions, which consumed quite a bit of time and attention.

Ryan, the senior of their group at the ripe old age of thirty-eight, held up his cell phone. "I don't know if anyone else got the messages, but Zaide and Theo aren't gonna make it. So, Brother Jase, you won't get to meet the other single guys tonight. And Alex and Elise bowed out, too."

281

Lori wasn't surprised about Alex and Elise. The youngest couple in the group were brand-new parents of a three-week-old. Although volunteers from the sixties-plus Sunday school class provided childcare for the younger groups' get-togethers, Alex and Elise probably didn't want to leave their baby with anyone yet, not even for a few hours.

Melissa, Ryan's wife, sent a smile around the group. "But isn't this a great turnout?"

Lori clapped her agreement. Several joined the applause, and someone exclaimed, "Hear! Hear!"

While the others cheered, one of the younger husbands, Brad, pointed his finger at each person by turn, presumably counting. "I dunno, guys. It's a great turnout, but with seventeen of us, we're probably going to have to split up over four lanes."

"Nah." Another of the younger men, Nathan, waved his hand as if erasing Brad's comment. "Let's divide into two teams and get lanes next to each other. It'll take a while to get through the game, and maybe we'll only end up playing one, but it'll keep us together. What do you all think?"

"Together," Lori blurted, and several members laughed. She gave Jase a sheepish look. "It'll be easier for Brother Jase to get to know everybody if we stay together."

Brad and Nathan held a lively discussion on the pros and cons of playing on two lanes or four, and finally Mark stepped in. "How about we vote?"

To Lori's relief, staying together won. With everybody in one group, she could keep an eye on Jase and Kenzie. She couldn't rid her mind of the picture of the two of them holding hands on Kenzie's couch. Even though they hadn't been smiling, the sight reminded her of the photograph in Jase's office. They'd looked too perfect together.

Two of the women, Ginny and Courtney, trotted off to order the pizzas, and the rest of the group moved en masse to the shoe counter. Armed with proper footwear, Ryan left to reserve two lanes, and Lori led the pack to benches, where they sat and traded out their shoes. All around her, voices jabbered and she listened intently, ready to shift the focus if Kenzie or Jase or anyone else mentioned brownies.

Ryan returned and directed the group to their assigned lanes. On the way, he glanced at Kenzie. "Are you bowling tonight, or do you plan to watch?"

She pointed to her feet. She still wore her tennis shoes, unlike everyone else, who'd changed into scuffed red, white, and blue bowling shoes. "I'll just watch."

No matter how many times Lori encouraged Kenzie to participate in activities, she always stuck to spectating. Sometimes it bugged her — couldn't Kenzie let down her guard and join in once in a while? — but tonight she was grateful. The couples would play on the same team, the way they always did for these bowling nights. Kenzie bowling out meant Lori and Jase would have to pair up to make the teams even. Being paired with Jase was exactly what she'd hoped would happen when he called and asked to go with her.

Another noisy, laughter-filled discussion ensued when they divided into teams. She and Jase joined Mark and Ginny, Nathan and Kara, and Ryan and Melissa. They shouted playful insults across the ball return at Brad and Courtney, Drew and Kendra, Nick and Abby, and Lucas and Macey, but only between throws. Lori insisted that everyone follow bowling etiquette and remain respectfully quiet when someone went up to the lane.

Ordinarily, Lori loved pizza. Ordinarily, she loved bowling. Dad had signed her and her brothers up for a bowling league when they were kids, and she'd gotten pretty good at it. Even Dad had acknowledged she was good for a girl, the best compliment she could remember receiving from him once she hit puberty. But tonight she couldn't swallow a bite. And no matter how hard she tried, she couldn't get into her groove.

Jase and Kenzie had looked so comfortable together — so *right* together — side by side. No man in his right mind would choose Lori over someone cute and petite and reserved like Kenzie. She'd put the two of them together and sunk her own potential romance. Plus, worry that Kenzie and Jase would resume their conversation about brownies, which would uncover her gluttonous act, left her on edge. She could make up a story about where the brownies had gone, but lying would only make things worse. Why hadn't she given those brownies to Jase the way she was supposed to? And why hadn't she figured out a way to clean up after work somewhere other than Kenzie's apartment, which had thrown the two of them together?

As Nathan had predicted, with so many bowlers, it took the better part of two hours to finish one game. Lori and Jase's team lost by only three pins, and Lori berated herself for being so off. If she'd bowled her average, her team would've won by more than ten times that number. And maybe she would've impressed Jase. Drew and Kendra volunteered to pay for a second game, but a quick vote ruled the majority were content to leave it at one. Lori regretted ending so soon. She wanted a chance to prove she could actually bowl well. But she was also relieved. So far, the subject of brownies had remained unspoken. Maybe she would end this evening with her secret intact.

The losing team cleaned up the pizza mess, and the winners returned everyone's bowling shoes. Then the group ambled to the exit. At the edge of the parking lot, they gathered for their customary closing prayer. They formed a circle and joined hands, the same way they always did at the end of a Sunday school hour. Kenzie and Jase reached for each other, and Lori quickly stepped between them.

Ryan smiled from across the circle. "Brother Jase, would you mind praying for us?"

"Um, sure. I'd be glad to." Jase seemed to cringe. Or was he only gathering his thoughts? "Let's bow, huh?"

Lori bowed her head and closed her eyes. Within her hand, Jase's fingers twitched. Was he nervous? Of course he'd be nervous his first time with these people — yikes trikes, he probably still hadn't memorized all of their names! — and then being put on the spot. Even if he was a minister, he was human and needed time to settle in. One of the others should've prayed instead. She squeezed Jase's hand, hoping it would communicate her support.

"Dear God . . ." His hand continued to quiver, but his voice was strong. Jase expressed gratitude for the enjoyable evening, then asked God to get everyone home safely. He cleared his throat, a barely discernible *ahem,* and he spoke again. " 'The LORD bless you and keep you . . .' "

Lori recognized the beginning of a passage from Numbers. Brother Kraft often read it to end their services, and she automatically began reciting with him. " 'The LORD make his face shine on you and be gracious to you.' "

The others joined. " 'The LORD turn his face toward you and give you peace.' "

Jase said, "Amen," and he released her hand.

The couples in the circle paired off and spread across the parking lot, waving goodbye to one another. Lori, Jase, and Kenzie went, too, but it felt awkward walking three abreast when all the others moved in twos. Jealousy wove itself through Lori with such intensity her skin tingled. Would she ever know the pleasure of walking hand in hand with a man who truly loved her? She glanced down at herself. At her chubby knees sticking out beneath the hem of her tentlike top. Doubt brought the sting of tears. Kenzie'd said she was a good person, and she was. She worked hard, she loved God, she was fun to be around — all positive traits. But men her age cared a lot more about having a pretty girlfriend. No one, not even Kenzie, would call Lori Fowler pretty. And now that she'd started her down-on-herself roll, she couldn't seem to stop.

They reached Lori's car, and Jase turned to Kenzie. "Do you want to ride shotgun? You had the back seat on the way over, so it's only fair."

Lori read the unspoken message. He didn't want to sit next to her. She flounced around to the driver's side of the car. "Yeah, Kenz, I'm gonna let Brother Jase off at your apartment anyway, so it doesn't really matter who rides up front."

Kenzie shrugged. "Okay."

Jase opened the passenger door for Kenzie, and she climbed in. Then he got in the back, leaving Lori to open her door for herself. The last time he'd walked her and Kenzie to the car, he'd opened her door for her. So why not this time? Had she scared him when she squeezed his hand? He'd seen it as a come-on probably, and now he'd try to avoid her. It'd happened with guys in the past — her meaning to be friendly and them taking it as more. She'd blown it with Jase before they could even begin to form a friendship.

Jase and Kenzie talked all the way from the bowling alley to Kenzie's apartment, but Lori set her lips in a grim line and refused to participate. Her heart hurt. And she was hungry. She'd skipped lunch, the same as she'd done every day since Monday — her self-induced punishment for indulging herself with those brownies — and then she hadn't finished even one piece of pizza at the bowling alley. Now she was famished, and all she could think about was food.

At least food was always there for her, ready and available when she needed it.

She pulled into the parking area of Kenzie's apartment complex, located an empty spot for visitors, then put the car in park. "Well, here we are, end of the road. Kenz, I'll see you at work tomorrow. Brother Jase, I'll see you Sunday."

Jase reached forward and gave her shoulder a light squeeze. "Thanks a lot for taking me with y'all. I really had a good time. I worked at a bowling alley in San Antonio, but I didn't get to bowl very often, so this was a treat."

Lori flashed him a tight grin, then faced forward again. "I'm glad. Now that you've met most of the group, it ought to be easy for you to make friends. You'll get lots of chances to do things with the group, and the men'll probably include you in their guys-only activities. You won't feel like you're stuck with Kenzie and me."

"Lori . . ." Only an idiot would miss the disapproval in Kenzie's tone.

Lori glared at her friend. "I'm not being rude. I'm being honest. Up until tonight, we were the only young people from church who've socialized with him. But that'll change, and he probably wants it to. I mean, why wouldn't he want to hang out with the guys or make lots of friends?"

Jase cleared his throat. "Well, since you're being honest, I'll be honest, too."

The scent of pepperoni on his breath drifted from the back seat. She filled her lungs with air and braced herself for the rejection to come.

"I hope you won't exclude me just because I've met the others. Y'all are my first friends at Beech Street, and I'd kinda like to keep seeing you." He scooted across the seat and opened the door. "Kenzie, I hope you're still thinking about sharing your testimony with the youth sometime. Lemme know when you decide, huh? Oh. Keep listening for answers."

Lori frowned. Did intimacy tinge his lowered tone on that last comment?

"And, Lori? Thanks again for the ride. Y'all have a good rest of the evening." He got out, closed the door, and crossed beneath the streetlamps to his vehicle.

Lori's breath whooshed out, and she slumped forward until her forehead met the steering wheel. "Are you getting out, too, Kenz?"

"I thought you'd want to come in. Your clothes are in there. Or do you want me to bring them to the fabric shop tomorrow?"

"Bring 'em tomorrow." Lori needed to leave. To find something to eat.

"I can do that, but I have to say . . . I'm surprised at you. I thought you liked Brother Jase, but you weren't very kind just now."

Lori sat up. "Neither were you earlier."

Confusion marred Kenzie's face. "What?"

"You know I like Jase, but you were holding his hand on your sofa." The hurt billowed in Lori's chest. If she couldn't trust Kenzie, she couldn't trust anyone. "Then, at the bowling alley when we got ready to pray, you tried to do it again."

Kenzie's mouth fell open. "We were standing next to each other. It could have been anybody standing there and I would've reached for them."

Lori squinted her eyes. "What about on your sofa? There wasn't anybody else around then."

"We weren't holding hands on my sofa."

Lori snorted.

"He was praying for me."

"Why?"

"Because I've been struggling with something, not knowing whether I should do it or even if I could, and I asked his advice." Kenzie shrugged, holding out her hands. "He's a minister. I figured he'd know what I should do."

Lori cocked her head. "You haven't said anything to me about a struggle."

"I will talk to you about it, but not tonight." Kenzie reached for the door handle. "It's getting late, and we're both on the morning schedule tomorrow, so let's wait for another time, okay?"

"Don't keep secrets with Jase." Lori barked the order as gruffly as any command her dad had given her.

Kenzie's eyes widened. "I won't." She

292

cupped her hand over Lori's wrist. "I'm not."

Shame washed through Lori. What was she doing, attacking Kenzie? Her emotions were running amok. Between feeling guilty for her feeding frenzy and wishing she could change her looks to be worthy of Jase's affection, she was all mixed up. She should apologize. She licked her lips, seeking courage.

"I'll see you tomorrow morning. Drive careful, okay?" Kenzie left the car and ran for her apartment, her shiny blond hair bouncing on her shoulders as she went.

Lori did the right thing. She stayed put, not leaving until she saw Kenzie close herself in her apartment. But when she pulled onto the street, she turned in the direction of a late-night ready-made pizza vendor. She had a hunger that needed to be filled, and a pepperoni pizza with extra cheese would help. For a while.

TWENTY-ONE

Bradleyville
Jase

On his third Wednesday of teaching the youth, Jase congratulated himself for correctly greeting all the members by name as they arrived. Sure, it was a small group, only twelve in all, but recalling names had never been his strong suit, and he was proud of himself for remembering them. Now to learn the names of the guests Emma, Charmaine, and Jennifer each brought.

While the kids enjoyed the supper provided by the kitchen team, Jase sought Sister Kraft. Neither Lori nor Kenzie had shown up for church last Sunday. He'd heard the vacuum cleaner's hum in the sanctuary yesterday, proof Lori was in the building, but she hadn't come to his office. At least not when he was in it. He'd found a folded sheet of paper with activity ideas in her handwriting on the corner of his desk this morning. But she wasn't here tonight, even though she'd helped with the last two youth suppers.

Concern sat like a weight on his chest. She'd been her usual bouncy self — maybe even bouncier than usual — during the bowling party last Thursday, but on the drive to Kenzie's apartment, she'd become what he could only define as aloof. Had he done something to offend her? Or was she not feeling well? He hoped the minister's wife, who seemed to know everything happening with each member of Beech Street Bible Fellowship, would shed some light on the problem. If a problem existed.

Sister Kraft was at the sink washing the baking sheets used for the kids' ham-and-cheese turnovers. Jase snagged a dish towel and stood close. "Fun dinner. The kids are enjoying it."

She glanced at him, her eyes glinting with humor. "You didn't say anything about last week's lasagna, but you praise the glorified sandwiches?"

He shrugged. "You put pimento cheese with plain ol' ham inside a garlic bread wrap. I'm impressed."

Her laughter rolled. "Well, I'm glad you enjoyed them. And I'm glad we made extra." She handed him the pan. "Looks like the group grew by a few."

He nodded, peeking out the serving window while drying the pan. "Yep. That's what y'all wanted, right? To expand the program?" Funny how, despite his feelings of inadequacy, the kids were responding to him. At least the girls, Raul, and Zack were. He wasn't sure about Cullen and Brent yet. Especially not Cullen, even though he'd stayed put through all of the service Sunday morning. Thank goodness. Jase laid the pan aside.

"That's what we prayed for." Sister Kraft scrubbed the second pan, her gaze aimed at him. "But you didn't come in here to dry dishes or even to praise the addition of pimento cheese with the ham. What's on your mind?"

His eyebrows shot up.

She nodded. "It's plain as the nose on a clown's face that something's eating at you. Are you worried about Merlin?" She lowered her voice and sent a glance around the kitchen at the other workers. "His blood pressure's coming down since he started his new prescription, so things are looking positive."

Jase's arms drooped. "He's having trouble with his blood pressure?"

Sister Kraft frowned. "He didn't tell you?"

She rolled her eyes, grabbed him by the sleeve, and led him out of the kitchen and into the narrow entry, out of sight of everyone else. "He and I agreed not to alarm the congregation, but I thought he'd at least mention it to you."

Jase's heart began to pound. "What is it?"

"The doctor diagnosed him with congestive heart failure."

Jase's entire frame jolted. "Are you kidding me?"

Sister Kraft patted his arm, creating a damp patch. "He's on medication and a special diet, and the prognosis is good. That's why he didn't want the congregation to know. No sense in unnecessarily scaring everyone. He did, however, promise to tell the deacons in confidence. Since you're his associate, I presumed he'd tell you, too. I'm sorry he didn't." She growled under her breath. "I'll let him know I spilled the beans."

Jase's worry about Lori fled in light of this information. "Are you sure he'll be okay? I mean, hearts are kind of important."

A sad smile formed on her lips. "Yes, they certainly are. Even though they aren't meant to tick forever, we're doing what we can to keep Merlin's ticking. While we wait for these lifestyle changes to take effect, we're trusting God to bring healing as He sees fit."

Wait and trust God. Isn't that what he'd told Kenzie to do? He shook his head. "I'm sure sorry y'all are dealing with this. If I can do anything to take some of the stress off, have him let me know." Had he really offered to take over some of the preacher's responsibilities? His mouth was getting ahead of his brain.

Sister Kraft grabbed him in a hug. "Thank you, Brother Jase. Your arrival to Bradley-ville couldn't have been more timely. I'm so glad you're here."

"There you are."

Sister Kraft released Jase, and they both looked toward the voice. Ruby frowned at them from the opposite end of the entry. "Are you paying attention to the youth? They're done and getting restless, Brother Jase. Time to shoo 'em out of here."

Despite his worry for Brother Kraft, a bubble of laughter formed and found its way from Jase's chest. "Yes, ma'am, I'll see to them."

"Good." She disappeared.

Sister Kraft gave Jase a gentle nudge toward the fellowship hall. "Remember, mum's the word. Merlin doesn't want to alarm everyone. Pray for him, but don't talk about him."

He swallowed. Should he make a promise he might not keep? He wouldn't tell anybody, but his prayer life had become nearly nonexistent. He chose a generic "Yes, ma'am," as his answer, then jogged around the corner and clapped his hands rapidly three times, his signal for the kids to listen. They ceased their rough-housing and shifted to face him. He waved his hand toward the back door. "Let's go play a quick game of mushball."

With a collective whoop, the kids raced for the door. Jase followed them out. Although he usually played, too, tonight he wasn't needed. The extra guests filled the teams, so he observed instead. The not-quite-seventy temperature was perfect for an outdoor activity, and the kids had a great time whacking the soft rubber ball and running bases. He checked his watch periodically, and at 7:10 he cupped his mouth and hollered, "Last bat and then inside."

The kitchen team had left a cooler of canned pop and bottled water inside the door of the youth room, like always, and the kids grabbed their choice of drink as they entered and then settled in chairs. Cullen sauntered in last. He grabbed a chair from the last row, slid it all the way to the wall, then slouched into it, his cap at its usual angle.

Jase caught the boy's eyes and tapped his own forehead. With a grunt, Cullen yanked off the cap and plunked it on his knee. Then he folded his arms and gazed at Jase through narrowed lids.

Jase scanned the group. "Who wants to open with prayer?"

Ari, a quiet senior with shiny dark brown hair and stunning blue eyes, raised her hand. While she prayed, Jase got the uncomfortable feeling of being watched. He peeked and, sure enough, Cullen hadn't closed his eyes. Their gazes collided, and a grin lifted one corner of the boy's mouth. Jase snapped his eyes closed until Ari's "amen."

While the kids sipped their drinks and fidgeted in their chairs, Jase delivered his planned lesson about Jesus's first miracle, turning water into wine at the wedding in Cana. Jase had always pondered why, after telling His mother that His time hadn't yet come, Jesus had gone ahead and performed the miracle anyway. He read aloud Mary's comment to the servants, "Do whatever he tells you," then angled a curious look at the kids.

"Why do you think Jesus's mother gave the servants that direction after Jesus told her He wasn't ready yet to perform miracles?"

Zack thrust his hand into the air. "Because she believed in Him and she wanted others to see who He was, too."

"Or maybe she wanted to show Him off." Sienna didn't bother to raise her hand. "Moms are like that."

Several kids laughed, but Jase didn't see humor in the comment. His own mother had been more interested in passing him off than showing him off. He cleared his throat. "Maybe. Any other ideas?"

Cullen shrugged. "She was thirsty, they were out of wine, and the liquor store was closed?"

"Cullen . . ." Zack groaned the name, and several other kids turned and gaped at him, muttering their shock or disapproval.

Cullen gave an innocent look. "What? He asked a question, and it's a possible answer, isn't it? If I was old enough, I bet my mom would —"

Jase needed to cut this off at the pass. "Somebody read verses six through eleven, please." To his relief, Emma read in a loud voice, occasionally sending a withering frown over her shoulder at Cullen. When she finished, Jase thanked her, then turned his attention to the group. "Okay, now, why did Jesus go ahead and turn the water into wine after telling His mother it wasn't His time yet?"

For a moment the kids sat quietly, glancing at one other or looking at their Bibles. Finally Kaia, who hadn't yet spoken or volunteered to read, lifted her hand.

Jase smiled at her. "Yes, Kaia? What do you think?"

"I think . . ." She licked her lips, sending a sideways glance at Sienna, who bobbed her head in a silent cheer of encouragement. "I think He saw a chance to let people see God, and He took it." She sagged against the chair's metal backrest and let out a huge sigh.

Leesa, sitting behind Kaia, peeked past her to Jase. "I agree with Kaia. Even though He didn't feel quite ready, when the door opened, He walked through it. Not to show off for His mom, and not to show off for Himself, but because like it said in verse eleven, it was a sign meant to reveal His glory."

"And whenever Jesus revealed His glory," Zack said, "it was meant to point to the Father."

Jennifer's friend, a girl named Krystal, twisted around in her chair and looked at Zack. "So all the miracles Jesus did, like healing and stuff, wasn't for the people, but for God?"

A lively discussion followed, during which Jase listened and moderated more than participated. He allowed several minutes of free exchanges and brought them back on track when the subject started to drift. When they drew the conclusion that Jesus performed the miracle so His disciples would start to really see who He was and who He served, Jase gave three claps.

Silence fell. He smiled at the group. "Y'all did some great thinking tonight. You understand Jesus's reasons for doing what He did. Now, how do we take what Jesus did and apply it to our lives? I mean, none of us can change water into wine." Snickers rolled. "So what do we do?"

Zack's hand went up, but Kaia spoke first. "When we do stuff for others, we don't do it to impress someone or so people will notice us. We do it because we love God and want people to see Him. In us."

Zack nodded so hard his shaggy bangs bounced. "Yep. She nailed it." Several others added their agreement.

Kaia's cheeks blushed scarlet, but she smiled.

Another of the guests, the girl who'd come with Emma, sent a scowl in Jase's direction.

"But, like, how? Gimme an example."

"Mowing somebody's lawn without them asking, and don't tell them you're the one who did it."

"Being respectful and obedient. Not 'cause you'll get in trouble if you don't but because it's the right thing to do."

"Not talking smack about someone even though other people are doing it."

"Praying before you eat in public places. Even in the cafeteria. People'll know you're grateful."

Answers flew, one on top of the other.

"Smiling at grumpy people." Sienna's comment earned a light round of laughter, and she hunched her shoulders and giggled. "Well, giving somebody something good that they didn't earn or maybe don't deserve is kind of God's business, isn't it?"

"No *kind of* about it," Jase said. "Everything God gives us is undeserved because He is holy and majestic and we are not." Was he listening to himself? He cleared his throat. "Y'all are really getting it. Any other ideas for" — what was the guest's name again? — "Ashley?"

"Yeah." Cullen sat forward and played with his cap. "When you find a wallet, and you look inside, and there's money and credit cards, and you could really use those 'cause your dad's a deadbeat who doesn't help, and even though your mom's working two jobs, you're still behind on rent, but you take it to the police station and turn it in anyway. And then when the owner wants to give you a reward, you don't take it because doing the right thing is reward enough in itself."

A prickle attacked Jase's scalp. His gaze locked on Cullen's unsmiling face, and he nodded. "That's a great example. Thanks, Cullen."

Cullen sat back and fiddled with the brim of his cap, his expression bland.

Since Cullen had mentioned finding a lost item, Jase grabbed the lead-in. "Cullen's example reminded me . . . I've lost something pretty important."

Leesa tilted her head. "Valuable monetarily or sentimentally?"

Jase swallowed. "Both."

Sienna sat up like a chipmunk, her eyes wide. "What is it?"

Jase glanced at Cullen, who seemed very interested in removing a loose thread from the embroidered design on his cap. "I'd rather not say." The kids knew about Rachel. Losing her was part of the reason he'd come to Bradleyville, and he'd shared his testimony with the congregation his first

Sunday here. He didn't want to get into the nitty-gritty details of things with these kids. "But I'd really appreciate it if y'all would pray that it's found."

Brent grinned. "Is there a reward?"

Sienna whacked him on the shoulder. "That's terrible! What did we just talk about?"

"I was kidding. Sheesh . . ." Brent slunk low in his chair, as far from Sienna as he could get without leaving his seat.

Jase chuckled. "My eternal gratitude is about all I can offer, but I hope that's motivation enough for some of y'all to pray it finds its way back to me." Time to turn the focus. "All right, I have an assignment for next week."

Exaggerated groans and mutters rumbled for a few seconds, and Jase shook his head and laughed. "It's not gonna be that bad." He waited until they quieted. "As Christians, we're called to be 'little Christs.' In other words, we're to follow His example. So for the next week, look for ways you can be like Jesus. When we get together next, we'll talk about what all you saw and we'll pick a few things we can do as a group to bless somebody else. Okay?" The idea had been on Lori's list, and he liked it. He hoped the kids would.

A few nods, a few smiles, and a few grimaces. But most seemed on board. "Good. Now, Zack, you wanna get your guitar? Lead us in a couple songs, then we'll pray and head y'all out of here."

Back in his apartment, Jase flopped onto his sofa and replayed Cullen's contribution to the group's discussion. Had the boy's example about finding a wallet and the reasons for wanting to keep it been something he'd pulled out of the air, or was it more personal — a way of sharing the truth of his family life? Sympathy pinched Jase's heart. At the same time, he still wasn't convinced Cullen hadn't taken Rachel's ring. He'd seen Cullen's sneaky side often enough to be wary of taking everything he said at face value. The boy definitely warranted watching. He should probably ask Brother and Sister Kraft about his home life, too.

He slapped his forehead. He'd intended to ask Sister Kraft about Lori's unusual absence. Now, at almost nine o'clock, he shouldn't bother her. Lori had come in and cleaned last Thursday, so she'd probably do the same tomorrow. He'd catch her himself and talk to her then.

TWENTY-TWO

Wichita
Lori

Lori was past due at the church to perform her custodial duties after the Wednesday-night activities. Vacuuming, dusting, floor mopping, and bathrooms and kitchen cleanup took about five hours, and it was four o'clock already. She should get to the church. But she rounded another aisle in the pharmacy and slowly perused the shelves. There had to be a supplement that would carve off these pounds. Or at least one that would make her not want to eat. It was here, and she would find it. She had to find it.

A little sign announcing Weight Loss Products hung above a section, and she stood beneath it, gathering the courage to pick up one of the bottles and read the details. There were security cameras everywhere, which meant right now someone was probably watching the fat woman in aisle four search for a miracle. Was he laughing at her size? And why didn't any of the names on the containers sound like something a person would actually consider putting in their mouth?

A skinny-as-a-rail older woman wearing a shirt with the store's emblem on its breast pocket breezed around the corner and came directly to Lori. Had whoever monitored the security cameras sent her?

The woman gave Lori a bright smile. "Can I help you with anything, hon?"

Lori shrugged and flicked her hand. "No, I'm fine. Browsing. You know, seeing what all's new." She tugged the ribbed bottom band of her sweat suit jacket lower on her hips. Crazy Kansas weather. Did it have to drop fifteen degrees overnight and make her need a jacket? Of course, the one she'd grabbed from the hook was at least one size too small. The dryer must've shrunk it. *Uh-huh, right.* Holding down the hem with one hand, she reached for a bottle marked Green Tea Extract.

The woman stepped around Lori. "All right. Let me know if you change your mind." She hurried to the other end of the aisle, where a weary-looking young mother batted her toddler's hands away from the vitamins.

With the others in the aisle occupied, Lori selected two bottles of unpronounceable pills — one for boosting metabolism, the other for suppressing appetite — in addition to the green tea capsules. Her hands full, she headed for the checkout counter. She plopped the items on the counter and dug in her little crossbody purse for her debit card while the gum-chewing young man at the register rang up her purchases.

"Forty-one ninety-three."

Lori's head bounced up. "W-what?"

"Forty-one dollars and ninety-three cents."

She dropped her astounded gaze to the trio of plastic containers. "Are you kidding me?"

He shook his head. "No, ma'am."

The amount and being called *ma'am* — yikes trikes, she was only twenty-six years old! — were both very, very upsetting. "But that can't be right." She waved her hand. "They're only vitamins."

He pivoted a small digital screen and pointed at it.

She scowled at the numbers. Two of the supplements were ten dollars each, but one was nineteen by itself. She couldn't figure out which one, though. She pointed to the amount. "Take this one off."

He slid the metabolism booster over the scanner, hit a button on the register, and looked at her. "Twenty-one fifty."

She stuck her debit card in the card reader, shaking her head in disbelief. How many bags of store-brand chips and cases of generic soda could she buy with twenty bucks?

In her car, she popped the lid off both bottles and dumped capsules into her hand. The Styrofoam cup of pop she'd bought at a gas station before coming to the pharmacy was almost full, and she guzzled at least a fourth of it, washing the pills down her throat. She hated swallowing pills. When she was a kid, if a doctor prescribed medicine for her, she begged for an elephant-sized shot instead of pills. But if these things would stomp out her feeding frenzies, it'd be worth it.

By the time she reached the church, her dash clock showed a quarter of five. Brother and Sister Kraft kept what she'd teasingly called banker's hours, coming in at eight in the morning, taking an hour break midday, then heading home at five. Of course, they had duties outside of those hours, but she could clean their offices any weekday after five. Jase, on the other hand, was less predictable. She'd seen his office light glowing in the hallway as late as ten o'clock.

Lori blew out a breath. She'd avoided him for an entire week, which had nearly killed her. Or at least given her food poisoning. Her loneliness had driven her to buy a clearance-priced ring of cocktail shrimp. Forty boiled shrimp and a cup of cocktail sauce. Dad would've had beer with it, but she drank lemon-lime soda. A full liter while she ate the whole ring in one sitting Saturday evening. Then spent most of Sunday in the bathroom. She might never eat shrimp again. But her upset stomach hadn't kept her from downing an entire box of cream-filled snack cakes Monday, snarfing a twenty-count box of chicken nuggets and a large order of curly fries Tuesday, and taking advantage of the buy-one-get-one burger deal at a fast-food restaurant yesterday. She bought two deals and ate them in front of the television. She'd probably gained five pounds in one week. All because of Jase.

She really wanted to see him. To find out if he'd meant what he said about wanting to spend time with her. Well, with her and Kenzie. But at the same time, she'd die a thousand deaths if they came face to face. She'd said as much to Kenzie before leaving the fabric shop this afternoon. Kenzie told her she'd feel better if she apologized for the cold way she'd treated him after the bowling party. But didn't he owe her an apology, too? After all, he'd pulled away from her when she was only trying to be supportive and then wouldn't even sit across the console from her in her car. No one would call his behavior warm and cuddly, either. Still, Mom had taught her that two wrongs never made a right. She knew better. So she would apologize. After a few days. When the pills had done their duty and the evidence of her gorging sessions wasn't so obvious.

She grabbed the bottle of green tea extract and shook it. "You better work, you aggravating expenditure, you!"

Something tapped the driver's side window, and she let out a shriek. Her pulse galloping as fast as she used to chase the ice cream truck, she jerked around and spotted Jase smiling from the other side. She shoved the pill bottle into the console's storage space and rolled down the window. "Jase. You scared me."

"I figured so by the way you tried to shatter glass with that high note." His expression was contrite, but his dimples showed. He was fighting a grin. "The engine's been idling out here for a while, but you weren't getting out. Since you missed church Sunday and Wednesday, I was afraid you might be sick or something. I wanted to check on you. I'm sorry I startled you." He tilted his head, giving him a boyish look. "Are you okay?"

She shut off the ignition, swung the door open, and stood in the wedge of space created by the door and car body. "Yeah, I'm fine. Was just . . . thinking. Kind of waiting until after five so I wouldn't bother anybody with the noise of the vacuum." How slovenly she felt in her faded sweat suit next to him in his neat twill trousers and navy-blue polo shirt. The fabric lay smooth over his flat belly and was tucked into his pants. She couldn't wear anything tucked in. And her tops couldn't lay smooth because her belly wasn't flat.

She jammed her hands into her pockets and tried to crisscross the open jacket tails over her stomach. The zipper halves overlapped, but that was it, leaving her feeling exposed and embarrassed. "Is everybody done for the day?"

"Brother and Sister Kraft went to visit a couple of members who recently moved into a retirement home. I doubt they'll come back to the church after their visit. I can be done for the day if it'd be easier for you to do your work with me out of the way."

Did he have to be so nice? He was kind. And good looking. Smart. A minister. He was perfect. Too perfect for her. Her head knew it. But how would she convince her heart? She opened her mouth to tell him yes, it would be easier to clean the place if she was by herself, but her traitorous tongue went rogue. "You can stay if you want to."

"Good." He bobbed his neatly bearded chin toward the front doors. "Let's both go in, then, huh? It's cold out here, and I wasn't savvy enough to put on a jacket today."

She stepped away from the car, and Jase pushed the door shut. Then he escorted her to the front double doors and opened one for her. Inside, he paused and turned a serious look on her. "Have you been sick?"

A squiggly strand of hair had come loose from her ponytail and tickled her cheek. She anchored it behind her ear, then returned her hand to her pocket. "Yeah. I was pretty sick on Sunday. A touch of the flu, I think." Liar.

"Is that why you didn't pop in and say hi when you were here cleaning on Tuesday?"

Did he have to give her the third degree? How was she supposed to answer? Honesty would make her look like a dolt. If she lied, the resulting guilt would send her diving headfirst into a pint — no, a quart — of ice cream. "Well . . ."

He smiled, his eyes sad. "I think I know why."

Her heart went *ka-wump.* "Y-you do?"

"Yeah." He slipped his hands into his trouser pockets and lowered his head, peering at her past the hank of red-brown hair flopping over his forehead. "I think I might have offended you by praying with Kenzie."

What kind of person would take offense at a prayer? If he wanted to make her feel even more ashamed, he'd found the means.

"I've been thinking about it, and I can imagine what it looked like from your point of view when you came into the room. But honestly, all I did was hold her hand and pray. We weren't doing anything sneaky behind your back."

"That's what Kenzie told me." Hands in her pockets, she straightened her arms and stretched the fabric across her stomach. "And I believed her. She said she'd tell me what y'all" — had she really said *y'all?* — "were praying about, but she hasn't had a chance yet. She and I, um, haven't really been together much since I didn't pick her up for church Sunday and my job here takes up some evenings." She'd missed Kenzie, too. The past evenings had been as lonely as when she'd hidden away in her room during her teenage years.

Jase smiled, and the outer corners of his eyes crinkled. "Well, I hope y'all will get together now that you're feeling better." He paused and curiosity lit his face. "Say, speaking of Kenzie, do you know if she brought a pan of brownies by the church last week?"

Lori's eyes bulged, and her frame went stiff. "What did she tell you?"

"She didn't say anything. But one day when I was leaving the church, I smelled brownies. I think it was Monday." He rolled his eyes upward. "Yeah, Monday, and I found brownies. I'm pretty sure they were made from Kenzie's recipe. There's something different about the way they smell. Richer. Darker, if you know what I mean."

Lori knew what he meant. Her mouth went dry, and she felt as if her tongue fastened itself to the roof of her mouth.

"Anyway, I found them, but when I looked in the pan . . . whoa." He jerked backward, like a gust of wind had blasted him. "What a mess. I was pretty sure some kind of animal had dug through them."

An animal? Fire attacked Lori's face. She tried to laugh, but it came out more like a strangled squawk. "Really? Oh, wow. That's awful."

"Yeah. I thought about throwing them away, but I put them back where I'd found them. Later that night, they were gone. I figured you must've thrown them out when you cleaned." He shook his head, making a *tsk-tsk* sound. "What a shame to waste them. I hope there aren't mice — or gophers! — in the kitchen." He laughed.

Lori couldn't laugh. She'd dug in that pan. And he thought an animal had done it. An *animal.* Humiliation rolled through her in waves of heat that seared her face and sped her pulse until her chest heaved with quick breaths. His description was right. When she started one of her binges, she was animalistic. Stuffing herself. Eating without thought. Making a pig of herself. A whimper crept from her throat.

Jase's smile disappeared beneath an expression of deep concern. "Are you getting sick again?"

Her chest puffed up and down like a bellows, and tears distorted her vision. Her chin quivered uncontrollably. More whimpers squeaked out. Mouse squeaks. Or maybe gopher squeaks. Did gophers squeak? She wanted to tell him she was okay, but she wasn't okay. She wasn't anywhere close to okay. Something inside her was very not okay. Why else would she stuff herself the way she did? And there stood Jase, witnessing her fall apart.

"Lori?"

Embarrassment, shame, emptiness, and the longing to be loved all rushed together in a giant mass of emotion she couldn't quell. She turned her back on Jase and shook her hands from her pockets, then clamped them over her mouth. It didn't help. A sob broke free, then another, and she dissolved into harsh wails.

TWENTY-THREE

Wichita
Kenzie

Kenzie picked up the scissors and aimed the open blades at the taut strings holding the latest place mat on the loom. A few snips, then some knots, and another set of four would be ready to send to the mission store. Just as she positioned the shears for the first cut, her cell phone rang from its spot on top of the pony wall, where she'd laid it for easy access when she sat at the loom earlier. She glanced at the incoming number. Lori.

Thank You, Lord. Things had been tense between them since last week's bowling party. Maybe Lori was ready to really be friends again, as Kenzie had been praying. She put down the scissors and picked up her phone. "Hi, Lori."

"Actually, Kenzie, this is Brother Jase."

She frowned. "Why do you have Lori's

phone? Where's Lori?"

"She's at the church. With me." A strange background noise accompanied his voice, like someone was gargling and singing opera at the same time. "She's having kind of a . . . I'm not sure what to call it. I guess I'd say an emotional meltdown."

Lori? In the years of their friendship, Kenzie had seen Lori worried, sad, and even aggravated, but she'd always kept a grip on her emotions. Kenzie sank onto the stool and clamped her phone to her ear with both hands. "What happened?"

"I don't really know."

A muffled click sounded, and the background noise disappeared. Brother Jase must have closed himself in a room away from Lori. If she was that overwrought, she shouldn't be alone. Kenzie stood up.

"We were talking about a pan of brownies I found in the kitchen, how I started to eat one but it looked like something had burrowed through the pan, and it set her off." Brother Jase sounded worried, frightened, and panicky at the same time. "I'd take her to Brother and Sister Kraft's house, but they aren't there. I didn't know who else to call. Can you come?"

"Yes." She stomped her foot. "I mean, no. Not if you're at the church. I don't have a way to get there."

A groan met her ear. "Of course. You don't drive. What should I do? Call her dad? His number's in her phone."

"No!" Kenzie had never met Lori's father, but she knew he'd be no help at all. He'd be, as her daed would put it, a full hindrance. "Have her drive here."

"Kenzie, you don't understand. She's in no condition to drive. Seriously, she's falling apart. She's scaring me."

His statement scared her. She bit her lip. Why hadn't she purchased a vehicle and learned to drive? Then she could help both Lori and Brother Jase. But maybe she could still help. "Do you remember where I live?"

"Um . . . it was off West Central Avenue. I remember that much."

"If I text you the address, can you put it in your phone's GPS and find it?" Amazing how easily the terms flowed from her tongue. She hadn't learned to drive, but she'd learned quite a lot in her years of living in the world.

"Yeah, I can do that."

"Good. Are you calm enough to drive?"

"Yeah. Yeah, I think so." He sounded calmer now. Maybe having someone else make a plan was already helping him.

"Okay. Bring her here."

"Thanks, Kenzie." Such relief colored his tone that tears stung Kenzie's eyes. "We'll be there as soon as I can get her in the car."

The distance from Beech Street Bible Fellowship to Kenzie's apartment was only eight miles — a fifteen-minute drive, depending on streetlights and traffic. While she waited, Kenzie paced, prayed, chewed her thumbnail to the quick, and counted the number of times the second hand made it around the clock. By the twelfth round, the walls were closing in on her, so she moved out onto her little landing and stared at the street, continuing to pray.

When Lori's familiar green compact sedan pulled into the parking lot, her knees went weak. She kept a grip on the handrail as she half ran, half stumbled down the stairs. Pinching her skirt above her knees, she raced to the car and met Brother Jase as he stepped out.

He grabbed her hand. His palm was sweaty and his lips looked white. "Yikes trikes, Kenzie, I'm glad you're here. She's not even making sense."

Neither was he. He'd said *yikes trikes,* a completely nonsensical exclamation Kenzie'd never heard anyone but Lori use.

"I'm supposed to be a minister, but —" His voice broke. "I don't know what to do for her. I almost drove to a hospital, but she insisted she wanted to come here."

Kenzie wished she had the courage to hug him. He seemed to need it. But she wasn't even good at receiving hugs. She should leave the comforting to Lori. When she felt better. Still holding his hand, Kenzie said, "Then let's get her inside."

She guided him around the hood to the passenger side. Brother Jase let go of her hand and pulled the door wide. Kenzie crouched down and peered in at Lori. Her friend's red-blotched face and tear-stained cheeks made her heart ache. She forced herself to smile. "Hi. Brother Jase said you're not feeling good."

Lori shook her head.

"Did something happen after you left the fabric shop? You were okay at work."

Lori raised her trembling hand and swiped at her nose. "Nothing happened t-today. Yet. But yesterday . . . and Tuesday . . ." She gulped, tears welling in her eyes. She held a bottle of vitamins to Kenzie. "I got these, but I think it's too late."

Kenzie patted Lori's leg. "Can you walk?"

"Of course I can walk."

"Come on out of there, then." Kenzie straightened and moved aside.

Lori exited the car, and Brother Jase took

324

a step toward her. She scurried away from him and looped her arm around Kenzie's waist. Hurt flickered in Brother Jase's eyes, but he closed the car door without a word and gestured the two of them ahead. Kenzie slipped her arm around Lori's shoulders and guided her forward. They climbed the stairs together, Brother Jase following.

In the apartment, Lori sank onto the sofa and, after a moment's pause, Brother Jase took Kenzie's stool.

Kenzie sat close to Lori and put her hand on her friend's arm. "Do you need something to drink? To eat?" Maybe Lori had low blood sugar. Van from work was hypoglycemic, and when her blood sugar dropped, she got dizzy and snapped at everybody. But after she ate something, she was fine. "Maybe it would help."

"I don't need anything to drink, and I for sure don't need anything to eat." Lori snapped as sharply as Van ever had. Then she hung her head. "I'm sorry. I'm not mad at you. I'm mad at me. Disappointed in me. And you will be, too, when you know."

Brother Jase sat with his spine stiff, hands on his knees, and gaze locked on Lori's face. "Know what?"

"What happened to those brownies. The ones you said a gopher ate."

Kenzie bounced a puzzled frown from Lori to Brother Jase to Lori again. "A gopher ate some brownies?"

Lori lifted her head and gave Kenzie a sorrowful look. "Not just *some* brownies. The brownies I asked you to bake for Jase. And it wasn't a gopher. It was me. I got into them. Dug through the pan with my fingers." She held her hand up and glared at it. Then she smacked it onto her leg. "That's why I hid them above the refrigerator. No one was supposed to see them there. I planned to at least salvage the ones around the edges, the ones I hadn't touched, and give them to Jase. The way you expected me to, Kenz. But then I saw the photograph."

She shifted her gaze to Brother Jase. "Rachel was so pretty. Dainty looking, like Kenzie. I got . . . jealous. And I wanted the feeling to go away. So I took the rest of the brownies and ate them."

Suddenly Kenzie remembered the trash bag Lori had carried out of the church. "Is that what you had? Not a dirty empty dish but the brownies?"

Lori nodded. Her chin quivered. "They fell out of the pan on the way home, but that didn't matter. I ate them out of a trash bag. Like some starving homeless person would've done. Except I don't have an excuse, because I'm not homeless, and it's pretty obvious I'm not starving." Her sad tone turned hard. "How could I be starving when I eat all the time?" She balled her fists and banged them on her thighs. "All the time, Kenzie!" Tears rolled.

Kenzie got up, hurried to her bathroom, and grabbed the box of tissues from the back of the toilet. When she returned, she saw that Brother Jase had moved to the sofa beside Lori and sat with his hand between her shoulder blades. Kenzie put the box in Lori's lap and went to the stool.

Brother Jase pulled out a tissue and pressed it into Lori's hand. "Lori, can I ask you something?"

Lori wiped her eyes and nose. "I guess."

"Did someone mistreat you when you were a child?"

Lori's eyes went wide. She drew away from Brother Jase. "No. Of course not."

Kenzie huffed. "Lori, tell the truth."

Lori glowered at Kenzie. "I am. Nobody hit me or . . . or hurt me."

"Maybe not physically, but someone did hurt you."

Lori hung her head. "I don't wanna talk about it."

Brother Jase glanced at Kenzie, sympathy in his eyes, then faced Lori. "Yeah, when someone hurts us, we don't want to talk about it. We don't want to acknowledge it. Maybe because we blame ourselves, like we think we did something to deserve it, and it embarrasses us to admit it. Maybe because we want to pretend it isn't real, and by not talking about it, we can keep it hidden."

Slowly Lori raised her head and looked at Brother Jase. "How do you know that?"

A sad smile formed on his lips. "Because that's how I felt when I was little. My mom didn't take care of me, so I figured I wasn't worth taking care of. Then the state took me from her, and I went to different foster families. But none of those places were really my home. Just someplace to be. I felt pretty worthless. Empty, you know?"

Kenzie battled the desire to cry. She'd never been mistreated, but constant worry about failing to follow the rules of her sect had left her feeling hopeless. Uncertainty about her standing before God had carved a hole in her heart and sent her seeking to plug it up with perfection. Until grace washed away her fears and filled her life.

Lori nodded. "Yeah, I know. When I get that way, I . . . I eat."

Brother Jase smiled. "To fill yourself up?"

Lori hung her head again. "Yeah."

"But it doesn't really help."

Lori's chin bounced up. "It sure doesn't. Not for the long haul."

Kenzie gazed at Brother Jase in amazement. On the phone, he'd said he didn't know how to help, but clearly he did. His understanding had soothed Lori and erased her tears.

Brother Jase eased backward and slid his arm across the back of the sofa, no longer touching Lori but staying close. "When I was in seventh grade, my school counselor diagnosed me with obsessive-compulsive disorder. Most of my life was out of my control, so I controlled what I could. Everything had to be in order, as perfect as I could make it, you know? My books stacked alphabetically in my locker, my shirt tucked in just so, pencils lined up on the edge of my desk, that kind of thing. When I was scared, I refolded all my T-shirts so they were all the same size square. Nervous? I organized my closet. Mad? Upset? Bored? I found something to straighten up. I got teased a lot, and I felt really stupid for being so picky about stuff. But even so, when I felt empty or insecure, I tried to make something perfect since I couldn't make myself perfect."

Lori's jaw went slack. "That can't be. You're so . . . so . . ."

He arched a brow. "What?"

Lori sputtered and couldn't seem to find words.

Kenzie moved to the sofa and perched on the arm next to Lori. "You always seem so confident."

He slowly shook his head, his eyes sad. "Looks can be deceiving. I still battle the need for order. But I'm better, thanks to counseling and a church family that loved on me and helped me believe I was worth something." For a moment, his forehead pinched, as if a sudden pain claimed him. But he took in a breath, and the expression cleared. "If habits can be made, they can be broken. You can break your overeating habit, Lori."

Lori released a rueful chuckle. "I don't know. When I start, it's like . . ." She rolled her eyes toward the ceiling, then looked at Kenzie. "Kenz, remember when you came over last summer and we watched that documentary about the ocean? There was a segment about sharks."

Kenzie cringed. She'd had nightmares after seeing a shark tear apart an injured fish. "I'd rather not think about it."

"But it's the best way I can explain what happens inside of me." Lori shifted toward Brother Jase and steepled her hands under her chin. "When the shark got the scent of blood, it went crazy. It ripped into the food source like it was battling for survival, and it didn't stop until every piece of that fish was either eaten or so shredded it wasn't worth grabbing." She pressed her palms to her chest. "That's how I am when I'm sad or lonely or feeling bad about myself. I start eating and I can't stop. I keep going and going until my stomach is so full it hurts and I feel sick. But even though I know it's going to make me feel that way, I still do it. Like I have no control."

Lori covered her face with her hands. "I can't believe I just told you that. You'll never be able to look at me again without envisioning me gorging myself on brownies or . . . or tearing apart a fish."

Kenzie slid to her knees in front of Lori and took hold of her wrists. "I love you, Lori, and nothing you said changes that. You use food to fill yourself up. It's not that different than me trying to do everything right so I'd be complete."

Lori lowered her hands and peered at Kenzie from the corners of her eyes. "What do you mean?"

"In my community, we lived by the *Ordnung* — an unwritten list of dos and don'ts. People who didn't abide by it suffered disapproval, sometimes even shunning."

Lori sniffled. "What's that?"

"Being treated like you're dead."

Lori shuddered. "That's awful."

Kenzie nodded. "I didn't want to be shunned. So I tried to keep all the rules. But I couldn't. Because no one can. No one in human skin, anyway."

She let go of Lori's wrists and stood, facing Lori and Brother Jase. "I got filled up when I found Jesus. Now when I mess up, I ask for forgiveness and God makes me whole again. The missionaries who told me about Jesus said the Holy Spirit would come to me. Jesus called Him the Comforter, and I know He's in me. He keeps me filled up. He can fill you, too, Lori."

Jase

He'd stayed quiet and listened, but the excitement stirring in Jase's chest couldn't be squelched. He sat up and looked at Lori. "Have you asked Jesus to be your Savior?"

Lori nodded. "Yes. At church camp when I was thirteen. My dad sent me to camp mostly to get me out of his hair for a week. I prayed with my counselor one night and accepted Jesus, and I got baptized at Beech Street by Brother Kraft after I got back from camp."

"Then you have the Holy Spirit in you."
Beneath his breastbone, Jase felt as if
something danced. As if his heart was coming to life again. "You have what Kenzie
called the Comforter. You don't need food,
Lori. With the Holy Spirit's help, you can
break your habit of using food as your filler.
You already know it's ineffective. So why
not choose something that will fill you
permanently? Why not let the Holy Spirit
be your comforter and let God be your
filler? God made Kenzie whole. He'll do it
for you, too."

Lori looked from Jase to Kenzie to Jase
again. "How? I don't know how."

How well he understood. Jase didn't know
how to let go of his resentment toward God
for taking Rachel from him. He didn't know
how to restore his relationship with the
Father. He didn't know how to lead the kids
from Beech Street. He couldn't do any of
it. At least, not on his own. A memory verse
from his time as a teenager at Grace Chapel
tiptoed through his mind and found its way
to his tongue. " 'I know what it is to be in
need, and I know what it is to have plenty. I
have learned the secret of being content in
any and every situation, whether well fed or
hungry, whether living in plenty or in want.
I can do all this through him who gives me

strength.' "

Kenzie smiled and nodded. "Philippians 4, right?"

Jase flashed her a grin. "Verses 12 through 13. We all have need for various types of filling. And we gain the strength to find contentment when we lean into the giver of strength. Do you know who that is, Lori?"

Tears filled her eyes. "It's Jesus."

"Yes. If you let Him, He'll help you break the habit of overeating."

Kenzie bent down and touched Lori's knees. "I'll help, too, by praying for you and encouraging you and not baking any more pans of brownies to tempt you."

Jase reared back. "Wait a minute. No more brownies? That's cruel and unusual punishment." To his delight, Lori laughed. He grinned at her. "And I'll do what I can, too, to help you. When you feel tempted, call me. I won't judge you or ridicule you. We'll just talk it through. Okay?"

Lori pulled in a shuddering breath and released it. "Okay. Okay, I'll try."

Jase stroked his chin, thinking. "You know, my psychology professor told us that to break a habit, it's not enough to stop doing the unhealthy thing. We need to replace it with something beneficial or it leaves a hole we might try to fill with something else that isn't healthy. Like people who replace cigarettes with food, or people who are addicted to gambling play computer games, which can also be addicting. So you need to choose something healthy or beneficial you want to do in place of eating. Any ideas?"

Lori sat for several seconds, her brow puckered and her lips sucked in. Then she gave a firm nod. "I want to pray more."

Something jabbed like an arrow through Jase's middle.

"I want to do something to get my mind off me and on somebody else — maybe learn a craft and donate the projects to missions, like Kenzie does with her rugs."

Kenzie gave a little jolt and looked aside.

"And I want . . . I want . . ." Lori's chin wobbled. "So much of the time I start gorging myself because of something I remember my dad saying to me. I think it would really help if I made peace with my dad."

TWENTY-FOUR

Bradleyville
Merlin

Merlin eased his car into the middle stall of the garage, then put the vehicle in park and turned off the ignition. He angled a smile at Leah, who dozed in the seat across the console. No matter how short the drive, she fell asleep when she was the passenger. But never behind the wheel, she always said with a firmness that tickled him. They were home now, so it was time to get out, but he hated to disturb her. She hadn't slept well since he told her about his CHF diagnosis. Such irony, her telling him not to worry but taking all the worry on herself.

He touched her arm. "Leah?"

"Hmph?" She snuffled and popped her eyes open. She looked around. "Oh, we're home."

He chuckled. "Yep."

Her sleepy expression morphed into a firm

scowl. "And what are you going to do now?"

Another chuckle threatened, but he swallowed and erased it. She meant to be fierce. A man shouldn't laugh at a lioness. Even if her sleep-tousled hair resembled a kitten's fluff. "Talk to Jase."

"Good. And while you're doing that, I'll start supper."

"Something light."

"How about creamed canary tongues on toast?"

He burst out laughing. When the kids were young and asked what was for dinner, if Leah hadn't yet decided what to cook or was feeling a little ornery, she teasingly told them creamed canary tongues on toast. But it'd been years since she'd thrown the option at him. It brought back sweet memories. He opened his door and got out, still chuckling. "Maybe not tonight. It's after six, and technically I'm not supposed to eat anything after six thirty, according to the cardiologist."

She got out and rounded the car's hood. "I read the instructions, Merlin. I've got makings for a tossed salad in the fridge, and I'll chop up the leftover broiled chicken breasts to add some protein. Let me take care of supper. You take care of Jase."

"Yes, ma'am." He gave a mischievous

salute and followed her out of the garage. She headed for the house, and he climbed the staircase to Jase's apartment and knocked. He waited several seconds, but Jase didn't answer. Was he still in his office? He spent a lot of time in there. The man was dedicated. A good trait for a minister.

Merlin plodded down the stairs, then paused at the bottom with his fingers pressed to his opposite wrist, monitoring his pulse. When it slowed to a reasonable beats-per-minute count and he could draw a deep breath, he ambled around the garage and across the grassy lot toward the church. He used his key and let himself in through the back door. As he walked through the fellowship hall, he stepped in something sticky. He paused and frowned at the spot. Hadn't the floor been mopped yet? Lori was supposed to clean on Thursdays. Maybe she hadn't gotten to the fellowship hall yet.

He entered the hallway. Everything was dark, including the corridor where the offices were. Both doors were closed, and not even a sliver of light showed under Jase's door. So he wasn't here. Merlin scratched his temple, frowning. Jase's car was in its stall, but the man himself wasn't at home or at the church. And the church obviously hadn't been cleaned, so Lori was also missing. A puzzle. Or, more accurately, two puzzles.

Merlin changed direction, intending to go home to let Leah know about their MIA employees, when the click of the front-door lock caught his attention. He hurried around the corner and saw Jase and Lori enter the foyer. He put his hands on his hips and grinned. "There you are."

Jase rubbed his knuckles against his chin, and Lori fiddled with her key ring. The two of them looked as guilty as a pair of red-headed foxes caught in the henhouse. Lori hunched her shoulders and grimaced. "Oh. Hi, Brother Kraft."

Merlin strode forward, chuckling under his breath. "Hi, yourself. I'm mighty glad to see you. I was just fixing to worry since I couldn't find either one of you." He examined their unsmiling faces. Maybe he shouldn't set aside his worry just yet. "Everything all right?"

"Yes and no." Jase placed his hand on Lori's shoulder. "Could we talk to you?"

From the serious looks in their eyes, whatever they needed might take a while to talk through. He hadn't eaten yet, and his window for opportunity would soon close. "Have you had your supper?"

They shook their heads in perfect synchronization, the way his twins had when they were little. Merlin smiled. "Well, Leah's putting a tossed salad on the table, and you know her — she always makes plenty. Why don't you two come eat with us? We can talk at the table, or we can come back here afterward if you need a more private chat." He lowered his brows slightly. "Unless it's too pressing to wait."

Jase looked at Lori, and she looked at him. She shrugged. "It can wait."

Jase turned to Brother Kraft. "Okay, sounds good. Thanks."

The three of them exited the front door, and Lori locked it behind them. Merlin led them through the gravel parking area toward the lot between the church and parsonage. Curiosity writhed through his middle. What was up with these two? Acid burned in his throat, and he inwardly berated himself. The verse from Matthew he'd used in last night's Bible study replayed in his memory. "Can any one of you by worrying add a single hour to your life?" Of course not, but worry could sure carve some hours away. He turned his thoughts into prayer, and by the time they stepped through the back door into the screened porch, the burn in his throat had retreated.

He ushered them into the kitchen and announced, "Company for supper, Ma."

Leah turned from the counter, a butcher knife in her hand, and smiled. "Well, what a nice surprise. And with these extra hands, it'll be ready before you know it. Merlin, would you set the table? Jase, there's a pitcher of tea in the refrigerator. Please pour. And, Lori, those cucumbers need sliced. There are knives in the drawer next to the sink. You can use the pull-out cutting board above the drawer."

A teasing grin lit Lori's somber face. "And I know what I should do — shake a leg, right?"

Leah laughed. "You got it."

Working together to put the meal on the table reminded Merlin of the days when their children were still in the house. How quickly the years had gone. He'd spent more than thirty of them right here in what most folks would call a nothing town, shepherding the flock at Beech Street Bible Fellowship. Some people would probably think he'd wasted his life staying in such a small place and preaching to such a small congregation. But Merlin thought otherwise. God called him to plant seeds and love on people, and that's exactly what he'd done. He could go to his grave content, knowing he'd poured himself out on the ones God brought to him.

He shifted his attention to Jase, who'd finished his Leah-assigned task and now leaned against the counter, sneaking cucumber slices from Lori. A smile tugged at Merlin's lips. The two young people looked comfortable together. Jase had come for a job, but he might find something even more here in Bradleyville. Wouldn't that be something?

Leah turned with the salad bowl cradled in her hands. "Lori, scoop those cumber slices on top of everything else and let's eat. We're burning daylight."

Wichita
Kenzie

Friday morning, Ruby welcomed Kenzie with a hug and a huge smile. "Guess what?"

Despite her restless, nearly sleepless night, Kenzie found her boss's joy contagious, and she smiled. "What?"

Ruby kept hold of Kenzie's shoulders. "Four. Already four people have signed up for the crazy-quilt wall-hanging class I advertised. And the ad's only been up since Tuesday! With so much interest right out of the starting gate, we might have a full group for our very first class. Wouldn't that be a blessing?"

Kenzie unsnapped her fanny pack and cradled it against her chest. "That's wonderful, Ruby. I'm so happy for you."

Ruby slid her arm around Kenzie's waist and guided her to the checkout counter. "I'm happy for me, for you, for Barbara and Van and Lori. If these classes take off the way you said they did at the shop in Indiana, I can put everyone back on full-time status." She took the fanny pack from Kenzie and placed it in Kenzie's cubby. Then she put her fists on her hips and beamed. "Are you ready for good news item number two?"

Kenzie hid a yawn behind her hand. "Sure."

"Van did some investigating, and she found a supplier that's willing to send us three table looms on a consignment basis, plus a used model that can serve as a sample." Ruby's eyes glittered like newly polished sapphires.

Kenzie had never seen her boss so excited. Should she stomp on Ruby's good mood by telling her the decision she'd made somewhere around three that morning?

Ruby aimed a thoughtful frown in the direction of the yarn department. "I need to clear a spot to set it up, but it'll be worth it. Having a loom available will be quite a novelty. People can try their hand at weaving, and then maybe they'll get hooked the way you did and end up buying one for themselves." She drummed her fingers on the counter. "Of course, I'll need to invest in rug warp or some other more sturdy yarns than I've carried in the past, but that shouldn't be an overwhelming financial burden. Especially if the classes bring in extra revenue."

Her smile returned, and she grabbed Kenzie in another hug. "And apparently they will, because four people have already signed up." She sighed and stepped back. "I know it isn't wise to count your chickens before they've hatched, but I feel so much more positive than I have for at least a year. And much of my change in attitude has to do with the knowledge you shared. Thank you, Kenzie."

Kenzie gave what she hoped was a genuine smile. "You're welcome. I'm glad you liked some of the ideas."

Ruby shook her finger, her eyes glinting impishly. "I liked *all* the ideas, young lady. But we can't incorporate everything at once. So we'll go with the ones that best suit the store and are a little easier to navigate."

Kenzie leaned against the counter. "Will you teach the crazy-quilt class?"

"Oh, no." Ruby made a face. "I'm better

at doing than explaining. Bev and Peggy, the two women who organize the quilt group at the rest home our church ministers to, have agreed to teach. I included their fee when I figured the cost. If we don't get a full class, I'll probably have to pay some of their stipend out of pocket, but I'll recoup that from students buying their materials. I know the women'll do a great job, and then the students will tell other people about the class." She nudged Kenzie with her elbow and winked. "Word-of-mouth advertising is the best kind. Happy customers make a business flourish."

Flourish . . . A knot formed in Kenzie's throat. She needed to tell Ruby her plans. She pulled in a breath. "Ruby, I —"

"Oh, Kenzie, I've been meaning to ask." Ruby spoke at the same time. "The ring post has been floating in cyberspace for almost three weeks now. Have you had any promising bites?"

Kenzie crinkled her nose. "Lots of bites and inquiries, but none promising."

Ruby squeezed Kenzie's shoulder. "Well, don't give up hope. People will keep sharing, and we'll keep praying, and surely the rightful owner will contact you."

Kenzie sighed. "Yes, ma'am."

Ruby glanced at her wristwatch. "Gracious, we've been chatting for almost ten minutes. Barbara should be here soon. She'll straighten shelves and man the cash register. Right before closing yesterday, I sold the little kitty-trio wall hanging from the front window, and I need to put up something else to grab attention, so would you please work on another wall hanging? Something summery and cheerful . . ." She snapped her fingers. "Ah, yes, the pattern with the appliquéd sunflower medallion. Pick out some jewel-toned fat quarters for the log cabin border. That should set off the sunflower nicely."

Kenzie wove her fingers together and fidgeted in place. "All right. But, Ruby, I need —"

Ruby turned Kenzie in the direction of the sewing corner. "You need to get busy, and so do I. We'll talk at lunch break, all right?"

Kenzie scuffed toward the sewing corner, her heart heavy. She loved Ruby. And all the other women at Prairie Meadowlark. It would break her heart to tell them goodbye. But she didn't have a choice. God had very clearly instructed her to return to Indiana. She still didn't know how she'd get there or when she'd go, but she was going. She wouldn't be able to rest until she'd told

Mamm and Daed and Grossmammi and her brothers how to be truly filled up.

TWENTY-FIVE

Bradleyville
Jase

Jase laid his Bible aside and leaned back in his squeaky chair. He wished his office had a window he could look out. Sister Kraft had found an old four-paned window frame somewhere and put a picture of a rolling flower-dotted prairie behind the glass. She'd hung it on the wall next to his desk, then said, "Now, that's a pretty, relaxing scene. Don't you agree?"

He agreed the picture was both pretty and relaxing, but it was also unchanging. Not the same as the view outside a real window. And he needed a distraction from his thoughts.

Several recent promises he'd made weighed on him. Namely, promises to pray for people. For Brother Kraft. For Kenzie. Lori. Even Cullen. Truth be told, he should pray for all the kids in his youth group every day. He knew what it was like in public high school. The pressures to fit in, to adopt the popular belief systems instead of following God's instruction, the general disdain toward Christian values, even from some of the teachers. He'd encountered it all in high school, and it was worse now. The kids needed prayer coverage.

But every time he bowed his head and closed his eyes, nothing happened. He prayed with the youth group every time they came together. He'd prayed with the young adult Sunday school class. He'd prayed with Kenzie last week and with Lori and Brother Kraft last night. Why could he pray in group settings but on his own he was so dry and empty? Maybe because he was all alone inside his heart and head.

He shouldn't be alone. He'd told Lori the Holy Spirit was always with her and would help her. Kenzie had pretty much said the same thing. It was true, too, according to the Bible. Believers who accepted Christ's salvation received the gift of the Holy Spirit, God's own Spirit, inside them. He'd been so sure of God's presence before he lost Rachel. Maybe the car accident had knocked the Holy Spirit out of him. Maybe his prayers were only repetition of other phrases he'd heard or bits of verses he'd read.

Maybe the whole relationship-with-God thing had always been a farce but he just hadn't known it until after he sobbed and prayed and trusted that somehow Rachel would live but she didn't.

He slammed his hands on the desk and stood, his pulse racing. Had he seen proof of God's presence in people's lives, or had he only seen happenstance? He needed to know for sure. If it was real, he wanted it back. Maybe he wanted it back even if it wasn't real. Because he'd been content then. And contentment, even born of ignorance, was so much better than this constant flip-flopping of emotion and attitude.

Somewhere in the building, a vacuum cleaner was running. Which meant Lori had come back this morning to finish what they hadn't done last night. She'd argued with him about helping, but after her meltdown and emotional confession at Kenzie's and then her long conversation with Brother Kraft, it'd been late and she'd seemed as weak as a newborn kitten. So he'd cleaned the bathrooms, and she'd taken care of the kitchen and fellowship hall. But they hadn't gotten to the classrooms, hallways, and sanctuary. Maybe he could help her. He wasn't getting anything else done.

He stepped into the hall, and at the same

time, Brother Kraft came out of the main office. The men stopped, face to face. Jase pointed toward the sanctuary's closed doors. "I was going to check on Lori."

Brother Kraft smiled, his eyes twinkling. "Great minds think alike. Leah heard the vacuum start up and suggested I peek in on her. How about if we go together?"

Jase didn't want to be rude, but neither did he want to go to Lori with someone else in tow.

"Then after we assure ourselves she's doing all right, I'd like to talk to you. I'd intended to chat with you yesterday evening, but things went a different direction."

Jase and Lori had invaded the minister's supper, derailed his plans, and monopolized a good chunk of his evening, but Brother Kraft spoke of it as casually as if his personal time held no value at all. But of course it held great value. Jase cringed. "I'm sorry we messed up your night. But I'm also glad you were available." There he went with the flip-flopping again. Couldn't he hold to one feeling or opinion at a time?

Sister Kraft stepped into the main-office doorway, one fist on her hip and fire sparking in her blue eyes. "You did not mess up our night. There's no reason for apologizing. But Merlin does need to talk to you, so

I'll go check on Lori. Merlin and Jase, choose an office — I don't care whose, as long as it isn't mine — and have a sit-down. I'll be right back." She charged between them up the hall and disappeared around the corner.

Brother Kraft watched after her, then winked at Jase. "Now you know who really runs this outfit. So . . . your office or mine?"

His had windows. "Yours, please."

Brother Kraft turned around. "This way, then."

Jase followed him through the secretary's office to his study. The room was three times the size of Jase's with floor-to-ceiling bookcases along one wall and windows on two — a pleasant place to sit. Instead of going behind his desk, which actually resembled an old farm-kitchen table, Brother Kraft gestured to two brown leather wing-back chairs. The far one faced the north and looked out over an empty field. Jase took it.

Brother Kraft settled in the other chair, folded his hands, and bowed his head. "My dear Father, thank You for this beautiful day and the opportunity it provides for us to serve You."

It took a moment for Jase to realize the man had launched into prayer. He quickly closed his eyes and bowed his head. While he listened to the older man repeatedly refer to God as "Father," a pressure built in his chest. When Jase talked to God, he said "God" or "Lord." "Father" seemed more intimate but, to Jase, alien. He'd never called anyone "father" because he'd gone his whole life without one, and he'd never missed it as much as he did in those minutes while Brother Kraft spoke to his heavenly Father with such ease and familiarity.

"Amen."

Jase echoed, "Amen," more in response to the intimate tone the pastor had used when talking to God the Father than to the actual prayer. He met the man's smiling gaze and held out his hands in query. "What did Sister Kraft send us in here to talk about?"

Brother Kraft laughed. "Lots of stuff. But for starters, would you consider doing some preaching?" He asked Jase to fill the pulpit on the few fifth Sundays of the year. Jase checked his cell phone calendar and discovered a fifth Sunday ended May. Just over five weeks away. Not much time, especially considering how empty he was faithwise. Would he be able to find something of value to say between now and then? Yet how could he refuse? Gritting his teeth, Jase gave a nod of agreement. Then Brother Kraft asked if he'd take over visiting prospective families with high school–age children.

"It probably would be good for you to make a schedule and try to visit the homes of the kids who are members of our church and therefore members of our youth group, too." Brother Kraft linked his hands over his belly and crossed his leg, giving Jase the impression this conversation would be lengthy. "It'll help you get to know the kids better, and it'll let the parents get to know you. Familiarity improves relationship."

Jase's insides jumped. Familiarity . . . Maybe seeing God as more than the Creator — trying to see Him as Father, someone personally interested in his life — would improve his relationship with Him.

"I generally plan visits on Monday and Thursday evenings. Around here, most school events are on Tuesdays and Fridays, so you're less likely to find people home on those evenings."

Jase nodded, his mind still pondering the title *father*. Lori's confession about the way she viewed herself seemed rooted in a poor relationship with a fault-finding, emotionally abusive father. Maybe that's why she had trouble feeling complete. When he was in college, he'd kind of scoffed at his psychology professor's lecture on the importance of a father's influence. At the time, it had seemed to Jase that the man's prediction of diminished self-concept, emotional insecurity, and self-loathing in children who didn't have involved fathers in their homes was just psychological mumbo jumbo. But after listening to Lori and honestly reflecting on his own childhood, he wondered if the professor had really hit the mark.

Was that why God invented the two parent household? And why He called Himself "a father to the fatherless"? Was His intention, from the beginning of time, for all children to have what they needed to grow up emotionally healthy?

"Jase?"

Jase gave a start. "Huh?"

Brother Kraft grinned at him. "I asked you if you were good with taking over the tradition of honoring the graduating seniors the fourth Sunday in May?"

Jase scratched his prickly cheek. "I'm sorry. I drifted off and didn't quite catch what you did in the past."

The minister released a laugh and shook his head. "All right, let me say it again."

This time Jase listened, and even though he had some qualms about standing up and making speeches about each of the kids who would graduate from high school this year, he thought he could do it. Zack, Leesa, and Ari were all good kids, and he already knew a few things he'd be able to say about them. Next year with Cullen, though? That might be tough.

He nodded. "Yeah, I can do it. If you have some kind of program written out that you've followed in the past, I'd like to see it. I think it would help me."

"Leah keeps meticulous records of everything we do here at Beech Street. Check with her."

"Okay, I will." Jase braced his hands on the armrests, ready to rise.

"There's one more thing . . ."

He eased back into the chair.

"Leah confessed she told you I'm having a little challenge, healthwise."

Jase wouldn't call congestive heart failure a *little* challenge, but he nodded.

"She encouraged me to ask you to take over some of the preaching and visitations, in part, to reduce my load and hopefully my blood pressure." He grinned, and Jase couldn't help but smile back. The man oozed friendliness and could probably put a grizzly bear at ease. "But there's another reason, one Leah doesn't know about, and I'd appreciate it if we kept it between you and me."

How many secrets would the two of them share? They weren't telling anyone else about Rachel's lost ring or Cullen's uninvited visit to his apartment, and no one beyond the deacons and Jase was supposed to know about the minister's health situation. He hadn't been sworn to so much secrecy since he joined a backyard club with a bunch of other grade school boys in a foster family's neighborhood. "Okay."

Brother Kraft pulled in a deep breath, as if he was trying to gather strength. "I've been the senior pastor — well, the only pastor, really — at Beech Street since 1988. Thirty-two years now. Our twins were born the year before we came, and our boys were early grade school age, so pretty young. I raised my family in this church. It means a lot to me."

Jase couldn't imagine being tied to a congregation, or to anything else, for that length of time. He released a soft whistle. "It's quite a legacy you've built here."

Brother Kraft smiled, but it held an element of sadness. "It's fairly unusual for a church to keep the same minister for that length of time. I feel honored to have been accepted as the shepherd of this flock for so many years. But I'm getting older. I was sixty-eight my last birthday. I guess you

357

could say I'm getting tired."

Jase frowned, unpleasant scenarios crowding his brain. "Are you planning to retire?"

Brother Kraft shook his head slowly and puckered his lips. "Noooo . . ."

Jase released a sigh of relief.

"Not right now. But eventually? When the Father says it's time? Then yes. I'll hand the title of shepherd to someone else." He sat forward, resting his elbows on his knees and fixing Jase with a serious look. "When that day comes, the people here will need something familiar, some*one* familiar, so they'll feel secure during the transition. I've been praying for more than three years already for the person who will help my flock transition to a new shepherd, and God sent you."

His smile, which expressed godly love and acceptance and confidence, rounded his cheeks. "Will you join me in praying for God's perfect timing for my stepping down from leadership here? This ticker of mine is trying to call the shots right now, but I've told it someone else is in charge. Everything needs to be according to God's timing. And who knows? Maybe God's using my heart trouble to bring my pastorate to a close. I'm not sure yet. But He'll let me know. In His time and in His way."

Brother Kraft sat up and folded his hands

over his stomach again, contentment in his features — a contentment Jase longed to have for himself. "It would sure ease my mind to know you're praying for my discernment and for the church family's peaceful adjustment." He held Jase's gaze with a penetrating look. "Will you do that, Brother Jase?"

Lori

Someone tapped Lori's shoulder, and she gave an all-over start. She smacked her toe on the vacuum cleaner's power button and turned. Sister Kraft stood behind her, an ornery glint in her eyes.

Lori jammed her fist on her hip. "Sister Kraft, you nearly scared me out of a year's growth."

The woman had the audacity to laugh. "Well, if someone did that to me, I'd be grateful."

Lori scrunched her brow in confusion.

The minister's wife laughed again. "Honey, at my age, the only direction I'm apt to grow is out, so being scared out of a year's worth of growth would be a blessing."

Maybe Lori should ask Sister Kraft to scare her again. And again. And again.

"I came to check on you several minutes

ago, and I tried to wait until that thing" — she glared at the vacuum cleaner — "stopped yelling, but I gave up on the idea of you turning it off. So I interrupted." She folded her arms and tilted her head. "Did you have a good night's sleep? Any . . . problems . . . when you got home and were by yourself?"

Lori understood the real question, and pride squared her shoulders. Although she'd been emotionally drained and extremely lonely after her intensely personal talk with the Krafts and Jase, she hadn't put so much as a single M&M in her mouth. In fact, she'd dumped the entire bag of candy-coated chocolates down her garbage disposal and removed the temptation. "No problems, and I slept pretty well." Not surprising. She'd been exhausted. But nights when she wouldn't be too exhausted to eat surely waited ahead. Would she be able to stand strong during those evenings, or would she fall into the old habit of seeking comfort in the pantry?

Sister Kraft patted Lori's back. "Good for you. Answered prayer, yes?"

Lori nodded. "Definitely." She gestured to the vacuum cleaner. "I gotta finish up in here, then hit the classrooms. I'm due at the fabric shop by noon."

"Then I'll let you get back to it." The minister's wife eased backward, her smile intact. "Remember what Brother Kraft told you last night. If you hit a rough spot and need to talk, call."

Lori smiled. Jase had told her the same thing.

Sister Kraft touched Lori's arm, her expression serious. "And be sure and let us know if you decide to go talk to your dad. We'd be happy to go with you, if that's what you want, but at the very least, we'll want to be in prayer while you're with him."

Lori nodded, gratitude swelling in her heart. "Thanks. I appreciate it."

Sister Kraft waved and left, and Lori reactivated the vacuum cleaner. She pushed the noisy machine up and down between the pews, stopping frequently to free the cord — the corners of the pews made great cord catchers — and occasionally to empty the dust canister. The mindless task left too much time for thinking, and today she couldn't stop thinking about her dad. And her mom. And how her relationships with them tied into her practice of gorging herself.

She'd told Kenzie and Jase and then Brother and Sister Kraft that she needed to hash things out with her dad, get to the heart of his dissatisfaction with her, and hopefully find a way to mend what was broken. Or at the very least bring an end to the flow of criticism and resentment. If she thought clear back to her early childhood, she harbored good memories of Dad. Of being carried on his shoulders, of watching cartoons together on Saturday mornings, of trailing him in the yard when he pulled weeds from Mom's garden. Even when she'd peppered him with questions, he'd answered them patiently. He'd liked her then. She'd adored him. Was it possible to recapture that relationship?

She appreciated the Krafts' willingness to go with her. They were good people, supportive and smart. But if she went to Dad's place with her pastor and his wife in tow, he'd consider it an attack. He wouldn't mince words. She couldn't subject them to the awfulness she knew could come out of his mouth. They didn't deserve it.

And neither do you.

The internal voice, louder even than the obnoxious vacuum cleaner, startled her nearly as much as Sister Kraft's tap on the shoulder had. She turned off the vacuum and looked behind her. Then in front of her. She searched the sides and corners of the sanctuary — the very quiet sanctuary —

and not a soul was around. Yet she had heard someone answer her thoughts.

She shook her head like a dog shaking loose a burr, trying to convince herself she'd been imagining things. But the words inside her brain refused to dislodge. So it was real. It had to be real. A shiver caused her entire frame to tremble. She didn't deserve a verbal attack from Dad. The comforting words gave her courage. But did they mean that she shouldn't go to him alone or that she shouldn't go at all?

TWENTY-SIX

How had she let a full week slip by without talking to Ruby about needing to return to Indiana? The pull was so strong that sometimes Kenzie was amazed her heart was still in her chest. But each time she tried to bring up the subject, Ruby changed it. Did the woman know Kenzie's intention and was she trying to prevent Kenzie from terminating her position at the shop, or was she so caught up in improving her store's success that she was unaware of anything else?

Today, May Day, was bustling with customers. And small wonder, considering everything available to them. Shoppers took advantage of the free blueberry-infused lemonade and sugar cookies decorated to look like sunflowers, opportunities to dabble in various crafts, and special discounts in every corner of the shop. Prairie Meadowlark Fabrics & Quilting hadn't seen this much activity since the after-Christmas sale. Ruby, plus all four employees, spent the whole day on the floor, and despite Kenzie's inward struggle, she celebrated the busyness. Ruby had worked so hard to put the details of the event together in such a short amount of time. She deserved this success.

Kenzie had been given the responsibility of showing customers how to operate the loom, which had arrived a few days before the big May Day Extravaganza. Ruby had set it up on a table in front of a window where passersby could look in and see Kenzie work. This newer loom was different from Grossmammi's vintage model in shape and size, but its similarities in function made it easy for her to use. Sometimes she felt a little like a monkey on display in a zoo, but she enjoyed instructing interested customers and letting them add to a table runner made of multicolor yarn as thick as a rope.

As a customer thanked Kenzie for the demonstration and turned away from the loom, Lori came up behind her. "Ruby says you should take your lunch break now. I just finished mine."

Kenzie had hoped she and Lori would be able to take their break together. They'd already seen each other every day for the past week and enjoyed several evening meals with Brother Jase. But with her time in Kansas coming to a close, she didn't want to miss any chances to be with Lori. However, given the activity in the store, they probably shouldn't leave the floor in pairs.

"Okay, thanks." Kenzie hung the handmade "Taking a Break — Back Soon" sign on the loom and headed in the direction of the break room.

Lori walked with her. "Twenty minutes instead of thirty, Ruby said." She sighed. "That barely gave me time to eat my salad and call Jase for our regular noontime chat."

Kenzie shot Lori a startled look. Since when did Lori and Brother Jase have a daily chat time? Sure, friendship was in full bloom between them. She'd noticed it taking off the night Brother Jase brought Lori to Kenzie's apartment. But she must've missed something significant if they'd established a daily talk-to-each-other routine.

"But" — Lori's tone brightened — "we're going to get four breaks today instead of only one to make up for having to cut lunch short. Jase said to call or text when I'm free and he'd make time to chat for a few minutes. And guess what? I'm helping with a youth project after work, so I'll get to see him tonight." She sighed and caught Kenzie's hand. "He's wonderful, Kenz. He really is." She gave a quick squeeze and let go. "Gotta get back to the sewing nook. See ya later!"

Lori hustled off, and Kenzie entered the break room. She opened her lunch bag and took out the sandwich and carrot sticks she'd packed that morning. Lori's bright smile lingered in her memory. Back in Flourish, if a man and woman spent so much time together, the fellowship considered them in a courtship. Were Lori and Brother Jase courting? Maybe they were, since Lori hadn't asked Kenzie to join their activity this evening. Had Lori only forgotten to invite Kenzie, or did she want the time alone with Brother Jase? Kenzie could hardly blame her — as Lori had said, Brother Jase was wonderful. But she didn't like this feeling of being left out.

Sitting alone in the break room with no one to talk to didn't help chase away the uncomfortable feeling. She needed a distraction. She pulled out her cell phone and checked her email. The inbox set up for the missing ring had several more messages, and she read through them while she ate. She finished reading as she took her last bite of the sandwich. Then she wadded up her napkin and threw it into the wastebasket with a frustrated huff.

It'd been almost a full month now since she posted about the ring. When she returned to Indiana, if she moved back in with Mamm and Daed, she'd probably have to give up her cell phone. Some people might be tempted by her worldly possession, and the Bible advised her not to tempt others into sin. Even if she didn't consider using a cell phone a sin, they did, and she respected the fellowship's beliefs enough not to create strife. Unless the real owner of the ring came forward soon, she might never find her. So what to do with it?

She snorted a short laugh. Why hadn't she thought of it before? She could give it to the police. They'd put it in a safe place and look for the owner, wouldn't they? Then she'd be free of the responsibility and could be sure it wouldn't fall into the wrong hands. A weight seemed to roll from her, and she smiled. She still had much to figure out, most notably the financing, before she could actually leave Kansas. But determining a means of dealing with the ring relieved a major concern. And maybe Lori growing close to Brother Jase was also a blessing. Her friend wouldn't be so lonely if she was with him.

With a bounce in her step, she returned to the loom.

Bradleyville
Jase

Jase snipped another cluster of purplish-white blossoms from the rhinoceros-sized lilac bush and laid it carefully in the box near his feet. The smell from the flowers was sweet, almost overpowering with him so close to the bush. Sister Kraft, on the other side, repeatedly sniffed and released exaggerated sighs. Obviously she liked the fragrance.

When Sienna had asked if the youth group could get together on the first day of May and leave May baskets on people's door-steps, Jase had figured the kids would consider it a babyish activity. But no one, not even Cullen or Brent, made a disparaging remark. So Wednesday evening, while he shared the Bible lesson, the youth made simple baskets by rolling colored paper into cones and stapling handles to the cones. Some of the kids were involved in track, so they wouldn't be able to participate, but Sienna, Kaia, Tobi, Jennifer, Zack, and

369

Cullen had promised to show up and distribute the baskets. Then Jase intended to treat them to pizza.

Thank goodness Sister Kraft agreed to make said pizzas. She also gave him a packet of Scripture cards — like business cards but with pretty images and verses — to tuck into the baskets. And when Jase asked her advice about what kind of flowers to buy, she'd volunteered the blooms from the lilac bushes growing behind the parsonage.

She leaned sideways and peeked at Jase, a huge smile on her face. "Isn't it fortuitous the lilacs blossomed early this year? I guess those extra-warm days in April coaxed the buds to open. And right on time for your baskets." She disappeared again behind the leaves and purple flowers. "I've always considered lilacs one of spring's harbingers."

"Your sister always said robins are spring's harbingers." Loneliness for Sister Eileen — and Brother Tony — pinched Jase's chest. He needed to do a better job of keeping in touch with his former minister and his family.

"Oh, of course. Robins, too. And those little marshmallow treats shaped like ducks and rabbits." Her face poked around the bush again, like a puppet popping onstage. "Do you know what I'm talking about?"

Jase laughed. He'd never considered what some folks thought of as an Easter basket staple to be a sign of spring's arrival. "I do. Too bad I didn't stock up on those during the after-Easter sales. We could have put one or two in each of the baskets."

She snickered. "I have at least seven boxes of them in my pantry."

Jase gaped at her. "Seven?"

"There were twelve. We've eaten quite a few."

He burst out laughing.

Her expression turned defensive, and she settled her fist on her hip in a pose he now knew well. "Who can pass up seventy-five-percent-off goodies?" With a shrug, she slipped behind the bush again, and he heard the *snip-snip* of her scissors. "Of course, with Merlin needing to cut back on sweets and such, I should probably get rid of the temptation. How about I donate them to your May Day party and you let the kids eat them? Oh!"

Jase almost dropped his scissors at her shrill exclamation. He darted to her, expecting to find her fighting off a wasp or a bee.

She grabbed his arm, her smile bright. "I had a great idea. It's cool enough today for the kids to sit around a firepit. Those crazy marshmallow things are actually really good roasted. The sugar caramelizes and gets crisp." She licked her lips. "Merlin and I have a whole stack of hot dog sticks in the garage, and we have leftover firewood for the basement's wood-burning stove. So how about it? Do you want to make your May Day party a real party?"

Memories of bonfires behind the church when he was a teen flooded Jase's mind. Of roasting hot dogs and marshmallows, then singing praise songs while the logs crackled, smoke stung his eyes, and stars twinkled overhead. He'd felt close to his fellow students and also to God during those evenings. And hadn't Lori put *Have a bonfire and make s'mores* on the list she'd given him?

He nodded. "I like the idea a lot, but do we have time to get it pulled together? Besides, several of the kids didn't plan to come tonight because of the track meet, and they might feel left out if they hear about it after the fact."

She handed him her scissors and swished her palms together. "You finish cutting flowers. I'll go phone each of the families and alert them to the change in plans. We'll make the get-together an hour later, and maybe instead of pizza, we can roast hot dogs. I'm sure I have a big package of them in the freezer, but I'd need to buy buns."

Jase raised one hand like a traffic cop. "Cullen doesn't like hot dogs."

She frowned at him. "Who told you that?"

"He did."

She rolled her eyes. "That boy . . . At the end-of-the-school-year party last May, he and Zack had a contest to see who could eat the most, and he won. Eight of them! On buns with toppings." She shook her head, tsk-tsking. "He's like the little boy who cried wolf — it's hard to believe what he says sometimes."

Jase chuckled, but inwardly he wanted to groan. If Cullen had lied about disliking hot dogs, what else had he lied about?

She wagged a finger at Jase, her gaze narrowing. "But I know what he'll eat, and that includes hot dogs, so let's plan on a wiener roast tonight. All right?"

"Sounds fine. Lori's coming to help deliver the baskets. I'll ask her to pick up buns on her way. Okay?"

"Yes. Four packages should be enough, and have her grab a couple big bags of potato chips, too. Tell her to use the church's credit card. Merlin gave her one when she took the position as custodian." Sister Kraft headed for the house, whirling one hand in the air the way a cowboy swung a lariat.

"Keep cutting! Keep cutting! We want those baskets to overflow!"

Jase snipped another sprig and laid it in the box. With a cool breeze teasing the back of his exposed neck and the scent of the lilacs filling his nose, a thought — or was it a prayer? — formed unconsciously. If Cullen had taken Rachel's ring, and if he fessed up and returned it, it might be enough to convince Jase that God was listening.

He flicked a glance at the clear sky. *So, are You, God?*

TWENTY-SEVEN

Wichita

Kenzie

Kenzie had hoped to ask Lori to drive her home to retrieve the ring and then give her a ride to the police station after work, but Lori flew out of the shop the moment Ruby turned over the Closed sign. Kenzie gazed forlornly after her. Now what?

Ruby put her arm around Kenzie's shoulders and squeezed. "Miss Kenzie Stetler, thank you, thank you, thank you from the bottom of my heart. This day went better than I could have anticipated. I haven't balanced the cash drawer yet, but Van said we did booming business all day. I expect, even considering our freebies and discounts, it'll show tangible evidence of a successful May Day Extravaganza."

"I'm glad." Kenzie tried to smile, but her lips refused to cooperate.

Ruby's joyful expression faded. "What's

the matter, honey?"

Kenzie sighed. "I was hoping Lori would take me on an errand, but she left without even telling me goodbye."

"Is that all?" Ruby stepped away from Kenzie and gathered her jacket and purse. "I can come back later and do all the closing responsibilities. Where do you need to go?"

Kenzie cringed. "I wasn't hinting."

Ruby laughed. "Oh, I know, but I owe you at least a car ride after you gave me such a great idea for bringing in new business." She pulled on her jacket, smiling. "Where am I taking you?"

"Well . . ." Kenzie wrung her hands. "My apartment, and then the police station."

Ruby's eyes widened. "The police station? Did something happen?"

She hadn't meant to alarm her boss. She shook her head emphatically. "No, no, nothing bad."

Ruby heaved a huge sigh. "Thank goodness. Then what do you need there?"

Kenzie explained her intention to turn the ring over to the officers' keeping. "I don't want to take it with me when I go back to Indiana since I won't have access to the internet anymore, and it seemed like —"

"Wait." Ruby cocked her head and

scowled. "What do you mean when you go back to Indiana? Are you planning a visit?"

Kenzie closed her eyes, swallowing a groan. She'd practiced the speech in her head so many times, it felt as if she'd already delivered it. But she hadn't, and now she'd alarmed her boss again. She opened her eyes and fixed Ruby with a repentant look. "I'm sorry. I've tried to talk to you, but you've been so busy getting the loom set up and preparing for today's event, you haven't had time to listen."

Ruby folded her arms over her chest. "I'm listening now."

Tears unexpectedly flooded Kenzie's eyes. "I need to go home, Ruby. I left because I couldn't join a church that based the promise of heaven on a list of things a person had to do or not do. There was no security in it. I discovered true security when I accepted Jesus as my Savior and received His forgiveness. And lately, I can't stop thinking about my family. How they're still living under a . . . a cloud of uncertainty. Grace is available to them, but they don't know it because they haven't been told. I need to tell them. Mamm and Daed are getting older. Grossmammi is almost eighty already. If I wait, it might be too late. I have to go back."

Ruby grabbed Kenzie and held her tight. "Oh, honey . . ." Her voice broke, and she pressed a kiss on Kenzie's temple.

Kenzie hadn't been held that way since she was a little girl, when Grossmammi would grab her close and place her warm lips on the patch of skin not covered by Kenzie's kapp. Kenzie closed her eyes and savored the embrace while anticipating a similar warm hug when she saw her dear grossmammi again.

Ruby released Kenzie but kept hold of her upper arms. "I understand. Are you intending to move back, or only visit?"

Kenzie blinked several times, clearing her vision. "I . . . I'm not sure. I hadn't thought that far ahead. To be honest, I'm still not sure how I'm going to get there." She grimaced. "It costs a lot. But I keep remembering what Daed always said — God provides for the ravens, and He'll provide for His children. I know for sure I'm one of His children, so He'll provide the way for me to get there."

"Yes, He will." Ruby gave Kenzie's arms several brisk pats, then stepped back. "Get your things. We'll pick up the ring, and I'll help you file the report with the police. And then I'm taking you out for dinner."

Kenzie paused midway to the employee

cubbies. "Oh, Ruby, no. You don't need to do that. Taking me to the station is more than enough."

"Honey, I want to." Tears winked in Ruby's blue eyes. "You're very special to me, and I'll miss you like crazy when you're gone. I want as many minutes with you as I can grab before you pack your bags and return to Indiana."

Kenzie's heart rolled over. "All right. Thank you." As she retrieved her jacket and fanny pack, she battled tears. She was going home. She had to. But she would miss Ruby and the others so much. Leaving her dear friends was going to be a lot harder than she'd realized.

Bradleyville
Lori

Lori sat across the crackling fire from Jase and enjoyed the glow bringing out the gold in his hair and beard. Each contour of his face, including his whisker-covered dimples, became prominent as light from the flickering flames danced across his features. Ribbons of smoke twirled upward, inviting her gaze to follow the wisps and take in the expanse of heavens above, but she couldn't tear her focus from Jase. She recognized the light, fluttery feeling in her chest. She felt the way Mom had told her she'd someday feel when the right man came into her life. She'd fallen in love.

When she'd called Jase during her noon break, she hadn't expected to be invited to participate in the youth group's May Day basket delivery. She hadn't been completely sure she wanted to participate. Hang out with a bunch of teenagers? She hadn't enjoyed being around teen girls even when she was one. But she'd offered to help as needed, and she couldn't turn down an opportunity to be with Jase. And she'd enjoyed the evening. Every part of it — going house to house and leaving fragrant bunches of lilacs on porches, watching the kids joke with one another and call "Happy May Day! God bless you!" to the people who caught them making the deliveries, and handing out the roasting sticks, hot dogs, and colorful marshmallow chicks to the kids.

Mostly, she enjoyed being included.

Maybe being included contributed to the wonderful airy lift in her chest. She'd wanted a place to belong — a feeling of family — and she had it in church, but tonight was different. Better. Because of Jase. He'd been in Bradleyville only a month, but from all appearances, he'd settled in completely. As ridiculous as it sounded even to her, it seemed as if he'd been with them forever.

She'd never had a boyfriend, not even in high school. She'd wondered if she ever would. As Dad had often told her, what boy would want a wild-haired, tubby, too-prone-to-giggles girlfriend? But Jase had accepted her as is. She couldn't call him her boyfriend. But he was her friend. Her supportive, attentive, accepting friend. And even if that was all he ever was, she thought she could be content. Because with his help and lots of prayers, she was starting to like herself. Which was a really good feeling, too.

Zack, sitting on her left, set his roasting stick aside. "Hey, Brother Jase, is it okay if we sing a couple songs?"

Jase smiled across the fire. "Did you bring your guitar?"

Cullen, who slouched between Jase and Emma, rolled his eyes. "Doesn't he always bring his guitar? I swear, it's like an extra appendage."

Emma nudged Cullen with her elbow, her eyes widening in mock surprise. "Why, Cullen Wade, how impressive."

He frowned at her. "What?"

"You know the word *appendage*." Emma patted his shoulder. "You even used it correctly in a sentence. Good job." Several other kids laughed.

Cullen scowled. "Ah, knock it off."

Emma grinned. She turned to Zack. "C'mon, Zack, make use of that extra appendage."

Cullen unfolded himself from the blanket he and Jase were sitting on. "I'll get it." He left the circle and trotted to a car at the edge of the parking lot. He dug in the back seat and returned with Zack's guitar. He handed it to Zack and then plopped onto the grass behind Jennifer.

Zack put the guitar in position and accidentally elbowed Lori. "Oh. Sorry."

"It's okay." Lori scooted over and bumped into Ari. "Whoops! Excuse me."

"Sister Lori, come over here. There's room."

Goose bumps broke out over Lori's frame at Jase's smooth invitation. She looked at him, and he patted the spot Cullen had vacated. Whispers rolled around the circle, and all eyes seemed to watch her as she made her way behind the kids to the opposite side of the fire. When she sat next to Jase, Sienna and Kaia bumped shoulders and giggled. Lori winked at them, and they giggled harder.

"All right, gang, how 'bout this . . ." Zack strummed a chord and began to sing. " 'You called me from the grave by name. You called me out of all my shame . . .' "

Jase and the kids joined Zack, but Lori couldn't sing. Even though she had what her high school music teacher had called a pure soprano and she'd always enjoyed singing, at that moment, a huge knot tangled her vocal cords. Not one note could escape. *"You called me out of all my shame."* God had used Jase to call her from her shame, and she would never be the same.

While the others sang through the verses and chorus of the song, she inwardly praised the One who loved her the way she was but loved her too much to leave her incomplete. Her chains were falling away. Alleluia!

Jase

Jase sang, but with less enthusiasm than the kids exhibited. Mainly because he was afraid he'd made a mistake by inviting Lori to sit beside him. He'd sent a message to the kids, for sure. Their smirks, nudges, and snickers had let him know what they thought his invitation meant. Did Lori assume the same thing?

Maybe a part of him *had* intended to send a message. He liked Lori. Liked her a lot. When she smiled and her dimples deepened in her rosy cheeks, she lit up the whole room. She had an infectious laugh, and she wasn't hesitant about using it. Joy seemed to explode out of her at times, and it drew him in. When she'd fallen apart in front of him last week, it'd been all he could do not to take her in his arms and comfort her. He'd kept himself from giving in, though, because he didn't want to send mixed signals.

They were supposed to be friends. Him and Lori and Kenzie. Only friends. And they needed to stay that way for lots of reasons. The most pressing one being he wasn't sure where he stood with God. Lori was dealing with enough emotional angst without him dumping his uncertainties on her. Besides, as much as he liked Lori, he still thought about Rachel. Even more since he'd lost her ring. No. The timing was all wrong for him to dive into a new relationship. He shouldn't allow anything more than friendship to develop.

While they transitioned into another song, the fire retreated to bright coals with a few little bluish flames licking at the remaining chunks of charred birch. The air cooled significantly, and full dark surrounded them. Time to end the gathering. Jase waited until Zack strummed the final cord, and then he stood. "All right, y'all, let's join hands."

The kids muttered, but they stood and took hold. Lori slid her hand into Jase's and at the same time gave him a sweet smile. Yep, he needed to wrestle these rioting feelings into submission. And quick.

He prayed, then asked the kids to gather up the leftover food and roasting sticks and take them all to the Krafts' house. Lori supervised them. Cullen stood to the side and watched Zack and Jase pour buckets of water over the coals until the whole pit was a soggy mess. Jase gave Zack a light clap on the shoulder. "Okay, that looks good. Thanks. Would you mind putting the buckets on the Krafts' back porch?"

"Sure." Zack slung his guitar over his shoulder, stacked the buckets, and headed for the parsonage. Cullen started to follow.

"Cullen, hold up."

The boy turned around. With the only light from a single streetlamp at the edge of the church's parking lot and Cullen's face shadowed by the brim of his ever-present cap, Jase couldn't make out the boy's features, but he surmised he was being given a scowl. "What?"

"Can we talk a minute?"

Cullen's heels dragged, carving paths in

the gravel as he scuffed near. "What about?"

They should've gone inside, where Jase could see the boy's face. Then again, maybe it was better out here in the dark, where he wouldn't know if Cullen was shooting belligerent glares. He placed his hand on Cullen's shoulder, deliberately keeping a light grip. "Something I hope you'll be honest with me about."

Cullen's muscles tensed. "What?"

"The afternoon I found you in my apartment."

"I already told you, man, I didn't *break* and enter. I just entered."

Defensiveness colored the boy's tone. Jase paused for a moment, gathering patience. "I know. But when you were in my apartment, before I got there, did you . . . take anything?"

Silence fell. A heavy silence, as black as the night. Cullen's jaw twitched, and Jase waited for a denial. An angry outburst. Anything. But the youth kept his lips closed tight.

Jase sighed. "Listen, Cullen, I just need to know. I want you to be honest with me so I feel like I can trust you. I wanna be able to get along with you, but it's hard to do when I'm not sure I believe you."

Cullen knocked Jase's hand aside. "Okay,

yeah, so I took something. Sheesh, why's it such a big deal? It's not like you've got a girl living with you. You didn't need it. And I thought my mom might like it."

Jase's pulse seemed to blast into overdrive, and his ears began to buzz. If he hadn't known better, he'd say his mouth filled with cotton. He wasn't sure he could talk, but he pushed the question past his dry throat. "What did you take?"

Twenty-Eight

Jase

"A magazine."

Jase drew back. He'd heard wrong. He didn't subscribe to any magazines. Was Cullen making up another story? "A magazine? Are you sure?"

"Yeah. One of those sales magazines."

"You mean a catalog?"

"Whatever. It had ladies' clothes in it."

Jase recalled finding a thin catalog from an online women's retailer in his mailbox, but he'd thrown the thing in his recycling bin. Cullen had gone through his recycling?

"My mom doesn't have time to go shopping in actual stores. She buys everything from the internet. I didn't think you'd wear anything from it." Cullen coughed a laugh. "Would you?"

Jase held back a sharp retort. If Cullen had dug through a recycling bin, he might've rummaged through other containers. Including Jase's whatnot box. "You're sure you didn't take anything else?"

"Like what?"

"Like a piece of jewelry?"

"Jewelry? There wasn't nothin' like that around. Just mail." He jammed his hands into his hoodie pocket and dropped his head back, face aimed at the sky. "So maybe I should've left your mail alone. But, sheesh, most of it was addressed to Occupant. Not like I stole your Social Security check or something."

The crunch of shoes on gravel intruded from behind Jase. He glanced back. Lori stopped several feet away, her puzzled expression touched by the streetlamp's glow.

She pointed over her shoulder with her thumb. "Cullen, Zack asked me to let you know he's ready to leave."

Cullen took a sideways step. "He's giving me a ride home. My mom's working second shift at the gas station in Derby."

Jase nodded at the boy. "All right. You better go."

Cullen turned.

"And, Cullen?"

Cullen didn't face Jase, but he stood still.

"Thanks for being honest with me."

"Yeah. Okay." Cullen took off at a trot. He passed Lori and returned her soft "Bye" before he hopped into Zack's car. As Zack drove away, Lori ambled to Jase.

"Everything okay?"

Jase considered Lori's question. So many things weren't okay. Yet with her smiling up at him under a starlit sky, her unruly mass of copper-colored corkscrews waving in the breeze, he didn't want to list them. He wanted to enjoy the moment. And it scared him. Should he enjoy a peaceful, almost intimate moment with another woman? Or would his actions betray Rachel?

He hung his head. "I don't know." Lori couldn't possibly realize he'd answered his inner questions rather than her spoken one.

"Look, the whole church knows that Cullen's a handful." She released a light laugh. The breeze tossed her curls across her cheek, and one strand caught in her shiny lip gloss. She tugged it loose and pushed it behind her ear. "He always has been, so don't feel bad if he gives you a hard time."

Jase watched her hair lift and bounce in the breeze. "You seemed to get along with him pretty well tonight. With all the kids, really. Have you worked with the youth before?"

She shook her head. The stubborn strand came loose and blew across her cheek again.

She grimaced and tucked it aside. "Nope. I've fed 'em but never really hung out with 'em." She sighed, a contented-cat look on her face. "It was kind of fun. Surprised me a little." She eased a few inches closer, tipping her head slightly and keeping her eyes locked on his. "You surprised me, too."

He forced a laugh. "Oh, yeah? How?"

"By asking me to help tonight. I mean, Sister Kraft and Brother Kraft were right here. They could've done it."

Given Brother Kraft's recent health situation, Jase wouldn't ask him. But he couldn't tell Lori without breaking a confidence. "Well, Sister Kraft did quite a bit. She cut a bunch of flowers, gave us the cards we put in the baskets, and provided most of the food and the wood for the fire."

Lori's frame shivered. "Speaking of fires, it's a lot colder than I realized now that the fire is out. Could we maybe go inside the church to talk? Or someplace else? Your apartment, maybe?"

He'd invited Lori and Kenzie to his apartment for Chinese takeout earlier in the week and he hadn't thought anything of it. But Lori by herself? It'd send another message, and if he wasn't willing to follow the presumptions with reality, he shouldn't lead her on. Turning her down would probably hurt her feelings, but telling her yes could get her hopes up for something more than friendship. What was best? They couldn't stand out here in the cool breeze indefinitely. Somebody needed to make a decision.

She sighed. "It is kinda late, and tomorrow's my Saturday at the shop. We had a really full house today so it'll need quite a bit of sweeping and straightening, I'm sure. I guess I should go ahead and —"

Jase reached for her but didn't touch her. "Lori, it isn't you."

Her eyebrows came together.

"You're an amazing woman. I like you." His hand hung in the space between them like a broken bridge. "I like you a lot."

Her cheeks glowed bold pink. She ducked her head. "I like you, too."

"But there are so many things I don't — I'm still so new here, and — I don't want to let you down."

Her face lifted, and she gave him the sweetest smile. "That was a very ferhoodled speech."

He frowned. "A what speech?"

"Ferhoodled. It's a Kenzie word. It means kind of mixed up."

An accurate description, then. For his speech. For his life.

392

She shook her head, sending her wind-tossed curls aside, and grinned. "Look, I don't expect anything more than friendship from you."

Her words were confident, even a little smug, but something in her eyes made him wonder if she was being honest with him and with herself. He started to lower his hand, but she caught hold of it between both of hers.

"I realize you've only been here a short time. I realize you still miss Rachel. I won't push myself on you. But when you need help with the youth again, gimme a holler. If you wanna go grab a bite to eat after church on Sundays or some evening, I'm game. And if you just wanna pray for me from afar, that's worth a lot. No need to get all ferhoodled. Okay?"

Ferhoodled. What a fun word. It made a serious topic feel not so heavy. "Lori, I —" His cell phone vibrated in his jacket pocket, and he jumped.

She squeezed his hand, then let go. "You take that. I'm gonna head on home. See you Sunday, Brother Jase."

There was much he should say. Only a coward would keep quiet about his unfitness as a minister and let her think she held no place in his heart. He was definitely a

393

coward, because he watched her get into her car, listened to the engine start, then watched her drive away. All while he stood still as a statue at the edge of the parking area and his cell phone went to voice mail.

When her taillights disappeared, he walked to his apartment and let himself in. The little fixture above the kitchen sink he always left burning provided enough light for him to find his way to the couch. He flopped onto the center cushion, let out a mighty whoosh of breath, then pulled his cell phone free from his pocket. He scowled at the number showing as a missed call. Probably spam. But they'd left a message. Might as well listen to it before deleting it. It'd give him a distraction from his troubled thoughts. He pushed the voice mail icon, set the phone to speaker, and plopped the phone on the side table.

"Mr. Edgar, this is Officer Pratt from the Sedgwick County Police Department. You turned in a report on a missing diamond ring. Today a ring was turned into the office, and it closely matches the description you gave us."

Jase shot off the sofa and stood trembling in the middle of the shadowy living room.

"Please come by any Monday through Friday between 8:00 a.m. and 6:00 p.m. to look at it. If you have a photograph of your ring, please

bring it with you for comparison. Again, this is Officer Pratt. You can ask for me, but if I'm not here, reference case number —"

He scrambled for a pencil and paper to write the series of digits. His hands shook so badly he doubted he'd be able to read his own writing later on. The recording ended, and Jase remained in place with his fingers curled around the pencil so tightly he was surprised it didn't break.

Hope beat like the wings of a moth against the sides of a jar. Was it possible? Had Rachel's ring been found?

Wichita
Lori

Lucky her, working the Saturday after the store's May Day Extravaganza. Lori pushed the broom between aisles. How many cookie crumbs had she swept up already? And here were more, clear at the opposite end of the store from where Ruby had set up the treats table. People were messy. And sadder yet? The sight of those crumbs made her stomach rumble and saliva pool under her tongue.

She'd been really good last night — only ate one hot dog and three chips at the youth party. And even though being basically dismissed by Jase at the end of the evening had stung her heart mightily, she hadn't eaten a thing when she got home. But this morning, after a night of wrestling with feelings of insignificance and doubt, if there were leftover cookies in the store, she'd want to snarf them as fast as Cookie Monster on *Sesame Street* ever had. Thanks to words of advice from both Jase and Kenzie and wise counsel from Brother Kraft, she could recognize her food-frenzy triggers. Recognition, Brother Kraft had told her, would help her remember to stop and process her feelings before diving headfirst into a pizza box or an ice cream carton or a —

"Lori?"

Lori paused in sweeping and looked to the end of the aisle. Barbara balanced a platter on her palm the way servers at fancy social gatherings offered guests hors d'oeuvres. Lori'd only seen it in movies, never in real life. Before now.

"Ruby put together a snack tray to reward us for our hard work yesterday." Barbara's gaze roved the large plastic platter. "Crackers and cheese, olives, hard salami, grapes, gingersnaps, and chocolate-covered fancy mixed nuts."

Until Barbara mentioned the chocolate-covered nuts, Lori's temptation remained in check. But . . . chocolate. Sweet, creamy, satisfying chocolate. Feet still planted on the tile floor, she strained toward the platter.

"I'm putting it in the break room refrigerator, so help yourself when you go in." Barbara departed, taking the tray and its tempting treats with her.

Lori wrapped her hands around the broom handle and squeezed. Last night they'd sung around the firepit about the Holy Spirit living inside a believer, about God's resurrection power. While the kids sang, she inwardly celebrated how her shame was falling away. She had a choice — resist temptation and walk in freedom or submit to it and wallow in shame.

But chocolate . . .

Help me, Holy Spirit. Be my filler-upper, the way Jase said You'd be. Gimme Your power, like You gave Jase. Don't let me cave. Please, please don't let me cave.

Kenzie

After a half hour or so of frustration, Kenzie finally managed to deactivate the email account Ruby had set up for people to contact her about the ring. According to Ruby, Eileen had already deleted the original post and said the action should take it off the internet completely. She hoped so.

With the ring and the post taken care of, she turned to a fresh page in the spiral notebook she used to record her loom projects, and she began a list.

Things to Do Before I Can Leave

1. Find the money to buy a bus ticket to Indianapolis and arrange ride to Flourish
2. Decide if I'm going for good or for a while

She stared at the second item on her list. Maybe she should make it first instead. Everything hinged on whether she intended to move home or only stay for a visit. After living away from the sect and its strict confines and after experiencing the freedom granted by living under grace, the thought of making Flourish her permanent home created a rock in her belly. God wanted her to go. She'd never deny His tug. But did He expect her to stay?

As much as she hated to bother Brother Kraft on a Saturday, she needed advice, and he would give her godly counsel. She pulled up the Krafts' number on her cell phone and pushed Call.

"Hello?" Brother Kraft's warm, fatherly voice greeted her.

Kenzie automatically smiled. "Good morning, Brother Kraft. This is Kenzie Stetler. Am I bothering you?"

"No, not at all. What can I do for you?"

"Well, I hope you can help me know for sure what I'm supposed to do." Before she called, her stomach had felt tangled in knots. But as she shared God's prompting for her to return to Indiana and the uncertainties surrounding the move, her taut muscles relaxed. Brother Kraft occasionally murmured "Mm-hmm" or said "I see," letting her know he was listening closely. She finished with "What do you think God is asking of me? To stay in Flourish or only visit Flourish?"

A long silence fell at the other end of the line, and Kenzie stayed quiet, too. She sensed her advisor was seeking his advisor's wisdom, and she wouldn't interrupt.

"Kenzie, may I ask you some questions?"

She pressed the phone tight to her head. "Yes."

"The reasons you decided not to join the church and stay in Flourish, do those still apply?"

"Yes, sir."

"Do you believe God brought you to

399

Wichita?"

She thought back to the circumstances that led her to this city. "Yes, sir, I do."

"What happens if someone with flour on her apron asks to hug you and you say yes?"

The question seemed so out of place that Kenzie released a puzzled laugh. "Well, I probably get flour on me."

"And then if you offer to hug someone else and they agree, does flour transfer to them?"

Had Brother Kraft forgotten what they were talking about? She shrugged. "I guess it can."

His chuckle carried through the connection. "That's right. It certainly can. Now, Kenzie, replace the idea of flour with the gospel message. When you were on your rumspringe, someone told you about Jesus and you accepted Him for yourself. They could deliver the message because at some time in the past, they'd accepted the message of salvation through Christ."

A light was dawning in the back of Kenzie's mind. She nodded slowly. "Yes. Yes, they could."

"God is prompting you to carry the message to Flourish and share it with your family. If they accept Jesus's gift of salvation, will they be able to tell someone else?"

She imagined a dusting of flour being transferred from her dress to Grossmammi's apron to Daed's coveralls to Caleb's twill shirt, and a smile tugged at her cheeks. "Of course they can."

"Good. Good." The approval in his tone warmed Kenzie and completely chased away the boulder of nervousness. "All right. One more question. Before you make the trip, would you find time to come to my office so Sister Kraft, Brother Jase, and I may pray with you?"

Kenzie's vision went blurry. She blinked, sniffing, and nodded. "I'd like that very much."

TWENTY-NINE

Bradleyville
Jase

He knew it was coming. Brother Kraft had called Jase yesterday about Kenzie's intention to visit her Amish family and his plan to send her off with the prayerful support of the congregation. So the minister's request for him to come to the front of the church at the end of the service didn't take Jase by surprise. But it still sent butterflies through his stomach.

He eased out of the second pew, careful not to step on Cullen's feet, and met Brother Kraft and Kenzie at the front. What else could he do? He was a minister in the church. He'd be a member of the Sunday school class Kenzie attended if he wasn't teaching the youth during the same hour. Of course he should be part of Kenzie's commissioning to take the gospel to her former community. But how awkward he

402

felt. How many memories it stirred. A little over a year ago, he and Rachel had knelt together at the front of the church while Brother Tony and two deacons prayed for them. Look where those prayers had led.

God, if You're there, give me words to say. Something helpful. Something meaningful. And fulfill Kenzie's call. Not a request, a command. *Don't yank it away from her, the way You stole mine and left me rudderless.*

Brother Kraft draped his arm around Kenzie's shoulders and smiled at the congregation. "Folks, you all know Kenzie. She's been a faithful, active member of Beech Street Bible Fellowship for over two years now, works at the fabric shop with Leah's sister Ruby, and bakes some of the meanest brownies in the history of the world."

Light laughter rolled, and Kenzie's cheeks blotched bright pink. Jase couldn't resist grinning at her reaction. Her modest way of dressing and humble spirit were as sweet and uncommon as the flavor of her wonderful brownies.

"Some of you might not know, though, that she was raised in an Amish sect. Until she was introduced to Jesus, she thought she had to earn her way to heaven by obeying the laws of her community. But she discovered the freedom that comes from grace, and now God is leading her to return to her former home and share His truth with her family."

Applause broke out over the congregation, and Jase joined in. The clapping tapered off, and Brother Kraft gestured to the prayer bench in front of the pulpit.

"Kenzie, would you kneel, please?" Brother Kraft waited until Kenzie knelt and folded her hands. Then he placed his hand on her shoulder. He shifted his attention to the congregation. "If there's anyone else who would like to come forward and pray for Kenzie, feel free to join us."

Jase wasn't surprised at all when Sister Kraft and Lori left their seats and came up. Two of the couples and the teacher from the young adult Sunday school class joined them, followed by ladies from the kitchen team and three of the deacons. They created quite a crowd, and those who couldn't reach Kenzie placed their hands on the ones who could, connecting all of them.

A shudder went through Jase's frame. The firm pressure of a hand cupped on his shoulder and another against his spine sent him backward in time to the church in San Antonio. Longing to return to the faith and assurance he'd had the day the deacons prayed for him and Rachel became so intense he began to quiver, and he couldn't make it stop.

"Our dear heavenly Father, the one who calls us to service meant to bring glory to God and joy to the obedient one's heart . . ."

Jase closed his eyes so tightly stars danced behind his lids. He listened to Brother Kraft's request for God to grant Kenzie courage and strength and wisdom, to bless her and open the hearts of her family members to receive true salvation. The words were similar to those offered for him and Rachel. Beautiful words. Soul-stirring words. Sincere words offered from a sincere heart. Words that had come to nothing for him.

Brother Kraft finished, and one of the deacons prayed. Then Sister Kraft, then a kitchen lady, and then Lori, who spoke so softly and brokenly Jase could barely hear her. His heart went out to her. She and Kenzie were so close. She'd miss her friend. He hoped Kenzie's departure wouldn't send Lori down a path of uncontrolled eating. She'd need prayer, too.

With a shuddering breath, Lori fell silent.

Seconds ticked by.

Jase was supposed to close the time of commissioning. Brother Kraft had given him the responsibility. He needed to say something. He cleared his throat. "God . . ." Whoever was touching his back gave him an encouraging pat. He searched his anguished mind for something worth saying out loud and cleared his throat again. "God, thank You for Kenzie's willingness to serve You. Bless her. Amen."

"Amen," everyone echoed, and the group surrounding the prayer bench stepped back.

Kenzie rose, her tearstained cheeks glowing pink, and sent a shy smile around the circle of faces. "Thank you."

Brother Kraft put his arm around her again and beamed at the congregation. "Everyone, keep this young lady in your prayers. She has quite a journey ahead of her, and God hasn't put all the pieces in place yet." He turned his warm smile on Kenzie, giving a little nod. "But when He calls, He also equips, and we trust He'll make the way, yes?"

Kenzie smiled through tears. "Yes."

Jase remembered being so sure. He wanted it again. *Show up, God. Show up for Kenzie.* He gulped. *And show up for me.*

Lori

Brother Kraft had Kenzie remain at the front and invited people to come up and give her a "holy hug" before leaving. Lori gave Kenzie a tight, lengthy squeeze and whispered, "We're doing lunch, right?" At Kenzie's nod, she exited through the sanctuary's side door and walked around to the foyer.

Jase was already there, holding the front door open with his hip and shaking hands with folks as they left. Lori hung back, half of her wanting to approach him and the other half afraid to go. But why the fear? They'd enjoyed how many meals as a trio of friends? Today didn't need to be different. But somehow, underneath, it was, and she hated it.

At a break in the line, she forced her feet to carry her forward, and she touched Jase's elbow. "Hey. Kenz and me are going to a pizza bar for lunch. Wanna come?"

Relief seemed to flood his features. He nodded, the movement exuberant. "I do. Thanks, Lori."

She gave a quick smile and darted off, her heart pounding in happiness. Their friendship must not be demolished if he wanted to continue their Sunday noon get-togethers. Especially knowing she'd be without Kenzie's company soon, maintaining her relationship with Jase mattered. She didn't want to lose both of her best friends.

Lori followed the routine that had become second nature over the past couple of weeks. She locked the back door, turned off all but the emergency lights, and made sure no one had left a faucet running in the kitchen or bathrooms. She returned to the front doors as Brother and Sister Kraft escorted Kenzie from the sanctuary.

Sister Kraft bounced a grin over Jase, Lori, and Kenzie. "I've got a roast, potatoes, and carrots in the oven. Brother James and his wife are joining us, but there's plenty if you'd like to come, too."

Jase looked at Lori, and Lori looked at Kenzie. Kenzie looked back, uncertainty etched in her features.

Sister Kraft laughed. "All right, it's clear you three have other plans and don't want to hurt an old lady's feelings. Go — enjoy your time together." She slipped her hand through the bend of Brother Kraft's elbow, and the two left.

Lori caught hold of Kenzie's arm the same way, then sent a hesitant smile at Jase. "Wanna ride with us?"

"Sounds perfect."

His answer filled her with happiness.

"And today's lunch is on me." His green-blue gaze met Lori's eyes and held. "No arguments. I owe you."

He didn't owe her anything, but she chose to accept his offer. She gave Kenzie's arm a little tug. "Let's go."

Lori's mouth watered at the aroma of pepperoni, sausage, and onion rising from the pies lined up on the buffet counter, and it took every bit of self-control she possessed to leave the pizza slices behind. But she couldn't deny a feeling of pride as she settled in a booth next to Kenzie with a healthy salad in hand.

Jase slid in across from Lori and offered a brief prayer. Then they ate. Without talking, except for requests for salt or Parmesan or saying excuse me for bumping elbows or knees. Jase returned to the bar for seconds, and Lori slumped against the booth's padded back. She breathed out a long sigh.

Kenzie sent her a sidelong look. "Are you mad at me?"

Lori zipped her attention to her friend. "No! Why would you think that?"

Kenzie shrugged, fiddling with her fork. "You're so quiet."

Lori cringed. "It's not because of you, Kenz. Jase and me had a . . . I don't know what to call it . . . weird Friday, and I think we aren't sure where to go now."

Kenzie put her hand on Lori's arm.

"Don't blow it."

Lori scrunched her brow. "Don't blow what? My friendship with Jase? That's not all up to me, you know."

Kenzie shook her head. Tears brightened her sky-blue eyes. "Don't blow your new habit. Don't let his quietness make you feel empty."

Now Lori understood. She patted Kenzie's hand. "Don't worry, okay? I admit, it's a constant temptation. But I'm praying extra hard and reminding myself human relationships aren't nearly as important as my relationship with God."

Kenzie's chin quivered, but her eyes smiled. "Who fills you."

Lori nodded. "Yes. When I let Him, He sure does."

Jase returned with a huge salad nearly hidden by a sea of ranch dressing. He jabbed his fork into the mess, looking at Kenzie. "So what's the plan? Do you have a set date to leave?"

Kenzie pushed her empty plate aside and played with her napkin. "A date is the only thing I don't have set. And everything else is on hold until I have the money to buy the ticket."

Lori frowned. "Why didn't Brother Kraft take up a collection for you? I bet people would've given you the money."

Kenzie shook her head, her expression firm. "No. Getting to Indiana is my responsibility. And I told God it's in His timing. When He's ready for me to go, He'll provide. In the meantime, I've got lots to do so I'll be ready to leave when He makes the way."

Jase chewed and swallowed a bite. "What can we do to help?"

"Ruby and Barbara came over last night. They asked if Barbara's niece could sublet my apartment while I'm gone, and of course I said yes." Kenzie rolled the napkin into a tube and formed a cinnamon-roll shape with it while she talked. "I didn't know how I'd pay for it if I wasn't working, and I didn't want to give it up. It's in such a perfect location for me with my job at the fabric shop."

Jase stabbed his salad again. "Ah. So you're not quitting, just taking a leave?"

"Yes." Kenzie dropped the napkin on top of her plate, and it slowly unrolled. "I'm glad Ruby is willing to be flexible. She's been very kind to me."

Lori grinned. "What a relief. I'm glad you plan to come back. I think it'll be bearable to let you go if I know I'll see you again."

Kenzie leaned over and bumped shoulders

411

with Lori — her way of hugging.

Jase carried a dripping bite toward his mouth. "Will Barbara's niece use your furniture and all so you don't have to move things out?"

Kenzie crinkled her nose. "Sort of. I'm fine with her using my furniture, but I didn't feel good about leaving Gross-mammi's loom or my personal things behind. Ruby said I could store the loom and whatever else I needed to in her basement until I get back. We even started boxing some stuff last night."

Jealousy twined through Lori's chest. She should be the one helping Kenzie. They were best friends, after all. "What about all the clothes for weaving your projects? Your hall closet was stacked almost to the ceiling. Do you need help boxing those up?" An idea struck. She grabbed Kenzie's arm. "Oh, hey, instead of storing your loom and all the clothes in Ruby's basement, could they come to my apartment? If you give me some more weaving lessons before you go, I'll make things to send to the mission store for you."

Kenzie's face paled, and Lori realized her mistake. She wasn't supposed to talk about Kenzie's projects. Not in front of anyone outside the store. She bit her lower lip and sent a furtive glance at Jase. He was looking at Kenzie with curiosity lighting his features.

Lori waved her hands, wishing she could scrub her statement from Jase's memory. "Never mind. Stick to your original plan. It'll probably be safer with Ruby than with me, anyway."

To her relief, her ploy turned the tide, and Jase asked about Kenzie's family. Lori already knew about the family's dairy, how many brothers Kenzie had, and that her grandmother lived in a little addition on the back of the farmhouse, so she listened with half an ear. Until Jase spoke her name.

She jolted and looked at him. "What?"

"Kenzie's going home to see her parents. It made me wonder if you've gone to see your dad yet."

Lori swallowed. She shook her head.

"Do you have plans to go anytime soon?"

She'd thought about going to see Dad. She'd thought about it every day since her major meltdown. She needed to do it. She sensed she wouldn't find complete healing from her past until she'd confronted it full on. But beyond thinking and praying, she'd done nothing. Again, Lori shook her head.

"When you do go, you won't go alone, right? You'll take Brother Kraft or somebody with you?"

Lori appreciated the Krafts' willingness to go, but she still worried her dad would see the minister and his wife's arrival as an attack. Layton Fowler had never responded well to people exerting authority over him. Not that Brother Kraft would be pushy. He was a very kind man. But Dad would interpret his presence as pushiness.

Lori lifted one shoulder in an awkward half shrug. "I don't know yet."

Jase put his fork down, his expression stern. "Well, I do know. I'm not at all comfortable with you talking to him by yourself. Not if he's been emotionally abusive in the past. You don't deserve an attack —"

Tingles tiptoed over her scalp. Hadn't her internal voice said the same thing?

"— and shouldn't have to face him unsupported."

Kenzie nodded, her ponytail bouncing. "Exactly. When you go, take Jase with you." She pulled in a breath and sat straight up. "And I want to go, too."

THIRTY

Wichita

Jase

At eight o'clock sharp Monday morning, Jase strode up the sidewalk to the sprawling gray-painted building where he'd filed his report about the missing ring. In his wallet he carried the jeweler's receipt, a black-and-white grainy image provided by the jeweler for insurance purposes, and the receipt for the engraving. He'd come so close to throwing the paperwork away before he moved to Kansas. But he'd decided if he ever wanted to sell the ring, having its value recorded on some kind of official documentation was wise. Now he might use those documents to reclaim what should have been on Rachel's finger. Assuming the ring turned in was Rachel's.

He entered the office, and like last time, the smell of scorched coffee assaulted his nose. His stomach whirled. But it wasn't

415

the odor upsetting him. No, his gut rolled from the effort of tamping down the bubble of hope trying to rise in his chest. He wouldn't let himself believe. Not yet.

He pressed his palm to his belly and crossed to the tall desk. "Good morning."

The middle-aged woman in a blue uniform looked up and smiled. "Good morning. Can I help you?"

"Yes, ma'am. I'm looking for Officer Pratt."

"I'll page him. Please wait over there." She pointed to a row of wooden chairs pressed against the wall beneath a bank of windows.

Jase took a seat in the first chair and tried not to breathe too deep. Maybe the smell did bother him. He took out the receipts and pinched them between his fingers, then rested his elbows on his knees. While shuffling the slips of paper front to back like a hand of cards, he listened to the ring of phones, the mutter of voices, and the click-click of soles on a hard floor. A pair of polished shoes at the end of crisply ironed blue trousers moved into his line of vision.

He lifted his head and met the gaze of the tall dark-haired man who'd taken his report. Jase rose on shaky legs and stuck out his hand. "Officer Pratt." Too late he realized he held the receipts. He grimaced, switched them to his other hand, and tried again.

The officer shook Jase's hand, then pointed to the receipts. "Are these your proof-of-ownership papers?"

"Yes, sir."

Pratt took the items without looking at them, then turned toward a hallway. "Come with me." He led Jase to a long narrow room and walked him to a chest-high desk. He nodded to the man on the other side. "Box fourteen, Barry."

The man bent out of sight, then popped up with a metal box. He handed it across to Pratt. The officer tucked it under his arm and gestured to a table in the corner. "This way."

Jase sat, and Pratt took the chair across from him. Jase chewed the inside of his cheek while the officer used a key and unlocked the box. With the lid up, blocking his view, Jase couldn't see the contents, but he watched Pratt's face. The man examined the paperwork, his gaze flicking to the box's interior from time to time. Then he gave a nod, as if agreeing with something someone said, and turned the box to face Jase.

Jase leaned forward slightly and looked inside. His heart gave such a leap he gasped. He lifted out the small plastic bag holding a wide white-gold band with a single round solitaire diamond. He didn't remove it from the plastic, but he didn't have to. When he tilted the ring, the simple message he'd chosen to prove his lifelong commitment came into view.

From this moment into eternity.

Jase's eyes filled with tears. He hid them with one hand and gripped the little plastic bag with the other. So many emotions crashed through him — gratitude, disbelief, joy, curiosity, even sorrow — he couldn't contain them all. Eyes closed, he clung to Rachel's ring and told himself over and over this moment was real. He had it again. He didn't have her, but he had her ring.

God had shown up.

He gave his eyes a swipe with the heel of his hand and opened them. "Who found it? Can you tell me the person's name?"

"We generally keep that information confidential."

But Jase needed to know if Cullen had been the one. "I — I'd like to thank whoever returned it."

Officer Pratt slid the paperwork for the ring to Jase and shifted the metal box out of the way. "If you'd like to leave a message, we can relay it to the woman who brought it in."

A woman? Then it hadn't been Cullen.

Unless Cullen's mother had brought it. "By any chance, was her last name Wade?"

The officer shook his head. "No. The woman who brought it in said she found it in the pocket of a pair of pants someone had donated for a mission project."

All at once, realization struck with the force of a bucket of cold water thrown in his face, carrying him backward through a series of events, each so clear in his memory the room seemed to disappear behind the images.

Putting her ring in his pocket before picking up Rachel for their date.

Sitting at the stoplight, laughing and talking the way they always did.

Seeing the light turn green and pulling forward, eager to see her reaction when he said, "Oh, look what I picked up today," and handed the newly sized and freshly engraved ring to her.

A flash of motion in his peripheral vision, a crash, and . . . nothing.

His memories faded to blackness, like an old television set losing its picture, and the room in the police station came into focus again. What a fool he'd been. In his grief-numbed state, he'd discarded everything he'd worn that night, not wanting any reminders of the night he lost the woman he loved. And somehow he'd forgotten he put the ring in his pocket.

It hadn't been stolen. It hadn't even been lost. He'd given it away. Strange how his donated pants ended up in Wichita, Kansas. But thanks to the honesty of whoever purchased them, the ring was in his hand again. He wanted to repay the person somehow. Reward them. He had a little over three hundred dollars left in the emergency fund he'd set aside from the insurance payout for his totaled car. He'd gladly hand it over as a token of appreciation.

Jase pressed the fist holding the ring against his galloping heart. "Officer Pratt, you said you could get a message to the person who returned the ring. Would you ask if she'd be willing to meet me? I'd like to give her a reward, and I'd like to give it to her in person. Because what she did . . ." He swallowed. "She gave me back my hope."

Kenzie

Kenzie adjusted the tension on the table loom's warp. Someone, probably a curious child, had fiddled with the dials when she wasn't looking, and now the last few rows were uneven. She slipped the shuttle through the shed, then pulled the beam, taking care with each step of operation and watching the various parts for signs of problems. All went smoothly.

She clamped the tension dial to keep it tight, then reached for the shuttle. Before she could release it through the shed, Ruby rounded the corner, waving her cell phone over her head.

"Kenzie, you'll never guess who just called."

Someone important, based on Ruby's excitement. She gave her boss her full attention. "Who?"

"Officer Dillard Pratt from the Sedgwick County Police Department. The owner of the ring has been identified, has picked it up, and" — her voice rose in pitch and volume with every phrase — "wants to meet with you and give you a reward!"

Kenzie's jaw dropped. When they'd filled out the paperwork at the police station, they'd put Ruby as the finder since Kenzie intended to discontinue using cell service when she went to Indiana. She hadn't expected to know what happened to the ring, and her heart gave a flip of joy. "They found the owner already?" She couldn't hold back a laugh. "All those emails I read through, and all the worrying I did was for *nichts* — for nothing. I guess I should've taken it there as soon as I found it."

Ruby laughed, too. "Well, blame me for the delay. The social media search was my idea." She bounced the cell phone on her palm. "I'm supposed to call the officer back and let him know when we can meet the owner."

Kenzie chewed her lip. "Why should I be rewarded for giving something back that was never mine to start with? Besides, I feel funny about meeting up with someone I don't know. I don't think my daed would approve."

Ruby released a little huff. "Now, I wouldn't send you off on a dangerous rendezvous. The meeting will be at the police station, so no worries about safety." She clasped her hands as if she were praying. "I'd like to know who owned that beautiful ring with its romantic inscription. I don't get a lot of excitement, so humor me. Let's meet the owner."

Kenzie looked into Ruby's hopeful face, and she melted. "Okay. Set it up. But not for today. Brother Jase and I have an errand with Lori."

Ruby tapped her chin with her finger. "How about we try to arrange it on your off-schedule day? You're not working on Wednesday this week, right?"

Kenzie nodded.

"I'll make sure both Barbara and Van are here. Then I'll be free to drive you over." She clapped her hands. "Oh, this is fun! A real-life mystery solved." She winked. "I can't wait to tell Eileen. She'll be so tickled!" She hurried off.

Kenzie sat for a moment, frowning at the end of the aisle where Ruby had disappeared from view. Meeting the ring's owner might be okay. Especially at a safe place with Ruby along. But she wasn't sure about accepting a reward. Shouldn't doing good be reward enough? She'd thank the person for the offer but not take the money. Then her conscience would be clear.

THIRTY-ONE

Lori

Lori stopped on the concrete slab outside the door to her family's modest 1950s ranch-style home. When Mom was alive, potted flowers sat at both corners and a bent wire holder with different flags for each month of the year hung on the door. May's had tulips on it. Where were those flags now?

Kenzie and Jase stepped up onto the stoop beside her. Kenzie gave Lori a worried look. "Are you going in?"

Lori huffed out a mighty breath. "I don't know, guys. Maybe this isn't smart. Maybe it'd be better for me to let sleeping dogs lie, you know what I mean?"

Jase placed his hand on her shoulder, barely a touch. "If you really want to change your mind, we won't argue with you. But as I recall, you set three goals. To pray more, to put your focus on someone besides yourself, and to make peace with your dad."

How had he remembered all that? He must really listen when she talked. She found it both flattering and intimidating. "I know, and I am praying more. I'm saving up to buy one of the looms at the shop so I can contribute to" — she glanced at Kenzie, choosing her words carefully — "an important cause. Two out of three. That's worth something, isn't it?"

Kenzie nodded. "It is. It's worth a lot. But, Lori, be honest with yourself. What will you regret more — failing at an honest attempt to reconcile or not even trying and spending the rest of your life wondering what might have been?"

The pressure of Jase's hand increased. "She gave you some wise advice there. I'd listen to her, if I was you."

Lori stared at Kenzie for a few seconds, then at Jase, and she let out another huff. "All right. You're right. If I don't at least try, there's no hope. We should always grab for hope, right?"

A smile curved Jase's lips, a content, almost secretive smile she'd never seen on his face before. It raised myriad questions in her mind, but she didn't have a chance to ask even one. He reached past her and rang the doorbell.

Lori held her breath, watching the door,

waiting, silently counting seconds to distract herself . . . *eight, nine, ten, el*— The door creaked open, and her youngest brother, Laban, stood on the other side of the threshold.

Lori gave a little jolt, just as she'd done on Easter Sunday when he answered the door. Had he grown even more since then? Laban was so tall. As tall as Jase. He didn't look like a boy anymore, either. He'd been a lanky fourteen-year-old eager to take over her room when she moved out of the house. Since she'd only seen him on holidays over the past five years, she was always taken by surprise at how much he'd changed. She needed to spend more time with her brothers. She'd let her issues with Dad keep them apart, but she needed to make a better effort to be in their lives.

Laban rolled his eyes. "Why'd ya ring the bell, goofball? You used to live here. It's still kinda your house, you know." Then his gaze skittered to Jase and Kenzie, and his brow puckered. "Who're they?"

Lori forced her quivering lips to smile. "These are my friends. We came to see Dad. Is he home?"

Laban glanced over his shoulder. "He's home. Watching the sports channel." He leaned closer, pulling the door halfway closed behind him. "He's already had a few. Sure you wanna come in?"

She'd had to gather up so much courage to come this time, she wasn't sure she'd be able to do it again. Besides, she had re-inforcements with her and lots of prayers behind her. She whispered, " 'The LORD is with me; I will not be afraid. What can mere mortals do to me?' "

Laban drew back. "Are you quoting Shakespeare?"

Lori laughed, and it refreshed her more than she could express. "No. That's Psalm 118:6." She tossed a grin at Kenzie and Jase. "Let's go in, and I'll introduce you to my dad."

Laban led them through the familiar living room with its same 1980s floral sofa and matching side chairs arranged in a rectangle on the burnt-orange shag carpet and then past the eat-in kitchen. A wide cased opening gave her a view of the room Dad and a couple of his pals added on to the back of the house the year after Laban was born. Dad called it a family room, but they'd all known it was Dad's room. Apparently it still was.

He sat in his recliner, its footrest up, with a can of beer in his hand and his attention glued to the big-screen television mounted on the opposite wall. The drapes were drawn and the floor lamp beside his chair was off. The only light came from the television set, giving the room a gloomy appearance. Lori stifled a shiver.

Dad didn't even look over when they entered. "Who was at the door?"

Laban glanced at Lori, a warning in his eyes. "Lori. And some friends of hers."

Dad kicked the footrest down. "What's the matter?"

Laban quietly left the room.

"Nothing's the matter, Dad." Lori crossed in front of her dad's chair, gesturing for Jase and Kenzie to follow. The three of them sat on the sofa, with Lori closest to Dad's recliner and Jase in the middle. "I wanted to talk to you, and my good friends came with me so I could introduce you. They wanted to meet you."

"Why?" He smoothed his hand over his age-speckled head. He'd been bald on top for as long as Lori could remember. In her younger years, he grew the hair on the right side of his head long and combed the strands toward his left ear, but she'd noticed at Easter he'd given up the comb-over. She thought his gray hair looked better cropped short, even if it did mean having no coverage up top.

"Like I said, my friends wanted to meet you." She held her hand toward Jase. "Dad, this is Jase Edgar. He's the new youth minister at Beech Street Bible Fellowship." She flipped her hand toward Kenzie. "And maybe you remember me talking about Kenzie. She works with me at Prairie Meadowlark. Jase and Kenzie, this is my dad, Layton Fowler."

Both Jase and Kenzie said hello, but Dad acted like he didn't hear them. He shifted his focus to the television.

Lori cleared her throat. "Dad?"

He grunted.

"Can you turn off the TV for a minute? I'd like to talk to you."

He glowered at the television for a few seconds, then punched the button on the remote. "Make it quick. I have things to do."

Lori glanced at Jase, and he gave her an encouraging nod. She turned to her dad. "I came to apologize." Now, why had she said that? She'd meant to ask questions, not ask for forgiveness.

"What for?"

She couldn't backtrack now. And she realized she didn't want to. "For not getting along with you. It bothers me. We weren't always at odds. I remember when I was little. We had fun then." Her nose stung, a

429

sure sign tears were coming. "But it's so different now. What'd I do to make you dislike me?"

His thick brows, still dark, formed a sharp V. "You're not easy. The boys, they were easy. But you?" He snorted, shaking his head. "Moody. Absentminded. Especially after Estella died. It's like you lost your mind."

Lori bit back a protest. She'd only been twelve when Mom died. She'd missed her like crazy. Maybe she had lost her mind a little bit. She'd nearly lost herself under a layer of fat, trying to eat herself to a place of peace.

Dad tapped the armrest with the remote, his scowl deep. "I didn't know what to do with you. The boys, they bucked up. But you? You didn't want me. You only wanted your mother. There wasn't one single thing I could do for you, so I quit trying. Easier that way."

Easier? Easier for who? Instead of rejecting her, couldn't Dad have told her she'd be okay? They'd get through it together? She'd been lost without Mom. She'd needed comfort. Badly.

But maybe so had Dad.

Had he felt as empty as she had? A memory crept from the recesses of her mind —

of her big, strong dad sobbing late one night when she should've been asleep. She'd stood outside his bedroom door, silent tears rolling warm down her cheeks. Oh, how she'd wanted to make things better, but she couldn't bring Mom back. She'd been helpless against Dad's sorrow, so she'd scuffed back to her room and cried, alone, under her covers. Maybe he'd been helpless against her sorrow, too.

Back then, he'd been the adult and she the child. But she was an adult now. She could offer the understanding he'd needed and hadn't received. She leaned forward. "My mourning must've tormented you. I know you missed her. It must've been hard."

"I still miss her. It's still hard." He lifted the can to his lips and took several noisy gulps.

Lori put her hand on the recliner's armrest, next to Dad's arm. "I know."

"And I don't need you and your sad face reminding me of her. Reminding me what I don't have." He turned a watery frown on her. "Every time you come around, you're morose, morose, morose."

She hung her head. "You're right. I am sad when I'm here." She forced herself to meet his unsmiling gaze. "But my sad face isn't because of Mom anymore. The way you talk to me, using a gruff voice and saying things that are unkind . . . those things make me sad, Dad."

He faced the black television screen. "How else am I supposed to make you buck up? You can't spend the rest of your life looking back. You gotta go forward."

Was he talking to her now or to himself? She sent up a silent prayer for wisdom, then spoke softly. "You're right. We've gotta go forward." She pulled in a deep breath. "I miss having a mom, and I also miss having a dad. I can't get Mom back. But, Dad, can we maybe try to be father and daughter? I'd really like to try."

His stiff frame drooped, and his head sagged. "What do you expect from me?"

"Nothing more than I'm willing to give you. Understanding. Acceptance." She gulped. "Love."

He clicked the remote, and the TV roared to life. "I'll try." He'd spoken as if to the television screen, but Lori's heart ignited with hope.

She slipped from the sofa and curled both hands over his forearm. "I'll try, too."

"I wanna watch my game."

She swallowed a sad smile. It'd probably be a long journey to reconciliation, but at least they'd taken a first baby step. "Okay,

Dad. We'll go."

Jase and Kenzie paused by Dad's chair and said goodbye, and he flicked a glance at them and nodded. Then they trailed through the house and out onto the stoop.

Outside, Lori wilted against the door and let her breath ease out. She hadn't realized how tense she'd been until her muscles relaxed. She was surprised her legs held her up. "Wow. That was hard."

Jase gave her a one-arm hug. "You did good in there. You were kind, and you got through."

Lori angled a weary smile at him. "I got through the first layer. He's like an onion. There's a whole bunch more to go."

Kenzie folded her arms. "You know, when you've talked about him, I thought he was just plain mean. But I've changed my mind. He's just plain sad. And bitter. He's held on to his hurt for a lot of years, so it might take a long time for him to let go. You're going to need lots of patience."

"And I know how you can practice patience." Jase's eyes glinted with impishness. "Hang out with the youth group every week. Moody, hormonal teenagers aren't much different from crotchety, sour-faced old men."

Lori laughed. "I'll think about it." She

sobered. "But I know one thing. From this moment, I've got to stop looking back and keep my focus forward when it comes to a relationship with my dad. It's the only way I'll avoid falling into bitterness, too."

Jase nodded. "Very wise."

Kenzie squeezed her hand. "Reach for hope. Always reach for hope."

THIRTY-TWO

Jase

Jase paced the foyer area of the police station. Ridiculous to be nervous, but his feet refused to stand still. Maybe part of his nervousness was the envelope of twenty-dollar bills tucked into the hidden pocket inside his jacket flap. Fifteen of them made a nice stack. He'd never been one to walk around with a lot of cash in hand. Why tempt someone to knock him over the head? But it seemed the best way to repay his heroine. If she ever showed up.

Officer Pratt waited behind the welcome desk, presumably doing paperwork. He'd set up a two o'clock meeting between Jase and the person who'd turned in Rachel's ring, and the huge round clock on the wall showed five past. Not terribly late. It only felt that way because he'd arrived fifteen minutes early. Twenty minutes' worth of pacing so far. At least he was getting some exercise.

The doors opened for the sixth time since his arrival. He turned his attention to the entrance. Jase gave a little "Huh?" of surprise. What were Ruby and Kenzie doing here? There must've been a problem at the store. He rushed to greet them.

"Hey, you two. Are you all right?"

Ruby gave him a startled look. "We're fine. Are you?"

Kenzie's forehead puckered in worry. "Why are you here?"

Ruby folded her arms over her chest. "You haven't been arrested, have you?"

He laughed. "No, I'm —"

Officer Pratt stepped between them. "Do you all know each other?"

Ruby nodded, her expression stern. "Yes. Brother Jase here is the youth pastor at our church. He's a fine young man, so whatever the problem is, I'm more than happy to vouch for him."

Confusion clouded the officer's face. He turned to Jase. "Why did we need to set up a meeting if you already know each other?" Understanding dawned. "Unless . . ."

Ruby pulled in a gasp. "Are you trying to tell me . . ."

Snippets from conversations over the past weeks collided in Jase's brain. Clothes for a mission project. Kenzie using clothes to make woven items for missions. His ring found in a pair of donated pants . . .

His mouth fell open and he gaped at Kenzie. "It was you."

She drew back, her fingers on her collarbone.

He pointed at her. "You're FinderzNotKeeperz."

"Wait . . ." Her blue eyes widened into twin saucers. She pointed at him. "It was yours?"

Officer Pratt grinned like a jack-o'-lantern. "Oh, this is rich. The guys in lost and found are gonna love it. I gotta go tell them about this." He trotted off.

Ruby shook her head, wonder in her eyes. "To think the owner was so close all the time, and we didn't know it."

A red flush brightened Kenzie's cheeks. "Oh, my goodness, I'm so embarrassed. You emailed me, and I told you the ring wasn't yours. I didn't think it could be because you said it was an engagement ring, and I honestly thought it was a wedding ring. Besides, you didn't include the inscription. I figured the owner would include the inscription."

A wry chuckle found its way from his throat. "I did include it. But then I deleted it. That message was supposed to be between Rachel and me, and I didn't want to share it with a stranger. But then, you're hardly a stranger."

Ruby laughed and grabbed him in a hug. "I've always known the Lord works in mysterious ways, but this is almost beyond belief."

Jase returned Ruby's hug, then reached inside his jacket and pulled out the envelope. "I came prepared to give this to my heroine. I guess that's you." He held it toward her.

She moved backward a step, her hands in the air like she was under arrest. "I can't take anything. Especially not after I goofed up and told you I didn't have it."

"That wasn't your fault." He waved the bulky packet. "Take it."

"I can't."

"Why not?"

"Because we're friends."

He smiled. "All the more reason you should."

Her forehead pinched again. "Huh?"

That unusual sensation of warm, scented liquid flowing over his head and down his shoulders returned. All at once, he understood it. An anointing. That's what it was — an anointing. In Jase's mind, puzzle pieces were sliding into place and forming a picture. A wondrous picture he could never have painted on his own. "Kenzie, Rachel and I intended to be church planters. We wanted to share the gospel with people who hadn't yet heard the story of God's love and grace. When she died, our dream died with her. I didn't think I'd have the chance to carry the salvation message to those who needed to hear it. To be honest, I wasn't sure I even believed it myself anymore. I was so . . . broken . . . by my loss."

Tears swam in her blue eyes, and he battled them, too. God's ability to make beauty out of ashes was stirring the neglected embers of his faith to life again. He sought words to help her understand. For her to see how God meant this moment to happen.

"You want to take a trip. It's a mission trip, because you intend to carry the story of salvation to your family members, who are ensnared by legalism. It's exactly the kind of trip Rachel and I had hoped to make. But now it's you going. And if this money" — he lifted her hand and pressed the envelope into her palm — "funds your trip, it'll be as if Rachel and I have a part in it. Don't you see?"

Her gaze dropped to the envelope, then

shifted to his face. Indecision played in her eyes.

He closed her fingers around the envelope and leaned down slightly. "Take it, Kenzie. Rachel and I prayed to see souls saved. When your family members find Jesus, their lives will change from that moment into eternity. It will be an answer to our prayers. Let us send you. Please?"

Ruby sniffled and put her arms around both of them. "Listen, you two. I don't believe in coincidence. Kenzie, I think that ring was meant to find you because God knew you'd be honest and try to return it. Jase, I think you were meant to come to Bradleyville so you'd be where the ring was found." She'd looked back and forth at them, but now she aimed her gaze ahead, as if drifting off somewhere. "I think Kenzie's pull to go home and Jase's desire to reward the ring's finder were prompted by the Almighty." She gave a jolt, dropped her hands to her hips, and fixed a stern glower on Kenzie. "And I think if you don't take that money to buy a bus ticket to Indiana, young lady, you're a stubborn fool."

Jase laughed, and Kenzie dipped her head and giggled. When she raised her face, she was smiling. She hugged the envelope to her chest.

"All right, Brother Jase. I'll buy a ticket with the reward money and go home. And I'll tell my family the story of how I was able to come. It'll be evidence of God's work in our lives."

Jase closed his eyes. *I asked You to show up, and You did. Bigger and better than I imagined. Thank You, Father.*

Bradleyville

The evening of the fifth Sunday of May, Jase stepped behind the pulpit in the Beech Street Bible Fellowship sanctuary. Bats flopped around in his stomach. They had to be bats. Much too big and active for butterflies. Yes, he was nervous, but not the same kind of apprehension he'd experienced weeks ago when Brother Kraft had asked him to speak this evening.

Back then, he'd worried about finding something of value to say. Today, he had something to share — a story that had restored his faith and given him fresh hope — but how would the congregation react? They might feel duped and fire him on the spot. He remembered the sensation of warmth flowing over him at the police station. Instantly, the bats stopped circling and settled, bringing an element of calm in Jase's soul. If they fired him, he'd take it as

God's means of moving him elsewhere.

"If you have your Bible, feel free to turn to the book of Jeremiah, the twenty-ninth chapter, verses eleven through thirteen." He opened his Bible and read the scriptures. He didn't need to read them. He knew the passage by heart, but he wanted to see the words printed on the pages of God's Holy Word as he stated them. He lifted his head and smiled at the people seated in the pews. A bigger crowd than usual for a Sunday evening, no doubt meant to offer him their support and encouragement for his very first official sermon. One person was notably absent. He and Lori had seen Kenzie off at the bus station more than a week ago already. But Lori was in her familiar spot. Ruby sat with her. And there in the front row beside Brother and Sister Kraft, his former minister, Brother Tony, and his spunky wife, Eileen, beamed up at him, proud as peacocks to hear him preach. They'd traveled over six hundred miles for this sermon. So he better make it good.

"Show of hands. How many of you have Jeremiah 29:11 underlined in your Bible or committed to memory?" Hands lifted all over the sanctuary. Jase nodded, chuckling. "I thought so. It's a pretty standard one for Christians to memorize and then pull out and chew on when they hit a rough spot in life. It's a good reminder, right?"

Heads bobbed.

"But what happens when a rough spot is so hard, so jarring, that it shakes the faith right out of you? The Lord's plan is to prosper us — and this is spiritual prosperity, just so we don't confuse it with financial prosperity — and give us hope. But I bet a lot of you can attest that some life situations feel pretty hopeless."

More nods and a few sheepish grins or sad frowns.

Jase pulled in a deep breath. "When I arrived in Bradleyville two months ago, I was in a pit of hopelessness. My plans, the ones I'd carefully laid out with a goal of honoring God with my life, had crumbled. The woman I loved and wanted to marry, taken from me. The goal for us to go out as a missionary team, crushed. We use the term *heartbroken* kind of flippantly sometimes, like it's a storybook word, but that's what I was. Heartbroken. Hopeless. If this was God's plan, I didn't want it. I couldn't see any kind of future anymore. Not with a God who allowed such devastation to fall on me."

The sanctuary was silent. Reverent. Maybe stunned. Jase's gaze skimmed across faces. Some seemed somber, others sympathetic, a few uncomfortable. He didn't blame them. He'd never known how to react to someone else's raw pain laid out in the open. But he needed to be honest, so he sent up a quick prayer for courage and continued.

"People told me God giveth and taketh and I should praise His name. People told me God knew the number of Rachel's days and it was His will for her to go home. People told me to find comfort in the hope of heaven. But I was angry. Angry at God. And bitter. I wanted *my* plans back. So when I came to Bradleyville, it wasn't so much out of obedience to God as a way to escape the bitterness, anger, and disbelief I'd wallowed in for a full year in San Antonio." He looked directly at Brother Tony. "Yes, disbelief. I wasn't sure anymore if God even existed."

The preacher who'd led Jase to salvation, who'd baptized him, mentored him, counseled him, and loved him didn't even flinch. Tears winked in his eyes, though, and those tears told Jase how deeply the man cared for him. Maybe as much as a father would.

Jase shifted his attention to the congregation again. What he planned to say next might disappoint some people. Might turn a few people against him. But he'd promised

God to be honest tonight, and he would keep his word. He glimpsed Brother Kraft's warm smile, and it bolstered him.

"Shortly after I arrived here, I realized the stupidity of why I'd come. Y'all needed someone to lead and guide your next generation. And here I was, empty as a buckshot-blasted rain barrel in a drought." A few laughs broke the tension. "I had nothing to pour out. You know that old song 'Just a Little Talk with Jesus'? Well, I had me one, and it wasn't very pretty. I told Him if He was really there, then He needed to show up. I told Him to prove Himself to me."

He cringed. "Pretty brazen, right? I know we're not supposed to talk disrespectfully to God Almighty or His Son. But at that moment, I didn't much care about offending God. That's how far from Him I'd slipped." He propped his elbows on the podium and leaned toward the people in the pews. "But here's the thing . . . When I told God to show up, even though I didn't realize it, what I was really doing was seeking Him. I missed Him so much. I missed being secure. I missed being able to trust Him. In the very center of my soul, I was aching for Him to fill me up the way He'd done before. I needed Him."

His voice broke, and he bowed his head,

silently praying for control. He swallowed a few times, rubbed his nose, and faced the congregation again. "Let me tell you something. When you seek Him, even when you seek Him from a place of bitter anger, He shows up. I have proof." He reached into his pocket and pulled out Rachel's ring. He pinched the band between his fingers, tilting it back and forth so the diamond caught the light. "This is the ring I bought Rachel. Shortly after I got here, I realized the ring was missing. I guess you'd say it ramped up my anger and bitterness. It sure didn't seem as if God was making much effort to prove Himself to me. I thought it'd been stolen, so I did what most anyone would do. I filed a police report. But I honestly never expected to see it again."

He placed the ring on the edge of the podium, with the diamond facing the congregation like a small spotlight. "Since I have it here tonight, you already know it was found. Kind of steals the tension from the story, doesn't it?"

A few chuckles. Jase's lips twitched in a grin. He planted his palms on the open Bible. "But there's still some surprise involved. The person who found it was one of our members, Kenzie Stetler, and she turned it in to the police." He shook his head, wonder blooming anew. "When an officer called me and told me the ring had been found, I wanted to reward the finder for her honesty. I had no idea I'd end up funding Kenzie's return to Indiana."

Tears filled his eyes, and he pressed his fist to his mouth for a moment, seeking control. "God not only gave me back my tie to Rachel, He gave me the chance to send Kenzie on a trip to share His good news with the people she loves most. He redeemed my dream of spreading the gospel. It wasn't the way I'd envisioned it, but it almost means more than what I'd planned. Because Kenzie is my friend, not a stranger, and I know how joyful she'll be if any of the people she loves accept Jesus as their Savior."

He picked up the ring again and angled it so he could see the inscription. Eyes locked on the words, he smiled. "Inside the band of Rachel's ring, I had a message inscribed. It says, 'From this moment into eternity.' I chose it as my solemn commitment to love, honor, and cherish her for as long as we lived. But those words hold a deeper meaning for me now. From the moment I received Jesus, I was secure into eternity as God's child. He never left me. He didn't forsake me. Even when I stormed heaven with angry outbursts, He went right on loving me."

Jase angled his gaze to the congregation. "I realize some of y'all may feel misled, knowing now that I came out of selfishness rather than a true desire to serve. If I've offended you, I ask your forgiveness. If you want me to step down as youth pastor, I'll do it without a fuss. But I want you to know that God used members of this congregation to restore my faith." He smiled at Brother and Sister Kraft, then shifted his gaze to Lori. "To convince my heart that it could love again." She blushed crimson. He swept a slow look across the congregation as a whole. "Y'all have played a role in helping to heal my aching soul, and regardless of where I go from here, I will always be grateful."

THIRTY-THREE

Lori

While Sister Kraft raised the roof with her exuberant piano playing, Brother Kraft led the congregation in their end-of-service song. The minister had chosen Lori's favorite hymn, "I Love to Tell the Story." It'd been Mom's favorite, too. Usually Lori sang it with gusto. But this evening, because of a huge knot of emotion blocking her vocal cords, she could only listen.

Beside her, Ruby sang in her rich alto, " 'I love to tell the story; more wonderful it seems than all the golden fancies of all our golden dreams . . .' "

Delightful shivers climbed her spine. Jase had shared his story of the dreams he'd been forced to set aside to see God's purpose fulfilled. In her pocket she carried a letter from Kenzie that would add a new chapter to his story. A happy chapter, one that would let him see another layer of

God's work in his life. Because Kenzie's beloved grossmammi was asking questions about how she could be secure for eternity. She swallowed a chortle. And there was something else in there sure to make him and a lot of other people squeal with delight.

After delivering a closing prayer, Brother Kraft dismissed everyone. Jase positioned himself at the doors to the foyer and shook people's hands as they left. Several folks paused and talked with him for a few minutes, and Lori battled impatience. When would she have the chance to talk to him? After what he'd said while looking straight at her, a hope was pounding beneath her breastbone. As soon as she'd shown him Kenzie's letter, she intended to ask straight out if he loved her.

What if he said he loved her as a sister in Christ? Would it devastate her? Would it send her burrowing into a box of dough-nuts? She shook her head. No. Because her identity — her true identity — was found in being a beloved daughter of the King. God had completely filled her from the top of her curly head to the soles of her feet. Temptation to use food as comfort still teased, probably always would, but the Holy Spirit was helping her overcome the long-held habit.

She huffed a breath. It would probably be a while before everybody cleared out. But she could make sure classroom lights were off, the back door was locked, and nobody'd left a stove burner on in the kitchen after the fellowship meal. She performed the custodial duties that had become second nature, then returned to the sanctuary.

Only Brother and Sister Kraft and the guests from San Antonio remained with Jase. She pulled the letter from the back pocket of her jeans and bounded over to the group. Jase's face lit when she stepped near, sending her heart into cartwheels.

He stretched his hand to her. "Did I do okay?"

She took hold and squeezed. She'd prayed with him in his office before the evening service and had teasingly promised to give a critique afterward. She nodded. "You did real good. Ten plus plus."

The entire group burst out laughing, Jase included. "You're awfully good for my ego." Then his expression turned tender. "Thanks. That means a lot."

Two more cartwheels inside her chest. She let go of his hand and waved Kenzie's letter. "Anybody interested in news from Indiana?"

Sister Kraft clapped her hands. "Absolutely!"

Lori started to open the envelope, but Brother Kraft put his hand over hers.

"Leah, how about you, me, Tony, and Eileen go to the house and let these two look at the letter together? Jase or Lori can fill us in later." A knowing glimmer in his eyes sent Lori's heart into another flip.

Brother Kraft caught hold of his wife's hand and headed for the doors. Tony and Eileen followed them. Sister Kraft peeked over her shoulder. "There's a no-sugar-added strawberry tart in our fridge, so come on over when you're done talking, if you'd like."

Lori was sure Jase would want to go. His former minister planned to head back to Texas in the morning, and he'd want time with the man who'd been so important to him. She nodded. "We'll be there soon. Thanks."

The others departed. For several seconds, she and Jase stood like a pair of statues in the doorway to the foyer. Then she flapped the envelope. "Well . . . wanna hear?"

He gave a little jolt, as if his engine had been jump-started. "Yeah. Sure." He pointed to the sanctuary. "Wanna sit?"

Lori crossed to the very back pew, the one

reserved for parents with small children, and sat. Jase sat next to her and stretched his arm across the back of the pew. He smiled at her, and her silly heart decided to spin again.

She blurted, "You looked at me during your sermon and said your heart has found a way to love again. You looked at me." She tipped her head and narrowed her gaze. "Did you mean to look at me?"

He rubbed his knuckles on his whiskered cheek. His dimples winked. "Yeah."

She held her breath for a moment, examining his green-blue eyes. "Tell me how." Her breath whooshed out with the words. "How'd I do it?"

A grin brought the dimples into prominence. "By being you. By being funny and kind and boisterous and unpredictable."

No storybook hero would choose the description Jase had just given, but she liked it. He'd taken the time to look beneath her surface. Even so, he probably only meant he loved her as a friend. Her chest pinched momentarily, but she reminded herself of the inscription inside the ring he'd bought for Rachel . . . *into eternity.* Even if Jase did love her as more than a friend, he couldn't love her forever. Not from the beginning to the never-end of time. Only God could do that. And He was her enough.

She leaned over slightly and brushed his arm with her temple, then lifted Kenzie's letter. "I'm glad. Now, do you wanna see —"

He put his finger on her lips. "Lori."

Her gaze zipped to meet his. No cartwheels in her chest this time. Nope. Her heart spun like a pinwheel on a windy Kansas day. She'd wondered if a man would ever look at her with love and admiration, and now she knew one would. Because Jase was. And the knowing was splendid.

"It's way too soon for us to make any kind of commitment. Our relationship is still so new. But there are lots of things I love about you already. First is how much you love God, and second is how much you love people. You have one of the most beautiful souls I've ever seen."

He saw her soul? Yikes trikes, no man had ever looked that hard at her. A happy laugh left her throat. "I love you for trying to see it."

He grinned and winked. "It's pretty hard to miss. Joy sticks out of you." His forehead pinched, a slight frown forming. "I'm gonna say this, and I don't want you to take it the wrong way, okay? But your joyful spirit . . . Rachel had that. It was the first thing that attracted me to her."

Lori's jaw dropped. "But Rachel was so beautiful. I saw her photo. You didn't notice that first?"

He shrugged. "I'm sure I noticed it. It's pretty hard for a man not to notice a beautiful woman. But that isn't what made me fall in love with her." He took Lori's hand. "There are different kinds of beauty, Lori, and the kind you have — the same kind Rachel had — is lasting."

Lori scrunched her shoulders. "But my goofy hair. And my round face. You don't notice those things? They don't make you . . . cringe?"

His soft laugh and warm eyes melted her. "Cringe? No. You have your own very unique beauty. And what are looks anyway? Over time, they always fade. But a beautiful soul? That lasts into eternity." He released her hand and slipped his fingers into the strands of her wild hair, pressing his palm lightly against her cheek. "I want to get to know you more and more. Because I think the more I know you, the more I'll love you. Do you want to know me more, too?"

She couldn't nod without dislodging his hand, and his touch was the most delightful thing she'd experienced. She wanted to stay there forever. "I do." Oh, what a poor choice of words. Sent her straight to a marriage ceremony, and hadn't he said he wasn't ready for that yet? "Yikes trikes . . ."

His laughter rolled. He snagged her in a hug, laughing against her hair, and then wheezed a sigh. "Ah, Lori, you make my heart spin."

She nestled her cheek on his shoulder. It fit so perfectly there. "Like a pinwheel in the Kansas wind?"

"Exactly like a pinwheel in the Kansas wind."

She smiled. "Good." She remained still for several more seconds, content, but there was something he needed to know. "Jase?"

"Hmm?" He stroked his hand down her hair.

Oh, what a glorious feeling. "Um . . . I forget."

He laughed again and sat up, releasing her. "I'm sorry. We're here alone, and if we don't head over to the Krafts' soon, we might start rumors. How about we go?"

My, he was a wise man. She started to rise, but her hand pressed down on the envelope and she remembered what she needed to tell him. "Oh! First, you need to hear this!" She opened the letter and read her favorite part, about Grossmammi asking Kenzie about Jesus's grace. Jase let out a whoop that echoed from the rafters and hugged Lori again. She hugged him back, then wriggled free.

"There's more." She pointed to a list of ingredients under the title *Kenzie's Secret Recipe Brownies.* "Look at that. She sent it to me! Isn't that the sweetest thing ever?"

He tapped the end of her nose with his fingertip and shook his head. "Nope. You, Lori Fowler, are the sweetest thing ever. And don't you forget it."

She wouldn't. Oh, no, she surely wouldn't.

KENZIE'S SECRET RECIPE BROWNIES

(That Isn't Secret Anymore)
1 stick of unsalted butter
1/2 cup coconut oil (or a second stick of
  butter)
3/4 cup plus 2 tablespoons packed brown
  sugar
3/4 cup plus 2 tablespoons white
  granulated sugar
1/4 teaspoon salt
2 teaspoons vanilla
3 large eggs
2 tablespoons sour cream
3/4 cup sifted Dutch cocoa powder
2/3 cup all-purpose (NOT self-rising) flour
8 ounces dark chocolate, coarsely chopped
  into chunks

Preheat oven to 350°F; line an 8 × 8-inch
baking pan with parchment paper.

Melt the butter and coconut oil over low
heat. Watch to make sure the butter doesn't

brown. When the butter and oil are liquid, remove from heat.

Add the sugars and salt to the pan; stir until the mixture is smooth and has cooled a bit.

Use a hand mixer to beat in the vanilla, eggs, and sour cream (at least 2 minutes on medium, until the batter is frothy, almost like a meringue).

Sift the Dutch cocoa powder and flour together. Using a rubber spatula, fold the flour-cocoa mixture into the wet ingredients until just incorporated. DO NOT overmix.

Gently fold in the chocolate chunks (you can add 1/2 cup chopped nutmeat, if desired).

Spread the batter evenly in the prepared pan.

Bake to preferred doneness: 30 minutes for a gooey center; 35 minutes for a fudgy center; 40 minutes for a chewy center (Kenzie's were fudgy). Cool completely (important: if you need to speed the process, since they'll be hard to resist, set uncovered pan in the refrigerator) before cutting into 16 squares with a warm, dry, clean knife.

READERS GUIDE

1. Jase receives a piece of advice from Merlin Kraft shortly after his arrival in Bradleyville: "God raises us up for His purposes so we have the opportunity to experience and share His power in a human life. . . . You might feel like your plans have been lost, but His plans are never forsaken. He will use you for His glory, and it'll be for your good, too." Have your plans ever crumbled? How did you adapt to the change in direction? Did you uncover new strength, wisdom, or ministry in the change?

2. How did Jase's tumultuous childhood prepare him to minister to the youth at Beech Street Bible Fellowship?

3. What role did Brother Tony play in Jase's life? Do you have a mentor who has inspired and guided you? Have you taken the time to thank this person for his or her influ-

ence? Have you ever mentored someone else? How has this blessed and challenged your life?

4. Kenzie left her Amish farm for the city and changed her name, but she held on to some elements of her simplistic upbringing. Why do you think she didn't cast off everything from her former life? Do you think she will stay in Indiana or come back to Kansas? Why?

5. Lori lost her mother when she was young, which left a hole in her life that she tried to fill with food. Why was this unhelpful? When you're feeling empty, how do you fill yourself? What role does God want to play in being our filler?

6. Because of her physical appearance, Lori felt unworthy. Society places great value on physical appearance. How does this align with Scripture? How can we help our daughters or the young women in our lives view themselves as valuable?

7. Jase used Jeremiah 29:11–13 as the basis for his first sermon at Beech Street. Are these verses familiar to you? Do you believe God is found when we seek Him even from a place of bitter anger? In what ways did

God reveal to Jase hope and a future? How has He revealed hope and a future to you?

8. Merlin contemplated the question, If God already has life pathways mapped, does prayer change the circumstance? How would you answer the question? What scriptures support your viewpoint?

9. Pretend a year has passed since Kenzie left for Indiana and Jase delivered his first sermon. Where do you see Kenzie, Jase, Lori, Merlin, and Cullen now?

ACKNOWLEDGMENTS

I always thank family first. So thanks, *Mom,* for all the prayers. They continue to bolster me even though you're no longer with me on earth. I miss you so much. Save me a seat (and a scoop of potato salad) at that banqueting table. *Daddy,* thank you for being such a great example of the heavenly Father. Believing in a God who truly loves me was an easy concept to accept because you love me so well. *Don,* thanks for your willingness to take care of yourself, the pets, and the house so I can escape into story world. That Dog and I are glad you're here. As for *my girls and my precious grand-darlings,* I love you more than I love chocolate, kittens, and sunsets, and that's sayin' something.

For more than a decade, the wonderful ladies I refer to as "the posse" have been my cheerleaders, prayer warriors, partners in adventure, and critique-group members.

Were it not for an article in a magazine and a full-of-laughter "what if" session, this story would not have come to life. So, *Eileen, Connie, Margie, Darlene,* and *Jalana,* thank you for the laughter and inspiration. Love y'all muchly.

And I've got to give extra props to *Eileen,* who found the article in the first place. She asked over and over, "When're you gonna write that story?" Well, it's written now, but she won't see it. She graduated to heaven in the middle of the edits. But that only means she's seeing more glorious things than a printed book. I miss you, my Texas tornado pal, but I'll see you soonly.

Gratitude and fond affection for my first minister, *Merlin Kraft,* and his wife, *Leah,* who were like surrogate grandparents to me. *Merlin,* thank you for mentoring my dad — I reaped the benefits of your gentle guidance; and, *Leah,* I treasure my first Christmas dress, which you so lovingly sewed for me. (Of course, the rabbit-shaped birthday cake is long gone! As is your unforgettable meatloaf.) Although both of you now reside in heaven, your influence lives on. And to *Merlin and Leah's children,* thank you for letting me borrow their names for this book. It was a joy to revisit them in memory while I wrote.

466

To the *young adult Sunday school class* at First Southern Baptist Church, thanks to those who graciously approved the use of your names for Lori's class in the story. It added a personal touch that made my heart smile. You are our future! I hope you all know how important you are. It's a joy to watch you grow in Jesus.

I am ever grateful for the prayers and support offered by my *Sunday school ladies* and the *Lit & Latte book club members.* You mean more to me than you'll ever know.

Thanks to my *team at WaterBrook* who work with me and help grow me as a writer. I appreciate all of you.

Oh, and to *Sharlene,* thanks for the expression *yikes trikes.* It fit Lori so perfectly.

Finally, and most importantly, thank You, *God,* for being my completer. You are my strength, my comforter, and the one who fills me up. Thank You for seeing something of value in this tarnished vessel. May any praise or glory be reflected back to You.

ABOUT THE AUTHOR

In 1966, **Kim Vogel Sawyer** told her kindergarten teacher that someday people would check out her books in libraries. That little-girl dream came true in 2006 with the release of *Waiting for Summer's Return*. Since then, Kim has watched God expand her dream beyond her childhood imaginings. With more than fifty titles on library shelves and more than 1.5 million copies of her books in print worldwide, she enjoys a full-time writing and speaking ministry. Kim and her retired military husband, Don, are empty nesters living in a small town in Kansas, the setting of many of Kim's novels. When she isn't writing, Kim stays active serving in her church's women's and music ministries, crafting quilts, petting cats, and spoiling her quiverful of granddarlings. You can learn more about Kim's writing at www.kimvogelsawyer.com.

The employees of Thorndike Press hope you have enjoyed this Large Print book. All our Thorndike, Wheeler, and Kennebec Large Print titles are designed for easy reading, and all our books are made to last. Other Thorndike Press Large Print books are available at your library, through selected bookstores, or directly from us.

For information about titles, please call:
(800) 223-1244

or visit our website at:
gale.com/thorndike

To share your comments, please write:
Publisher
Thorndike Press
10 Water St., Suite 310
Waterville, ME 04901